SCORE *to Settle*

SCORE *to Settle*

BELLA NORTH

bookouture

Published by Bookouture in 2025

An imprint of Storyfire Ltd.
Carmelite House
50 Victoria Embankment
London EC4Y 0DZ

www.bookouture.com

The authorised representative in the EEA is Hachette Ireland
8 Castlecourt Centre
Dublin 15 D15 XTP3
Ireland
(email: info@hbgi.ie)

ISBN: 978-1-80550-017-9
eBook ISBN: 978-1-80550-016-2

For the readers who fall in love with book boyfriends. You are my people! May your real-life standards forever be ruined and your TBR pile endless.

SCORE TO SETTLE PLAYLIST

Hit Me With Your Best Shot – Pat Benatar

good 4 u – Olivia Rodrigo

You're So Vain – Carly Simon

My Kink Is Karma – Chappell Roan

I Did Something Bad – Taylor Swift

Team – Lorde

Risk – Gracie Abrams

Picture You – Chappell Roan

Bed Chem – Sabrina Carpenter

Dangerous Woman – Ariana Grande

Don't Blame Me – Taylor Swift

Nonsense – Sabrina Carpenter

It Isn't Perfect But It Might Be – Olivia Dean

Cowboy Take Me Away – The Chicks

Still Into You – Paramore

Listen to the playlist on Spotify!

ONE

HARPER

"Yo, Sullivan. Who was that girl you were with last night?"

The football player turns to the camera, mischief dancing in his deep brown eyes. Every person in the editorial meeting is transfixed by the screen—the line of dark stubble showing from beneath the white slats of his helmet and the smile stretching across Jake Sullivan's face. *"Just a friend."* He grins, flashing perfect white teeth.

"Don't tell me you've broken another heart already?"

Jake pulls off his helmet, showing black hair styled away from his face. He tips back his head, his laugh deep and long.

Another voice comes from off-screen. *"Not if I break your bones first."*

A second later another teammate in the same bright red Denver Stormhawks jersey throws himself forward and the two men fall to the ground in a playful tussle as the person behind the camera laughs.

Tim, my editor at *Sports Magazine*, pauses the large flatscreen and rolls his eyes at the two women at the end of the table grinning from ear to ear. One of them fans her notebook across her face.

"OK," Tim says. "I get it. Jake Sullivan is a good-looking man, and at twenty-nine, he's the best tight end the Stormhawks have ever had. He knows how to catch a football, but what else do we know about him?"

Glances are exchanged. The team's four reporters and two juniors—of which I'm one—have been called into this meeting and none of us know where this is going.

Alison, one of the reporters fanning her face, flashes a smirk. "There was the thing in the parking lot with the three cheerleaders last summer."

Tim sighs, pinching the bridge of his nose. I've only been at the magazine for three months, but even I know this means to tread carefully. Tim is a decent guy. He's tall and wiry, thinning on top, but then, who wouldn't be with four kids at home and a fifth on the way? He buys the first drink on nights out and remembers birthdays, but he still comes with a short fuse. "Anything else?"

Silence.

"Maybe that's it," I say, regretting the words the moment they leave my mouth. I've survived this far at the magazine by keeping my head down and my mouth shut.

"She speaks," Tim says, his tone a little mocking but not unkind. "Would you like to expand on that, Harper?"

"OK..." I venture carefully now, tucking my shoulder-length chestnut brown hair behind my ears as I try to gauge where this meeting is going. All eyes land on me. "What if there isn't anything else about Jake Sullivan? What if he likes to screw women and play football and that's it?" I shrug, risking a glance across the table. Of course it's Callie's eye I catch. The other junior. Hired at the same time as me. We both have a four-month probationary period. At the end of it only one of us will keep our job, and I need it to be me. I can't lose two jobs in one year. It's bad enough that at the age of twenty-six I've had to come home to Denver after my short run at *Insight*—New

York's most prestigious news magazine, read by millions all over the world. Callie smirks and runs a perfectly manicured nail across her throat before flicking her long dark curls over her shoulder.

But to her surprise and mine, Tim points a finger at me and nods. "Exactly. Jake Sullivan is known for only two things. Football and women. Which brings me to why you're all here. *Sports Magazine* has been given a huge profile feature on Sullivan." Tim strides around the table as he continues, "Stormhawks management wants Jake to clean up his image and they're giving us five weeks of full access and all expenses paid to follow Jake as the team finishes its season. We need to go behind the scenes and get to know the real Jake. They're hoping our presence keeps him in line, and our profile shows the world what a good guy he really is. And they want it to come from a local outlet."

"But what if the real Jake is the same as the Jake everyone thinks he is?" I ask. "What if he *is* only about football and women?"

Tim shrugs. "Then that's what we write. We have full creative control, something Stormhawks management is aware of. I don't care what direction this piece takes, but we need to go deep. If Jake really is as bad as his reputation, then we need to learn why. This might be a big gamble for the Stormhawks, but for us it's simple: We write the truth, whatever that might be."

"So I'm writing gossip pieces now?" The guy beside me, Kevin Fielding, says, voice dripping with disdain. He's the senior reporter and the one almost certain to get this assignment. He's also an asshole. No doubt I'll be booking flights and hotels for him for the next five weeks and learning all the reasons why nothing I did was good enough.

"No, you're not," Tim says. The reply causes a shifting of bodies in seats. Sharks circling. Gossip piece or not, every reporter in this room except me wants this story and their name on the byline. It's the kind of piece sure to be picked up by bigger news outlets, which means one hell of a career boost.

The bickering begins as each reporter throws out the reasons why they'd be perfect for the job. I switch off. I'm new here—whatever comes next won't involve me. I let my gaze wander to the breathtaking view from the twentieth floor of the Arquette Media building. The towering skyscrapers on either side frame a picture-perfect scene of distant snowcapped mountains and a vast expanse of endless sky. New York was buzz and hustle and everything I wanted, but nothing compares to the skyline in Denver in November when the sky is bright blue, the sun pale yellow. Fall leaves in burnt orange cling to the trees, waiting for one more gust of wind before they drop. I can almost feel the crisp mountain air on my skin and hear the far-off calls of the golden eagles.

"Harper." Tim's voice jolts me back to the meeting.

I jump, surprised to hear my name come up.

"Her?" Kevin says beside me, his upper lip rising in an undisguised sneer. Definitely an asshole.

"Sorry? What's me?" I ask.

"You're doing the feature on Jake," Tim says. A pained expression crosses his face as a bolt of something shoots down my body. Adrenaline? Fear?

"You're kidding."

Tim shakes his head, still looking like this is the last thing he wants. "I was as surprised as you are. Believe me, you weren't my first choice. There's a lot of experience on the team and I don't enjoy throwing my juniors in the deep end like this. But," Tim continues, shooting me a sympathetic smile, "Jake's mom—who also happens to be his agent—wants you. I'm guessing you've heard of Mama Sullivan? She runs the show when it comes to her boys. And she's not someone you want to cross."

I nod dumbly. Mama Sullivan is one of the best agents in the NFL. Her head for business and loyalty to her three sons make her not just respected but feared by many in the industry. She's not someone you argue with, which I guess is the only reason Tim is allowing me to do this.

"Do you think it was the piece I wrote on the future of baseball at *Insight*?" I ask, trying to keep the grimace from my face at the mention of my last job. The article was my one byline at *Insight*, delving into the evolving identity of baseball, walking the line between keeping the traditions old fans love and modernizing to bring new fans in. It was the interview with pro baseball player Quincy Baltimore that gave depth to the piece, but it's nothing like what they're asking me to do with Jake Sullivan.

Tim frowns, like he can't believe it either. "Maybe."

"But—"

He holds up a hand and the protest dies on my lips. "I'm sorry to do this to you, Harper, but someone with your background shouldn't have any problem tackling this. Just don't screw it up. And remember—we want depth and we want truth. Good guy or not, I don't care, just get to the heart of what makes Jake tick."

I feel myself nod. My background? Is he referring to my dad or the details I embellished in my interview to get this job?

Callie shoots me a look of pure hate. "Don't expect any help from us." She talks like she's been at the magazine for a decade and isn't just as new and dumb to how things work as I am. Callie might be a total bitch to me, but she has become everyone else's friend in the last three months. I've tried to keep my head down, work hard and prove myself, but it hasn't made me well liked. No matter how hard I work, no one sees me as part of the team. She's right. This isn't going to help.

Tim reaches for the bridge of his nose again. Not a good sign for Callie.

"Do you know how much of our advertising money comes from companies targeting the NFL?" he asks.

I bite back a smile at the sight of Callie's reddening cheeks. Even though Tim is nothing like my father, I've been at enough family dinners with my dad when he's home from traveling to know what it is to be put on the spot.

"Um…" Callie opens her notebook, flipping through the pages as though the answer will be in there.

"It's millions, OK?" Tim answers for her. "It's not an exaggeration to say that Jake Sullivan is as high profile as they come in football. Thanks to his skills as tight end and his reputation, he's a household name. His reach goes a lot further than just Denver Stormhawks fans and a feature like this is going to sell a lot of magazines. So if Harper needs help from anyone on this team, we help. That's why I've called you all in here. This is going to be our lead feature for February to coincide with Super Bowl frenzy, which means after the five weeks of shadowing Jake, time is going to be tight. Callie, you'll be booking Harper's transport and accommodation for when she's traveling with the team. Harper, you'll send me weekly updates with your notes for the feature. And if you have any questions, Kevin and Alison or anyone here will help."

Tim's tone is final and no one offers another snarky reply. Even without it, it's clear not a single person in this room, including Tim, believes I can do this.

I swallow down the mountain of what-the-fuck-am-I-going-to-do fear and act like I was expecting nothing less than to be given a huge story and no time to write it in my fourth month on the job. "So when do I sit down for an interview with Jake?"

"Aren't you listening, Harper?" Tim replies. "This isn't a 'you ask, he answers' kind of feature. This needs to go beyond the sound bites and the bravado. Sullivan has spent years building a reputation as a bad boy and a womanizer. The Stormhawks management team has let it slide up 'til now, but they don't like the backlash they're getting in the press. Any time the Stormhawks get a mention it's followed with a story about Jake. Which means no more sex scandals or drunken brawls. Mama Sullivan has promised the Stormhawks he's a good boy really. If that's true, then they want everyone to see it in this feature. And if it isn't true, it's probably going to mark the end of his career at the Stormhawks. It's one of the last family-owned NFL teams, and its reputation and the reputation of its players means a lot to the higher-ups.

"So you'll be shadowing his every move for the next five weeks all the way to their penultimate game of the season at the end of December against the Kansas City Trailblazers. You'll be going to the games. Going to practice. Going wherever it is Jake goes. And Mama Sullivan has invited you to stay at Oakwood Ranch when you're not on the road. She told me to tell you to bring hiking boots."

Fuck!

"But Thanksgiving is next Thursday," I say, picturing a cozy dinner at my best friend Mia's mom's house. Heading out to watch the parade then eating more food than we should, including second helpings of Gloria's famous pumpkin pie. I've already got my holiday sweater ready.

Tim shakes his head. "You'll be in LA with the Stormhawks for Thanksgiving. But the Stormhawks aren't one of the teams playing on Christmas Day so you can see your family then."

"Right." A hard lump forms in my chest. I hate letting people down, but I know Mia and her family will understand. "When do I leave?"

"Now. There's a car downstairs waiting to take you to your apartment to pack a bag. You're due at Oakwood Ranch at five. It's about a thirty-minute drive west of Denver so don't be late. And a word to the wise—keep it professional." Tim strides out of the room without waiting for a reply, his meaning clear—don't sleep with Jake.

Not a chance, I think as my cheeks flush crimson. I get to my feet in the black Louis Vuitton stilettos I bought for my New

York life and leave the meeting room. The rest of the team is already talking about how badly I'm going to fuck this up before the door has even closed behind me.

I grab my jacket and bag and hit the elevator button. The editorial meeting replays in my mind as I climb into the waiting car and give him directions to Mia's apartment and the couch I've been sleeping on since returning from New York.

I wonder if there was a point I could've casually mentioned to Tim that I've been keeping a few tiny details to myself that feel important for this feature. Like how as a sports journalist I might know plenty about baseball, basketball, ice hockey, and golf, but I know nothing about football. Seriously nothing... What the hell is a tight end anyway?

And it's not like I can throw myself into research. There'll be no computer to hide behind for the Jake Sullivan feature. It's massive and they've given it to me. I have no idea why Mama Sullivan chose me, how she even knows who I am, but I'm in too deep to back out now. This assignment will finish at the same time as my trial period at *Sports Magazine*. If I mess this up, I'm out of another job.

The thought sends a flutter of unease through me. The humiliation of being fired from *Insight* in New York this past summer is still a wound that won't heal. It doesn't matter how many times Mia tells me it wasn't my fault, I can't shake the glaring knowledge that I've let people down, mostly myself.

I love journalism. I love finding the tiny details of a story that others miss and crafting just the right words to draw the reader in. And I especially love sports journalism. Even if my dad thinks it's not as important as the political stories he's built his career on. But sports has competition and passion. It has the drive of the athletes, the adoration of the fans. It's blood, sweat, and tears, and it fascinates me. All aside from the NFL. Football is a sport I've steered clear of since high school.

The junior position at *Sports Magazine* is a dream job, and one I was so lucky to get with no references. It was only thanks to Mia pulling strings that I got an interview—having a best friend whose family owns a media empire was bound to come in handy one day. It's why I wasn't exactly honest during my interview with Tim about my NFL knowledge. If I lose this job, Mia won't be able to help me again. My career will be over.

I won't let it happen. Being a journalist is all I've ever wanted to do. Without it, I'll have nothing. Not to mention having to see the look of disappointment on my dad's face if I fail again. As a Pulitzer Prize–winning journalist, he's hard enough to impress as it is.

Whether I like it or not, I'm going to have to write this feature on Jake. And if I want him to trust and open up to me, then I'm going to have to become his new best friend for the next five weeks.

Then another thought occurs to me—a tiny spark of an idea. Tim wants me to go beyond the sound bites to what really makes Jake tick, but Tim doesn't care if the feature is good or bad for Jake. Tim doesn't care if my story saves Jake's career or destroys it—as long as it's a damn good article. A ghost of a smile tugs at my lips.

Jake Sullivan has broken a lot of hearts over the years. But I'm pretty sure mine was the first. And that's the other small detail I should've told Tim just now. I might not know anything about the NFL, but I sure as hell know Jake Sullivan.

Looks like I might finally get my revenge.

TWO

JAKE

DYLAN: *Mama's looking for you, J. Where are you?*

DYLAN: *She's pissed!*

CHASE: *What's he done now?*

DYLAN: *He was supposed to be home by now. The reporter is here.*

CHASE: *LOL*

DYLAN: *Real helpful, Chase. Haven't you got a coach to impress?*

DYLAN: *Jake, are you on your way?*

DYLAN: *???*

The door at the back of the Stormhawks stadium gives easily. I ignore the "No Exit" sign and the one below reading "Door

Alarmed" and stride into the parking lot and the late-afternoon sun. This late in November my breath plumes in a white cloud from my mouth as I heave a long sigh. I'll get a grilling on Monday about this, but right now all I want is to be in my truck and driving home. Plus, sneaking out the back means I can avoid the pep talk from Coach Allen.

No amount of backslapping is going to change how much I sucked today. My passes were off, my catches clumsy. I just couldn't get in sync with the team. I'm a tight end. I'm supposed to be versatile. It's why I love the position. I'm a big receiver and a blocker. When I'm on, I'm the glue between the line and the skill players. I'm the safety valve for the quarterback when things go south. I'm the guy who can throw a chip block to spring a run or catch a tough pass. But today? I felt like dead weight. Every route, every block—it was like my brain knew what to do, but my body was running a second behind.

It's only one practice. Everyone has an off day. But with six games left to win our conference division and secure our place in the playoffs, plus contract renewals around the corner, I can't afford to give anything less than my best. Not to mention the Stormhawks haven't made the playoffs for the last three years, finishing second in the AFC West last year, narrowly missing out to the Kansas City Trailblazers by two points. Heads are gonna roll if the Stormhawks don't make it for a fourth. And considering the shit I'm already in with my reputation, I can't give them any more reasons to put my head on the block.

I pull my phone from the back pocket of my Levi's, groaning as an ache stretches across my lower back. I try to remember the last time everything didn't hurt and almost laugh. I'm twenty-nine years old not a hundred. But in football terms, I'm already old. I'll be lucky to get five more years on the team and that's only if I can stay injury-free. My mind flashes to Dylan, but I shut it down before the queasy guilt hits the pit of my stomach.

There are two missed calls from Oakwood Ranch. I briefly

wonder if she already knows how badly I sucked today. She must be pissed if she's asking Dylan to message me. Joanna Sullivan—known to the world as Mama Sullivan—might be the sole reason Dylan, Chase, and I play football as well as we do. She might be our agent and the driving force behind our pro careers, the reason I'm playing for my home team. She might be one step ahead of all of us, all of the time. But Mama doesn't text.

I cross the empty parking lot. On game days this whole area and every block for a five-mile radius will be jammed with vehicles. Banners and grilled burgers and shirtless men drinking beers from coolers.

My old pickup is sitting alone in the middle of the lot. It was ancient when I bought it a decade ago and I keep thinking about trading it in. It's not like I don't have the money. Thanks to Mama's unflinching negotiation skills, all three of us Sullivans are among some of the top-paid players in the NFL. But I'm not in this for the money and I like the way the seats of my truck are dipped and molded to my body, and how climbing in feels a little like being home.

I spot a small group of female fans leaning against the driver's side door and sigh inwardly. Some of the team brush the fans aside, but I always remember the eight-year-old me standing beside my dad, holding out my Stormhawks jersey for the legendary Mike Callaghan to sign. That scribble, followed by a hair ruffle, made my whole year. So I push aside my exhaustion and paste on a smile, giving them the full Jake Sullivan experience. I pose for selfies and sign posters and pieces of paper and flirt a little too.

I'm almost done when a blonde in cowboy boots and a tight denim shirt hands me a Sharpie before nodding to her cleavage.

I laugh, cocking an eyebrow. "Really?"

"You know it, baby." She grins and gives me the take-me-to-bed eyes I've seen a thousand times before. Then she unfastens the next button on her shirt, revealing the top of a black lace bra and a hell of a lot of breast to sign.

I shrug, never one to disappoint. As I lean close, I catch the scent of sweet perfume.

"Anyone ever tell you, you could be Rhysand from ACOTAR?" she says in a breathy whisper.

I frown, none of those words making sense to me. "Who?" I ask.

"Don't worry." She laughs. "It's a compliment."

I give her the roguish grin she wants and press the nib of the pen to her plump, tanned skin. Then a shout carries across the lot. "What the hell, Kelly?"

I turn in time to see a red-faced, angry-looking man charging toward me. He's half my height, skinny as fuck, and has a man bun, but his fists are bunched and he's coming at me swinging.

"Get your hands off my lady, Sullivan."

It would take zero effort to flatten this guy, but in a blink I see the story blowing up my socials. The backlash coming my way. A year ago, I wouldn't have cared, but I'm trying real hard to keep a low profile. Besides, I'm still sore from the cheerleaders thing last year no one will let me forget. So I hold my hands up in the universal sign for peace and give my best apologetic smile—the one even Mama softens at. "Just doing as your lady asked," I say.

His reply is a growl. "Well, don't. I know all about you and your ways."

The comment stings a touch but I say nothing as the man leads his girlfriend to an electric-blue Dodge, leaving in a roar of exhaust. It's a beauty, but no good for my wide shoulders and six-foot-four height. I sign a few more posters before hopping in my truck, and with a final wave, one more wink, I'm gone.

My phone buzzes with another message. If I was late leaving the locker room, I'm in real trouble now. And yet as I pass the sign for the exit that would take me into the city, I briefly consider stopping by The Hay Barn on the way home. A cold beer and banter with Flic at her bar sounds pretty appealing. But then a full-body wax would sound like a dream compared to what's waiting for me at the ranch.

The *Sports Magazine* feature was Mama's idea. A way to keep the Stormhawks management and Coach Allen happy. I'm playing for my dream team. My home team. It doesn't get better than this, and yet I'm fucking it up. She's worried about my career. We both are.

I know she's looking at Dylan. His words from the hospital bed after he busted his knee last year haunt her as much as they do me. *If all I have is football, and I don't have that anymore, then what's left?* I'm being unfair. If anyone can shake an injury that bad, it's Dylan.

I get that I need to do better. Change my reputation. I am. Or I'm trying to. It would help if the gossip sites gave me half a chance. But the *Sports Magazine* feature and a reporter jammed up my ass for five weeks—that's something I could seriously do without.

This is our one bye week—the only week in the season we don't have a game—and all I want is some peace and quiet. Walking Buck in the hills, some time at home at my family's ranch, halfway between Denver and Idaho Springs— surrounded by ranch land and state park and the distant Rockies.

I used to have an apartment in the city. I've lost count of the parties and fun I had there, but when Dylan tore his ACL and moved home to Mama and the ranch last year, I gave up the apartment and did the same. It was supposed to be temporary. A way to keep Dylan company and keep a low profile after the story broke about the cheerleaders in my truck. But over a year later, I'm still there. The truth is, I like being home. I like remembering my dad training the horses for the rodeo in the paddock by the barn and how perfect our lives were before he died and Mama sold the horses. I get it. Running the ranch with three unruly boys wasn't easy, even with Dad around. He died when I was ten and I still miss him, but I miss the horses too. A ranch without animals just doesn't feel right.

I keep telling myself I'll get my own place in the city again, but when I'm away with the team most weekends and for pre-season, Oakwood Ranch is the only place I want to come home to.

Dylan will be on my back this weekend like always. Mama too, although at least she'll be feeding me at the same time. I wish Chase was visiting. I haven't seen my little brother much this season. He's a quarterback for the Kansas City Trailblazers —our biggest division rivals—and even though he could get away with murder in Mama's eyes, I miss him. I make a mental note to give him a call tomorrow.

I resist the pull of The Hay Barn. A long, hot shower in my own bathroom and five minutes for some self-care would go a long way to easing the tension in my body. I'm playing again on Thanksgiving, away to LA Wildhorns. They're bottom of the AFC West and it's a game we should win, but I've been playing long enough to know there's no such thing as an easy victory. It's my favorite time of year—this stretch from Thanksgiving to New Year when the pressure mounts with every game but there's still everything to play for.

Five minutes on the road and I pass the electric-blue Dodge. It's pulled to the side, the man-bun boyfriend even angrier as he kicks at a flat. I think about flipping him the finger and driving on, but it's not my style. So I ignore my buzzing phone and pull over to help. Twenty minutes later, a hug from the not-so-angry boyfriend and another from Kelly, I'm back in my truck. Based on how eager Kelly was to slip me her digits on the back of a Starbucks receipt, I don't think she and the boyfriend will last the rest of the season.

I chuckle to myself and drop the receipt in the door to throw away later. Even Kelly and her lace bra and her cowboy boots can't take away my yearning to be home now. I hit the gas and leave the city behind. In the mirrors, the setting sun is hitting the glass high-rises in the city, but ahead it's all wide-open space.

Another turn and the peaks come into view. Low at first. Craggy dark ridges pushing up from the land, glowing orange in the setting sun. Beyond them, far in the distance, is James Peak and the other snowcapped mountains of the Rockies. I turn left on a dirt track and a few minutes later the ranch house—a sprawling property with a large red barn and rolling green paddocks—comes into view. Through the rich green spruce trees is a crystal-clear lake we swim in during the summer. There's not another ranch or building for miles. All that surrounds us is land and the foothills leading up to the mountains.

Like always, I feel the familiar pang of sadness when I see the empty paddocks. *One day*, I tell myself. One day, when football is over, I'll fill them with horses and pick up where my dad left off, breeding and training horses for the rodeo.

The horses were always Dad's joy. Mama's was football. A year after she sold the horses, she turned the back paddocks into a football field with goal posts and gridlines. Dylan, Chase, and I were out there every hour we weren't at school. Dawn until dusk in the summers, before girls came along anyway. We still play together on the Fourth of July when Mama cooks a turkey and declares it our own Thanksgiving, seeing how we're always with our teams, playing football, on the real holiday.

I kill the engine and open my truck door, filling my lungs with air that smells of my childhood—spruce and pine and dewy grass. My feet hit the dirt driveway and just for a moment I feel all the tension in my body unravel.

Then my three-year-old yellow Labrador retriever, Buck, is charging out the back door to greet me, ears flapping in the wind, tongue hanging out. I bend down and run my hands over his yellow coat, catching the stench of his seriously bad breath.

"You're gross, Bucky." I laugh and he barks his agreement, dancing around my legs as I head to the open back door.

The house has changed over the years. I always think of it as having grown with us. A kitchen extension on the back and another bedroom and bathroom above it when we got too big to share. When I'm in the city, I think of getting an apartment there again. But when I'm at the ranch, I think of building my own house on the edge of the land. Getting those horses I always dream about. I think my dad would like that. A connection to a man I wish I'd known better, wish I'd had more time with. People liked to tell me as a kid that time heals all wounds, but they were wrong. I might've learned to navigate my life without my dad, but it sure as hell doesn't hurt any less that he's not here to see it. That I don't have a chance to make him proud.

Becoming ranchers like Dad is something Dylan and I used to talk about doing together when we're too old to keep chasing our dreams. When I'm on the field and the ball is in my hands and I'm flying toward the endzone, feeling invincible, those horses seem far in the future. But on days like today, it doesn't seem so distant.

The kitchen smells of chili as I step inside. A woman I don't recognize is sitting at the end of the bench, a purple notebook already open on the long table that stretches the width of the kitchen. This must be the reporter. I knew she'd be here, but I still find myself taken aback. She isn't what I expected. Buck scampers over to her and flops beside her pointed-toe stilettos. *Traitor.*

My gaze snags on those shoes. Patent black, high, and sexy as hell. Then my eyes travel up her body, along a pair of tanned long legs, a cute ass wrapped in a tight pencil skirt, and a silk blouse just tight enough to hint at the kind of breasts that make a man weak at the knees. I keep going. Her hair is as sleek as the rest of her and rich brown, the exact color of chestnuts. Full lips, cute button nose, big Bambi eyes. But her gaze on me is cold. Why does it feel like she already hates me and we haven't even started yet? Her eyes are screaming "don't even try," and that suits me just fine.

Mama is by the stove, stirring a pot. She might be the fiercest person I know, but she's also tiny. She's barely reached my bicep since I was a teen. Not that her height ever stopped her giving me a grilling when she thought I deserved it. *One of these days, Jake, your carefree attitude is going to land you in the sort of trouble I won't be able to get you out of.* It's a variation on the talk she's given me for the best part of fifteen years. Only now do I wonder if we've finally reached that point. My stomach knots. *I'm still living the dream*, I remind myself. I just have to keep it that way.

"Just in time," Mama says as I kiss her cheek. She's pissed I'm late alright, but she knows to give me a minute.

"Sorry, Mama," I say in her ear.

She nods before waving a spoon toward the table. "Jake, this is Harper Cassidy, the reporter from *Sports Magazine*."

"I guess Kevin wasn't available," I say loud enough for Harper to hear as I steal a chunk of fresh bread, still warm from the oven. Mama shoots me a hard glare and I mouth another sorry. It was a dick comment, but Harper's unflinching dagger gaze makes my balls want to leap up into my body, and I wanted to even the playing field.

If my comment hits, she doesn't show it. Instead she stands, holding out her hand for me to shake. It's so formal. If the next five weeks are going to be like this, I'm going to be pulling over at a lot more broken-down Dodges. "Shall we get started now you're finally here?" she asks, cocking an eyebrow like she's daring me to carry on being a dick.

Happy to oblige, I throw a glance back to the stove. "Sorry, sweetheart." I grin, guessing she'll hate the endearment, and by the narrowed eyes I'm right. "The plates aren't out yet. I've got time for a shower."

"Excuse me?" Her look is pure disbelief, but I'm already by the door and Mama is coming to my rescue.

"House rules, I'm afraid," Mama says, flashing Harper a sympathetic smile. "They can shower if I haven't plated dinner. Believe me, raising three boys, you're grateful when they wash. Besides, there's plenty of time now that you're staying here."

I flinch. "Staying? At the ranch? You're kidding, right?"

Mama shakes her head. "I don't joke about business, Jake. You know that. Harper is here to go behind the scenes and get to know the real you so she can write a feature which will go a long way to saving your ass. She's hardly going to do that grabbing a few minutes with you after practice. So I invited her to stay. She's in Chase's room."

I sigh and disappear into the hall and up the stairs before the reporter can give me another of her glares. How the hell has this gone to shit so fast?

If my football career is hanging in the balance with only Harper Cassidy and this feature to save it, then I'm in a whole world of trouble. Because one thing is for sure—based on the looks she just fired my way, Harper already thinks she's got me all figured out. I really need to get out of this interview...

THREE

HARPER

Notes for feature: The first time I meet Jake Sullivan he walks in an hour late and reeking of cheap women's perfume.

"You're at Oakwood Ranch? Have you been kidnapped?"

"Very funny, Mia," I whisper as I close the door to Chase's bedroom.

"So that's it, then? You're leaving me without warning? How am I supposed to survive with nerdy Edward and his blender on my own? Who am I going to bitch about those gold diggers on *LA Love Hunt* with?"

I laugh into the phone. "Edward's not some creepy housemate. He's your boyfriend and you bought him that blender for Christmas last year after you broke his old one making margaritas. I thought you'd be glad to get your couch back for a while. Besides, we both know Edward only pretends to hate *LA Love Hunt*. Now that I'm gone, he can watch it with you."

Her cackle makes me grin. "True. So what's it like being there again?" she asks. "Is Jake still as hot in real life as he looks on TV?"

I think of those broad shoulders and muscles, the dark hair

he keeps pushed away from his face and the stubble across his strong jaw. *Hotter*, I think, but I keep it back. Mia needs no encouragement to start talking about hot men and my sex life, or lack of one.

I cast my eyes around Chase's bedroom. It looks the same as it did on the one time I came here when I was sixteen. Dragged along by Mia to third wheel while she had a brief thing with Chase in high school. I only said yes so I could see where Jake lived. And because Mia begged me.

There's still a teenage-boy feel to the space. There's a poster behind the door showing the back of a woman's naked body. She's wearing cowboy boots and leading a horse into the sunset, long hair flowing down her back toward a perfectly shaped ass.

There's a small desk and above it three shelves lined with shiny trophies. A Stormhawks flag hangs proudly on the wall, its bold red and white colors standing out against the plain walls. Chase might play for the Trailblazers now, but it's clear who his home team was growing up. A framed college football jersey with the number "10" and "Sullivan" printed in bold letters hangs above the bed.

"It feels the same," I say, remembering the instant sense of peace I felt staring across the paddocks and grassland as a sixteen-year-old madly in love with the star of the football team. The air fresh and dewy, the sky endless. Even on a cold November evening there's a warmth to the ranch I can't explain. It's hard not to compare it to my dad's house. How his minimalist décor creates the opposite effect to Oakwood Ranch—cold and uninviting. Or maybe that's just the way it's always felt with my dad after my mom died and it was just the two of us.

For a moment, the loneliness of my childhood threatens to consume me. I was only three when Mom died and I don't remember her. But I remember the emptiness. My dad working away more often than not. I grew up being raised by nannies—people who were paid to care for me. I didn't know any different until I started going to friends' houses and seeing what families really looked like. No surprise I spent most of high school at Mia's.

I glance out the window. Chase's room is over the kitchen, facing toward a large barn. Beyond the wide driveway and the two trucks lined up beside Jake's are a row of fenced paddocks, the grass rich green and overgrown. There's a stillness here, a wild beauty that makes me feel like I can breathe a little easier, despite every fiber of my being screaming at me that this is a bad idea.

"Are you ripping off your clothes around him yet?" Mia's laugh drags me back to the moment. Then she gasps. "Oh my God. Do you remember that story you wrote—"

"Mia," I cut her off, my face flaming at the memory she's yanking, kicking and screaming, to the surface of my thoughts. "That was a long time ago. I was sixteen. Now I'm a journalist and a professional and I'm here to do a job."

It might've been a long time ago, and I might be a different person now from the shy, nerdy girl I was in high school, but I haven't forgotten the story Mia is thinking of. It was an article about Jake—the star of the football team. But I made the mistake of showing one person, and it got out—copied and plastered all over the school. I'll never forget the hurt and humiliation from Jake's words after he read it.

Mia laughs again. "Do a job? Do Jake Sullivan, more like."

If it was anyone else, I'd carry on arguing, but instead I groan, not really minding. Mia has had my back since the seventh grade when her parents divorced and she moved from Michigan to be closer to her mom's side of the family and the family business—running Arquette Media, the home of *Sports Magazine* as well as a dozen other magazines and newspapers, and one news channel.

For all of five minutes we had plans for her mom to marry my dad, making us sisters. It quickly went out the window when we realized Mia's mom's corporate media head was the opposite of my dad's journalistic view of the world.

But we've been best friends through high school and college, and she was there to pick up the pieces when it all went wrong in New York this summer. No one makes me laugh like Mia.

I don't have many other friends. Despite my dad being away chasing stories most of my life, his love of journalism and his focus still rubbed off on me. But with a surname like Cassidy, I have big shoes to fill in the industry. I have to prove I'm professional, focused, and hardworking, and a good journalist in my own right. But somehow, my efforts always get read as stuck up and prickly. Like the team at *Sports Magazine* who love Callie but give me the side eye. It's always been this way. Mia is the only person in the world who really gets me, and I count myself lucky to have the best human on earth by my side.

"Just my job," I reply to Mia's innuendo. "Talking of which, Mia, what the hell is a tight end?"

She laughs again. "Are you serious?"

My silence says it all.

"OK," Mia says and I can hear the smile in her voice. "I'm not an expert or anything, but a tight end is the football player who does a little bit of everything. They're like a mix between a big, strong blocker and a receiver who catches the ball. So, on one play, they might be protecting the quarterback, and on the next, they're catching passes and scoring touchdowns. It's kind of a do-it-all position and one Jake Sullivan is very good at. He used to play quarterback in high school but moved to a different position in college and is now tight end for the Stormhawks. Talking of high school, did Jake mention—"

"No," I say quickly, before another memory I don't want rushes to the surface. "I'm one hundred percent sure no one in this family realizes I went to West Denver High and that's the way it's going to stay."

"Chase will remember you."

"Thankfully he's not here. I'm more than happy to be Harper Cassidy, the journalist from *Sports Magazine*."

"Is she all that different from Harper Cassidy, the high school girl hopelessly in love with the star football player? I quite liked that girl, you know."

"I'll be that girl again if you bring back your braces and your obsession with the rodeo."

We laugh back and forth a while longer, remembering versions of ourselves that feel like different people.

"Just remember to have some fun too, Harper," Mia says when the conversation moves back to my feature on Jake. "Work isn't everything. You need to have a life as well."

"Says the woman who works twelve-hour days and most weekends. Don't worry. I think I might find this fun. Jake already thinks he's God's gift to the world. I'm looking forward to digging deeper to find out if there's anything underneath."

"Uh-oh! I recognize that tone. Poor Jake. He's toast."

From somewhere in the house, a door slams. I lower my voice. "I better go."

"OK. Love you. Text me later."

"You know I will. Love you too," I say, catching my reflection in the mirror. My eyes are still dancing from laughing with Mia. I drop my phone on the red Stormhawks bedspread. Mia's mention of clothes makes me look down at my tailored skirt and blouse. I'm overdressed for a family dinner on a ranch.

As I unzip my suitcase and swap my outfit for a pair of tight, stone-washed jeans and a black sweater that hugs my curves, the window draws my gaze again. In the dusk, the view beyond the paddocks is almost lost, but I can just make out the first craggy foothills. I feel like I could walk straight into the mountains without meeting a single road, fence, or human along the way.

All my life, I've had pictures of the New York skyline on my walls, desperate to escape this state, but I'm still reeling from the reality of the city and there's something comforting about this room and this view. Is this feature on Jake out of my comfort zone? Yes. Is it going to be glaringly obvious within three seconds of speaking that I don't have a clue about football? Also yes. But maybe I can find some peace in the tranquility of the landscape while I'm stuck here.

Besides, anything has got to be better than trying to fake my way through editorial meetings and dodging Callie's snide remarks and constant attempts to undermine me. This could be the perfect spot to work on my novel too. I have no idea what I'm doing or why I'm doing it, but a buzz of excitement still shoots through me when I think about the novel I started when I moved back to Denver. A way to fill my evenings when Mia was working or out with Edward. Mia's right about one thing—I haven't exactly put much effort into building a social life since I got back, but I hate the thought of seeing people I know and what they'll think when they realize I'm back in Denver after messing up my shot in New York.

Quietly, I slip out of the bedroom. From the room next to mine, I catch the sound of a drawer opening then closing. I think of Jake, wet from the shower. I swallow and shove the image aside. I'm not a drooling teen with a major crush anymore. That version of me died the day I realized Jake wasn't the golden boy I thought he was. Ten years on and the cruelty of his words still echo in my mind like it was yesterday: *I'd rather die than meet the loser who wrote that!*

I push the memory aside and head for the stairs, taking in the framed family photos on the white walls. Dylan as a baby with a man in his twenties I guess is his father. Then Jake appears and it's the two of them and their dad for a few years, sitting on a paddock fence with the barn behind them. Then Chase joins them as a two-year-old, sporting overalls and the Afro curls I remember from high school. In the first photo, he looks uncomfortable in his adoptive father's arms, but by the second he's wedged in between Jake and Dylan on the fence and looks like one of the family.

With each photograph, the boys grow taller and broader and then suddenly their father is no longer with them in the shot. I feel a pang of grief for the first photo of the boys alone and the lost expressions hiding behind their smiles. Jake and I have one thing in common at least—we've both lost a parent. I hurry on before my own childhood memories fill my head.

Downstairs, the ranch is full of life and furniture. A home. Lived-in couches and plump cushions. Wood floors and a big fireplace in the living room.

"There you are."

I spin around to find Joanna Sullivan pulling a stack of placemats from a sideboard that looks straight out of an old John Wayne Western. Joanna is still wearing the oversized Stormhawks jersey and apron she greeted me in a few hours ago. She's in her fifties or early sixties with short, blonde-gray hair, a round face and body, and a knowing smile that seems to cut right through me. Mama Sullivan might look like everyone's dream American mom, but I have the sense that's all part of the subterfuge to draw people in. You don't raise three high-profile NFL players without being hardworking, whip-smart, and tough as nails.

It's on my lips to ask her a question about Jake and start getting the background to the feature, but then I remember Tim's warning about Mama. *She runs the show when it comes to her boys. And she's not someone you want to cross.* And so I ask, "Can I help set the table, Mrs. Sullivan?"

The woman laughs, a merry dancing chuckle. "In the thirty-seven years I've lived in this house, you're the first person to ever offer that." She stacks the mats in my open arms. "And call me Mama. Not even my doctor calls me Mrs. Sullivan."

I follow her into the kitchen, already my favorite room in the house. It's a vast, open space, with modern units lining one wall and a large, chrome stove. The long bench table stands in the center, easily long enough for three hulking football players to sit around. The décor is a mix of modern and classic, mirroring the rest of the ranch. There's a door propped open that leads to the garden, barn, and paddocks I saw from Chase's window.

The aromas of home cooking fill the air. I try to remember the last time I ate anything that wasn't at a restaurant or from a takeout carton. The only thing I make in the kitchen of Mia's apartment is grilled cheese, and I burn them more often than not.

"I won't interfere in you getting to know Jake for yourself," Mama says as I lay the table mats. "But I will say this—Dylan is the strong silent type, while Jake and Chase act like life is one big joke. But it is just an act, I can assure you. Jake especially is a hard nut to crack. Don't give up. He's sweet as sugar in the middle and I want the world to know it. This feature wasn't his idea, so you can expect some pushback from him. If you want my advice, don't hammer him with questions. He doesn't like opening up at the best of times so let him do it at his own pace. It's why I wanted you to stay here. He also feeds off emotions, which is why he performs best in front of a cheering crowd. Be patient. Relax around him and he'll do the same."

I can't stop the grimace from reaching my face. Relaxed. Patient. They're not words anyone has ever used to describe me before. "I can handle it," I say, hoping it's true.

Mama's penetrating gaze finds me again. She pauses for a moment and then nods. "I think you can." Her confidence in me should be a boost but it has the opposite effect. A crushing wave of what-the-fuck-am-I-doing anxiety sweeps through me again. I have no experience in writing profiles like this on anyone, least of all football stars. I lied to get this job, pretending I knew as much about football as I do other sports. And I didn't tell Tim that I knew Jake in high school. If Tim learns the truth, I'm finished. And even if he doesn't, there's a high chance I'm going to fail so badly, *Sports Magazine* is going to fire my ass before the week is out. I'll be humiliated again, but worse because this time my career in journalism will be done and I'll have nothing.

But before I can freak out any more, Mama is calling up the stairs, "Get your asses down here. Dinner is ready." She then places a steaming pot of chili on the table in front of me and I take a deep breath as footsteps crash down the stairs.

Relax. I can do that... right?

FOUR

JAKE

DYLAN: *Quit being a pussy and get your ass down here. You're hiding!*

JAKE: *I'm not!*

CHASE: *What's he hiding from?*

DYLAN: *The reporter is here. Worried she's going to realize you're full of shit, Jake?*

CHASE: *Give her some of the Sullivan charm.*

JAKE: *Pretty sure she's immune. Wish you were here, little bro!*

DYLAN: *If you're not downstairs in 60 seconds, I'm telling her about the time we stole your clothes after swimming in the lake and you had to walk home butt naked while those scouts were visiting.*

I'm royally pissed as I grab Buck's ball and stride out the back door in the direction of the lake. Does Harper think going barefoot with red polish on her toes, wearing tight jeans and a tighter sweater, laughing along to Mama's favorite stories from our childhoods, is fooling anyone into thinking she's anything but a hard-nosed journalist out for my blood?

Harper barely looked at me over dinner, let alone asked me a question. I groan, catching the irony. I don't want a reporter up my ass and she's not, and I'm still not happy. But it rubs me the wrong way that she's here twenty-four-seven. Sleeping in Chase's bedroom. In the room next to mine. It's not what I signed up for.

One thing she needs to learn is how thin the walls are.

Jake already thinks he's God's gift to the world. I'm looking forward to digging deeper to find out if there's anything underneath.

Even from my bedroom I heard the mocking tone to her *if*, like she already knew the answer. Harper clearly has her own opinion of me and her own agenda. But she still needs me to open up if she wants her story. If she thinks I'm going to make this easy for her, she can think again.

I didn't say a word over dinner. Eating up and getting out, heading to the lake to throw the ball for Buck while Dylan bobs in the water a few meters away, working on his knee exercises. Without the sun, the temperature has dropped. I'm grateful for my old college sweatshirt as the first stars appear over our heads. Based on the sprinkling of water I felt when Buck shook his fur a minute ago, the lake is cold as fuck.

"That grumpy ass face of yours is ruining the view," I call to Dylan, unable to resist the goad. "Have your balls dropped off in that water yet?"

Dylan grits his teeth and ignores me, twisting his body one way then the other.

Buck drops the ball at my feet and barks.

"You wanna go again?" I laugh.

He barks his reply, and I throw the ball so it lands a foot away from Dylan's face. Buck throws himself after it with an almighty splash, almost drowning Dylan's angry, "Watch out!"

"Sorry!" I grin, not sorry at all and we both know it.

"You're a giant dick, Jake."

I cup a hand to my ear. "What's that? I have a giant dick? So I'm told. No need to be jealous, Dyl. I hear there's medication you can get for that now."

Two years ago, Dylan would've grabbed me and pulled me into the lake, the both of us laughing, but now he just growls at me. The guilt hits like a football flying into my gut. We used to be inseparable, especially after Dad died. Dylan is only a year older than me, but he's always had my back. I don't think I'd have made it through high school without him breaking up fights and sometimes diving in and throwing a few punches himself before hauling me away.

He hasn't been the same since his knee popped on the fifty-yard line. I feel sick thinking of the moment I watched from the benches as he went down. It was the third quarter against the Indianapolis Riverrunners. Stormhawks were down by four and needed the win. All eyes were on Dylan as he dropped back for a big pass play. As soon as the ball left his hands, I saw a linebacker barreling toward him at full speed. Dylan tried to jump out the way, but it was too late. The linebacker's helmet crashed into his knee and I swear I heard the pop from the sideline. I definitely heard the scream of pain he unleashed. I tore across the field and was first by his side as he writhed in agony.

The worst of it is I should've had his back and protected him from that tackle and we both know it. The whole world knows it. Since the injury at the end of last summer Dylan has thrown his walls up. He can't take a joke anymore, but I keep trying. Those walls are higher for me than anyone else. I get it, but I miss my brother.

Dylan's injury was a complete ACL tear. It looked like his football career was over. But after two operations and months of sitting with his leg up, he's got a shot at a full recovery and being back on the field. He's thrown himself into a grueling physical therapy and weights routine set by the Stormhawks trainers and private physical therapists Mama's hired for him, including stretching exercises in ice water. He even broke up with his long-term girlfriend, Kate—a fitness instructor in the city—so he could concentrate on his recovery. I get the dedication, but I swear he wouldn't be so grumpy if he gave his dick even a fraction of the attention he's giving his recovery.

Although I've hardly been my usual self with women either, since his injury. I never used to care that every move I made with women blew up my socials, but now that it comes with a grilling from Coach Allen and Mama, it's not worth it. Especially when most of the rumors about me aren't even true.

"What's up with you today anyway?" Dylan asks, wading back to the shore. "Bad practice?"

I think about telling him how shit I was today, but Dylan is the last person I can complain to about my clumsy catches. We both know how lucky I am to be playing when he's stuck here. I know it eats at Dylan that Coach Allen moved me into his position as tight end after his injury. It's become an unspoken wedge between us. But what was I supposed to do—turn it down? The team needed a tight end and considering how close I'd come to being cut from the team last year, I had no choice but to take it. Someone had to fill Dylan's role. It's not like I don't feel terrible about it every time I step onto the field.

Buck barks beside me, nudging a wet face against my leg, but I'm lost in thought and not quick enough. In the next second, he's jumping, all seventy pounds plus the wet fur, bounding into me. You'd think I'd be used to being tackled like this, but he catches me off balance and suddenly I'm falling back on my ass with a, "Hey."

He barks in my ear while standing on top of me, dripping wet and panting breath. I laugh and rub my hands over his damp golden fur. Then just as fast he's darting from my arms and I turn to see Harper a few feet away.

She arches an eyebrow in amusement. "Am I interrupting?"

"Yes," I say at the same moment Dylan steps out the water—a giant hulk of a man. Taller than me by an inch, with a thick beard covering half his face. His hours pumping weights in his bedroom have paid off. The man is ripped. I catch Harper having the same thought, eyes flicking over him in appraisal, and feel another stab of annoyance that she's here. But Dylan is already shaking his head and grabbing a towel.

"Not interrupting at all," he says.

"How's the injury?" she asks him, nodding to the support Dylan is wrapping around his knee.

I wait for Dylan to explode in his usual anger like he does with me when I ask this question. It's not fair, but I'm looking forward to watching someone rip into this woman who's not only invaded my life but, based on what I've seen and heard so far, is out to ruin it. But of course Dylan is nice to Harper. Any frustration he feels at the question is hidden beneath that big beard of his.

"It's improving slowly," he says.

"That's great." She smiles.

Great is not the word for it. The longer Dylan is out with injury, the less chance there is he'll make it back, which is why he's working so hard and why he's so fucking miserable. He has nine months until the next team selection and pre-season. If he can't get back by then, he'll have been out too long and will likely never make it back. Something Harper should know as a sports journalist.

Dylan gives a short nod and moves away. "I'm going for a shower. He's all yours."

And just like that I'm alone with Harper Cassidy. She fixes me with a look as though this whole thing is a colossal waste of her time.

I've never cared what people think of me. If they want to believe that all I'm about is fucking women and playing football, that's fine with me. And it's not like I haven't earned that reputation in the past. It never used to matter, but then the story hit about me spending time in my truck in the stadium parking lot with three cheerleaders after practice last September. The story took on a life of its own. Threesomes and cheating stories flew out of corners everywhere. There was even a story about a secret love child.

No one seemed to care that the Stormhawks, like most NFL teams, have strict rules against players dating cheerleaders. I was benched for one game, but I wasn't dropped from the team because the stories were total bull. Even Coach Allen could see that. But since then, my reputation has become its own thing that I can't get a hold of. I can't go anywhere without being linked to a woman or slammed for a drunken night I wasn't even drunk on.

One stupid move and over a year later I'm still paying for it. People can't see beyond the reputation. The Dodge driver's comment runs through my thoughts. *I know all about you and your ways.* Even so, it annoys me more than it should that Harper thinks this way too. I thought a journalist from *Sports Magazine* would be supportive. Or at the very least have an open mind.

Neither of us speak as we stare over the lake. I'm more than happy with the silence. There's a rustle from the undergrowth nearby making Harper jump back and then laugh at her own reaction as Buck appears by her side again. I watch her toss her brown hair over her shoulder before taking a long inhale like she's preparing herself for battle.

"I thought we could make a plan for tomorrow," she says. "For us to spend some time together. It would be good to get a bit of background. What you do when you're not playing football, that kind of thing."

My jaw clenches and I see my weekend ruined. "I've got plans tomorrow."

She's silent for another moment, and then she says, "I'll join you."

I swallow down a groan. "I'm hiking Golden Gate Canyon in the morning. Me and Buck. Just the two of us."

"I hike," she says.

"Not based on those killer heels I saw in the kitchen earlier."

She rolls her eyes. "Staring at my legs, Sullivan? What a surprise."

"The only surprise is that you think you're fit enough to hike with me and Buck in the mountains." I sigh. Why am I letting this journalist get under my skin? "I'm going early and I'm going alone. We can talk at lunch."

"Early works for me," she says, like I haven't just spoken. "Shall we leave at seven? And for the record, I'm not one of your fans or your bar hookups. I can handle anything you throw at me."

And there it is. What she really thinks of me—fans and hookups. This woman is getting on my nerves.

"Let's get one thing straight—I don't want you here any more than you want to be here. And you don't know the first thing about me, sweetheart." I scowl, but Harper's eyes light in victory like I've just given her the invitation she needs.

"That's two things," she replies with a knowing smirk. "You won't even know I'm there." And before I can say another word, she's striding back to the ranch, Buck dancing at her heels. I'm still all kinds of pissed with Harper and this situation and I'm in no hurry to follow.

Won't even know she's there? Yeah, right! Harper can think we're meeting at seven all she likes, but I'll be halfway to the canyon by then.

FIVE

HARPER

MIA: *Enjoying the riding at the ranch?*

HARPER: *They don't have horses!*

MIA: *I didn't mean that kind of riding.*

HARPER: *FML*

Notes for feature: Sullivan sulks better than a toddler whose favorite toy just broke.

It's hard not to laugh at Jake's grumpiness as he strides two paces ahead of me on the trail. Every so often he throws a look back my way like he's checking I'm still here. The scowl on his face tells me he's hoping I'm not. Or maybe he just doesn't like Buck trotting obediently by my side, stopping every so often to sniff at the undergrowth before scampering to catch up. Each time Jake looks at me I smile sweetly, like I did in the kitchen when he found me in my workout leggings and a sweatshirt, bag packed and boots laced, ready to go an hour earlier than we agreed last night. Does he think I was born yesterday? Clearly, Jake's used to women fawning over him instead of challenging him.

The morning air has a bite to it as we make our way up the winding trail to Golden Gate Canyon. The sun has just begun to peek above the horizon, casting the first streaks of orange over the distant ridges of the mountains. Frost shimmers on the grass. Fallen leaves crunch beneath my boots with every step.

The trail curves up the side of the canyon, following a small stream that trickles over rocks and fallen logs. I pause, closing my eyes and inhaling the scent of pines and earth. If it wasn't for the fact my assignment is giving all the vibes of a sulky teen being forced to do homework, it would be the perfect hike.

Even with Jake's mood, it beats the gym workouts I usually drag myself to on Saturday mornings, spinning then weights followed by Pilates for three hours with thirty other men and women, all of us sweating, all of us hating and loving it in equal measure. At least my regular gym habit means I can easily keep up with Jake's determined march. He's lost in thought and seems oblivious to the natural beauty around us.

Alone together on the trail, no escape, is the perfect time to get him talking. I can practically feel Tim pinching the bridge of his nose at my hesitance, but I'm pretty sure any questions I ask Jake in his current mood will elicit little more than a growl. For now, I'm content to enjoy the views of the canyon.

The path widens as we reach the ridge and I step beside Jake, glancing at him from the corner of my eye. He towers over me, with broad shoulders filling out his long-sleeved hiking top. His black hair is hidden beneath a Stormhawks baseball cap and his stubble is just short enough not to be considered a beard. He looks manly and rugged and exactly the kind of bad boy fathers warn their daughters about.

He's also not my type. Not since high school, anyway. Considering the number of women who've thrown themselves at him in the years since, it's no surprise he doesn't remember me. I'm more than happy for it to stay that way. I was a different person in high school. Big glasses and frizzy hair, a few extra pounds on me before I realized what healthy eating and exercise could do for my body. Without a mom to teach me, I didn't have the first clue about makeup or clothes. It was only when I left for college that I realized it was up to me to take an interest. With Mia's guidance, I tamed my brown locks and started making the most of my appearance.

In college, I veered away from jocks and focused my attention on clean-shaven, button-down shirt types. Someone I could take home for dinner with my dad. Someone who could keep up with his sparring on politics and current affairs, rather than someone I could really fall in love with. That's when I met Scott. He was a year ahead of me on my journalism course. I took him home to meet my dad, hoping they'd hit it off. I never expected for it to feel like my dad liked him better than he did me.

I quickly discovered that men like Scott, who see themselves as smart and focused, are also entitled pricks. We broke up after a year, but not before my dad took Scott under his wing, helping him get his first job and then promotions along the way. Something he never did for me. He saw helping his daughter as nepotism. As if I cared. The only thing I've ever wanted from him is his love and his approval. But it doesn't mean I like the fact he's still close to Scott. Since then, I've pretty much avoided relationships. Never letting things go beyond a handful of dates. Never falling in love. Something Mia is desperate to change.

Jake steps ahead of me again as the trail winds around the curve of the ridge. I take in the vast landscape stretching below us, bathed in the pumpkin-orange glow from the morning sun.

There was a time this past summer when I thought I'd never live down the humiliation of being fired from *Insight*. When it would never stop being my first waking thought. But it's slowly gotten easier, thanks to Mia and my job at *Sports Magazine*, and maybe in part the novel I started as a way to distract myself, choosing something crazy and never expecting to fall a little bit in love with it. Who knew vampire romances in ancient Egypt could be so much fun?

I've been back in Denver for four months and working at the magazine for the last three, but it's only now—staring across the vast beauty of the landscape—that New York feels more like my past than my present.

"Wow," I say. "This view is unbelievable."

Jake is a step ahead and he turns, flashing me a roguish grin. "Checking out my ass, Harper?"

I roll my eyes and wave a hand to the endless forest below us. "Come on. You have to admit this is something special."

He pauses, following my gaze. I take the opportunity to step up beside him, watching him drink in the view. His chest rises and falls like it's the first breath he's taken all morning. "Yeah," he says. "It's nice."

"Nice? Is that all you've got? It's spectacular." I reach to rub Buck's ear. He tilts his head and leans his warm body against my leg, tail thumping in the dirt.

Jake shoots the retriever a traitorous look before gazing once more to the landscape. "Sometimes I think this is as close to perfect as I'm ever gonna see. Other times nothing in the world can beat the feeling of standing in a stadium of cheering fans."

The comment takes me by surprise. It's the closest to a real thing he's said to me since we met yesterday and I want to pull out my purple notebook tucked in my bag and write it down before firing a dozen more questions at him, but I heed Mama's warning not to push Jake and decide to tread carefully instead.

"It's a lot of pressure though, right?" I say, keeping my focus on stroking Buck, hoping Jake will open up.

"Like you wouldn't believe," he replies.

For a moment it seems like Jake might say more, but then the scowl is back and he's scooping up his bag. "We should get back," he says.

"You want breakfast first?" I ask.

The first hint of a smile twitches on his lips. "You brought food?"

I take the pack from him and unclip the top, pulling out the two wrapped sandwiches I made with Mama last night.

"You didn't? Looks like you'll be going hungry then." I smirk and take a bite.

He huffs, swiping the second sandwich from my hands. "Thanks."

Jake takes a big bite, his jaw working, before he swallows and looks at me, a glint in his eye I don't like the look of. "Not bad, sweetheart."

"Wow, a compliment from the great Jake Sullivan. I'm truly honored." My voice drips with sarcasm. "I'll be sure to add sandwich-making to my résumé under special skills."

He barks a laugh, more surprise than humor, the sound echoing across the canyon. "You do that. Right under pain in the ass." The way he grumbles the reply leaves me in no doubt he means it. For a man who wants to prove he's a decent guy at heart, he's not exactly trying hard to convince me. No doubt he thinks I'm the type to fall for his good looks and write a drooling, fluffy feature on how great he is.

Think again, Jake Sullivan!

"Funny, I was going to say the same about you," I say, matching his tone. I take another bite of my sandwich, savoring the crisp lettuce and salty bacon, stopping myself saying anything more.

Buck looks up at me, his brown eyes wide and pleading. I sigh and give him the last bite before tucking the wrapper away.

After we've eaten, we set off down the trail, walking in frosty silence again. By the time we're back at the ranch, the sun has inched over the horizon, and despite it being November, I can feel the hint of warmth on my skin. I need a shower and my hair straightener. The air here is seriously bad for my kinks. And then I need coffee and to pin Jake down to answer a few questions. So far all I have to send to Tim next week is cheap perfume, toddler tantrums, and pages of me ranting about what kind of person Jake really is...

It's late afternoon by the time I find Jake in the kitchen. He's showered and he's wearing jeans and a plaid shirt with the sleeves rolled up to show off some impressive arm muscles. I catch him giving my simple white tee and stone-washed jeans an appraising glance before he eyes the laptop tucked under my arm and makes a face.

I reply with a bright smile, pushing aside any hope of asking him some background questions and choosing a different tack. "I thought we could look at your schedule over the coming weeks. I'll need to book flights and hotels for your away games and it would be good to find some times for us to hang out that isn't just me trailing behind you."

Jake replies with his usual scowl but drops onto the bench at the table, staring at the back door like he's willing someone to charge through it and rescue him. I sit opposite and open my laptop to the Denver Stormhawks schedule. "So there are games every week on Thursdays and Sundays between now and the start of January, when it becomes about the finals and then the Super Bowl. Starting on Thursday with the Thanksgiving game against LA—"

"Playoffs," Jake cuts in.

I frown, pushing my hair behind my ears. "Sorry?"

Another eyeroll. "They're not called finals, they're called playoffs. At the end of the season, the division winners from each conference—the AFC and NFC—make the playoffs, along with three wild-card teams from each conference. Please tell me you know the NFL is split into two conferences: the American Football Conference and the National Football Conference? That each has sixteen teams, divided into four divisions— North, South, East, and West. The Denver Stormhawks are in the AFC West, along with Chase's team—the Kansas City Trailblazers—plus the Las Vegas Desertraptors and the LA Wildhorns. Each season, teams play games within their division as well as against teams in other divisions from their conference.

"When the playoffs start, it's elimination games. Division winners and wild-card teams face off, and the last two teams standing meet in the Super Bowl. That's the biggest game of the year. For the Stormhawks to make the playoffs for the first time in four years, we need to win the AFC West. But you already know all that, right?"

"Right." I nod, hoping my cheeks aren't burning as I pull my laptop closer and duck my head, typing a string of nonsense just to look busy. "Playoffs. That's what I meant."

He frowns and moves to the side so he can see my face. "You do know about the NFL, don't you?"

I laugh and give an outraged, "Yes."

"Good. Because a sports journalist who didn't know anything about the game writing a profile on a tight end would be pretty stupid."

Fuuuuuck! I grit my teeth and cringe inwardly at how accurate Jake's comment is. What was it Mia said about tight end positions? They're a do-it-all player, whatever that means.

"Don't worry. I know the game." I force a light laugh before steering the conversation back to our plans. "So on Thursday we travel to Los Angeles for the Thanksgiving game against the LA Wildhorns," I say.

He nods. "We stay over and we'll fly back on Friday. And before that, I'll be at practice at Stormhawks Park, our training facility, or at the stadium with the team most days. We usually get a rest day after games, but that's it."

We go back and forth on the schedule and I make notes on what flights and hotels I need for the two away games the Stormhawks are playing during our five weeks together.

I make him give me his number so we can arrange places to meet after practice. And even though it's kind of dumb and I hate myself for it, there's still a tiny part of me that can't believe I've got Jake Sullivan's digits in my phone. I can imagine Mia's squeal of delight when I call her later.

Jake's looking like he's ready to make a run for the back door when it flies open and Mama steps in with a bag of groceries in her arms and a beaming smile. Jake leaps up and takes the bag from her and she stands on her tiptoes and kisses his cheek.

"You won't believe who I found on my way back from the store," she says.

"Who?" Jake asks as Dylan appears from somewhere in the house, leaning against the kitchen doorframe. He's trying to look casual but there's something about his posture that seems stiff. It makes me wonder if he's in more pain than he's letting on.

Before Mama can reply, Buck tears through the open back door, barking with delight, dancing in circles, looking between us as though he wants to be the one to answer.

"Buck only ever looks this happy for one reason." Jake's face breaks into a huge grin as he throws himself at the door and drags his younger brother into the kitchen.

"Surprise." Chase laughs before struggling out of the hugs Jake and Dylan are trying to give him.

"Go easy on my baby," Mama warns, although she's

beaming with pride and delight at her three boys all in the same room together.

Chase is exactly how I remember him. Tall and athletic with a smile that makes me think he's only ever one step away from mischief. The only difference from the Chase in high school is his hair—the Afro curls have been replaced with a close shave. And even though I know he's not Dylan and Jake's brother by blood, he has the same air of confidence about him, like all three of them are exactly where they're supposed to be in the world.

I smile, one part of me happy to remember the times in senior year when we hung out together—two sets of best friends. Mia and me, and him and Serena. This was the year after Chase and Mia's short romance fizzled and they realized they were better as friends. Back then, I felt like I didn't really belong, but Chase always went out of his way to be nice to me and often had us cracking up with his silly jokes. But another—larger—part of me is dying inside for the car crash about to happen. I was really hoping to get through the next five weeks without Jake learning I was only two grades below him at West Denver High. And that meant not seeing Chase.

It'll be fine, I tell myself without confidence. Even if high school comes up, it's not like Jake knows I'm the one who wrote that story about him. I never put my name on it, thank God. My cheeks still burn at the memory of my story plastered over lockers and walls, and Jake's response to his friends, those cutting words.

In hindsight the article I wrote was more of a love letter, questioning if the star of the football team was really quite lonely. It ended with a time and place to meet if he wanted to know who I was. I still remember the hope I felt slipping it into his locker in the last week of the semester before Jake left for college. The excitement that he might come to find me in an empty top floor classroom. My last chance before he was gone to tell him who I was and how I felt about him.

I cringe thinking about that version of myself. But I was just a dumb kid who was lonely and thought she was in love. The article was never meant for anyone but him. But Jake made a joke of it and then he made copies for the rest of the school to laugh at too. He might not have known who wrote that article, but it didn't reduce the sting of humiliation I felt seeing him and the entire school laughing over my words.

I lost two things that day: my faith in Jake—the boy I thought I was madly in love with—and any shred of confidence in myself and my choices. Years later, I still battle with the latter. Still question everything I do, everyone I let into my life, while Jake continues to walk around messing with people's lives and not giving a damn. At least with this feature, the rest of the world will see Jake is every bit his reputation and then some. I just have to let him prove he is who they all think he is...

"What the hell are you doing here?" Dylan asks Chase. "Tell me you didn't get benched," he adds, shooting a side-eyed look to Jake.

Chase laughs. "For your information, the doc says my shoulder needs another week of rest and Coach wants his star quarterback ready for the big games. The Trailblazers are going to crush the Skychargers tonight, anyway."

"Good to see you haven't lost your ego in joining the Trailblazers," Jake quips, slapping him on the back. "Seriously though, it's good to see you."

"You too, bro."

Jake nudges Chase. "Hey, let's hit the field for some throwing practice in the morning like old times."

Chase sighs but he's grinning too. "Here we go. This is about my throw in the second quarter of the Desertraptors game, right?"

Dylan laughs. "You mean the throw even Mama could make?"

"Leave me out of this, thank you," Mama calls out.

I watch as the three brothers fall into an easy banter about Chase's last game. It's impossible to miss the strong bond between them and how being with his little brother brings out a softer side in Jake. It's not just the absence of his usual scowl. He's holding himself differently. He looks happier.

Quietly, I close the lid of my laptop, about to head for the door. I might be here to get to know Jake, but right now I'm intruding on some precious family time. Except Mama is calling across the kitchen before I've made it two steps. "You can sit your ass back down, Harper." I swear she hasn't even turned around. "While you're staying in this house, you're part of this family," she adds as though reading my mind.

I smile and sink back on the bench. The truth is, even with Chase here and the looming knowledge Jake is going to find out we went to high school together, I'm enjoying myself. The kitchen is warm and cozy and it's not the stove. It's this family and the love they obviously share. It's impossible not to compare it to the TV dinners I grew up with when my dad was working late or on the other side of the world, barely registering my existence either way. The times we ate together were formal. Stilted conversations about grades and staying on track. It's why, when I came back to Denver with my Louis Vuitton heels and my suitcase full of shattered dreams, I chose Mia's couch over my old room at Dad's place in Lakewood.

Chase looks my way before doing a comical double take and a wide grin spreads over his face. "Harper?" He steps away from Jake and Dylan. "Harper Cassidy."

My face reddens but I smile at Chase's shocked grin.

"But the last time I saw you..." he starts. "I mean you used to look... You were..." He laughs at the words he's stumbling over. The last time he saw me would've been high school graduation, before I started taking better care of myself. "You look gorgeous," he finishes with a shrug, stepping forward and enveloping me in a bear hug. "It's so good to see you."

Dylan chuckles. "Why am I not surprised you know Harper, Chase? Is there a beautiful woman in Denver you don't know?"

"You too," I say to Chase as we step apart, the blush still burning my face. Maybe it's Dylan's comment. Or maybe it's because I don't know if Mia ever told Chase about the enormous crush I had on Jake and how my professionalism is going to fly out the window the second he tells his brother.

"Oh, Harper and I go way back," Chase says.

Jake looks between us, a question knitting his brow, but thankfully Mama calls us all to help with dinner and Chase launches into telling us about his life with the Kansas City Trailblazers. It isn't long before the kitchen table is filled with plates piled high with food. Roast chicken and chunks of fresh bread. Potatoes and steaming vegetables, and huge yellow cobs of corn glistening with butter. My mouth waters as I realize how hungry I am.

"How long are you back for?" Dylan asks Chase as everyone digs in, reaching over each other for spoons and handing dishes back and forth.

"Just tonight. I fly back tomorrow afternoon."

A thought hits me and my head shoots up, eyes finding Chase as I gasp. "Your room." I clamp a hand to my mouth, thinking of my clothes over the back of the chair, my notebook open on the bed. I've made myself at home. "I can move my stuff," I say quickly.

Chase grins. "Don't worry, I'll sleep on the pullout in Jake's room. It'll be like old times sharing a room together." He punches his brother lightly on the arm, but it's not enough to wipe the look of annoyance crossing Jake's face. Just when I thought he couldn't hate me more.

"Please," I say. "It's your room. I can take the pullout."

Chase cocks an eyebrow, all mischief and trouble as he looks from Jake to me. "You wanna take the pullout?"

I start to nod.

"In Jake's room?" he continues with a wicked grin.

Heat burns my cheeks. Did I really just offer to share a bedroom with Jake? *Kill me now!* "No," I fire the word. "I didn't mean that... What I meant... I just..." I sigh. Why does this feel like high school all over again, me tripping over my words around cute guys? All I need is Mia at my side, jabbing me in the ribs and pointing out what a fool I'm making of myself. I take a breath and get a hold of myself. I'm not a lost teen anymore. "I will not be sharing a room with Jake at any point, but I can take the couch. It's your room, Chase, and you should have it."

Dylan and Chase share a look and burst out laughing. Dylan claps a strong hand on Jake's shoulder. "Well, it had to happen sometime."

"What?" Jake groans like he knows what's coming.

"Being turned down." Dylan grins. "Most women can't wait to share a room and a bed with you. That must hurt a bit, hey, Jakey?"

"Harper's not most women," Jake replies before turning his attention to his plate of food.

I can tell by the looks shooting between Dylan and Chase that they don't know if Jake's comment is a dig or a compliment. Obviously it's a dig, although I'm happy to be different from the women Jake knows.

"You boys gonna take Harper out tonight?" Mama asks as she looks over her boys. "It will do you all good to head to The Hay Barn and see Flic. Get you out from under my feet while you're at it."

I'm certain she doesn't mean that last part. Mama hasn't

stopped smiling all evening. It's easy to tell she lives for these moments.

I shake my head. "I probably shouldn't," I say before Jake can pitch in with some jibe about being stuck spending more time with me. "I don't think I brought anything to wear." And I really need to spend the evening reading the *Football for Dummies* guide I bought on my Kindle. Jake's comment earlier was way too close to the truth. If he finds out I know nothing about the NFL and calls Tim, I'm as good as fired. This might be the worst assignment I've ever had, but at least I still have a job. The thought causes another fluttering of anxiety in my chest. I can't believe the career I love is hanging by a thread, and the likes of Jake Sullivan is the one holding it.

Mama smiles and shakes her head. "Girly, in those Levi's and tee you'll fit in just fine. Especially with..." She stands and disappears into the mud room by the back door before appearing again a moment later with a pair of cowboy boots. "These."

My resolve to stay in my room and read disintegrates at the sight of the boots. They're the most gorgeous cowboy boots I've ever seen. Soft tan leather etched with an intricate stitch pattern and a low heel. "Mama, thank you, but I couldn't," I say, feeling strangely close to tears. It's the kindness, I think. I'm not used to it. Growing up with a journalist father who barely remembered me from one month to the next and then following in his footsteps into the most cutthroat industry in existence hardly leaves room for kindness. "They're too nice," I say quietly. The comment comes with the familiar pang of grief for a mother I don't remember.

She throws an arm around me, pulling me close and squeezing me to her side as she presses the boots into my hands. "Nonsense. You can and you will. My days of wearing them are long gone. And if I'm not mistaken, they'll be the perfect fit."

Later, when I slip my feet into the boots, I realize Mama was right. They're perfect. I just hope she's right about Jake opening up to me if I give him time. She might have faith in him being a good boy at heart, but I don't. When he opens up, he'll reveal all I need for the sort of feature I have planned. He's not capable of anything else...

If he opens up, I correct. Because unless that happens there won't be a feature. Somehow I need to convince Jake I'm on his side, even though I most certainly am not.

SIX

JAKE

After dinner I slide behind the wheel of my truck and the others pile in. Dylan, then Chase, then Harper. I'm reminded of a hundred trips I've taken with my brothers. To high school and Stormhawks games, and more recently, like tonight, to The Hay Barn. It feels easy and uncomplicated, which is just how I like things. With Chase home, even Dylan doesn't look so close to killing someone—namely me.

It's a squeeze with four of us and I find my gaze dragging to where Chase's leg is touching Harper's, not liking it one bit. Chase needs to focus on his game, not women. I don't want him making the same mistakes I did, building a reputation I can't take back. Mama is convinced Harper's feature will be the key to the bad-boy-turned-good story she's trying to build for me. Except she has no idea Harper hates my guts. And I have no idea why, but it feels like it's about more than me turning up late for our first meeting.

We chat about football on the journey. Chase and Dylan bickering over plays and when to punt. Like always, Chase falls right into Dylan's goading.

"When you're in the fourth down, you gotta go for it all the way," Chase says with an exasperated sigh. "That's football 101, man!"

Dylan groans. "That's a rookie move. On the fourth down, you punt it and then you pin them back. Let your defense work!"

"That's so old-school." Chase laughs. "This isn't 1985, Dyl. The league is all about offense now. You keep the ball and control the game. Help me out here, Harper." Chase nudges Harper's arm. "If you're on your final attempt to move the ball down the field and you're about to lose possession, do you keep fighting or go for the punt?"

"Er... I think it depends," she starts.

"Exactly," Dylan jumps in. "You can't say you'll keep on fighting unless you're there in the moment to make that call."

I grin, throwing myself in. "You're both wrong, anyway. If you're in the fourth, you go for the field goal."

Chase and Dylan groan in unison and we battle back and forth on different plays until we hit the outskirts of West Denver and turn into the parking lot for The Hay Barn. It's still early, but from the number of trucks already here, Flic's having a good Saturday night. It's the only bar we drink at when we're home. It's got cozy booths and a small-town vibe to it. Plus it's a Stormhawks bar and it's owned by my best friend.

The cold night air hits my face as I jump out of the truck and walk around the hood to open Harper's door. She slides out, murmuring a quiet thanks as I catch the scent of her shampoo—coconut and something fruity. Chase follows a beat later, clapping a hand on my shoulder. "Bit late for the gentleman routine, don't you think?" He flashes me a shit-eating grin as Dylan follows behind. I swing the door shut and make to punch my little brother, but he ducks away, throwing an arm around Dylan as the three of them walk inside.

The warmth and noise envelop me as I step through the door behind the others. I'm hit with the familiar scents of beer, sawdust, and barbecue. The walls are decorated with license plates, Stormhawks memorabilia, and a giant set of bull horns mounted over the bar. Country tunes drift from the jukebox in the corner, mixing with the chatter of the Saturday night crowd.

Flic is behind the bar in her usual black tank top and tight black jeans, long blonde hair pulled back in two braids that hang down her back. She's a dead ringer for Angelina Jolie in *Gone in 60 Seconds*, something she rolls her eyes at whenever anyone mentions it.

She grins as she sees us, already reaching for the bottles of light beer she knows we'll order.

"Jake," she calls with a wink. "I thought you were hiding from me."

I give a rueful smile. "Just been busy." It's true but I feel a pang of guilt too. Flic and I were photographed having lunch together last month and it blew up in the media when two of my teammates, Billy and Gordon, decided to question me at practice, catching the whole thing on Gordon's phone. It hit the gossip sites in under a day. My "just a friend" line not enough to stop Billy jokingly threatening to break my bones. Billy is a good friend and he was only messing around, but the leaked video caused a ton of ridiculous rumors hitting the gossip sites. The last thing I want is to drag Flic into the spotlight. She's always valued her privacy and I respect that.

Flic keeps her eyes on me another moment, searching for more, but then Chase's white Trailblazers baseball cap catches her eye and she's yelling a, "Hell no, Chase," and whipping it from his head.

"Come on, Flic," Chase groans, rubbing at his now bare head. I still think of him as the shy kid with the Afro and overalls who joined our family when he was two and I was five, but the shaved look suits him. "You know I'm a Stormhawks fan, but Trailblazers are my team now."

"And that's why I still let you drink in here. That and

because I love your sorry ass. But you know the rules." In another second, Flic is reaching for the staple gun she keeps by the liquor and jumping onto the dark mahogany bar in her black cowboy boots, jamming Chase's cap to her wall of shame on the beam that runs above the bar.

I chuckle and watch Harper take in the row of confiscated football team hats and tees and one piece of men's underwear with the New York Steelguards logo all over them. I wasn't here the night they got taken but I heard it was a good one. For a moment, my eyes linger on Harper and the way her jeans are tight in all the right places. Then I catch myself and look away. Harper might be objectively sexy, but I like my relationships like I like my life—uncomplicated and fun. Or at least I did when I was dating. Either way, Harper is none of those things. Plus, I can't stand her.

A cheer erupts as Flic hops down and finishes serving the beers. I cast my gaze around the place, nodding to a few old-timers who knew my dad. They're the type to buy me a beer and tell me how proud he'd be. Lately, comments like that make me think about my reputation and Coach Allen's look of despair every time a new story breaks about me, and I feel like I've let a dead man down alongside everyone else.

In the corner by the jukebox is the younger crowd. I spot the blond head of my Stormhawks teammate and linebacker, Gordon. I sigh. Just what I need. Of all my teammates, Gordon Jenkins is my least favorite, and that's putting it mildly. Maybe it's because his squeaky-clean rep is far from deserved, and yet he gets away with treating women like shit. I've dated my share over the years, but at least I know how to respect women. Or maybe it's just because I don't like the guy.

He's towering over a group of female fans in tank tops and denim skirts. I know a few of them by name and recognize the others. Cherry—a box-dye redhead and Stormhawks fan— catches my eye and I look away before she decides to saunter over. Cherry has made her feelings and her intentions for me clear. She's not looking for anything serious. A few years ago, I'd have gone along with it, but I don't want to be a notch on her bedpost or her on mine. I don't want that life anymore—it's why I've been single for over a year now. The truth is I don't know what I want.

As Dylan and Chase get dragged into a conversation with a group of fans at the bar, I grab our beers and Harper follows me to our usual booth in the corner. She perches on the edge of the scuffed leather seat while I spread myself out opposite and we do a good job of ignoring each other. If Harper is bothered by the silence, she doesn't show it. If she wasn't out for my blood, I'd admire her patience.

The journalists I've met have one setting: rapid-fire questioning. She's not what I expected, and as she draws the bottle of beer to her red-painted lips, I get a sudden image of all the places on my body those lips could be right now. The thought takes me by surprise and I shake it away, annoyed at myself. Whatever the reason, Harper Cassidy hates my guts and the feeling is more than mutual.

It's a relief when Chase and Dylan arrive with another woman in a gypsy skirt and tight top I recognize as one of Chase's old high school friends. She's with a dude with red-brown hair wearing a pale pink shirt and glasses who looks like he took a wrong turn at a golf tournament and wound up here.

"Mia!" Harper exclaims, scooching around the booth to make space until she's squeezed in next to me, our legs touching. I drink my beer and pretend not to notice the heat radiating up my leg. The other woman slides in beside Harper and the two hug.

"What are you doing here?" Harper grins. It's hard not to notice how happy Harper looks compared to the version of her I've seen so far.

Mia's skin shimmers with glittery makeup as she tilts her

head and levels Harper with a knowing look. "I tell you what I'm not doing here, shall I? I'm not here because my best friend in the whole world decided to go out for the first time in forever and thought to invite me."

"Hey, I go out," Harper protests.

"Hitting the gym and browsing bookstores doesn't count as out. But fortunately for you, Chase dropped me and Serena a message. And while Serena might be on a date tonight, my schedule was wide open."

I look around the table. To Chase. Then Mia. Then Harper. I remember Mia from high school. Loud, confident, beautiful, and hanging off Chase's arm for a few months—she's hard to forget. And I know Serena. She's been Chase's best friend since high school and is now on the Stormhawks cheer team. And it's clear from the way Mia and Harper are talking that they're close. High school friends close. But no matter how hard I try, I can't place Harper beside Mia in any of my memories. I was too busy playing football to notice the girls in Chase's grade.

Everyone squeezes in and introductions are made. The guy in the shirt and glasses is Mia's boyfriend, Edward. He's wedged in between Chase and Dylan and looks out of his depth as he's dragged into football talk.

Mia leans across Harper, fixing me with a fierce gaze. "Harper is my best friend," she declares, "so you'd better be nice to her, Jake, and treat her like the queen she is or you'll have me to answer to. And I'm no pushover."

A smile pulls at my lips, but I nod. "Yes, ma'am."

Mia and Harper fall into an easy conversation and I sit back, enjoying the buzz of the bar and being with my brothers. I can't remember the last time we were all together like this, only that it's been a while.

Then Dylan claps his hands and leans across the table, pointing at Mia. "I've just figured out where I know you from," he says with a broad smile.

"Yeah, dummy." Chase laughs. "High school. Mia, Harper, and I had homeroom together."

I glance to Harper, catching the flush to her cheeks, and wonder again why she's kept it quiet that we went to the same high school. Most people can't wait to tell me about a connection, although usually it's someone's friend's cousin who sat behind me on a flight once.

"I was three grades above you, bro. No way I remember you two from high school. But I do know that you're Mia Arquette," Dylan says, turning back to Mia with a grin. "You used to do barrel racing at the rodeo, right?"

Arquette. The last name snags in my thoughts. She isn't connected to Arquette Media, is she? The same company who owns *Sports Magazine* where Harper now works? I file that thought away for later as Mia's face lights up.

"Sure did." She tips her imaginary cowboy hat and we all laugh.

"Why'd you stop?" Dylan asks. "I never saw anyone ride like that."

The light in Mia's eyes fades in an instant and it's obvious it's a sore topic. But Mia shrugs and takes a long sip of wine. "Had to grow up sometime," she says like it was no big deal.

"Hey, Harper, why didn't you mention you went to our high school?" Dylan asks and I wonder if he senses the awkwardness of Mia's reply and is trying to move the conversation along. Although from the look of terror crossing Harper's face, he's waltzed us right into another awkward moment.

"Oh... I... didn't think it was important," she stammers.

"Really?" I turn to Harper, making sure she feels my gaze on her. I'm not sure why Harper is so embarrassed but I'm enjoying watching her squirm.

"It's not like I actually knew either of you. Just Chase..." she says, her voice trailing off.

Mia nudges her friend. "Harper doesn't like to remember high school. Seeing what a total nerd she was back then."

"Hey." Harper swipes Mia's arm but the comment lightens the tension in Harper's face.

Mia flashes Harper a wicked grin. "It's true. You even used to—"

Before Mia can finish, Harper leaps up, half shoving Mia out the booth. "We need more drinks. Mia, come help me."

They huddle close as they step to the bar, talking back and forth, and when Mia whispers something in Harper's ear, she throws her head back, laughing in a way that has my gaze pulling to those red lips again.

I'm clearly not the only one to notice because a beat later, Gordon is leaning casually beside them. He places his hand on Harper's arm as he talks, and whatever he says, it makes all three of them laugh. I shift in my seat, annoyance rising inside me.

Gordon is always pulling crap like this—swooping in on women, charming them into his bed with his preppy blond hair and clean-shaven look. I don't give a shit what the likes of Gordon do in their spare time, but it pisses me off when his reputation remains squeaky clean. Especially when he seems to enjoy making sure mine stays in the mud. I'm certain he was the one who released the video of me at practice last month. Even if he denies it, blaming one of the other players after he'd shared it on the team group chat.

Chase and Dylan are still deep in conversation about game play with Edward sitting silently between them. As much as I'd love to join them, I can't take my eyes off Harper as she shifts away from Gordon's touch and tries to catch Flic's attention to order. There's something in the uncertainty in Harper's eyes that makes my protective instinct kick in. I might not like Harper, but no one deserves Gordon hitting on them. I'm by her side in three strides.

"You ladies look like you need a hand," I say with a wink to Harper and a wave to Flic. "Mia, you might want to rescue Edward. He looks about as comfortable as a Stormhawks fan at a Vegas Desertraptors convention."

Mia's mouth makes a perfect "O" shape and then she laughs. "I'm on it." She flashes Harper a grin, conveying a silent message that makes Harper roll her eyes at Mia's back as she heads to the table.

"Hey, Jake, we're good here," Gordon says, barely acknowledging me as he focuses on Harper.

I resist the urge to shove him away, reminding myself we're in public. Instead, I turn my body, blocking his view of Harper as I give our drinks order to Flic before turning to Gordon. For a second, we're locked in a silent standoff, neither wanting to back down.

Then Harper's voice cuts in. "I'm fine, Jake. You don't need to be here. Gordon was just being friendly."

That's not what I'd call it, but I don't argue. "Sure thing. Hey, let me make the introductions. Harper, it looks like you've met Gordon Jenkins."

"People call me Flash," Gordon says with that grin of his that makes me want to break his nose.

I smirk. "Only your mother, Gordon. That name ain't catching on." I nod to Harper. "This is Harper Cassidy, a journalist from *Sports Magazine*."

I don't mention the feature she's writing on me. It's only a matter of time before the team finds out and corners Harper to share every embarrassing story about me. The longer I can keep it quiet for, the better. But as I expected, the mention of Harper's profession is enough for Gordon to back down. He's looking for a woman to warm his bed tonight, but he's not stupid enough to make a move on a journalist and risk damaging his reputation.

He shakes Harper's hand and immediately backs up. "Nice

to meet you, Harper," he says, turning away. "See you at practice, Sullivan," he calls over his shoulder.

Flic slides our drinks across the bar and smiles. "Rescuing women again, Jake?"

I shrug. "I'm pretty sure Harper can take care of herself."

"Yes, I can," Harper says from beside me. From the edge to her voice, she's none too pleased by the rescue. "And isn't he on your team? You acted like you hate each other."

"Gordon is my teammate. I trust him on the field to bring down the opposing team but off the field, it's different." The truth is, I wouldn't trust him not to step over a sweet little grandmother who's fallen down if it meant getting his dick serviced.

"Come on," Harper replies. "The man rescues puppies in his spare time. What's not to like?"

A muscle ticks in my jaw. How can she buy into that crap Gordon posts all over his socials? "Not all reputations are justified."

"Is yours?" she shoots back, fixing me with a questioning look.

I hold her gaze, noticing how those big brown eyes of hers are flecked with gold. The kind of eyes that draw someone in. I think of leaning in, brushing Harper's hair away from her face, and whispering in her ear how happy I'd be to show her just how true my reputation is. It's the kind of move that would really piss her off. But the short-term win of annoying Harper isn't going to help my rep. So I settle for honesty instead. "I'm not going to pretend I don't enjoy sex, but I'm not into one-time hookups anymore and I haven't been for a long time. Most of the stuff about me isn't true."

"Why don't you ever deny it then?" she fires back.

"Because I don't give a shit what people think of me. If they want to think I'm that person, why do I care? But now it's affecting the team and my career." I shrug.

Harper stares at me like I'm a math equation she's trying to solve. Then she gives a shake of her head. "So you're telling me you've changed?"

"I guess that's what you're here to find out." I scoop up the beer bottles and my soda and head back to the booth before she can ask any more questions. My thoughts pull to the comment I overheard her make on the phone last night.

Jake already thinks he's God's gift to the world.

Suddenly I'm wishing I'd left Harper to the likes of Gordon. The last thing I want tonight is to answer questions. I don't buy Harper's curiosity for a second. She's probably no better than the gossip sites that twist everything I say. That's the last time I go out of my way to rescue her ungrateful ass.

It's 2 a.m. before I give up trying to sleep. From across the room, Chase is snoring lightly on the pullout. *Just like old times*, I think, trying to be annoyed he's bunking in with me, but still finding myself happy he's home. Besides, it's not Chase keeping me awake. It's thinking about Harper and her questions tonight.

So you're telling me you've changed?

I usually don't care what people think, so why does the disbelief in her tone annoy the hell out of me?

I make my way barefoot to the kitchen, being careful to avoid the creaking floorboards engrained in my memory from an adolescence of sneaking around this house without Mama knowing. I smirk to myself at the thought. Without fail, any time I snuck out to a party or a hookup, Mama would yank me out of bed early the next morning with a list of chores as long as my arm. Of course she knew.

But as soon as I step through the doorway into the kitchen, I see Harper at one end of the table, the glow of her laptop illuminating her face in the dim room. She looks up, eyes widening in surprise.

"Oh! I'm sorry, I didn't think anyone else would be up," she says. "I can go to my room."

"Don't leave on my account," I reply, moving to the fridge to grab some water, aware of her watching me. I'm suddenly conscious I'm shirtless and wearing only a pair of basketball shorts low on my hips. Based on the glimpse I caught before I turned away, she's wearing a tee and not much else. "I couldn't sleep."

"Me neither," Harper says.

I lean against the counter and take a sip of water, watching her over the lip of my glass. Her hair is pulled up in a messy bun, strands falling loose to frame her face. The oversized tee she's wearing slips off one shoulder, exposing a delicate collarbone. From the way her breasts swell against the fabric, she's not wearing a bra.

I feel my dick harden and snap my eyes up to her face instead, but the way she's biting her lip in concentration as she stares at her laptop doesn't help the straining I can feel starting to happen against my shorts. This is clearly the side effect of not dating anyone for so long. Harper might be sexy as hell and scantily dressed in the middle of the night in my house, but she also looks like she's one step away from throwing me under a bus. Something my head isn't going to forget, even if my dick has.

I take a seat on the bench opposite before she can see the raging hard-on about to make a tent out of my shorts.

"Are you writing the feature about me already?" I ask, uneasy at the thought.

She shakes her head and shoots me a look. "I'd need to actually know something about you to start writing."

Ouch. She's got a point, although I notice she doesn't expand her answer to tell me what she is working on. I lean across the table to take a peek but she closes the laptop quickly.

"Working on your master plan?" I quip.

She frowns. "Master plan?"

"You know… a grand plan for how you're going to take over the world. You seem like the type."

Harper smiles but it doesn't reach her eyes. "You think I've got my life together? You think I've got a plan?"

"You don't?"

She shakes her head. "I did once, but it sort of crashed and burned earlier this year."

I raise an eyebrow and she pulls in a deep breath that draws my eyes back down to her tee and the place where her nipples are pushing against the fabric. I force my gaze up. *What the hell, Sullivan! This woman will eat you alive if you give her half a chance.*

"Earlier this year I landed a dream job. It was an internship for a features writer at *Insight*. I thought I'd made it. I found a New York apartment I could barely afford and signed a one-year lease. I blew the last of my money on a pair of designer shoes and walked into that office with my grand plan to take over the world."

"What happened?" I ask.

"I wasn't cut out for it," she replies. There's more to the story, but she pushes on before I can ask. "So yeah, this isn't the dream for me either, you know? Following you around like some kind of groupie. But if I don't do a good job on this feature, I'll be fired again."

Her honesty takes me by surprise. "Seems like we've both got a lot to lose if this doesn't go well then," I say.

She shoots me another hard look. "So maybe we need to find a way to work together."

"Hey," I shoot back. "You're the one who's already made up your mind about me. Do you even care what I have to say?"

She scoops a stray lock of chestnut hair behind her ear. "Of course I do. It's my job to care."

"Yeah, right."

"What's that supposed to mean?" she snaps.

"It means, I heard what you said about me."

"And what did I say?" She folds her arms. The movement pulls the fabric of her tee tighter around her breasts. It's a fight to keep my eyes from dragging down.

"Last night before dinner. You were on the phone," I reply. "I would guess you were talking to your friend Mia. Something about me thinking I'm God's gift to the world and you looking forward to finding out *if* there's anything more to me. It's pretty obvious you think every one of those stories about me is true and you can't wait to destroy me."

If I didn't know better I'd think Harper looks almost sheepish. "You're right, I did say that. I didn't mean for you to hear it and I'm sorry. But in my defense, you were an hour late to our first meeting."

She's got a point, but no way am I giving up the high ground.

Harper sighs. "We're not on the same team, Jake. I've been sent to write an in-depth feature on you. My job is to write the truth. If you want what I write to be positive, then you need to let me in and show me you're a good guy."

Her words hang in the silence. Anger hums beneath my skin, even if a part of me can see her point. I grit my teeth. Storming out seems like a pretty good option right now, but I'll be damned if I'm being chased from my own kitchen. However much I might hate this situation, I'm stuck with this woman for the next five weeks. Something's got to give.

I push a hand through my hair. "This is getting us nowhere," I sigh. "You're right, we're not on the same team, and we do need to find a way to work together."

"What do you suggest?" she asks, and even though I can't be sure, I think something in her softens too.

"We're going to be spending a lot of time together. How about we set some ground rules?" I reply.

"Like what?"

I think for a moment. "Like, I don't want to feel like I'm constantly being interviewed. You can ask me two questions a day."

"Four," she fires back.

"Three."

She rolls her eyes. "Fine, but you have to answer them. No jokes or evasion."

I nod my agreement. "And I get to ask you questions back."

Her eyes narrow on me. "Why?"

I shrug, not really sure myself. "Because it won't feel so one-way then."

She nods slowly. "OK, but no more scowling at me."

I laugh in disbelief. "I'll stop scowling if you stop shooting me dagger eyes."

Her lips tighten and she looks like she's about to narrow her eyes, but stops herself. "Fine."

A silence settles over our tentative truce.

"I'm starting now," she says.

"Of course you are." I start to frown but stop and she laughs. It's a nice sound. Light and delicate.

Harper tilts her head to one side as she looks at me. "Have you ever dated Flic?"

I laugh. "That's your question? No, I haven't ever dated Flic."

"Why not?"

I smile, thinking of my best friend. "Before Flic took over the bar, it belonged to her parents. But her dad was a useless drunk and left her mom to run the place on her own. Flic would hang around the bar all hours, collecting glasses and getting under people's feet. It was no way for a kid to grow up. One day my dad came home and announced that from then on, Flic would come home after school with us on Fridays and stay for the weekend. Chase got put in with me and Flic got Chase's bedroom, which is why my little brother said it was like old times sleeping on the pullout. And why none of us have ever dated Flic. She stayed with us pretty much every weekend through part of elementary school, all of middle school and most of high school, even after my dad died. She's like my little sister."

Harper seems to think about this for a while. "I can see that. She seems really nice."

"She is," I say. "My turn. Why were you really fired from your job in New York?"

"Hey," she frowns. "I started easy on you."

I smirk. "I never promised I'd do the same."

She runs a hand through her hair, hurt radiating from her body. "It's the biggest cliché in the book. I was working late on a story one night and the editor I was working with made a pass at me. I turned him down. The next thing I know, I was told I wasn't cut out for journalism and was fired."

A heat burns beneath my skin. The same protectiveness I felt in the bar watching Gordon make a pass floods back through me, taking me by surprise. "They can't do that."

"It happened," she says with a shrug. "I'm over it."

It's pretty clear she isn't, but I don't push it. I still have a feeling there's more she's not saying, but it's none of my business and it's not like I even care.

She's quiet a while before she speaks again. "Is the story about you and the three cheerleaders in the parking lot true?"

My jaw tightens at the mention of last September. But at least Harper is considering the possibility there might be more to me than the headlines and that fucking photo.

"Not even a little bit," I reply.

"What happened?" she asks.

A tension pulls across my shoulders. It was the lowest point in my career and no one will let me forget it. "Sorry, sweetheart, that's your questions done for today."

Harper rolls her eyes and gets to her feet, tucking her laptop under one arm. I catch a glimpse of a pair of tiny shorts beneath her tee and the smooth skin of her thighs. "No more sweethearts, either," she says when she reaches the doorway.

"Goodnight, Cassidy," I reply, watching her disappear.

As I slip beneath my covers ten minutes later, I find myself thinking about the perfect ass I tried to stop myself from watching walk out of the kitchen. I push the image aside. A 2 a.m. business truce in the kitchen doesn't change the fact that Harper thinks I'm a player, and she sure as hell is still a giant pain in my ass.

SEVEN
HARPER

MIA: *Did the hot tight end try to get into your pants last night?*

HARPER: *No, he did not.*

MIA: *And how disappointed are you?*

HARPER: *Hello! Professional journalist working here. I'm taking my job seriously!*

MIA: *The only serious thing about this is how seriously you have the hots for Jake.*

HARPER: *This is why I don't invite you out.*

MIA: *You love me really.*

HARPER: *True!*

Notes for the feature: I still haven't seen any sign of a sweeter

side to Jake. If it's in there, it's well hidden behind a cocky
confidence that irritates the hell out of me.

The embarrassment hits the second I wake the following morning.

Have you and Flic ever dated?

Seriously? Jake agrees to answer questions and that's the one I go for? I can't even use it in the feature. My cheeks burn with heat and I want to bury my head in the covers. I sounded like a jealous girlfriend and nothing like the professional sports journalist I'm trying to be. I need facts I can use. Jake can say all he wants that he's nothing like the man behind his reputation, but I've yet to see it. I'm still certain, given time, this feature will be his undoing. It's just a bonus at this point that I'll finally get some payback for him humiliating me in high school.

And yet something about seeing him in the middle of the night like that when I'd been lost in my novel—it knocked me off guard. I wasn't thinking straight. I shiver, remembering the way he leaned against the counter bare chested. Huge shoulders and defined muscles tapering to a toned waist, and that line of dark hair that disappeared into his shorts...

I could've asked him what he loves about football or what his first memory is from playing the game. I could've asked him what his biggest fear is or why there's an edge to his and Dylan's relationship that isn't there with Chase. But I remembered Flic from high school and how close she and Jake were, how they looked like the perfect couple back then, and I was more than a little curious. She was just as beautiful and self-assured in high school as the woman behind the bar last night, and I couldn't believe in all their years of friendship it hadn't got physical.

In comparison, Jake's first question cut right to one of the worst times of my life. Am I really so easy to read? The familiar burn of humiliation scorches through my body and I throw back the covers and force myself up. No good can come of dwelling on New York. I need to clear my head. I throw on my running clothes, scoop my hair into a ponytail, and make my way to the kitchen for a caffeine hit before I exercise.

I find Mama sitting at the table with a laptop and papers stacked in neat piles. It's a reminder that as well as cooking the best chili I've ever tasted and welcoming me into her home, she's also the driving force behind her boys' success, acting as their agent and a hell of a lot more, I suspect.

Mama's gray-blonde hair is pinned away from her face with a clip and she's wearing black-framed glasses and overalls over a red sweater. She lifts her head as I enter and smiles.

"Coffee's hot," she says.

"Thanks." I grab a mug and sit opposite.

"Sunday mornings are for admin," she says, waving a hand over the papers. I catch the name of a medical company at the top of one of the piles and wonder how much Dylan's knee injury is costing.

"Don't worry," Mama says, nodding to the medical bills like I've asked the question running through my mind. "The team is covering most of the costs for the ACL tear. These bills are just the extras we're putting in place, trying to give Dylan the best shot of getting back on the field. There's a specialist ACL treatment center in LA I'm trying to get him into next week. We're lucky Dylan can easily afford it. Players who get injured earlier in their careers don't have it so easy."

I add Dylan's injury to the growing list of things I need to research. It's a reminder I still haven't read up on the basics of football.

Mama straightens her papers and fixes me with a look. "So tell me—how's it going with my other boy?"

I think of the man I met on Friday who was the wrong side of cocky and a major dick. Then I think of the uneasy truce we agreed last night. "Slowly," I reply.

She nods like she gets it. "It's only been two days. You'll get there. This is why it had to be this way. You and him together for five weeks. He's got a lot of walls up and does a good job hiding behind them. A sit-down interview would've given you nothing but the same bull he's been feeding to the press and the fans his whole career."

"Jake said last night he doesn't care what people think of him. Is that true?"

Mama pulls off her glasses and gives a sad smile. "Jake was ten when his father died. It's an age when boys start to really look up to their dads and seek their approval. Harry died before Jake could see he already had it. That man was practically bursting with pride for all three of his boys. I'm no psychologist, but I think because Jake never felt he had his dad's approval, he decided he didn't want anyone else's either. So on the surface, it's true he doesn't care what people think. He's resilient and he's focused and he's a fantastic player. If he was signed with any other team, his reputation probably wouldn't matter. There are plenty of bad boys in the NFL. Plenty of players doing things far worse than Jake, although I will say this—people do love hearing stories about him.

"But the Denver Stormhawks are still family owned," Mama explains. "It's been that way since Larry Hubert started the team in 1959. They've resisted every offer from the big corporates and the fans love them for it. They do a lot for the Denver community and they care about their reputation and the reputations of their players. It's one of the few teams in the NFL where it's not just about the players' skills on the field. Jake knows this, and however much he pretends not to care, Stormhawks are his team. He feels like he's letting them down and the fans too and that's eating him up inside." She slips her glasses back on. "I'm hoping you'll be able to break the pattern with your feature."

My head shoots up. Guilt jabs me in the space between my ribs. The Jake I know might deserve what's coming to him, but

Mama doesn't. I feel suddenly uncomfortable about the fallout my feature will cause for her. But then Jake didn't care about my heart when he stomped all over it in high school—and I don't think he cared about any of the other hearts he's trampled since. Whether or not Mama believes the stories about him, the old saying still rings true: No smoke without fire...

Mama makes a move to stand. "I'd better get this packed away and put some breakfast on for those boys."

"It must be nice having them all home," I say, pushing aside the guilt. I'm only doing my job. I'm here to write the truth. It's just a case of waiting for Jake to show it to me.

Her smile widens. "Best feeling in the world to have my three boys sleeping under this roof. I know how lucky I am. At their age they could be on the other side of the world."

"When did Chase come to live with you?" I ask, remembering the family photos running up the wall and Chase looking so young in those first photos. I can guess the answer, but really I'm asking how it came about.

Mama's face softens. "He was nearly three, although he could barely speak. He's my nephew by blood, did you know?"

I shake my head.

"My sister and I have always been big Stormhawks fans. But my love of the game never stretched to loving the players the way some of the female fans do, if you catch my meaning."

An image of the woman with the bright red hair from last night flashes in my thoughts. The way she snaked an arm around Jake's neck as we were leaving. The way she pressed her face to his for a selfie was almost proprietary.

"I met Harry in my early twenties and we settled here. Dylan and Jake came along in quick succession and our lives became about running the ranch and raising our boys, but Leanna still went to every game. One night she hooked up with Jamel Bishop, a wide receiver who played for the Stormhawks for one season. She got knocked up. Jamel wanted nothing to do with her or the baby. He offered Leanna a chunk of money and signed with a team in Canada." She pauses and shoots me a look. "Chase knows who his father is, but he's kept it to himself. I've always believed it's his story to tell if he wants to, so I'd appreciate it if—"

I give a furious shake of my head. "I won't write about it."

"Thank you. Anyway, from day one Leanna struggled. The money didn't go far and Jamel wrapped her up in a lot of legal stuff when she asked for more. We tried to help where we could, but it wasn't like we had much ourselves. Then one day she knocked on our door at midnight and handed Chase over. She said she couldn't do it anymore." Mama purses her lips. "She kept the engine of her truck running as she handed him to me. That's how fast it happened. She left and we took Chase in. He's been my son and Jake and Dylan's brother ever since." Her eyes glisten and it's obvious to see the love she has for Chase.

Mama brushes down her overalls as though physically pushing the memory aside.

"The thing about football players, Harper, is that they're always hungry. I feel like I've spent the last two decades trying to make enough food to fill their bellies." She rolls her eyes, but I can tell she loves it. "By the way," she adds a moment later, "if you ever need a break, the keys for my truck are hanging by the door. Use it anytime you like."

"Thank you," I say. Emotion feels suddenly thick in my throat. It's the same feeling I had when Mama lent me her cowboy boots. I'm pulled away, wondering what my childhood would've been like if my mom hadn't died in a car accident when I was three. What kind of person would I be now? Would I be happier? Kinder? More outgoing? Would I still be a journalist? Would I still feel the need to prove myself to everyone I meet? I guess that's where Jake and I differ. He doesn't feel the need to seek approval from anyone because the one person he looked up to died. Whereas my mom's death left me trying to fill a hole inside me where her love should've been.

There are no answers to these questions, so I swallow them down with my coffee, reminding myself that my childhood wasn't bad. I had a father. I had a home. I had enough food and clothes. I even had people who seemed to love me sometimes. Like Stephanie, my first nanny. She came soon after Mom died and stayed for four years, leaving when I was seven to start her own family. She was kind and mothering, baking cookies with me and reading me bedtime stories. I cried every night for a month when she left.

Then came Penny. She was young and lazy and only stayed for the three months my dad was chasing a story in Colombia. Penny left when Dad returned to find the house in a state and his daughter dirty and sullen. I can't remember the names of all the nannies that came after her. Some stayed for a few weeks, others for months, but none stuck around for as long as Stephanie. With each new nanny, I told myself that if I was good, maybe she'd be the mom I needed. It became my mission to win them over and make them love me. Each time they left I felt the sting of failure.

I shut the memories down, finish my coffee, and step into another chilly November morning.

Ahead of me the land rolls out, dotted with trees with leaves in brilliant shades of red and gold. Frost glitters on the ground, crunching under my sneakers as I start to run. The beauty and stillness of this place takes my breath away. I choose a path that takes me around the lake and then to the perimeter of the ranch land. I pick up my pace and for a while I forget everything but the cold air hitting my lungs and putting one foot in front of the other.

I run for an hour until the sting of cold on my cheeks starts to bite and my legs ache. By the time I'm heading back to the ranch, my mind is clear. My resolve strengthened. Jake made a good point last night. I've been letting my own opinion of him cloud my judgment. I need to at least pretend to be open-minded if I want him to open up. Even if I already know the angle this feature will take, I still need the facts and the depth Tim asked for. With that thought in my mind, I head inside to start the day.

Jake is alone in the kitchen fixing coffee as I step through the back door. He's leaning against the counter, staring blankly at the coffee maker. His shoulders are tense and he's radiating a quiet fury.

"Whoa! Who peed in your cereal this morning?" I quip, flashing a smirk I hope will lighten whatever mood I've just walked into.

Jake's head snaps up at the sound of my voice. His frown deepens into that familiar scowl. *So much for our truce last night*, I think.

"Not in the mood, Cassidy," he says, and yep, I definitely dreamt last night. Either that or he's having second thoughts about our deal.

I could walk away and have the hot shower I desperately need, but two things make me stay. I'm cold and want another coffee, and it's still on my mind I need to show Jake I'm not the enemy.

I raise an eyebrow but say nothing as I take two mugs from the cupboard and place them beside the machine, studying him from the corner of my eye as I move. This isn't the cocky, doesn't-want-me-around vibe I've felt from him before. This is sullen and brooding, and the journalist in me wants to know what the hell happened between two and eight this morning to cause the shift.

A beat passes in the silence then Jake runs a hand through

his thick dark hair. "Sorry," he mumbles. "I didn't mean to take it out on you."

"And what exactly are you taking out on me?" I ask, pouring the coffee into the two mugs and sliding one across the counter toward him. I cup mine in my hands, warming my frozen fingers.

He taps the screen of his phone, turning it for me to read. It's from a Denver gossip site and the headline in bold red letters reads: JAKE'S WILD NIGHT OUT. Beneath it is the selfie of him and the redhead taken as we were leaving. His eyes are half closed because he wasn't expecting the photo. It's not his best shot. If I didn't know better, I'd think he was drunk, but he had one light beer before moving to soda for the rest of the night.

Beside it are two more photos, both grainy and taken from a distance. The first is Jake carrying a round of beers and the third is him standing close to a woman at the bar, her back to the wall. It takes me a beat to realize it's me in the photo.

"This is total bullshit," I say, surprised by the flash of annoyance I feel on Jake's behalf. "Those drinks weren't even for you."

"Does it matter?" He bites off the reply before slamming his phone onto the counter like it's to blame for the story. "I've already had a message from Coach Allen wanting my ass in his office first thing tomorrow. This is our one bye weekend of the season. The one week we don't have a game. We were all told to rest. This is exactly the kind of story that's going to ruin my career."

"Gordon was out too," I say.

Jake scoffs. "Yeah, funny how there aren't photos of him." He grabs his phone. "You're right, this is bullshit. I've been letting people say what they want and letting this rep grow, but I've had enough. I'm gonna tell the fans how fucking wrong this is."

"Maybe you should take a minute first," I say carefully.

He ignores me and starts to tap the screen, fingers moving with fury and precision, and even though it's not my business or place to intervene, and even though I don't care what Jake does, I can't stop myself from snatching the phone from his hands.

"Hey." Jake scowls but I stand my ground. *I'm doing this one for Mama,* I tell myself. And to prove to Jake I can have his back so he'll let me in.

"Maybe posting something is a good idea," I say. "Or maybe it's not. Either way, waiting an hour until you've calmed down seems like the safest option."

"Are you seriously telling me what to do now?" he asks, but the edge has left his voice and his eyes are no longer murderous.

I shrug, realizing what Jake needs in this moment is a distraction. "Did you know my dad is a two-time Pulitzer Prize–winning journalist?"

Jake raises his brows at my change of direction but shakes his head, so I carry on.

"He's spent his career covering every hard-hitting topic you can imagine from wars in the Middle East to election fraud. He's the most impressive person you'll ever meet. He's always thinking of the next story and where it will take him.

"Can you imagine following in those footsteps? It might not be a stadium full of fans and millions watching on TV, but believe me, I understand the weight of expectation. Ever since high school, people have read my work with an insane level of scrutiny, wanting to know if I'm as good as my dad. So I get it."

He shakes his head again, jaw tightening. "It's not the same, Cassidy. I've never cared what people think or say about me, but now this kind of made-up bull is going to ruin my career."

"Can't you play football for another team?" I ask, remembering what Mama said about players with far worse reputations than Jake playing in the NFL.

He shoots me a look like I've slapped him. "If I don't do something about my reputation, then come the end of the season, I'm gone. They'll sell me or trade me, and yeah I'll still be playing football but it won't be the same. Stormhawks are my team."

I drink my coffee, allowing the heat to slip down my throat and warm my body.

"What did you do?" he asks then.

"About what?"

"About everyone comparing you to your dad?" Jake's tone somehow manages to seem both interested and annoyed.

"To start with, I freaked out. I didn't exactly have a lot of confidence after high school," I say, fighting to keep the bitter edge from my voice. Because the reason for how much I struggled with my self-belief and making sound decisions after sophomore year and into college and even now is leaning against the counter beside me, drinking a cup of coffee, and he has no idea how much his thoughtless actions affected me." I take a breath. "By the time I hit my second year of college, I was second-guessing every word and hit a massive block. I was so close to flunking out. So I faked it. I acted like I was the best journalist on that course even if I felt like the worst. It didn't make me popular but after a while it didn't feel like pretend anymore. I graduated top of my class."

"Wouldn't it have been easier to stop caring what people think of you?"

I huff a laugh like what he's suggested is easy. "That's not me."

"Yeah, well, it suits me just fine," he fires back.

"If you didn't care what people think, you wouldn't be all kinds of grumpy about this story right now," I say, waving his phone at him.

He sighs but doesn't argue. He rubs a hand over his face and when he looks at me again the anger burning in his eyes has fizzled. I find myself wondering how the hell he looks so good when he's just gotten out of bed. Suddenly I remember I've spent the last hour running and I'm a windswept mess in desperate need of a shower.

"You can have this back in an hour, Sullivan." I back away to the door, tucking his phone in the pocket of my leggings.

I step out the room and swear I can feel the heat of Jake's eyes follow me down the hall. I shiver—cold from my run, I think. What am I doing? Helping Jake. Telling him about myself. My job might be to knock down Jake's walls, but I need to keep mine firmly up. I'm the journalist and he's my assignment.

EIGHT
JAKE

JAKE: *Can you get your hands on a swimsuit for later?*

HARPER: *There's no way I'm going in that freezing lake!*

JAKE: *Does a sauna sound better?*

HARPER: *It does, but I'm a professional and I'm here to do a job, not hang out in saunas with you.*

JAKE: *A professional pain in my ass. Bring your swimsuit!*

Stormhawks Park is a brand-new, state-of-the-art training facility a few miles south of the stadium. It has everything we need to be in peak condition, including three full-sized football fields and a huge weights room packed with free weights, cables, and machines. There's also a cafeteria that serves healthy meals customized for each player's nutritional needs. Funny though, I actually prefer practice at the stadium sometimes. There's a buzz that comes from staring at the 70,000 empty seats I know will be packed come game day.

But this place gives us everything we need to train hard and be game ready, and the creature comforts don't hurt either. It makes the long hours and physical toll worthwhile knowing we have a space like this to come back to. Especially now with a pool and sauna in the basement and Harper stepping toward me in a little red two-piece.

Damn! She looks good. Her body is all woman—toned, but with curves too. My eyes drag instantly to her pert breasts, barely contained inside the tiny triangles of red fabric. I realize I'm staring and drop my eyes, only for them to snag on the string tied in bows either side of the tiny red bottoms.

"Eyes up, Sullivan," Harper says and my gaze shoots to her face.

"Can't blame a man for looking when you're wearing something like that."

She rolls her eyes before turning to survey the empty pool. "Are you sure we're allowed to be here? What if people find out?"

I fix her with a sly grin. "Not much of a rule-breaker are you, Cassidy?"

"No! And I don't intend to start now, so if—"

I chuckle and hold my hands up in defeat. "I'm joking. It's fine to be here. It's just luck there aren't twenty of my teammates in here too."

That's not entirely true. I made sure to wait an hour after practice so any players using the pool, sauna, or ice baths would be long gone before bringing Harper down here. My teammates still don't know about the *Sports Magazine* profile feature and I'd like to keep it that way for as long as possible.

It might not be breaking any rules bringing Harper to the pool, but I'm still not sure if it's a good idea. Every conversation we have ends in sharp words or an argument, but she had my back yesterday when I was about to post a stupid rant on my socials. Even if she did do it in the most annoying way possible and confiscate my phone in the process. I'm still not happy she's here, still pissed about her comment to Mia on the phone. But the fake story about me yesterday was a reminder of how much I've got to lose and how easily I could lose it. Which means I need to find a way to change Harper's opinion of me. Not exactly easy, considering our rocky start. But I figure it wouldn't kill me to be a bit more accommodating.

Harper steps to the edge of the pool and without a second of hesitation, she executes a perfect dive, disappearing beneath the surface with barely a splash before appearing a few feet away and cutting through the water effortlessly.

"You coming in?" she calls, and I grin before cannonballing into the pool, causing a burst of laughter from Harper. "Real smooth, Jake," she taunts before throwing herself into her lengths.

For the next thirty minutes we swim in silence and I lose myself replaying the day. I didn't expect it to go as well as it did, and I have to begrudgingly admit that's down to Harper. Starting with being hauled into Coach Allen's office this morning. Thanks to Harper being with me and talking to Coach, he believed me when I said there was no truth to the story from the bar that now has over five million views and counting.

The message from Coach was clear though—true or not, Stormhawks management doesn't want any more bad press about me. I need to keep a low profile for the rest of the season. Fine by me. All I want is to get my team to the playoffs and make sure my contract is renewed, something that feels a lot more possible after how I trained today.

It was one of those sessions where the instinctual rhythm of the game felt like it lived in my bones. Effortlessly weaving between my teammates, like the turf was super-charged beneath my cleats. For the entire three hours of practice, I was acutely aware of Harper sitting in the indoor viewing platform. After every move I found myself turning to check if she was there watching.

∽

By the end of the swim, we're both breathless as we hit the sauna. It's a fight not to stare at the water droplets glistening on Harper's chest, rising and falling as she catches her breath. I close my eyes and rest my head against the warm wood. Only when the heat has wrapped itself around my muscles from the inside out do I open my eyes again and find Harper staring at me.

"My eyes are up here, Cassidy," I say, my voice husky from the yelling during practice.

I know it's hot in the wood cabin and sweat is covering our skin, but the way her cheeks redden is kind of cute.

"What did you think of your first practice?" I ask.

She hesitates, shifting on the bench so she's leaning against the wall opposite, long legs stretching toward me. "It was impressive."

I quirk an eyebrow. Something has been nagging at me since my first sit-down with Harper on Saturday. In the last three days, any time talk turns to football, she starts to fidget like she is now. Her answers to questions about the game are always vague. It's almost like she doesn't know the first thing about football. Then I remember what she said about her writing at college and how she faked confidence until it came.

She wouldn't...

Nah!

I almost laugh off my suspicions. Harper works for *Sports Magazine*. No way has she been faking knowledge of the NFL for the whole time she's worked there. That would be next-level crazy. Still, no harm in testing the theory...

"Hey, by the way, Dylan interrupted you in the truck on

Saturday. You were going to tell us if you think a team should punt if they're in the fourth down."

She scoops her hair back before she answers. "I was happy to stay out of that argument."

"Seriously, I want to know. What would you do?"

She hesitates like maybe she's thinking about it. "I'd probably punt."

I nod like I don't think she's full of shit. "What if there's a switch play at the two-hundred-yard marker?"

"I'd still punt," she says. I don't miss the question in her tone though. She looks at me, eyes a little wide, like maybe she knows what I'm about to say.

"That's funny, because there's no such thing as a switch play and the field is only a hundred yards long."

Her eyes widen another fraction, like her thoughts are scrambling. "Oh! I..."

I let her squirm a little before going in for the kill. "I think you were probably about to admit that you know nothing about football."

The second my words are out, Harper's hands fly up, covering her face. And even though it's unbelievable, I can't help but laugh at her reaction. *Gotcha!*

"It's not funny," she says in a small voice as she moves her hands away and looks at me with fear in her eyes. "How did you guess?"

"It wasn't that hard to figure out," I reply. "You always fidget when we talk about football. Your questions and comments about the game are always vague, and you called the playoffs the finals. Do you even know what a punt is?"

She shakes her head and I roll my eyes. "It's when a player drops the ball and kicks it before it touches the ground. The aim is to send the ball as far downfield as possible to push the opposing team into a worse starting position when you're about to lose possession anyway."

Harper looks at me like I'm talking in another language.

I shake my head in disbelief. "How the hell did you get given this feature without knowing a thing about football?"

Her face takes on a pained expression. "Because my editor, Tim, has no idea. Hit me with baseball questions or basketball or ice hockey, and I'm your gal. But not football."

"I get that. Don't most sports journalists have sports they know more about? But how did you get this feature?"

She looks uncomfortable. "After being fired from *Insight*, Mia got me an interview at the magazine and I really wanted the job, so... I sort of embellished my experience and knowledge of football."

"Embellished?" I smirk.

"Lied," she admits with a groan.

"How long have you been working at the magazine?"

"Three months," Harper admits.

"Fake it 'til you make it?" I ask.

"I thought so, but I've hated lying. I've been waiting for someone to find me out. And now you have. Even if Tim forgives me for lying in the interview, he'll be all kinds of pissed I said I could do this feature without mentioning I was seriously lacking in football knowledge. I'm still in a probationary period so it looks like I'm about to be fired from my second job in journalism in a year."

It's impossible to miss how crushed Harper looks. I think about what she's saying. I've wanted out of this interview since I stepped into the kitchen and caught sight of Harper's "don't mess with me" glare. But getting rid of Harper doesn't change the fact that I need this profile. If it's not Harper being a pain in my ass for the next five weeks, it'll be someone else. I'm not about to admit this to her, but after how she spoke to Coach earlier when he dragged me into his office before practice, and how she had my back yesterday, I'm thawing to the idea of having her around for a little while. Better the devil you know, isn't that what they say?

I fix my gaze on Harper. I don't miss the fear flashing in her eyes. A reminder of how much we both need this to work. "Last time I checked, Cassidy, I'm no tattletale."

Confusion pulls at her features. "You're not going to call the magazine and get me fired? I thought I was a giant pain in your ass."

I grin. "Oh, you're definitely that, but you're nicer to look at than Kevin, if I'm remembering him correctly. The lead reporter with the beard who seems to like the sound of his own voice more than the person he's interviewing?"

"That sounds like Kevin." She smiles before biting her lip, looking shy for the first time since she waltzed into my life. "What are you going to do then?"

I lean my head against the sauna wall. "Teach you about football, I guess."

"You'd do that?" There's a level of surprise in her voice that hits me the wrong way.

"No need to sound so shocked." My tone is sharper than I intend and just like that we're glaring at each other and I'm wondering if keeping Harper around is such a good idea after all.

"I'm not... I just... Thank you. That would be great," Harper says, her reluctant gratitude doing nothing to shift the sudden tension between us. Just when I thought we were making progress. It's like on the field, gaining five yards in the first down only to lose ten in the second.

I heave a sigh. "Lesson one—know your positions. What's the difference between a quarterback and a linebacker?"

"A quarterback throws the ball and a linebacker tackles people?" she hazards.

I huff a laugh. "Close enough. But we've got a long way to go if you're gonna understand what the hell is going on when we play the LA Wildhorns on their home turf on Thanksgiving, not to mention write a feature on the best tight end of all time."

A teasing grin lights up her face. "I thought I was writing a feature on you."

"Ouch, Cassidy. That was cruel." I laugh and the tension lifts. For now, anyway. Something tells me I might live to regret keeping her around. Harper Cassidy is making my head spin and not in a good way.

NINE

HARPER

TIM: *Good work so far, Harper.*

HARPER: *Thanks.*

TIM: *Send me a few more paragraphs by the end of next week. And don't forget to send Callie your travel itinerary so she can book your flights and hotels. Enjoy the trip to LA!*

HARPER: Will do.

Notes for feature: Beneath the playboy bravado, I've seen a gentler, patient quality to Jake. When it comes to talking about football, anyway.

"How's it going with the grumpy but very gorgeous football player?" Mia asks by way of hello on Thursday evening as I make my way into the Hank Stadium and the home of the Los Angeles Wildhorns, phone pressed to my ear. There's a tapping in the background and I imagine her in her holiday sweater at her mom's house, full of turkey and pumpkin pie. And still she's working. Typical Mia.

"He's actually being a bit less grumpy," I admit, taking in the dome shape of the stadium rising high above my head. If the Wildhorns were aiming for imposing, they hit the right vibe. I'm jostled by the crowds of Wildhorns fans in bright yellow jerseys making their way to their seats. There's a buzz in the air, a sense of hope and camaraderie and excitement. Two Stormhawks fans in the familiar red weave through the crowd and there's a friendly yell of goading from a Wildhorns fan and a cheer among the groups.

I pull the zip of my jacket a little higher, hiding the red fan's tee Mama gave me this morning, wrapped in pretty pink tissue and tied with a bow. *So you feel at home at the game,* she'd said with another of her hugs.

"Really?" Mia's surprise rings in my ear.

I take a staircase to the left, pointing me toward the skybox, reserved for friends, family, and VIPs. I wonder if there'll be any celebrities catching the game tonight.

"Hey, why are you working on Thanksgiving?" I ask.

"Oh God, don't! It's too boring to talk about. But you on the other hand—tell me more about this less grumpy Jake. Is he actually answering your questions now?"

"Sort of. We made a deal on how we'd work together. It's going... OK, I think. I sent some notes to Tim and he seems happy with where I'm at so far."

"That's great," Mia cries.

It really is. I got so used to having my work torn apart at *Insight* that I'm glowing from Tim's message. Obviously I was a little selective in the notes I sent. No need to type up the pages of hate notes I scrawled in my notebook in the first couple of days...

"I can't believe you and Jake are actually getting along."

I laugh. "We're not exactly getting along. We've just

stopped acting like we hate each other as much. Him being less grumpy and answering my questions isn't going to make me forget what he did in high school, or who everyone thinks he is now. I've still got a job to do."

There's a pause on the other end.

"What?" I say, knowing Mia well enough to know there's a question in that silence.

"Have you asked him about that article you wrote about him?"

I give a fierce shake of my head even though she can't see me. Mia is the one person in the world who knows it was me who wrote the article about Jake. The one person who knows how badly Jake's behavior hurt me. "Why would I do that?"

I know how stupid it is to still be caught up on something that happened in high school, but that one moment—how Jake treated me, how he stomped on my heart and my confidence—has left an imprint on my entire life. I put myself on the line giving Jake that article and suggesting we meet. When he made a joke of it, it destroyed whatever faith I had in boys—and then men—and in myself. From that point on, I allowed men to treat me badly in relationships—to put me down and cheat on me—because I didn't think I deserved any better. Because I didn't have the confidence to walk away. I've been single for so long, I can't even remember what it is to go on a date. It took me a while to realize it, but now I know it was all because of Jake.

"He has no idea it was me who wrote the article he plastered all over school," I continue. "I know it was stupid to give it to him, and thank God I didn't put my name on it, but—"

"It wasn't stupid, it was sweet. You were such a nerd, Harper. A very lovable nerd. I can't believe we were even friends. Why the hell was someone as cool as me friends with you?" she teases.

"Because Serena was always at cheer practice and I let you copy my homework."

"Oh yeah." She pauses again for a beat. "And you're sure he doesn't know you were the girl he humiliated?"

"Not unless you told Chase I wrote the article. And Chase told Jake," I reply.

"No way. I'd never sell out your secrets to a boy."

I smile. "I know you wouldn't."

"I still can't believe Jake was such a dick about it," Mia says.

"Seriously?" I ask incredulously.

"Maybe he's changed."

I grit my teeth. I can't deny Jake's been a gentleman this week. Even in the pool, I swear I was checking out his body way more than he was admiring mine, but that doesn't mean he's changed.

"Hello?" I cry. "What about the cheerleader thing and about a million other stories like it?" Even as the words leave my mouth, I find myself wondering how much of what I've read about Jake over the years is true. I know for a fact the story on Sunday about his wild Saturday night was all lies. But Jake still hasn't told me what happened in the parking lot last year. All I know for sure is that there's something to the story. Every time I mention it, he throws his walls up and shuts me out, despite the ground rules of our truce.

"I'm not saying you should fall in love with him, Harp." Mia doesn't say "again" but it's there in her voice and I'm reminded of the countless hours I spent lying face down on her bed, crying into a pillow as my heart felt like it had been shattered into a million pieces. "But," she continues, voice teasing, making me smile, shoving thoughts of high school out of my head, "you could fuck his brains out. That man has total BDE."

"BDE? Dare I ask?"

"Big Dick Energy." Mia cackles in my ear.

I can't help the laugh that escapes. "I'm going now," I say. "Goodbye, Mia."

"Love you," she replies like always.

"Love you, too."

I slip my phone in my pocket, somehow managing to smile at Mia's comments and still feel angry at the memories from high school. Nearly one week in and I didn't think spending time with Jake would be this hard. He can be easygoing and funny, and when we're getting along, I forget he's the same boy who acted so callously. It's like I'm doing such a good job pretending to be on his side, I'm almost starting to believe it myself.

~

At the entrance to the skybox a security guard checks my pass before waving me through with a bored nod. The space is decked out in plush leather couches, a fully stocked bar, and floor-to-ceiling windows overlooking the field and the fans taking their seats. It feels a long way from the rickety bleachers I sat on as a teen, craning my neck to catch a glimpse of Jake as he raced down the school field.

There's a muted buzz to the room. It's nothing like the feeling of being among the fans as I walked into the stadium and I almost regret not being in the heart of it all, but there's no beating the view as I grab a soda and make my way to a seat at the front of the box. The sugar from the drink gives me an instant boost and I shrug off the exhaustion of the day as the Stormhawks burst from the tunnel. I spot Jake's number 80 jersey and a whole new kind of buzz hits me. He's got his helmet under his arm, waving to the fans with a wide grin.

It's been a long day of travel after leaving the ranch early with Jake. He was edgy and sullen from the moment he climbed in his truck, the familiar tension between us returning. I booked the same flight and hotel, but I've barely seen him since arriving at the airport when he joined the rest of his team. He's had his headphones on most of the day, getting into whatever mindset he needs to reach for the game. I know Tim told me to use Callie to book my travel, but it feels weird to ask someone to do something I can easily do myself, and if I'm honest, I don't trust her not to book me a flight to an obscure airfield a million miles from where I'm supposed to be.

All around me, the stadium explodes with noise as the yellow Wildhorns take their position on the field and I try to remember Jake's lessons this week, dragging me to the football field at the back of the ranch every evening before sunset.

It's a game of territory and plays, he said, throwing me the ball.

Of course I dropped it, but after roaring with laughter, Jake was patient with me, teaching me to catch and throw alongside explaining the basics of the game. It made me think of an ex-boyfriend from my first year of college who wanted to play base-ball rather than just watch it. He got so frustrated when I continually failed to hit the ball that he stormed off, leaving me to find my own way home from the batting cages. It was a relief when we broke up soon after. The guy had a habit of cutting me off, like nothing I had to say would be worth hearing. Last I heard, he was making a run for congress. With Jake, he's happy to make a joke about my terrible throws, but he's patient too. I've even found myself studying my *Football for Dummies* guide at night so I can answer Jake's questions before he explains the answer to me with that teasing smile of his.

Below, the Stormhawks win the coin toss and choose to receive the football first. They take their positions and I feel my pulse quicken as anticipation hangs in the air. Winning their division and reaching the playoffs is nowhere close to secure, according to Jake. This would be an important win, and Jake was feeling the pressure this morning. He was in no mood to talk as we made our way to the airport. I can't see him being any more willing if they lose tonight.

I try not to worry. When Jake walked into the ranch last

Friday, an hour late and reeking of women's perfume, I never expected we'd make the kind of progress we have in just a week. Last night, we walked the perimeter of the lake and I asked him how he got into playing football.

In case you haven't guessed by now, Mama is a big Stormhawks fan. I think I always would've played football, but maybe not to the level I've reached. But Mama threw us into youth football as a way to focus after Dad died. He walked me over to the back football field and stared at it like it was the best view in the world. *She knew we needed a distraction and a focus —a way to channel our grief. I don't know if she planned for us to take it as far as we did, but I wouldn't be surprised.* He pointed to the field. *When we weren't at practice, we were out here or we were watching games on TV.*

I stopped myself asking how his dad had died. The baby-step approach has worked so far, asking two light questions and one that digs a little deeper.

A flurry of excited talk from the commentators blasts from the speakers as the Wildhorns kick the ball toward the Stormhawks and the seats around me fill.

Having some knowledge about the game definitely enhances the enjoyment factor, thanks to Jake's continual tuition, filling our awkward silences this week with game play explanations. The crowd's energy is electric as the Stormhawks receive the kickoff and begin their first drive. A moment later, the offense lines up for the first play. The Stormhawks quarterback takes the snap and drops back, scanning the field for an open receiver. But the Wildhorns' defense is relentless. In a flash, a defender breaks through, forcing him to release the ball too fast. The stadium gasps as the pass sails into the hands of a Wildhorns defender. Just like that, they've taken over. A few plays later, they punch it in for a touchdown. The extra point is good, sailing cleanly through the uprights. The scoreboard reads 7-0, and my stomach knots as the stadium explodes with cheers.

The game is fierce and brutal. In the second quarter, the Wildhorns add three more points with a field goal, pushing their lead to 10–0. The Stormhawks answer in the third with a field goal of their own. Then a well-placed throw finds its target in the end zone, and we add the extra point to tie it at 10–10.

During the break before the last quarter, I watch Jake talking to his teammates down on the sideline. He's focused and totally in his element. I'm starting to understand the draw of the game, but that doesn't mean I don't wince at every tackle. It's hard to believe any player walks away uninjured.

I asked Jake as we walked to his truck this morning if there's anything he can do to avoid injury. A wild look crossed his face. "Keep my cleats laced tight and my head in the game."

"So that's a no then," I said.

"Hey, if you've got a nurse's uniform in that suitcase of yours, Cassidy, I might be a little more inclined to get injured." Such a typical Jake comment, using humor to hide his feelings. I shoved him and he staggered, pretending he was already hurt. "Nurse! I need a nurse!"

The teams take their positions for the start of the fourth quarter, the tension palpable. The Wildhorns offense strikes fast, breaking through the Stormhawks defense to score another touchdown. The kicker adds the extra point with ease. It's 17-10 to the LA Wildhorns.

But on their next possession, the Stormhawks march down the field with precision, earning a touchdown too. The crowd holds its breath as the kicker steps up—and the extra point is good. It's all tied at 17-17 with only minutes left on the clock.

Then it happens. Stormhawks have the ball, and suddenly Jake makes his move. He finds space, and the quarterback throws a quick and accurate pass. Jake catches it like it's second nature before powering forward, putting the Stormhawks close to the end zone before he's brought down by a defender. The crowd erupts and me with it. I can't believe how much I've learned from Jake about football this week and how excited I am.

As the team moves, I see Jake still on the ground and I gasp as the replay shows a late tackle from a Wildhorns defender, knocking Jake flying.

Play stops and so does my ability to draw in breath as a silence falls over the hospitality suite and the stadium.

I think of Dylan—more than a year into his recovery. My heart leaps into my throat. "Get up!" I whisper, surprised how much my heart is racing. How much I'm willing Jake to be OK.

Team medics race across the field as the seconds pass like hours. On the big screen, I watch as Jake's helmet is eased from his head. There's a trail of blood on his face. I stand, biting my lip, but a moment later he's jumping to his feet and waving at the cheering Stormhawks fans with a confidence that takes my breath away.

On the next play, the Stormhawks score a touchdown to put them in the lead: 17-23. They score the extra point and the final whistle blows. The game is over. The Stormhawks have won.

Just before Jake turns to celebrate the win with his team, I swear he lifts his head and looks right at me, a teasing smirk dancing on his lips. My face burns with heat and I'm sixteen all over again, watching him from those rickety bleachers the year before he left for college. I can almost hear him telling me not to put the nurse's uniform on just yet, and I laugh with relief and wonder how I'll cope for the next four weeks when one game has me feeling like I was right there with him on the field, taking every tackle.

TEN
JAKE

What a win! One we really needed. One *I* really needed. For the first time in a long time, the ache in my legs and shoulders actually feels good as I step from the shower in the hotel bathroom. Like I've got a hundred more games in me. Our next game is at home against the Miami Tidalrunners on Thursday and already I'm feeling pumped for it.

I half wonder if having Harper at practice this week and the game tonight, knowing she's there for me and me alone, made the difference. It's a stupid thought. Harper is still closer to being a pain in my ass than a lucky charm.

I pull on my basketball shorts and throw myself onto the bed as I relive the game in my thoughts, the adrenaline still pumping through my veins. The hotel room is like every other mid-range high-rise in this part of Los Angeles. Functional and sleek but lacking personality. Doors bang from down the hall followed by the laughter and shouts of my teammates. It feels strange not to be joining them. How many nights like this have we hit whichever city we've been in, downing shots and beers and enjoying the flirting of the female fans who always find their way to the same bar?

I feel a stab of frustration that I'm not part of it tonight. But Coach Allen's words from Monday are still ringing in my head.

I don't have to tell you, Jake, that one more screw-up like last year and you're done.

I can't risk any more bad press. So here I am, alone on Thanksgiving night after the biggest win of the season so far, stuck in a hotel room while everyone else parties. I sigh and flip on the TV, trying to distract myself, landing on a rerun of *Friends*.

When the knock on my door comes a minute later, I kill the TV and ease my aching body up.

"Go to hell," I say as I'm opening the door, expecting Billy or Rob wanting to coax me out.

Except it's not one of my teammates. It's Harper, wearing a pair of skimpy denim shorts and the red Stormhawks tee Mama gave her. Her sleek hair is up in a swishing ponytail and she looks just as hot as she did in her swimwear earlier this week.

"Good to see you, too." Harper smiles but there's an awkwardness to it, like maybe she's having second thoughts about knocking on my door. I realize she's missing Thanksgiving with her family. I can barely remember a time before I was playing football on the holiday, but I doubt this is Harper's idea of a fun Thanksgiving. And I've just told her to go to hell. *Good one, Jake!*

I smile, opening the door wide for her. She hesitates for another moment before stepping inside, filling my senses with her intoxicating perfume, like autumn rain and wildflowers.

She holds up a pack of four beers in one hand and a first-aid kit in the other. "I thought since you're not allowed out, I'd bring the party to you." She looks hesitant for a beat before adding, "Seeing as it's Thanksgiving."

"Thanks," I say, grabbing a beer from her. Our fingers touch for the briefest of seconds as she passes me a bottle, sending a zing of something unfamiliar up my arm.

We stand in silence for a long moment then Harper's face lights up, eyes gleaming. "You were amazing, by the way."

I'll be damned if that praise doesn't feel as good as all the fans in the Stormhawks stadium cheering my name.

"That catch you made was incredible."

"That was all Billy and his throw, but spoken like a true fan, Cassidy." I laugh and it suddenly doesn't seem so bad to be stuck in this hotel room. My gaze slides to Harper's lips as she takes that first sip. She's wearing the red lipstick again. The one that makes me think about all the places I'd like her lips on me.

I need to get a grip. This is Harper Cassidy. The journalist out for my blood. Even as the thought lands, I'm not sure if it's true. Maybe we're not on the same team, but I'm not sure we're pitted against each either. I have no idea where that leaves us.

Harper spins around, placing her beer on the table and unzipping a small green medical bag.

"Tell me you don't travel with that everywhere you go?" I ask.

She throws me a glance, those red lips curving into a smile. "Nothing wrong with being prepared. Now sit down so I can fix that cut above your eye so it doesn't scar that pretty face of yours."

"You think I've got a pretty face?" I tease, dropping onto the edge of the bed. I refused to see the team doc tonight, waving away any concern, but I find I'm more than happy to have Harper's hands on me.

"Shut up so I can concentrate." She closes the gap between us in two steps, positioning herself between my legs. She's so close I can feel the warmth of her breath on my neck and the heat radiating from her body.

My mouth is suddenly dry, palms sweaty. I can't think of anything to say, so I do what I always do and deflect with humor. "I thought we agreed you'd be wearing a nurse's uniform." I lift an eyebrow and wince, remembering the cut

Harper is trying to fix. It's short but deep and stings like a bitch.

I can't help but grin as Harper rolls her eyes at my joke. Even though she's trying to act serious, I can tell she's fighting back a smile.

"You know, most girls would be falling over themselves to play nurse for me," I say, unable to resist teasing her some more.

She presses the antiseptic wipe a little harder than necessary, making me flinch. "If there's a line of girls waiting to take over, then maybe you should call one of them."

I chuckle, enjoying our back and forth. Harper isn't like any woman I've ever known. She challenges me, calls me out on my bullshit, and right now it feels more playful than judgmental.

"No, thanks, I like you patching me up just fine," I say, holding her gaze, feeling myself getting lost in the gold flecks in her eyes.

The sarcastic retort she was clearly planning dies on her lips as the air between us becomes charged, like it could ignite at any moment.

Harper clears her throat and looks away first. "You're all set." She swipes her beer from the table and drinks deeply before taking a seat on the opposite side of the room.

I touch my fingertips to the Band-Aid above my eye. "Good as new. Thank you, Nurse Cassidy."

She fixes me with that same look I remember from the kitchen a week ago when I walked in and found her sitting at the table in her sky-high stilettos. "Don't push it, Sullivan," she says, but there's a lightness to her tone.

"Wouldn't dream of it." I take a long pull from my beer bottle.

"So what was it like being drafted for the Stormhawks and playing alongside Dylan?"

And just like that she's back in journalist mode and leaving me reeling.

"The best feeling in the world," I reply. "Obviously it was a dream to be drafted to my home team, but more than that, playing with Dylan, that was the best. Before Dylan was injured, he was totally unstoppable. He was tight end and I was his strongside linebacker. It was my job to protect him and it was easy because we'd played together so long, I could sense his moves before he made them."

"When did you start playing as a tight end?"

"I'd been moving into the role for a while."

My answer is purposefully vague. If Harper notices, she doesn't say. I realize where this is heading. Dylan's injury. The night I was benched. And the reason why. I know we'll have to talk about it, but right now all I want to do is enjoy my beer and Harper's company.

"So tell me more about this hard-hitting journalist dad of yours," I say, steering the conversation to safer waters. For me at least, I think, catching the hardness in Harper's eyes.

"I haven't seen him for six months. But he's back in Denver in a couple of weeks to collect a lifetime achievement award from the National Journalism Association. It's black tie and compulsory attendance for his proud daughter." There's an edge to her voice and a hell of a lot more to this, but I don't press further.

"What were you working on the other night when I came into the kitchen?" I ask instead. It's been bugging me how different she looked sitting at her laptop, like she was free in a way she isn't most of the time.

She makes a face, sipping at her beer. "I thought I was asking the questions."

"That isn't an answer," I reply.

She pushes her hair away from her face and smiles at me. "Promise not to laugh?"

I grin. "Nope."

She lifts her fingers, drawing them across those perfect lips like she's locking the words inside, making me grin.

"Fine," I say. "I promise not to laugh. Tell me."

"OK, but don't make a big deal out of it. It's just something I started as a way to distract myself from feeling like shit after I came back to Denver." She takes a breath and I can tell she's nervous. "I'm writing a novel." She makes another face, like she's waiting for me to make a joke.

"Why would I laugh? Writing a novel sounds pretty impressive to me. What kind of story is it?"

Her smile widens as her cheeks flush. "It's a vampire story. Like *Twilight* but more adult and set in ancient Egypt."

I cock an eyebrow. "Adult as in..." I wink.

She laughs and covers her face with her hands. "Yes."

"Why are you embarrassed? I think it's great."

She's quiet for a moment, picking the label on her beer bottle. "I remember my dad once said that people who can't handle real deadlines or hard stories run off to write novels. I just... I don't want him to think I've given up. Plus I know how hard it is to get a book published. Only the best books make it."

"Why wouldn't you try, though? If you love it."

She gives a small smile before shaking her head. "I do love it, but... people will think I'm selling out."

"So? The way I see it, people are going to think what they want, Harper. You do you."

She rolls her eyes again but she's smiling. "Considering you've landed yourself in the kind of trouble that means a pain in your ass journalist is following you around for the next four weeks, I'm not sure you're the best person to give advice on not caring what people think. You've done too much of that..."

I laugh. "I'll give you that." I'm aware this is the kind of exchange that could easily turn into another argument and I want to keep things light and maybe even a little flirty too, now the buzz of beer has hit my bloodstream.

But then Harper places her empty beer bottle on the table and stands. "I'd better go. Plenty of notes to write up."

She starts moving to the door but stops as she passes where I'm still sitting on the edge of the bed, her bare legs a whisper away from my own, as she reaches a hand to my face. Her fingers press gently against the Band-Aid above my eye and she gives an approving nod.

"That's better."

And with that, she's gone. Then it's just me and the giant fucking hard-on I hadn't felt creeping up on me. Except this feels like more than just my dick reminding me how long it's been since I got laid...

Bad idea, Jake! Very bad.

ELEVEN
HARPER

JAKE: *Where are you?*

HARPER: *Missing me already?*

JAKE: *As much as I miss a cleat to my ass.*

HARPER: *Charming, Sullivan. Real charming! I've had to stop by the office. I'll be there to watch the game.*

JAKE: *In the nurse's uniform?*

HARPER: *You wish!*

Notes for feature: There is more to Jake than football and women, but that doesn't mean he's not happy to flirt with anything with a pulse, including me. He uses his charm to put people at ease, but he also uses it to deflect difficult questions. The incident with the cheerleaders last September and his strained relationship with Dylan included.

Another week passes and my truce with Jake holds. We've fallen into a rhythm of talking in his truck on the way to practice, and walking with Buck around the ranch in the late afternoons, mixing our banter with questions. It's hard to believe nearly two weeks have gone by since I was last at the Arquette building being told I'd be following Jake Sullivan around for five weeks.

I take a deep breath as the elevator doors ping on the twentieth floor, opening to the *Sports Magazine* offices. I feel even less like I belong here than when I was sitting at my desk in the far corner every day. It feels equally strange to be wearing my blouse and pencil skirt and Louis Vuitton heels after living in jeans and sweaters and my new Stormhawks tee for the last couple of weeks. I don't need to wear such corporate attire to work here. Hell, I've never seen Tim in anything but bootcut jeans and sneakers. It's another reason I stick out like a sore thumb, but it's my armor while I'm here. Fake it 'til you make it, just like Jake said.

It's a reminder to myself too that I can handle myself when the what-the-fuck-am-I-doing anxiety starts to overwhelm me and I fear someone is going to ask me a football-related question. I really hate that I lied to Tim and the team. It seems stupid now. All journalists have their strengths and weaknesses, but I knew my dad was disappointed in me for being fired. I hated the thought of everyone knowing I was a failure. I was desperate and humiliated, but that's feeling more like a lame excuse with every passing week, and as bad as I feel about it, I'm stuck with the lie now.

The office is just how I left it. Chaos and mess and sports memorabilia scattered around the place. Stood by the printer is a life-sized cardboard cut-out of an ice hockey player in full uniform. Someone has stuck a speech bubble to the side of his head that reads, *Tidy your desks, a**holes!*

Heads turn as I make my way to my desk. A few people nod

and I smile back, but no one leaps up to ask me how I'm doing. It's nearly the end of the day. Everyone is counting down the minutes before they can go home. If I was Callie, I know Alison and the other women who work here would be whisking me off for a drink in one of the nearby bars, asking the juicy gossip about Jake, but I'm not.

I sigh as I reach my desk and see it's become the dumping ground for unwanted mail and whatever other crap people want off their desks. Callie looks up from her screen at the desk next to mine as I sit down to discover I've also been left with the chair with the broken wheel.

"Hi, Harper. Good to see you," Callie says in a tone that suggests otherwise. "I almost forgot you work here," she adds with a tinkling laugh.

"Hey," I reply.

Then she smirks, ducking her head back to her work. A second later I see why. On top of my keyboard is a printout of my latest paragraphs I sent to Tim yesterday. The entire page is scribbled over with red pen, and written in capital letters at the bottom is the word "*BORING.*"

A sharp hurt stabs my chest. Tim thinks my work is boring. He thinks I'm a terrible journalist. I'm going to be fired. It's *Insight* all over again. Except without the sleazy editor making a pass. That clammy hand on the bare skin of my thigh and the hot breath in my ear.

You know, Harper. I can make sure you go places here.

Maybe if I'd turned him down more gently things would've been different. Something less cutting than my scoffing reply: *I wouldn't sleep with you if you were the last man on earth. Now get your fucking hand off me!*

I'd marched out of the office, intending to contact HR the following day. But the asshole got there first, telling HR I'd propositioned him. He made sure word spread around the office that I'd tried to sleep my way to the top.

No wonder Callie is gleeful. Living in Jake's world, I'd forgotten only one of us will have a job come January. Three more weeks to finish my feature on Jake. Three more weeks in this job. A flash of anger chases my hurt away and I'm on my feet, marching in my heels across the floor and straight into Tim's office without knocking. I hate that he thinks my work isn't good enough, but that's no excuse to humiliate me in front of Callie.

Tim's gaze shoots up at my sudden entrance, but he smiles when he sees me. "Ah, Harper. Take a seat." Somewhere beyond my anger I register the friendly tone as he waves me to a chair I ignore.

"I didn't ask for this assignment!" I say as I stride to his desk.

He looks perplexed but nods in agreement. "I know. I gave it to you after—"

"I'm the one who's put my life on hold," I cut in, skirting over the small fact that watching *LA Love Hunt* with Mia, browsing bookshops, and hitting the gym on Saturdays hardly counts as a life, but Tim doesn't need to know that. And even if my life is pathetic, I still missed Mia's epic family Thanksgiving for the first time since I was thirteen. "I'm the one trying to get to know a man who does not want this any more than I do, and—"

"And you're doing a good job," Tim cuts in with a bemused smile.

His comment knocks the momentum out of my anger. "What?"

"You're doing a good job," he repeats. "I told you that in my message the other day. You're nailing it, Harper. I've already shared your latest notes with the team."

"But..." I glance down at the piece of paper screwed in my hands and the word "boring" written across the bottom. Tim might have a short fuse, but if he had concerns about my work, he'd have told me to my face. From the corner of my eye, I spot

Callie in fits of laughter at her desk. I just about stop myself from face-palming. I fell right into her trap.

"Thank you. Sorry," I stammer, dropping into the chair opposite Tim's desk. "What did you want to see me about?"

"I wanted to check in on how you're doing," Tim says, leaning back in his chair. If he's wondering what the hell my tantrum was about, he's not asking. "You're doing excellent work and I don't have any concerns at all, but I also know Sullivan can be... difficult to work with."

"He's not so bad when you get to know him."

Tim raises his brows and I almost laugh. I'm as surprised as he is by my comment. "He's... You and he... I mean, he's treating you well?"

It's almost funny to hear Tim trip over his words. "We're keeping it professional if that's what you're really asking." It is and we both know it.

"OK. It's just I've seen it many times before. On an assignment like this... spending so much time together, the lines can get blurred. It makes things messy and can damage the integrity of the magazine."

"You have nothing to worry about." I smile tightly.

"Have you asked him about the cheerleader scandal yet?" Tim asks. "It's what people want to know about and it's that story and the aftermath with his brother Dylan that will sell a lot of magazines."

I nod slowly, pretending I know what he means. What has Dylan got to do with the cheerleaders in the parking lot? It's definitely something I should know by now. I could push Jake for an answer, but I think of how closed off he gets when I broach the subject and decide it's better he tells me his version when he's ready.

"Jake knows it's a topic we need to cover," I reply. "And he wants to get his side across, but it's a little too soon."

"OK. You've still got three weeks. Just don't leave it until the end and give him the chance to duck out of it."

"I won't," I reply, resolving to try again tonight after the game. It occurs to me I might be the one avoiding the hard questions because maybe suddenly I actually want Jake to like me. To trust me. And things are surprisingly fun when we're not arguing.

Tim stands and shows me to the door. "Good. I'm looking forward to reading more from you soon. Now, haven't you got a game against the Miami Tidalrunners to get to?"

I grin back. "Yes, I do."

I'm still smiling when I reach my desk and send a quick email. A second later I hear the chime of it landing in Callie's inbox and feel her glare. I've just sent her my travel itinerary for the away game next week, making sure to include Tim in the email so she can't ignore me or send back the expletives I'm certain will be running through her head. Turns out I'm not above asking someone to book my flights and hotel for me.

"Oh," I say, grabbing my jacket as I stand, "if you could, make sure it's a window seat for the flights. Thanks, Callie."

I drop her scribbled notes in the trash, hiding my smirk as I stride out of the office to get ready for the Stormhawks home game.

TWELVE
HARPER

Notes for feature: Jake's power on the field is equal to his charm off it. It's easy to get sucked into both and forget the man underneath can't be trusted. Yet...

We won! Can I say we? Am I a Stormhawks fan now? Hell yes! And we didn't just win. It was a crushing defeat: 34-18. The Miami Tidalrunners didn't stand a chance. I'm buzzing. I can't stand still. Hopping from foot to foot like the energy inside me is electric.

Mama grins as we make our way from the skybox down to the field—a Stormhawks tradition for Thursday night home games according to Mama. I find myself looking forward to seeing the wide smile on Jake's face.

"It's like nothing else, is it?" Mama says from beside me.

I laugh and shake my head, ponytail swishing. I'm back in tight jeans and my red Stormhawks tee, teamed with a cute leather jacket of Mia's she threw at me earlier as I ducked into her apartment to say hi and change before the game.

Mama slips her arm in mine as we step into the tunnel. The noise of the stadium echoes around us in whoops and hollers and the stamping feet of the fans. We emerge from the tunnel into a cold night, bright floodlights, and the roar of 70,000 people. The energy of the stadium floods through me. I suddenly understand why Jake lives for these moments. It's electric. We join the line of family and VIPs at the sideline, waiting to congratulate the players as they head to the locker room. I spot Jake jogging across the field, helmet under his arm, dark hair damp from exertion and flopping over his forehead. He waves at the fans, basking in the glow of victory.

As Jake draws nearer, I'm suddenly shy. Under the bright lights, his sculpted arms and muscular thighs are on full display and my thoughts drag back to the moment in his hotel room last week when I smoothed the edge of his Band-Aid. The surprise on his face as I drew near, and the knowledge pounding through me that it didn't need fixing.

When his gaze lands on me, Jake's smile widens and he bounds over. For a crazy moment he opens his arms like he's going to sweep me up and spin me around. Then he stops short before leaning close and saying in my ear, "You're starting to feel like my good luck charm, Cassidy."

I laugh, certain he's joking. All I can think about is the heat radiating from where his hand is resting on my hip. I step back, putting some air between us.

"Where's my hug?" Mama asks from beside me and Jake bends down and wraps his arms around her. "Proud of you," she says, and then, "Right. I've got to see the physical therapist about Dylan and this trip to the ACL center in LA, and then I've got a late meeting with management. You'll take Harper back to the ranch?"

He nods. "Sure thing."

There's no mistaking the don't-fuck-with-me-air about Mama as her tiny frame moves past the players and coaching staff. I smile as a man twice her size leaps out of her path.

As Jake is surrounded by his teammates, one of the bigger,

bearded guys swoops in and plants a loud, smacking kiss on Jake's cheek. Jake bursts out laughing and gives the guy a playful shove.

"Alright, alright! Settle down," Jake says, still chuckling as he extracts himself from the mob. He spots me hovering on the outskirts and steps over. "This way," Jake murmurs, gently pressing a hand to my lower back and steering me toward the tunnel. A spark flickers in the pit of my stomach, which I hastily put down to the leftover excitement from the win.

We enter the dim, concrete tunnel, the sounds from the field fading behind us. It smells of dirt and sweat down here.

"I need a quick shower," Jake says, glancing down at me with an easy grin as we reach a long corridor inside the stadium. "You OK to wait here? I'll only be a few minutes."

I nod and Jake flashes me another smile before disappearing through a door and into the locker room.

I lean against the wall and wait, feeling like I shouldn't be here, but no one pays me any attention. After a while, the door opens and I'm already smiling, but it's not Jake. It's Gordon. He's wearing a shirt and sweater combo and looks like he's about to waltz into his first day of lectures at an Ivy League college.

"It's Harper, right?" he says, eyes twinkling like he's glad to see me.

I nod. "Hi."

"A few of us are heading to The Hay Barn. You're welcome to join us." He leans an arm against the wall, getting in my space. I remember Jake's warning about him and shift away. "I hear you're writing about Jake. The guys and I can tell you some stories. Although more than a few aren't for the delicate eyes of *Sports Magazine*'s readership." He adds a wink at the end just in case I don't catch the meaning in his words.

"Maybe another time," I say as the door to the changing rooms opens again and there's Jake. His hair is wet, almost black from the water, and pushed away from his face, and his tee is clinging to those broad shoulders, a gray sweatshirt in his hand. I still can't get used to being in the company of someone so hot.

"Everything OK here?" he asks, voice husky from shouting in the game. He throws a glare toward Gordon.

"Yep," I say.

Jake steps closer, his clean woodsy scent enveloping me. "Enjoy the game, Cassidy?" he asks.

"Yes!" I smile and it's goofy, and Jake tips back his head and gives a throaty laugh. I feel myself glow at the sound of it. "Seriously," I say. "You blew me away tonight."

Gordon makes a scoffing noise from beside us. "Jake knows all about being blown away, don't you, Sullivan? You've been blown by half the cheer team last I heard."

Jake seems to grow a foot in height as he rounds on his teammate. "You and I both know the rules, Gordon. No fraternizing with the cheer team. Or have you forgotten? Don't take your sorry excuse for defense tonight out on me. I carried your ass in the game and we both know it."

There's a beat of tense silence before Gordon chuckles to himself, having got the rise he was looking for from Jake, and strolls away. I take a step back, too. I'm begrudgingly starting to see that there's more to Jake than his reputation. But Gordon has reminded me that Jake is still the man who broke my heart. Even if it's getting harder to keep hold of that knowledge with every passing day. Even if I can still feel heat tingling on my hip from where Jake's hand touched me earlier, my heart can't afford for me to forget why I'm here.

THIRTEEN

JAKE

The drive home is frosty and it has nothing to do with the cold December wind blowing through the open window of my truck. I should be buzzing from the win tonight. All anyone can talk about is the playoffs and what it would mean to reach them for the first time in four years. With our last two wins and only four games left, it's finally feeling possible. But instead of being happy, I'm pissed.

Beside me, Harper is staring out the passenger window, her jaw set, her arms folded across her body. Tension radiates in the silence. She hasn't said a word since we left the stadium and I shot down the question she was halfway through asking. No way am I in the mood to chat.

I grip the steering wheel tightly as I drive, my knuckles turning white. I saw the change in her expression and the way she looked at me after Gordon's bullshit comment about the cheer team. I don't care what people think, so why am I letting this get to me?

I glance at Harper as we speed down the dark highway back to the ranch. No one has any business looking so damn attractive when they're mad. The thought surprises me and so I focus on her anger instead. What the hell has she got to be mad about? The only person who has any right to be pissed here is me. We've spent two weeks together and one comment from a prick like Gordon and she's fixing me with that look. The one where she thinks she's got me all figured out and there's nothing I can say or do to change that.

We leave the city behind and my headlights cut through the inky darkness. The mountains in the distance are lost to the night, shadows against a sky littered with stars. Not even the crunch of my wheels on the drive and the sight of Buck galloping out the back door eases my mood. I jump from my truck with only one thought in my head—getting as far away from Harper as I can. I whistle to Buck and we stride into the darkness in the direction of the lake.

A moment later, the passenger door slams and even in my current mood I feel like an ass for not opening it for her.

"Hey," Harper calls. Her footsteps hit the ground behind me. "Why are you so angry with me?" she asks, grabbing my arm and pulling me to a stop. An electrical heat pulses from her touch. I'm pulled back to the moment on the field when I saw her cheering from the sideline. How close I came to sweeping her into my arms and spinning her around.

"I'm not angry," I growl. It's a lie and we both know it.

"What is this then?" Her breath leaves a puff of air in the chill of the night. She shivers a little in her leather jacket. The fit suits her but it's doing nothing to ward off the cold.

"Don't I get to be a little annoyed that my team is celebrating another win at my favorite bar and I'm not?" I sigh and shrug off my sweatshirt before handing it to her. "Put this on. It's freezing out here."

She looks like she's going to refuse but a second later she's pulling it over her head. Damn, she looks cute with her arms lost in the sleeves.

"Come on, Buck." I whistle and make a step to leave, but Buck remains sitting by Harper's feet, tail wagging, ears pricked with interest. I have to swallow back a groan. Of course my dog loves Harper more than me.

Harper closes the gap I've made between us. Can't this girl take a hint? I'm not in the mood.

In the light from the ranch house, her eyes are fierce. "This is about more than missing a few drinks with the team. Tell me what's going on."

I rake a hand through my hair, hating that she's right. "Fine. You know what, I never said I was perfect. I like women. I like sex. And I'm not going to deny that I've enjoyed a few one-night stands in my time. But I told you I've changed. So don't look at me like I'm a bad person, Harper."

"So you are angry with me. I didn't look at—"

"You did. Outside the locker room when Gordon made his stupid remark. One of the coaching staff had just let slip about the feature and he wanted to annoy me by getting to you. And for your information, I've never dated any of the cheer team. Any player caught fraternizing with a cheerleader is dropped from the team for good."

"So what happened in the parking lot last September then?" She fires the question and it hits me right in the gut. She takes another step forward, getting in my space. "You keep telling me there's more to you. That I shouldn't believe this playboy rep you've built. But you give me nothing. You answer my questions if they're about football, but the second I try to push deeper, you shut down or make a joke or storm off into the night." She waves her hand in the air like she's proving her point.

The fact she's right again does nothing to defuse my anger. "I never said I'd be good at this, OK?"

"Are you telling me you're doing your best here? That you're giving me your all?"

"No. But I don't want to talk about what happened last year. Not yet. I know I have to and I will, but not now."

Harper's face is stony, lips pursed in a way that snags my eyes. Another bolt of electricity shoots through my body. I'm suddenly not sure if I want to close the gap between us or tell her to go to hell. Once again, Harper's got my head spinning.

"When, then?" she asks. "Because you realize I have a job to do."

"Yeah, but my job is making sure my team gets to the play-offs and then to the Super Bowl, not teaching you about football and telling you all my secrets. I get why you're here and why we both need this, but can't I have one night off? One night where I get five minutes to myself in my own home."

"You're pushing me away," she replies.

"And you're driving me crazy," I growl.

She huffs, more frustration than anything. "I don't want to be here any more than you want me here, Jake. But you're right—we do both need this. My career is on the line too. So I have to keep pushing you whether you like it or not. This isn't a game to me."

"And you think it is to me?"

She shakes her head. "I don't know what I think anymore." With that, she's striding back to the ranch with my damn dog trotting at her side.

For a moment my gaze pulls to where her jeans hug her perfect ass, and that's when it hits me. The way I lit up inside when I saw her on the sideline tonight. The heat that radiated through my body when she grabbed my arm just now.

Fuck!

Is this…?

It can't be.

I think back to my teen years and the girls in my life, but as the star football player in high school and college, girls tended to come to me. Is it possible that at the age of twenty-nine I've got my first crush? On Harper—who has the power to both make me laugh and infuriate me to hell all in the same five minutes?

Damn it, Sullivan.

FOURTEEN

HARPER

HARPER: Forget what I said. Jake's a dick!

MIA: Trouble in paradise?

HARPER: He's cocky and rude and I don't care what Mama says, there is not a sweet bone in his body.

MIA: It's still early and I'm not quite awake yet because I read that last part as "I want his boner in my body," which is probably what you meant, right?

HARPER: Seriously?!! Go back to sleep!

Notes for feature: Jake Sullivan is a dick!

I'm still frustrated when I wake on Saturday morning. My concentration is shot. I've tried working on my novel. I've tried working on Jake's feature. But I can't write anything that doesn't involve an expletive about Jake. How can he be so grumpy and yet in the middle of an argument take his sweatshirt off for me to wear because he can see I'm cold? I shoot a murderous look to the sweatshirt still sitting on the back of the chair. I meant to return it to Jake yesterday, but he spent most of his rest day in his room. I only saw him at dinner last night, and we barely said two words to each other. Plus, I kind of like it hanging there...

There's also a nagging in my gut that beneath his grumpiness after the game on Thursday night, he had a point. Gordon's comment served as a reminder that I'm here to get the truth, to do my job, not cheer Jake on when he wins a game. Maybe I did put my walls back up a notch. I don't know if I'm annoyed that Jake noticed or annoyed I let it happen when I'm trying to prove to Jake I'm not the enemy. Either way, I've woken this morning feeling surprisingly shitty about it.

I scrunch my eyes shut, frustration pulsing alongside my heartbeat. I meant what I said to Jake during our fight. I don't know what I think anymore. Only that after a day of Jake's grumpiness and avoidance, I need to get off this ranch. I need my life back. I throw on my workout clothes and grab my gym bag, hoping Mama meant what she said about me borrowing her truck. At the last minute, I snatch Jake's sweatshirt from the chair and pull it over my head, breathing in the woodsy citrus scent of him.

I'm at the bedroom door when there's a light tap on the wood and I open it to find Jake standing in the hallway. He's wearing a Stormhawks baseball cap, sweats, and his usual playful smirk.

"Going somewhere?" he asks, nodding to my bag.

"The gym," I reply, shooting him a defiant look that softens in a second. Maybe we both have some making up to do.

"Can you postpone?" He cocks an eyebrow. "I want to show you something."

"What is it?" I ask.

He leans against the doorway, hands in his pockets. "It's this thing I do once a month on a Saturday morning. It's fun, I promise."

So much for escaping. And yet I drop my gym bag without question and look down at my workout clothes.

"You'll be fine wearing that," he says, reading my mind. "Come on. I don't want to be late."

I follow him to his truck, my curiosity taking over my mood. Outside, the morning sun stretching over the mountains bathes the ranch in a soft glow. The air is icy cold. Frost glistens on the grass of the empty paddocks like scattered diamonds. The crunch of gravel beneath our feet is the only sound.

"It's so beautiful here," I say, my breath pluming in the cold air.

Jake's feet slow and he follows my gaze over the ranch. "It's my favorite place on earth." A beat passes before he continues. "Playing for the Stormhawks is my dream. It has been for as long as I can remember. When we win—when I play well—it's the best feeling in the world. When I have a bad game and the crowd turns against me, it's like being kicked in the balls and I think of buying myself some horses and a cowboy hat and stepping away from football."

I look up in surprise. "You ride?"

He shoots me a sideways glance and there's amusement dancing in his eyes. When he turns to face me, the full height of him towers over me. "How many people do you know who live on a ranch and can't ride, Cassidy?"

"How many ranches do you see without any horses?" I reply.

He laughs. "Good point."

'Why don't you keep any animals here?" I ask. "It's not like you don't have the barn and the paddocks."

Jake pulls his baseball cap from his head and runs a hand through his ruffled hair. His tone when he finally answers is brisk. "My dad was the rancher and he died."

"I'm sorry," I say, thinking of my mom and the photo of her on the fireplace at my dad's house. The blue dress and wide smile I wish I could remember. I say nothing. Grief isn't a competition.

"It was a long time ago. I miss him and I miss the horses. One day soon Dylan and I will be too old to play football. Then we'll pick up where my dad left off."

We reach the truck and Jake holds the door open for me. By now the gesture shouldn't feel strange, but it does. Jake and I... we're not dating. We barely make it an hour together before we're arguing, but he still gets the door. My thoughts drag to my college ex, Scott. I can't remember a single door he ever held for me, or a single act of kindness or chivalry in the year we dated.

"Thanks," I say to Jake as I settle into the worn leather seats. I'm kicking myself for asking about the horses. After our fight on Thursday night and yesterday's silence, the truce between us feels more tentative than ever, and I've just ruined the easiness between us again.

But then just as Jake is about to close the truck door, he leans against the frame and reaches a hand to my shoulder. "Is this my sweatshirt?" he asks, eyes narrowed but sparkling with amusement.

I flash my own sheepish smile. "It's warmer than mine."

"That's because all your clothes are tiny." He laughs and the tension seems to lift once more.

"Yeah, but I look good in them," I joke.

"You look good in anything, Cassidy. Including my sweatshirt."

The compliment takes me by surprise, but before I can find a reply, Jake's closing my door and whistling for Buck. "Come on, boy," he calls and a moment later Buck bounds through the open driver's door, settling in the middle seat, all wagging tail and panting breath.

"Where are we going?" I ask as the engine rumbles to life.

"You'll see," Jake says, turning the radio on low.

We don't talk on the journey, which suits me fine. I stroke Buck's head and watch dark clouds roll slowly over the sky. There'll be a storm here by the afternoon. I think of sitting by the open fire in the ranch, curled on the couch with my laptop and Buck at my feet, and Jake too.

I shove the daydream aside and hide my groan. One compliment and I'm that nerdy sixteen-year-old who would walk by Jake's locker, waiting for him to notice me.

"OK," Jake says as we reach the outskirts of the city. I glance at his face and realize he's nervous. "This thing I'm going to show you, it's... it's important to me."

On the road ahead, he turns the truck into the parking lot of a recreation ground. The lot is half full with vehicles. I don't know what this is yet or why I'm here, but it means something that Jake has brought me.

Buck barks his excitement and Jake and I both wince at the sound in our ears. "Alright, we're here," Jake soothes, rubbing Buck's back.

He opens his door and Buck shoots out, sprinting through the neat line of trees to a stretching flat grassy field and a group standing like they're waiting for someone.

"Is he OK?" I ask as Jake opens my door.

He follows my gaze to where Buck is dancing excitedly around a group of children. "Don't worry," he says with a grin. "Buck knows them."

Jake grabs a large duffel bag from the back, looping it over his shoulder before handing me a stack of small yellow cones, the kind used in school gym classes.

"No one but Mama knows about this," he says as we walk toward the group. "And that's how I want it to stay, please. You were right the other night. I've not been giving this interview my all. So I want you here, Cassidy, but you can't write about the specifics of what I'm going to show you."

I nod. "Am I going to find out what this is at any point?"

"Sure." He smiles and then steps ahead, striding into the group.

As I draw near, I see it's a mix of moms and dads along with children ranging in age from toddlers to a sullen teenage girl wearing headphones and looking bored. A woman in her mid-forties with short blonde hair, a clipboard, and a whistle around her neck shoots me a curious look as I approach the edge of the group.

"Hey, everyone," Jake says, shaking hands and giving hugs to the children. Instantly the energy changes and chatter breaks out among the group. A little boy who looks about six jumps up and down beside Jake, tugging on his sleeve.

"I got a Stormhawks jersey," he says and Jake whoops, giving him a high five.

Jake catches my eye, beckoning me forward. "Everyone, this is my friend Harper. She's going to help with the drinks and donuts table for us today."

There's a chorus of greetings and I smile back, still not sure what's going on, but happily taking my place behind a foldout table and putting out the cups, drinks, and food from the bag beside it as Jake takes control.

He's in his element as he organizes the parents and children into teams for a fun game of football. He has such an easy rapport with the kids, getting down on their level. Even the sullen teen has taken off her headphones and is happily joining in. I can't help but smile as he leads them through some silly warm-up stretches, the kids giggling as they reach for the sky and then touch their toes. It's obvious from the way the kids and parents interact that it's more about taking part and giving them all a chance than it is about winning.

I'm impressed by Jake's patience. He takes time with each child, especially a boy with leg braces who needs help maneu-vering with the ball. Jake doesn't make him feel different, just encourages him to take his time and cheers loudly when he finally scores.

Only when the dad of the teen girl comes puffing over to me, face red with exertion, do I ask him what this group is.

"Football." The man laughs, shooting me a look like I'm a total moron.

I say nothing, waiting for him to fill the gap.

"For kids who've lost a parent," he adds. I catch the bob of his Adam's apple and the hitch in his voice before he gulps down a cup of water and turns back to his daughter.

I look again at the group playing football with Jake and see them with fresh eyes. This is what Jake does on Saturdays once a month. He comes to a park and messes around with grieving kids and parents. The understanding and hurt cut into my throat. It's for these people. For what they've lost. But it's for Jake too and the reason he does this. The hurt he must've felt as a boy losing his own dad.

I press a finger to the corner of my eye and tell myself to get a grip. No one else here is crying or looking sad. It's all laughter and smiles. The little toddler squeals with delight as Jake passes him the football before swooping him into his arms and making a run for the goal line, Buck bouncing at his side. Jake swings the boy one way then the other as people pretend to rush in for the tackle, then Jake tips the toddler headfirst, guiding him giggling to the ground, where he touches the ball to the grass for a touchdown.

"How long has this group been running?" I ask the woman with the clipboard as I help dish out snacks in the break.

She smiles. "Oh, years. Jake set it up when he was eighteen. I was one of the first to join. I brought my son along after his dad died. It made the world of difference to both of us having this to look forward to. When my son went to college, I offered to help organize things. Jake can't make every month because of his football commitments but he's here more often than not."

The hour flies by with laughter and more touchdowns. At the end, Jake gathers everyone for a team picture, insisting I join in, and I realize this glimpse into Jake's world has thrown me. It's becoming increasingly difficult to remember that this man is the same one who humiliated me and broke my heart in high school—the man I thought I hated. I feel split in two by the realization. After the side Jake showed me today, I'm wondering if writing the truth about Jake will really be the payback I thought it would, or if payback is even what I want anymore.

FIFTEEN

HARPER

I'm still warm and fuzzy from the wholesomeness of Jake's volunteering when we make our way back to the truck. Above our heads, the sun has been swallowed by the clouds. We've got about another hour before the rain starts. Jake is quiet but I catch him glancing my way, like he's trying to read me.

"I could murder a coffee," I say.

"I know just the place." He swings the duffel bag into the truck and whistles for Buck to follow, leading me through the park to a coffee stand by a pavilion. We grab two tall, steaming cups of coffee and wander through the park with Buck trotting between us. The coffee is strong and bitter and just how I like it.

"Why does no one know about this?" I ask.

He shrugs. "It's not their business."

"But..." I choose my words carefully. "This is exactly the kind of thing that would completely reinvent your reputation. It's just... so fucking nice of you."

He huffs a laugh.

"Seriously," I push.

He shakes his head. "It's not a publicity stunt, which is exactly what people will think if I start posting it on my socials.

I can't stop the people who come here from talking about it, but I'm not going to advertise what I'm doing here."

"Why not?"

He gestures across the empty park. "You think it would be quiet like this if people knew? You think grieving families want groups of fans turning up? I know what you're saying, but this is too important to me, Harper."

"I get it," I say quietly. "I won't write about it."

We walk through the park, talking about some of the children he's helped over the years. His passion lights him up and I still find myself blindsided by this side of Jake.

We're right in the middle of the park when the first heavy droplets of rain hit. Instantly a wall of water falls from the sky and we're drenched in seconds. Thunder rumbles over our heads.

"Shit," Jake hisses. "Come on." We drop our cups in the nearest trash can and Jake grabs my hand, pulling me toward an underpass that leads us under a concrete bridge. There's colorful graffiti on the walls depicting a sunset and the Rocky Mountains. Above our heads is a road that cuts through the park. It's not the most glamorous of places, but it's out of the storm.

Buck shakes the water from his fur, sprinkling us with more raindrops. It makes no difference. I'm soaked through, water dripping down my face. I must look like a drowned rat whereas Jake, with wet clothes clinging to every line of defined muscle on his torso, and his hair drenched and falling over his face, looks so good it's criminal.

A streak of lightning cuts across the sky followed by thunder so loud it sounds like the world is cracking open above our heads. Buck barks then whimpers, cowering at our feet. Jake crouches down against the wall, rubbing Buck's back and whispering in his ear.

"I don't like storms either, Bucky," he says. "We'll be OK here."

"Why don't you like them?" I ask, taking a seat on the ground on the other side of Buck and giving his damp fur a reassuring pat.

Jake is silent for a while and I think he's going to make a joke or deflect, but he doesn't. "My dad died in a storm," he says.

"I'm sorry." Sympathy rushes through me.

"It was the October I was ten. The weather had been so good it felt like summer was never going to end. When the storm hit, we just weren't ready for it. It seemed like one minute the sun was setting and everything was perfect. The next the storm clouds were rolling off the mountains and it went so dark so fast it was like someone turned off the lights.

"The horses were still out in the paddocks. I remember the sound of their hooves hitting the ground as they ran in circles, restless and scared. The rain was like this." He nods toward the park as another streak of lightning cuts through the sky. Buck gives a whimper at the next roar of thunder, and Jake and I huddle closer, hugging him from both sides.

"Dad went to put the horses in the barn. Dylan and I ran after him to help. Mama wanted to come too, but Chase was trying to join us and he was too little to do anything but get in the way, so she stayed in the house with him. It was like diving into the lake. You couldn't hear anything but the rain and the storm. I could barely see my hand in front of my face.

"We got to the paddock and I went to get my horse, Dolly. She was a really gentle mare. She wouldn't hurt a fly. But Dad was already leading her into the barn. So I went to get his horse, Trigger. He was a lot bigger and the thunder had started by then so he was skittish. As I reached for the bridle to lead him in, I slipped on the wet grass and Trigger reared at the sudden movement. I remember seeing those huge front legs in the air, about to come pounding down on me. Dad pulled me out the way just in time, but one of Trigger's hooves caught the back of his head."

He pauses, his throat moving as he swallows. Goosebumps rage across my skin and it has nothing to do with the cold.

"The injury didn't seem that bad," Jake continues. "He said he was fine. We got the rest of the horses in and Mama made us all hot chocolates. I remember we were laughing about it. Everything was good. Dad seemed OK." Jake's voice cracks and I slip my hand into his. His fingers entwine with mine and he squeezes his thanks. "We went to bed and Dad never woke up."

"What happened?"

Jake takes a breath. "The blow to the head from Trigger's hoof caused a delayed brain bleed in the night. He died in his sleep."

Hurt radiates from my chest. "I'm so sorry. That must've been really hard for all of you."

"Yeah, and I had the added weight of knowing Dad would never have been hit if he hadn't been saving me."

"You don't know that," I say. "And I bet anything, even if he knew the outcome, he'd still have done it a thousand times over."

"Mama says the same, but sometimes it doesn't help." Tears pool in his eyes and I wonder how this tragic accident has impacted Jake. I wonder who he'd be if his dad was still alive. It's the same unanswerable question I've asked myself about my mom.

We fall silent, listening to the rain hit the path. The thunder becomes distant as the storm moves away. I shiver in my damp clothes. Jake must notice because he lifts his arm and I scooch closer. His body is solid and warm.

"Harper," he says.

"Yeah?" I tilt my head to look up to his face, now inches from mine.

"About what Gordon said—"

"I'm sorry," I blurt. "I did let his comment get to me."

"I just want you to know I haven't..." He swallows and my eyes linger on his throat. "I haven't dated or so much as kissed a woman for over a year. I really have changed."

The air around us shifts as his words settle in the silence. Suddenly I'm thinking about Jake and kissing and how what he's told me is important to him. He doesn't say it, but I think the lack of women is since whatever happened in the parking lot with the cheerleaders. Now isn't the time to ask, because the mention of kissing has my gaze dragging to his mouth. Our faces are so close. Jake's gaze burns into me with an intensity that makes my breath catch.

The air between us seems to crackle with an electric tension, like the lightning flashing in the sky. A lock of damp hair falls over his brow. Without thinking, I reach up and gently brush it back, my fingertips grazing his warm skin.

His gaze drops to my parted lips and I feel that look everywhere, desire coiling hot and tight in my core. Slowly, achingly slowly, he leans in, closing the last distance between us until I can smell the intoxicating scent of his cologne mixed with rain and fresh air and pure man.

I don't move. I can't. I'm frozen. My heart pounds erratically against my ribs as if it might burst out of my chest. Jake's eyes are dark with desire. His large hand comes up to cup my jaw. I feel surrounded by him, his solid warmth seeping into my chilled skin. My eyes close as his lips hover a whisper from mine. The anticipation has my nerve endings sizzling.

We're going to kiss. The thought spins like a tornado in my head. It's all I can think. All I want.

Then the moment shatters in a spray of shaking fur as Buck leaps out from between us, pushing us apart before bounding from the cover of the bridge. The storm has passed—the rain stopped—and we were so lost in each other, we didn't notice.

"We should get going," I manage to croak as Jake's hand still lingers on my jaw.

"Sure." There's a huskiness to the one-word reply that has me melting a little more.

I leap to my feet, Jake following a second later. I stare anywhere but at Jake as my face burns with the sudden realization of what we were about to do.

Fuck.

What was I thinking? I'm the journalist and Jake is the story. Kissing Jake would've been completely unprofessional. Tim has already warned me to be careful and not compromise the integrity of the magazine. Both our careers are hanging by a single thread. Kissing Jake would snap that in a heartbeat.

I swallow hard and take a step back, putting some much-needed distance between us. Boundaries. That's what we need. I make a mental note not to visit Jake's hotel room when we stay in Atlanta on Thursday night after the Stormhawks play the Atlanta Skychargers. Ahead of us, Buck romps happily through the wet grass, oblivious to the fact he just saved us from crossing a line that would've ruined everything.

And yet, even without the heated moment under the bridge, something has shifted between us. We walk back to the truck in silence and all I can think is how sometimes the heat between us feels like hate and other times it feels like something else entirely. And how in that moment when I thought Jake was going to kiss me, I wanted it so badly I ached for it.

SIXTEEN

JAKE

CHASE: *Unlucky tonight, bro!*

DYLAN: *Should've won. Skychargers have a shit offense.*

CHASE: *It was close and it was their home turf!*

CHASE: *Still three more games to go to hit the playoffs!*

DYLAN: *Against the toughest teams in the NFL.*

JAKE: *Shit way to make me feel better, guys.*

CHASE: *Maybe you can find a gorgeous reporter to kiss your bruised ego better.*

JAKE: *Dick!*

The away team locker room in the Atlanta Skychargers stadium is quiet, the air heavy with the tang of sweat and failure. We take our grilling from Coach Allen with our heads hanging low.

He rubs salt into the wound for five minutes before pivoting to his usual speech about learning from our mistakes and coming back stronger.

When it's over, I strip off my sweat-soaked jersey and shoulder pads, wincing as I peel the tape off my knees. I can already feel the bruises forming from the hits I took out there tonight. A hot shower in the stadium before I leave will help soothe my aching muscles, if not my ego.

Dylan is right, we should've won. Under the spray of water, I replay the game in my head, analyzing each play and pass, each missed tackle or blown coverage. We really were close. If only Billy hadn't overthrown that deep ball to Rob in the fourth quarter. Or if the refs had called that blatant pass interference when the Skychargers corner yanked Rob's arm before he could go for the catch on the last scoring drive.

We should've played better. Too many missed passes. Not enough momentum or drive in our plays. But "should" means shit now. And it's pointless to throw blame and dwell on the "if only" thoughts. All we can do as a team is regroup and focus on the next game. We still have a shot at the playoffs if we can pull off wins against the Las Vegas Desertraptors and Chase's Kansas City Trailblazers. Both are home games, so we'll have the crowds to lift us. Then we're away for our final game against the New York Steelguards, who haven't lost a game all season. We still have a shot at winning the AFC West and making the playoffs, but with the sting of defeat throbbing in my muscles, I'm not sure we can do it. Based on the grumbles and silence from the team as we board the bus to the hotel, I'm not the only one who thinks so.

I push in my earphones and allow the beat of my favorite album to soothe my exhaustion and frustration. By the time we reach the hotel, I'm feeling better. There's no use dwelling on what can't be changed. Win or lose, I left it all on the field tonight. I need a cold beer, a burger, and sleep.

The hotel is another boring high-rise, decorated in neutral tones. Ahead of me Gordon, Billy, JT, and Dwight pile into the elevator, heading up to their rooms. There's space for me, but I slow my pace, hanging back. The last thing I want is to hear Gordon running his mouth on the ways he thinks we all let the team down tonight.

The lobby is busy with fans and parents and kids standing in groups or sitting on the gray couches. The air smells of something synthetic and floral being pumped through the AC. There's the buzz of talk and laughter coming from a dimly lit bar in the corner. I think about grabbing a beer alone, but in a place like this, it will be seconds before a fan wants to buy me a drink and give me their analysis of the game. I love the energy of the Stormhawks fans, but right now I want some peace.

I'm stepping toward the elevators when my gaze snags on the front desk, curving in a modern crescent shape, with perky-looking staff members in navy suits. And standing on the other side of the desk, looking somehow both sexy as hell and stressed, is Harper. And she's arguing with the desk clerk. My pulse kicks up a notch and I pause, thinking of my realization last week that the time we're spending together has given me a teen-like crush. Another side effect of being single for so long, no doubt.

My mind drifts to that moment in the park on Saturday. The heat between us in the underpass. I can't stop thinking about what would've happened if Buck hadn't chosen that moment to interrupt us. I'm used to women who are dazzled by my fame and eager to please. Harper seems thoroughly unimpressed by my NFL star status.

She's also the first woman I've taken to my Saturday mornings in the park with the bereavement group. I told myself when I woke that morning that I was doing it to show Harper I could give her more of myself after she threw that comment at me during our fight and I then spent all of Friday ignoring her, proving her right. But deep down, my wanting to show Harper that part of me had nothing to do with the feature she's writing.

Three weeks in, I'm finally starting to let my guard down. But since the moment in the park, things between us have been strained. One moment it's effortless and fun. Walks with Buck and evenings in the kitchen with Mama telling every embarrassing story from my childhood. Me groaning every time the family photo albums make an appearance. Even Dylan's mood lifting long enough to tell Harper the story of him and Chase stealing my clothes at the lake and me walking back to the Ranch butt naked while Mama held meetings with college football scouts. The more I wanted the floor to open up and swallow me whole, the harder Harper laughed, promising me she'll be selective with what she writes.

Then other times it's still prickly and tense. Like when I drove us to the airport this morning and we went from something that felt light and even flirty to her accusing me of not taking the feature seriously.

"I hope you brought your nurse's uniform in that suitcase, Cassidy. I might be inclined to get another injury." I flashed her my most flirtatious grin.

Her eyes narrowed on me, but she was smiling too. "Not a chance."

"What if—" I began in my teasing voice again when she cut me off.

"Seriously, Jake," she said, the smile dropping. "If you want this feature to really show who you are and change the narrative around your reputation, you need to give me more than cocky quips."

The tension was instant. My grip tightened on the steering wheel. "I am giving you access. Hell, I took you to the park on Saturday, didn't I? We're talking, aren't we? What more do you want?"

"I want you to drop the act. To stop deflecting with jokes and actually talk to me."

"I am," I growled. "But you've got to stop pushing me. I'm getting there, OK?"

"Not quick enough," she shot back. "We've only got two weeks left together. I feel like I've barely scratched the surface. We still need to talk about—"

"Not now." I cut her off and turned the radio up loud, driving the rest of the way in silence.

From across the hotel lobby, I watch Harper unleash an exasperated sigh. I know I should head to my hotel room rather than risk another fight between us, but even as the thought lands, I'm crossing the lobby and leaning against the desk beside her.

"Hey," I say. "What's up?"

Harper whirls around at the sound of my voice. "Nothing. It's fine," she says, her tone saying otherwise.

The desk clerk flashes me a smile that tells me she knows exactly who I am. "It's like I was just telling your... friend?" she continues and I don't miss the question in her tone or the spark of interest in her eyes. "The booking for her room was canceled this morning and we're now fully booked. We're looking into whether this was done by the booker themselves or if our computer system may have malfunctioned. Unfortunately, it appears another guest had the same issue yesterday. But right now, there's really nothing I can do. I'm very sorry."

The clerk glances behind us to a long line of impatient guests and I take Harper's arm and guide her away.

"But I didn't book the room. My colleague did. And if she canceled, I still need—" she starts to say.

"They're fully booked. Arguing isn't going to change that."

"I know, but so is every hotel in a twenty-block radius. There's an Irish dance competition at the convention center. Apparently it's a very big deal."

As she speaks, I spot a group of five tween girls gliding across the lobby with ringlet-curled hair piled on top of their heads and frilly blue dresses and matching hairbands. Behind them is a group of stressed-looking moms overloaded with bags.

"So come sleep in my room," I say.

Harper rolls her eyes and I laugh. It's not the usual response I get when inviting a beautiful woman to my room. Then again, nothing about Harper is the usual for me.

"Not like that," I say. "Seriously, Cassidy. It's already late and we've got the fans breakfast tomorrow you wanted to come to. You can take the bed. I'll sleep on the floor, or a couch if there is one."

"It's your room. I can take the couch or the floor."

"Ain't gonna happen, Cassidy. You'll take the bed." I don't wait for her to give me all the reasons this is a terrible idea and instead call the elevator and pick up her bag. It pings its arrival and I hold the door for Harper. She hesitates for a final beat, then follows me inside. As the doors slide to a close, the faint scent of her familiar wildflower perfume wraps itself around me.

I glance over at her. She's chewing her bottom lip, a crease of concern between her brows. She's not wearing her red Stormhawks tee tonight, but a white tank top with the red Stormhawks logo stretched across her breasts in the most enticing way. It gives me a kick to think of Harper buying her own merch.

"Don't look so worried. I'm not some creep using this as an opportunity to lure you to my bed," I say, pushing away those exact thoughts from my head.

She gives me a wry smile, revealing a dimple in her right cheek. The worry lines between her brows soften and her eyes gleam with a hint of amusement. "I know. Believe it or not, I do actually trust you."

The comment takes me by surprise. I say nothing but feel

the smile tugging at my mouth as we hit the eighteenth floor. I pull out the key card handed to me as I walked off the bus earlier and tap it to the lock.

"Just think of this as a PG-rated—" The rest of the words die in my mouth as I open the door into the smallest hotel room I've ever seen.

To be fair to Harper, she sees the funny side, huffing a laugh as we both take in the space. The room has the same bland functionality as the rest of the hotel. Gray walls and gray carpet, teamed with green and gray curtains and a matching throw covering a queen-sized bed.

There's a TV on the wall and below it a small fridge. Beside the bed is a door leading into a bathroom. It has everything you'd expect from a hotel room, except space. One step into the room and my legs are already hitting the edge of the bed. There's barely enough room to stand, let alone lie down. It looks like the only place I'm sleeping tonight is in that bed with Harper beside me, and from the look of dawning horror on her face, she's realizing the same thing.

SEVENTEEN
HARPER

HARPER: *Help!!*

MIA: *Tell me everything.*

HARPER: *Long story. I'm sharing a hotel room with Jake.*

MIA: *OMG! Fuck his brains out.*

HARPER: *Mia!! You're not helping!*

MIA: *OK, fine. Stare longingly into his eyes and wish you were fucking his brains out. Better?*

HARPER: *No!!!!!*

Notes for feature: Beneath the cocky charm, there's an old-fashioned quality to Jake. It's in the little things he does, like pulling a chair out for me or checking on me from across the room with a single look. But just how much of a gentleman is he?

I'm drowning in what-the-fuck-am-I-doing anxiety as I hide in the bathroom of the tiniest hotel room in existence, questioning if I'm seriously going to spend the night sharing a bed with Jake. The man I'm supposed to be professional around...

The check-in clerk's words race through my thoughts. *We're looking into whether this was done by the booker themselves or if our computer system may have malfunctioned.*

This is exactly the kind of thing Callie would do. And the exact reason I didn't ask her to book my hotel and flights in the first place. What the hell was she thinking leaving me stranded in a city with no hotel rooms in a twenty-block radius? I know the answer—she was thinking how much she wants my job. *Fuck!*

I unzip my suitcase and stare at my favorite nightwear set— a cute ivory silk camisole and matching shorts. What was I thinking packing this? I know the answer. After sleeping on Mia's couch for months and then staying at the ranch with Jake, Mama, and Dylan, I've taken to wearing gym shorts and baggy tees to bed, and I was thinking a night alone in a hotel room seemed like the perfect time to wear something that made me feel a little sexier.

Now, as I slip on the set, all I see in the mirror above the sink is how much my nipples push at the fabric and how indecent these shorts are with the amount of ass they leave on show. I glance back to my suitcase, hoping to find a set of sweats or something equally undesirable, but I packed light and my only other clothes are the ones I've been wearing and what I need for tomorrow.

There's nothing for it but to brazen this out. I run a hand through my hair and lift my chin at my reflection. I'm a professional. I'm here to do a job. I will not think about having sex with Jake Sullivan.

Who am I kidding? I'm horny just thinking of getting into that bed beside him tonight. But I'm certain that's just my body's reaction to how attractive Jake is. The truth is, I don't know how I really feel about Jake right now. I've kept my distance this week, placing myself on the other side of whatever room we've found ourselves in, trying to regain my composure after we almost kissed last weekend. Something we're both pretending didn't happen. Something that can't happen again if I have any chance of keeping my job when this is over.

When Jake is cocky and joking, all I see is the pro football player, the boy from high school… But the more I see the other side of him—the one where he's thoughtful and says things about his past or his future that melt something in me—the more I find myself drawn to him.

Shit.

I'll wear the clothes I had on this evening. Sleeping in tight jeans isn't ideal but anything has to be better than this. I'm reaching for my bra when there's a knock at the door.

"Stop hiding, Cassidy. I've ordered us room service."

"I'm not hiding," I call back even though it's exactly what I've been doing.

Fine. Have it his way. I take a deep breath and open the bathroom door. Jake has changed into shorts and a tee and is stretched out on the bed. He looks at me and I watch his eyes flare wide, a slow smile starting to form on his lips; he must catch himself because it's gone in a second, hidden behind a mask of indifference.

"I thought you seemed like a burger type," he says.

"Thanks." There's no way I can eat right now, but my stomach has other ideas and gives a rumble that makes Jake chuckle.

"They said it won't be long. Can you survive?" He grins, rolling off the bed and pulling two beers from the mini bar. He pops the lids before handing a bottle to me. I try not to notice the electric charge that shoots through my body at our touch.

"The hotel room in LA wasn't this small," I say, perching on the edge of the bed and crossing my legs.

He huffs. "I know. Believe me, I'm going to be having words with the support staff when I get back."

"Maybe it's the Irish dance convention. Those girls looked like they take it pretty seriously."

"Not as serious as the parents. Did you hear that woman in the lobby yelling at her husband for buying the wrong brand of hairspray?"

I laugh, about to tell Jake the importance of hairspray brands when my phone rings. I think it'll be Mia with some filth to share, but I'm surprised to see it's Dad calling.

"Sorry," I say to Jake. "I need to take this." I stand, answering with a breezy, "Hi, Dad, are you back in Denver?" Because that's the only time he calls.

"Harper." Dad's voice is deep and serious, pulling me back to a childhood of awkward dinners spent with my father. "You're coming on Tuesday to the awards dinner?" he demands, without any preamble. After an entire life of his abrupt style, I know I should be used to it, but would a "how are you?" have killed him?

I groan inwardly. I've been doing a good job of ignoring the fact that Dad's lifetime achievement award is now this Tuesday. Dread floods my body. "Yes, Dad," I reply. "I'll be there."

"Seven sharp at the Arquette Media building."

I wonder if he's forgotten I work in that very building. Probably. I know he only wants me there for appearances.

"I'll be there," I say again.

"Are you still working at that magazine?" he asks.

The hurt is instant. "It's *Sports Magazine*, not a school paper." The retort surprises me as much as I imagine it does him. The second I hear his sigh of disappointment in my ear, I wish I hadn't bothered. "I'm working on a feature now, actually. I should go. I'll see you Tuesday."

I end the call before he can say more and dip my head, allowing a lifetime of hurt out of the box for just a second, feeling small and stupid. Feeling the hollowness of not being good enough. Of a life without a mom. It's been a long time since I've let Dad's remarks cut so deep, but knowing Jake heard every word makes it worse somehow.

The moment passes and I squash the hurt back into its hiding place.

"Hey." Jake moves from the bed so he's standing beside me.

He's so close I can feel the heat radiating from his body. I must still be feeling vulnerable because I have the urge to lean in.

"I'm not gonna pretend I know a thing about your relationship with your dad, but no one should make you feel less than the unstoppable, fierce woman you are."

I lift my gaze, expecting a playful smirk, but he looks serious, intense. I'm suddenly reminded of how skimpy my camisole is and the way the silk is brushing against my nipples. I open my mouth, searching for a reply. A joke—a way to make this moment less heated. But my mind blanks. Once again, I'm knocked sideways by this man. Is this how Jake sees me? Unstoppable and fierce? I want to tell him how wrong he is, how scared I am every day that someone is going to figure out that I'm a terrible journalist, that I'll be laughed at and ridiculed for spending my free time writing a vampire love story with characters who have more of a social life than I do. I want to tell him he's wrong. Except more than that, I want to be the fierce, unstoppable woman he sees in me. To be more like Jake and not care what people think or the repercussions of doing what I want.

I stare into Jake's dark, soulful eyes and allow myself to get lost for a moment in how hot this man is. The sharp angle of his jaw is dusted with dark stubble that I long to feel rasping against my skin. His full lips are parted slightly, drawing my eyes down to his mouth. I imagine how those lips would feel pressed against my own. My eyes drift lower, appreciating the strong column of his neck and the way his broad shoulders fill out his simple white tee. The thin cotton clings to his sculpted chest and abs, outlining every ripple of hard muscle.

Time slows. The room, the world, everything fades away until it's just me and Jake, alone in this moment. My breath catches in my throat as Jake gently brushes a stray lock of hair back from my face. His fingertips graze my cheek, igniting flames everywhere he touches.

His eyes flick down to my parted lips then back up again, a question in his eyes. I'm frozen, mesmerized, unwilling to break this spell weaving around us. My heart pounds so loudly I'm sure he must hear it. Slowly, giving me time to pull away, Jake leans in closer.

His hand moves into my hair and around the back of my neck, drawing me toward him. My insides burn. I stop thinking and move the last few inches until our bodies are pressed against each other. His lips brush against mine and it's electric and so fucking hot I feel it between my thighs.

And then his tongue slides into my mouth, stroking against my own. Every moment shoots another dart of need through my body. My nipples tingle against the silk of my top as I press against him. I can feel his rock-hard erection through the fabric of his shorts. I wrap my arms around his neck, pushing myself against him as our kiss deepens, wanting him. Wanting more. Wanting everything.

But then Jake pulls away a fraction and the spell is broken.

"Harper," he whispers, voice husky. "We shouldn't..."

Even as his words land with a crushing realization, another part of me wants to pull him close once more, whisper that we very much should. But then the knock at the door comes and we're both leaping away anyway. Jake's back hits the wall and suddenly we're grinning and laughing, even as my face burns crimson.

Jake reaches for the door and takes the tray from the waiter, and I lean against the wall, trying to stay upright as desire courses through me alongside the knowledge that Jake was pulling back, telling me we shouldn't go any further. He's right —of course he's right—but the rejection is sharp and stinging regardless. I cover my face with my hands and groan as Jake closes the door.

He puts the tray on the edge of the bed and I can feel him looking at me. "Harper—"

"I'm sorry," I blurt.

"I'm not," Jake says, and when I drop my hands and look at him, I realize I'm not sorry either, but that doesn't make it right. Or me any less embarrassed.

"We shouldn't have done that," I say. "It was so unprofessional. I'm supposed to be writing a feature about you." I think of my resolve to put some boundaries between us and Tim's warning against the lines being blurred. That's all this is. I was sad and a bit horny and Jake is... he's the hottest man I've ever met. "We can't let that happen again."

I think I catch a flash of disappointment on Jake's face, but it's gone in an instant and I'm already questioning if it was even there. *He's the one who pulled away*, I remind myself.

With a smile now playing on his lips, he raises a finger to his chest, drawing an X. "I promise not to kiss you again," he says, and I ignore another wave of heat flooding my body that I want to pretend is humiliation but I know is disappointment.

I nod and smile gratefully, telling myself this is for the best. We only have two more weeks together anyway. I'm a journalist who needs to stay professional. A journalist who could be out of a job come January. Jake is a pro football player with a bad reputation. We don't fit. And even if that wasn't all true, I can't afford to risk my heart for this man again.

Just two more weeks together, I remind myself. *Then we'll both get on with our lives. I can handle this.*

"Can we forget it happened?" I say.

"It's forgotten," he replies. "Let's eat and watch trashy TV."

"What's the deal with your dad?" Jake asks when we're finished and the tray is outside the room. After moving awkwardly around each other, we're now side by side beneath the bed covers. I stare into the darkness pretending my skin isn't tingling with the heat from Jake's body. Just like I pretend I don't notice Jake slide off his tee so he's now naked from the waist up.

"It's complicated," I reply.

"When isn't it?"

I remember the moment under the bridge in the storm on Saturday. Jake's honesty about his father's death. I'm surprised to find I want to be honest too.

"My mom died when I was three. A drunk driver slammed into our car when we were driving back from the store. I don't remember the crash and I'm not sure I remember my mom either. When I think of her, all I have is the photos I've seen and this feeling of warmth."

"Harper, I'm sorry," he says and I know he gets it. "Losing my dad was the worst thing that happened to me, but I can't imagine how much harder it would've been without the memories I have of him."

"Maybe it's easier if you can't remember," I say, but I don't really believe it. The truth is, I'd give anything for a memory of my mom. "At the time, Dad was at the height of his career. He was traveling all over the world. The last thing he wanted was to come home and look after me. So he didn't. He hired nannies to do it. I grew up raised by people who were paid to pretend to love and care for me. I remember wishing every single time that they'd fall in love with me and my dad and become the mom I wanted.

"I didn't know any different until I started going to friends' houses and seeing what families and love really looked like. I think my dad loves me in his own way, but he's very focused. When he was home, we'd talk about my homework and what I wanted to do with my life and the steps I needed to take to get there. I know he was disappointed when I chose to follow in his footsteps, even more so when I started getting interested in sports journalism. I guess I thought if I was a journalist too then we'd have something in common, but it seemed to only drive us further apart. He told me when I left for college he wouldn't support nepotism. It was fine. I never wanted his help. He comes back to Denver every few months when he's finished with whichever story he's chasing, and we see each other for a coffee or a bite to eat. That's it."

"And this awards dinner on Tuesday... you don't want to go?" Jake asks.

I let out a long exhale. "Not really. It makes me sound like a terrible daughter, doesn't it? I really am happy for him. But it's not just my dad at this dinner. It's going to be a room filled with award-winning journalists. I'm sure they all know George Cassidy's daughter was fired from *Insight*. It's going to be awful."

"Even though it was because a sleazy editor made a pass at you and it wasn't your fault?"

"No one knows that. My editor made sure no one believed my side of what happened."

"Well, who cares what they think? You like working at *Sports Magazine*, right?"

I stare straight up in the dark, aware of every dip of the mattress when Jake shifts, every breath I'm taking. "Yeah, I do."

I like Tim and the style of the magazine. And even though I hate that people see me as a failure, I like being back in Denver, too. "But just to make things worse, my ex, Scott, is going to be at the awards dinner too."

"He's a journalist?"

I nod. "And a total ass. He's close to my dad, though. Scott and I dated in college, and when I took him home, the two of them hit it off. Dad helped Scott out a lot with his career. And he's doing really well because of it."

"Your dad helped your ex but wouldn't help you?" Jake's surprise rings in the darkness.

"Yep. Scott and I broke up after a year. It turns out he was sleeping with half the girls on the course, including my college roommate. It wasn't a great loss, to be honest. I realized afterward what a prick he was. He always made me feel like I was in the wrong." I take a breath. I could say more about Scott. Of all the ways he's an entitled dick, but I push it aside, not wanting to give the man any more space in my thoughts. "But he stayed in touch with my dad. They're still close. He's going to be at the dinner and he's giving a speech to introduce my dad."

"Couldn't you have done that?" Jake asks.

I laugh. "That would've required my dad to see me as something other than a giant disappointment."

"Harp—"

"It's fine, Jake," I cut in, injecting a lightness into my voice and almost believing it. "I'm honestly doing fine. It's only one night, and despite everything, I do want to support my dad."

Jake is quiet for a long time and I think he's fallen asleep but then he whispers, "This won't mean anything because I'm just me, but you're fucking awesome. If your dad and the room full of journalists on Tuesday can't see that, then it's their loss."

I lie awake for a long time, remembering the loneliness of my childhood. All the nights I longed for a mom I'd never known but was acutely aware was missing in my life. And then as a teen, when sixteen-year-old me would fill that loneliness with dreams of Jake Sullivan noticing me for the first time and thinking I was awesome. Jake is wrong. His comment is everything.

EIGHTEEN

JAKE

I wake to find I'm on my side, with an arm flung over Harper's waist and a hard-on so big it's almost painful. My thoughts leap straight back to last night. The way Harper pressed against me when we kissed and how fucking good it felt. And that cute night-set she's wearing, the strap of which has fallen over her shoulder in her sleep. I was halfway to ruined when she stepped out of the bathroom wearing it last night. But it feels weird to stare while Harper's asleep.

Slowly, I move my arm away from Harper's body, trying not to wake her. The last thing she needs to see is the tent I'm pitching under the sheets. Man, I haven't woken up with morning wood like this since I was a teen.

I step to the bathroom and quietly close the door. I need to get it together. I'm acting like some horny frat boy around Harper and she deserves better. That's why I stopped things progressing last night. It took every ounce of my willpower to pull away from those beautiful full lips. All I wanted was to push her onto the bed and ravage every inch of her body. And I'm pretty sure from the sultry look in her eyes when I pulled back, she wanted it too.

But Harper had been sad after the call from her dad. It felt like I was taking advantage of a low moment. Besides, the whole reason Harper is spending so much time with me is so I can prove my reputation is bullshit. I can hardly do that and make a pass at her at the same time. Even if it did half kill me to promise I wouldn't try to kiss her again when, honestly, it's all I can think about.

Turning on the shower, I step under the hot spray and take my dick in my hand. I think of Harper's lips, her smooth skin, the soft sound she made in her throat when I touched her. It barely takes any time before I'm shuddering in release.

~

Harper is awake when I step out of the bathroom with a towel wrapped around my waist. Just looking at her tousled hair and that sheepish smile makes my dick twitch all over again.

"Morning," I say, trying to act like this is a completely normal situation.

"Hey." She bites her bottom lip then pulls her hair up into a bun. "Look, about last night..." she starts, but trails off.

"If you're going to start getting weird on me about the thing that is already forgotten, please don't," I say. "It happened. It's forgotten. So get up because we've got the meet-and-greet fans breakfast this morning and you're going to want to be taking notes on how amazing the fans think I am. It'll be good background for your feature."

Harper arches an eyebrow in reply. "Someone's woken up thinking pretty highly of himself."

"Maybe you bring out the best in me," I reply. I meant it as a throwaway comment, but it lands like it's more.

Harper shoots me a look like she isn't sure I'm joking. I'm not entirely sure I am either and the realization causes a nervous energy to thud through me. I think about how much better I've been playing for the last three weeks and wonder if there's some truth to my comment.

I reach for the edges of the towel slung around my hips. "Are you planning to watch me get dressed or—"

"No," she yelps, jumping up and heading for the bathroom.

I keep my eyes off her ass and focus on finding my clothes.

"Jake," she says, and I look up to find her standing in the doorway to the bathroom. Her eyes are wide, her face clear of makeup and just as beautiful. "I know we're not talking about the thing we've forgotten, but I just wanted to say thank you. You were kind to me last night when I needed it."

I smile, but then her next comment feels like a sucker punch even though I know it's coming.

"But we can't kiss again. We need to keep things—"

"Professional," I finish for her. "We're on the same page, Cassidy. Relax. I have no intention of breaking my promise."

Harper disappears into the bathroom and a moment later I hear the shower running. My mind reels as I get dressed. I think back to last night again. I've kissed a lot of women in my life, but none of them have ever made me feel the way Harper does. This is a problem...

I enjoy spending time with her. I love the way her mind works. The more time we spend together, the more layers it feels like I peel back from myself and from her, catching glimpses of the real Harper underneath—vulnerable and uncertain but also passionate and so smart it blows my mind. She's the kind of girl a guy takes seriously if he knows what's good for him. I want to know everything about her. I want to be the one she turns to, the one who makes her laugh, the one who holds her when she cries.

The realization hits me like a lightning bolt. I want Harper to like me. I care what she thinks about me. This is more than just finding her physically attractive. It's more than my dick feeling deprived of attention. A lot more. But I just promised I wouldn't kiss her again... and I know I have to stick to it.

NINETEEN

HARPER

MIA: *Where are you?*

HARPER: *Jake's just dropping me off. Be with you in a sec.*

MIA: *I've ordered you a cocktail.*

HARPER: *It's barely lunchtime.*

MIA: *What's your point?*

Notes for feature: Jake Sullivan has spent his life wanting the approval of one man—his father. With Harry Sullivan's tragic death when Jake was just ten years old, it seems as though Jake coped by deciding that without his father, he wouldn't be seeking approval from anyone else. Jake will say he doesn't care what anyone else thinks of him, and while a part of that is true, it's important to recognize that not caring what people think isn't the same as not caring, because Jake cares deeply about his family, football, and his friends.

The following Tuesday, we're back in Jake's truck as it rumbles down the dusty road away from the ranch, the midday sun streaking across the fields and hitting the dark crags of the hills that stretch toward the distant mountains. I catch a glimpse of the lake, just visible through the tall spruce trees, the water glistening in the sunlight. I'm going to miss this view when this assignment is over. I'm going to miss the ranch too, and Mama.

Jake's got one hand draped over the steering wheel, the other resting on the open window frame. I *know* I'm staring at his muscular forearm. It's been five days since we kissed in Atlanta and I can't stop thinking about the moment our lips touched and it felt like the entire world disappeared. Even if Jake has been true to his word and acting like he's forgotten it ever happened. He's been his usual easygoing self. A little bit cocky. A little bit flirty, but never taking it any further.

Last night, Mama cooked pot roast as a farewell dinner for her and Dylan. They left early this morning for LA and the specialist ACL treatment center, and I'm trying really hard not to think about the fact that Jake and I will be alone at the ranch for the next week.

"You gonna miss me tonight?" Jake asks as we hit the highway to the city.

I roll my eyes. "Please. I'm looking forward to a break from your ego."

He chuckles, unfazed. "Ouch, Cassidy. You wound me."

I can't help but smile. His playful banter is growing on me, though I'd never admit it.

"So what's the deal with Mia?" Jake asks.

I shoot him a questioning look. "What do you mean?"

"She used to do barrel racing in the rodeo and now she's some corporate hotshot. That's a hell of a change."

"Yeah." I remember the tears. The inconsolable sobs shuddering through my best friend's body after another fight with her mom. The realization that no matter what she did, Arquette Media would be hers one day. "She felt she had a responsibility to carry on the family legacy, which meant going to college and getting an education and starting on the bottom rung of the business. If things had been different, I think she'd have gone all in and dedicated her life to competing at the rodeo professionally. She loved horses."

"She doesn't ride anymore? Not even for fun?"

I shake my head, feeling a pang of sadness. "I think it was too painful for her. If she couldn't have her dream, she wanted to forget it was there."

Mia has a great apartment and a great job. She has Edward too, who treats her like a queen, even if he is the polar opposite of her first rodeo boyfriend, Cole. Not to mention she'll be running a media empire one day. She's happy, I think. It's just not the same kind of happy I remember from when she was leaping onto a horse and entering an arena.

As we hit the outskirts of the city, my phone buzzes with a text from Mia. She's at the restaurant already. I fire a reply before shooting another look to Jake. I'm not going to miss him, but there's no denying it will be strange not to see him for twenty-four hours. After Jake drops me off for lunch with Mia, he's going to Stormhawks Park—the training facility—and after lunch I'll head to Mia's apartment to get ready for Dad's awards dinner. It's being held in the top-floor banquet suite of the Arquette Media building, just around the corner from Mia's. It makes sense for me to stay in the city tonight and meet Jake at practice tomorrow.

I thought I'd look forward to a night in the city and sleeping on Mia's couch, but I miss the ranch already. The weeks I've spent there have made me realize I'm ready to find my own place. I can see now that sleeping on Mia's couch has been a form of denial that my dreams of a New York life are over. I need to move on. Denver is my home now. It's time I started acting like it.

We pull up outside Bill's and I see Mia already in our favorite window booth. I hop out before Jake can park and jump out to open my door. I'm still not used to that level of chivalry and I know Mia's jaw will hit the table if she sees it.

"See you tomorrow," I call.

"Hey," Jake says, and I turn back. "Have fun tonight."

A wave of discomfort hits me at the thought of Dad's awards dinner and what all those people will be thinking of me. Then there's the matter of my ex, Scott. I can already picture the slimy smile on his face and those hands reaching to touch my skin. I'm suddenly regretting the backless dress I plan to wear. There's a nagging sense that I haven't been entirely honest with Jake about Scott, but as I shout a thanks and wave goodbye, I shove the thought away, along with my concerns for tonight. I've been looking forward to my catch-up with Mia for days.

I push open the heavy wooden door of Bill's and the familiar warmth envelops me. I love everything about this place, from the cozy leather booths with their soft lighting to the black-and-white photos of old Denver on the walls. There's a rich smell of sizzling meats and fresh bread in the air that immediately makes me feel famished. Christmas lights twinkle around the dark, polished wood bar and mottled mirrors, sitting behind gleaming bottles of liquor. It's a reminder that Christmas is just around the corner. With my strained relationship with Dad, Christmas has always felt like something to get through. More often than not, Dad's away and I spend it with Mia and her mom anyway.

Mia looks up from her phone as I approach, grinning as I slide into the booth opposite her, the leather cushion creaking softly. Two Moscow Mule cocktails are already sitting on the table in tall glasses filled with ice and a wedge of lime balanced on the side. Mia has twisted her black braids up into a sophisticated bun, and in her pale gray suit jacket, she looks ready to take over the world—not just her family business.

"Hey," I say, matching her smile. Mia is more like a sister to me than a best friend, and being around her feels like a warm hug. Like coming home after a long day, which is probably why I've spent the last four months sleeping on her couch.

"How are things?" I ask.

She waves a hand dismissively in the air. "Exactly the same. Working all the hours. Missing living with you."

"No way. You have your living room back."

"I never minded. And neither did Edward. And you're coming back, right? When the feature on Jake is done?"

My five weeks tailing Jake officially end next Sunday after his game against Chase's team—the Kansas City Trailblazers. There are still twelve days left, but with Christmas in between, I'm not sure how much time we'll actually spend together or why every time I think about the end, something heavy sinks inside me.

I smile at my best friend. "I think it's time I got my own place."

Mia makes a dramatic sad face. "I guess I knew it couldn't last forever. Well, let's drink these and you can tell me everything about the devastatingly sexy tight end you've been spending all your time with."

I laugh. "It's my job, Mia."

"Yeah, yeah. Now spill. What happened when you spent the night in the hotel room together?"

Just thinking about that night makes my stomach flutter.

"Nothing happened," I say, taking a long sip of my cocktail, enjoying the fizz and spice of the ginger beer next to the kick of lime and that instant hit of vodka. It's a drink that will always remind me of this restaurant and these moments with my best friend. It was the first drink she ordered for me when I returned from New York, feeling like my life was over.

Mia's expression is one of utter disbelief. "Harper Jane Cassidy," she says with all the authority of a fifth-grade teacher who knows she's about to get a confession. "I've known you since you were twelve years old, don't you lie to me."

I groan. There's no way Mia will let up until she has the truth. "Fine. We kissed."

Mia punches the air and gives such a loud, "Yessssss," that every head in the place turns. "Tell me everything."

And so I do. It doesn't take long before I'm done and we're ordering food.

"He must really like you," she says.

I shake my head. "He pulled away first. He said we shouldn't. It was a stupid mistake."

I'm about to explain all the reasons why someone as hot as Jake isn't interested in me, why the two of us can never work, when a figure passes by the window. Dark hair and broad shoulders filling out his black sweater in a way that makes my mouth go dry.

"Oh God," I say as realization hits. "Mia, I'm begging you— don't embarrass me."

"Why?" She follows my gaze, her face lighting up as Jake pushes through the doors and in four long strides is sliding into the booth beside me. Our legs touch and there's a shot of electricity that reminds me why I've been trying to keep my distance from him this week.

"Hello ladies, mind if I join you?"

"Yes," I mutter as Mia shakes her head.

"I won't stay long." He grins, ignoring my reply. "I realized I didn't need to be at practice just yet, and thought I'd buy you lunch."

Before we can say another word, a waitress hurries over. "What do you need?" she asks like she's offering a lot more than what's on the menu.

"Just water for me, thanks," he replies, and I'm relieved when the smile he flashes her is polite, but nothing more. "Unless you ladies are ready for another cocktail?"

I shake my head. "I'm supposed to be spending the after-noon making sure I look presentable for tonight's dinner. One cocktail is already more than I need."

Mia takes a long sip from her own drink before she replies, "You're going to need way more than one cocktail to be in the same room as Scott tonight. I almost wish I was going so I could tell that piece of shit what I think of him."

"I think I would pay to see that," I grin. Mia's eyes light up and I know exactly what she's going to say, so I cut her off. "But it's my dad's night so I'm going to pretend he doesn't exist and not make a scene."

Only when the waitress has brought Jake's water does he stretch his arm over the back of the booth behind me, moving in close so I can smell the heady scent of him. "You always look a lot more than presentable," he says and there's something in his eyes that makes me think he's picturing the red two-piece swimsuit. Then just as quickly, the arm is gone and he's leaning across the table to Mia. "So, tell me all the embarrassing stories about Harper."

"Well, I'm guessing Harper has already mentioned the huge crush she had on you in high school?" Mia says with a devilish smile.

I yelp, almost spitting out my drink as heat floods my cheeks. "Mia," I warn, knowing exactly where this is going. "Don't you dare."

Jake winks at me before fixing his gaze back on my soon-to-be ex-best friend. "Oh Mia, I think you do dare."

She laughs. "I don't think crush really sums it up. She was madly in love with you."

I groan and concentrate on my cocktail as delight dances in Jake's eyes. I want to kill Mia for this. But of course, I won't. I know exactly what she's up to. She's trying to matchmake us.

"She had your timetable printed in the back of her note-book," Mia continues with that cackling laugh that, even while

I'm wishing the world would swallow me up, makes me laugh too. "She would hang around near your locker when she knew you'd be passing."

Jake shoots me a curious look and I can see him raking over his memories of high school before shaking his head. "I had no idea."

"That makes it worse," I mumble, flames burning my cheeks. "But I was a sophomore and you were a senior. Hardly surprising you didn't know I existed."

"I was a total idiot back in high school," Jake says. "And all my friends were bigger idiots. All I cared about was football. I'm glad you didn't know me back then because you'd probably hate me right now if you did." His comment lands at the exact moment Mia's foot nudges mine like she's making sure I'm listening. I can almost hear her voice in my head, reminding me that people change.

She's right. I think how much I've changed in the last ten years. I was so certain this feature would prove Jake was an awful person. That him opening up to me would be his downfall. I even thought it would serve as payback for how much he humiliated me, but the truth is, he's not the person I've spent the last ten years hating.

Mia cackles again, pulling me back to the restaurant. "And all those practices and games she made me watch. Sitting in the freezing cold."

"Made you watch?" I laugh. "You only came with me to copy my homework."

"Hang on." Jake turns in the seat and the warmth of his leg touching mine stirs a heat in me I try to ignore. "You came to high school practices and games?"

I pull a face and nod.

"And you still didn't pick up any of the rules or understanding of the game?"

I bury my head in my hands as Mia replies with another cackle of laughter. "She was watching you, not the game."

"I'm so sorry," Jake says, seeming genuinely apologetic. "I had no idea you had a crush on me. And honestly, you were better off without me back then."

But what about now? The question pops into my head unbidden and I bury it before I can think about the answer.

"Maybe so, but you went off to college and broke my heart," I say, shoving Jake's arm playfully, pretending like I didn't spend all those hours crying on Mia's bed.

Jake checks the time and pulls a face. "I need to get to practice. Good to see you, Mia. It's been very... informative." Then he leans toward me and whispers in my ear, "Have you forgiven me for breaking your heart yet?"

I burst out laughing as my face heats all over again. Jake has no idea how close he came to me not forgiving him. "Yes. Now go. I'll see you tomorrow. Try not to get into trouble while I'm not there to babysit you."

He flashes me a final grin and I watch him walk away, unable to tear my eyes from his ass and those muscular legs.

"Perv." Mia laughs, catching me staring.

"Mia," I growl the second the door closes behind him. "I can't believe you did that. I'm so telling Edward it was you who broke his blender. On purpose!"

She gives me a dismissive wave as our food arrives—two large plates of chicken salad with fries on the side. "I was doing you a favor. Besides, I could've told him you killed bunny rabbits in your spare time and he'd still have looked at you all googly-eyed. The sexual tension between you two is off the charts."

"No way." I shake my head.

"The hell it isn't. So if you want me to book a hotel tonight for me and Edward so you and Jake can have my apartment, that's cool with me." She waggles her eyebrows suggestively.

I bark a laugh. "Don't you dare. Jake will be at the ranch tonight. And even if he wasn't, nothing would happen between us."

"I'm just being a good friend," she says, popping a French fry into her mouth.

"Being a pimp, more like." I laugh, deciding not to mention that with Dylan and Mama in LA for the next six days, Jake and I have Oakwood Ranch to ourselves. The last thing I need is Mia's encouragement. I already feel like my professionalism is now hanging by the same tenuous thread as my career.

Mia grins, taking a long sip of her cocktail. When she fixes her gaze on me again, her expression is serious. "There's something I have to tell you about Jake."

"What is it?" I ask, my stomach knotting although I'm not sure why.

"Don't be mad, but I spoke to Serena about the article you wrote on Jake."

Heat floods my face. "Mia!"

"I didn't mention you. I swear. I was super vague. I just asked if she remembered it, and get this—she swears Chase told her back then that Jake told him he didn't make the copies. One of his friends did. Remember Bruno Arnolds?"

"Vaguely." Jake told Chase who told Serena who told Mia, who's now telling me. My head spins with how much this conversation sounds like high school.

"Apparently he snatched it from Jake's locker and made copies before Jake even got to see it. And I know that doesn't excuse what he said to his friends, but it kind of makes it not so bad, doesn't it?"

I nod slowly. There's still a pang of hurt when I think about what Jake said that day. *I'd rather die than meet the loser who wrote that!* Those words crushed me. Broke my heart. Destroyed my confidence. Made me think I wasn't good enough to be treated well in relationships. Made me question every decision I made. Except—can I really blame Jake for all of those things? I have a dad who's barely been there my whole life, a mom who died before I was old enough to remember her, not to mention having my fair share of teen hang-ups about myself and my body. And yet, all this time, as I've mostly steered clear of men to work on my own confidence, I've blamed Jake. Hated him for it.

Realization is hot beneath my skin. Jake might've been an idiot in high school, but I've been one ever since.

TWENTY
HARPER

JAKE: *What's your dress like?*

HARPER: *It's red.*

JAKE: *Send me a photo.*

HARPER: *Nope.*

JAKE: *Want to know what I'm wearing right now?*

HARPER: *No!*

Notes for feature: Jake Sullivan can switch from serious to playful to sweeping you off your feet all within the same minute. Considering his abilities on the football field, it's no surprise he's just as astute at reading people and situations away from it.

The twenty-sixth floor of the Arquette Media building is a huge open space with floor-to-ceiling windows providing a panoramic view of the glittering Denver skyline at night. Circular tables draped in white linen fill the room, each set with gleaming china and cut-glass stemware. There's a stage to one side decked with a glittering Christmas tree and a band playing instrumental Christmas classics.

In the center of the room is a large dance floor made of glossy parquet. Waiters in crisp white shirts glide between tables with trays of champagne and hors d'oeuvres. An ice sculpture of the sweeping "A" of the Arquette Media logo sits on the bar, slowly melting under the heat of the lights.

Everywhere I look, Denver's elite business owners, VIPs, and journalists mingle in tuxedos and ball gowns. Even with my hair blow-dried until shining and swept to one side, an hour spent on makeup, and a floor-length red silk dress that I know I look good in, I feel out of place. These are the movers and shakers of the media world, the titans Mia's family is part of. I cringe inwardly at what they must be thinking when they look at me. George Cassidy's daughter trying to follow in his footsteps but fired from her internship at *Insight*.

Nerves twist in my stomach. I don't belong among these people, and after what happened in New York, I never will. But Dad wants me here for appearances and so I'll drink the champagne, eat the food, and clap in all the right places, while spending the evening avoiding Scott.

Except when I make my way to the table and find my place name, there are only two other names I recognize. Dad's. And Scott's. Of course my ex is seated next to me. A memory crashes into my thoughts from the last time we saw each other, standing on the street in downtown New York. Me with a cardboard box of my belongings in my hands, fighting back tears. Scott with a smug grin on his face.

I heard what happened, he said, throwing a hand up to hail a cab. *There are winners in this world and there are losers, Harper. Not everyone has what it takes to be a winner.* He disappeared into a cab without a backward glance, leaving me to catch the subway back to the apartment I could no longer afford.

A waiter clinks a fork against a glass, announcing dinner is ready to be served, and there's a shuffling of bodies as people drift to their seats. I swallow down the memory and take my seat, avoiding eye contact with Scott as he takes the chair next to mine. The overwhelming scent of his cologne hits my senses, causing another barrage of memories I don't want.

I guess I only have myself to blame for the fact we're at the same table. I never told Dad what an asshole Scott is. By the time I realized, Dad was already helping Scott get his first job. Anything I said would've seemed petty. So I've kept quiet all these years and let Dad think Scott and I are still friends.

From the corner of my eye, I watch Scott straighten his place setting. There's no denying he's good-looking. Short brown hair and an attractive face, but after spending nearly four weeks with Jake's hulking frame, Scott looks weak and pathetic in comparison. He's also a chauvinistic prick who thinks the world and everything in it belongs to him, including me.

I angle my body to the left and talk to a war reporter in her fifties. She introduces herself as Lori and tells me she worked with Dad over fifteen years ago. The stories she shares of their time together sound more like an Indiana Jones movie than anything my dad would do.

"Your dad," Lori replies, shooting him a wistful look that makes me wonder if they were ever more than just colleagues. "He never shut up about you. He even showed me these cute stories you wrote about a horse named Whisper."

I laugh, surprised at the memories the name unleashes. I remember the stories I wrote as a kid about a naughty mare called Whisper, who kept running away to find her dad, having adventures along the way. I'd write them while Dad was away, leaving them on his desk for when he returned. He never told me he'd read them, let alone took them with him.

"I'd forgotten about those stories," I admit, following her gaze. Dad is in full swing, lecturing his half of the table on the future of the political landscape. It's his favorite topic and a lecture I've heard many times. His silver hair is as scruffy as ever and his tux looks like he wore it for a week-long stakeout in a car before coming here tonight. Knowing Dad, he probably did.

By the time the main courses have been cleared and a chocolate mousse is placed in front of me, I've almost forgotten Scott is beside me. Unfortunately, the same can't be said for him.

"Hello, Harper," he purrs in my ear when Lori is pulled into a conversation with her husband. Scott places a possessive hand on my upper arm that immediately gives me the creeps. "You look stunning as always."

"Hi, Scott," I say, shifting away from his touch. I hate everything about this guy, but the last thing I'm going to do is make a scene during Dad's big night.

He doesn't catch the hint and invades my space again. "I hear you're working at *Sports Magazine* now."

"Yep."

"I imagine that's a good fit for you. More on your level than *Insight*."

I'm about to tell him to shove his "good fit" up his ass when there's movement across the room and Mia's mom, Gloria, takes the stage in a beautiful emerald-green sequined dress. She sees me at my table and smiles, mouthing an "are you ok?" my way.

I nod and something in that brief moment of care makes me pull my shoulders back. I might have failed at my dreams of being a journalist in New York, be sleeping on my best friend's couch, and be way out of my depth with a gorgeous football player I never know from one minute to the next if I want to yell at or kiss, but I'm still ten times the human Scott is.

It's at that moment Scott's hand moves to the back of my chair, his fingers brushing my bare skin. I round on him, twisting quickly and getting in his face. I don't break the polite smile as I drop my voice and whisper, "Scott, keep your fucking hands to yourself. If you touch me again, I'm going to break your fingers."

He pulls back, mouth gaping, but I don't miss the darkness flashing in his eyes as Gloria begins her introduction to the evening's event. "We're here, of course, to recognize the lifetime achievement in journalism of George Cassidy. As a two-time Pulitzer Prize winner, George needs no introductions, but he's most certainly earned one. So I'd like to welcome his friend and self-confessed protégé, Scott Harrington, to present the award."

Scott stands, stepping around the table and shaking Dad's hand before taking to the stage. I focus on the wine in my glass and tune out Scott's speech. The last thing I need is to be reminded of how my ex-boyfriend owes his career to my dad.

A slow-burn anger simmers in my body as the room erupts in applause and my father makes his way to the stage, hugging Scott and taking the golden award in the shape of a quill.

"I'll keep this short," Dad says in the hard voice I remember from my childhood and teens. My anger softens. My dad has always had a commanding presence, and despite our awkward relationship, he's still my dad. I'm proud of him.

"I've spent my life reporting the news, not being part of it. But I'm honored to accept this lifetime achievement award tonight. When I started at the *Denver Chronicle* over forty years ago, journalism was a very different beast. We pounded the streets, chased leads and hoped we had enough to fill the next day's paper. Now news breaks online in an instant. Our biggest challenge in journalism has become to cut through the bullshit and the fake news to report the truth. It's a job I'm not done with yet."

He raises the award, his gaze traveling across the sea of faces until he finds mine. He gives a single nod before leaving the stage. Is that it? One terse nod to the daughter who always came second to his career? I almost laugh at myself. Was I really expecting anything more?

Dad steps down from the stage and I stand. Our hug is brief and awkward. "I'm glad you could make it," he says.

"Wouldn't miss it," I reply, smiling through the hollowness threatening to suck me away. I wish—like I always do in these moments—that my mom was here.

"I'm flying out again next week. Lunch tomorrow before I go?" he asks and I wonder if he even realizes next week is Christmas.

"Sounds good." I smile, already preparing myself for the apologetic message on my phone when I wake up tomorrow, telling me about an urgent story he needs to cover and canceling our lunch.

"I'll see if Scott can join us, too," he adds.

I feel myself wanting to nod, to say something bland and accepting like I always do, but the memory of Scott's fingers stroking my back is far too fresh for playing nice. "Let's make it just us. You might think the sun shines out of his ass, but Scott's a total asshole who deserves to rot in hell." I spin away, keeping my head high as I walk to the restrooms without waiting to see the look of surprise and probably disappointment on Dad's face. My heart hammers in my chest. I don't know if I feel mortified or gleeful. Either way, I can't believe I just said that.

I'm leaning against the wall in the corner with a glass of wine, hiding from Scott and a room full of people wanting to tell me how talented my dad is, when my gaze snags on a familiar figure moving toward me. Tall, broad, and smoking-hot in a way that makes my stomach flutter. It can't be...

I didn't think Jake could look hotter than he did in his low-slung basketball shorts in the gloom of the kitchen at the ranch on that first weekend together. Or coming off the field in his jersey and pads, muscular and unstoppable. But Jake in a tuxedo is utterly swoon-worthy. Our eyes lock. There's no doubt in my mind that I'm weak at the knees for this man. I don't bother to fight the grin spreading across my face.

"You're here," I say as he reaches my side, speaking up to be heard as the band starts again, this time with a singer and a lively beat.

"And you're breathtaking," he replies, lips brushing my cheek and causing a flash of heat to burn in my core.

"Seriously, you're here? Why? How? This is a private event. You can't just walk in from the street," I say, stumbling over my words as he pulls back.

Jake takes a glass of champagne from a passing waiter, replacing my near-empty wine glass. "The *how* is easy. I'm Jake Sullivan. That's an automatic ticket to any event in Denver." He winks.

I roll my eyes. "Fine. *Why* are you here?"

He smiles. "Cassidy, I'm a tight end. My job isn't just catching passes—it's blocking, protecting my teammates, making sure they're covered when they need it. Trust me, I know when someone needs a wingman."

"I'm fine." I laugh.

He narrows his eyes a fraction.

"I'm glad you're here," I correct. "Thank you."

He slips an arm around me and turns us so we're facing the room. The heat of his body, his fingers on my skin—it's electric. "Where is he, then?"

"Who?" I ask.

"The ex your dad chose over you."

"Oh." I nod to the table near the stage where Scott is holding court with a group of men and women, acting like the up-and-coming editor he is. "Brown hair. Smug smile."

I know there's more I should tell Jake about Scott, but now isn't the time.

"OK, then." He nods, and there's an intensity to his gaze that makes my stomach drop.

"OK, what?" I ask, nerves fluttering—but in a good way.

"Well, for starters, it's a crime for anyone to wear this dress and look this gorgeous and hide in the corner." He moves me to arm's length, turning me slowly around and flashing an appreciative smile. "So drink up. We're dancing."

I laugh and let Jake pull me to the dance floor. It feels like every pair of eyes in the room is on us, including Scott's. But Jake's confidence must be rubbing off on me, because with him by my side, I don't care what the people in this room think of me. All I care about is the heat of Jake's touch on my bare skin and that simmering tension between us. I know it isn't hate now. It's desire.

TWENTY-ONE

JAKE

Harper is stunning in red silk that clings to every curve. It's a dress made for her. It's also a dress made to be stepped out of, left as a pool on the floor while I explore every inch of her naked body. The thought makes my dick stir. I force my mind back to the dance floor and the feel of the smooth skin of Harper's back against the rough callouses on my hands.

This is going to be a lot harder than I thought. My plan tonight was simple—be Harper's knight in shining armor. But with her looking like this, I might have a harder time keeping my intentions purely chivalrous.

I remind myself of all the reasons making a move on Harper is a bad idea. For starters, we've only just stopped hating each other. I like the easy flirting between us and I don't want to spend the next twelve days together arguing. Plus, there's the feature to consider. I've been keeping a low profile. There have been no new bullshit rumors about me. But this close to the playoffs and contract negotiations, my career is riding on this feature. I need Harper to see the real me, not the player and womanizer she thought I was at the start. And I don't need to drag her reputation into the same mud I'm in. Which means not making a move. Not to mention the fact I promised I wouldn't kiss her.

"Remind me to send a thank you card to Mrs. Conley," Harper murmurs in my ear as we sway to the music, finding our rhythm together. In those strappy red heels, she's only a few inches shorter than me and her red lips are so close it would take nothing to lean in and kiss her.

I give a questioning look. "Mrs. Conley, the battle-axe principal of West Denver High? Why are we thanking her tonight?"

Harper grins. "Don't you remember she forced us all to take dance lessons in the weeks running up to prom? I think she hoped it would keep some decorum to the prom nights."

I tip my head back and laugh. "I'd completely forgotten that."

"Blocked it out, more like." Harper shudders. "Mia and Chase always danced together, leaving me slim pickings. Most of the boys were a head shorter than me."

I chuckle as Harper recounts those awkward high school dance lessons. "I definitely don't remember having a shortage of dance partners back then."

"Star player on the football team. What a surprise every girl was clamoring to be your partner."

"You can't tell me it wasn't the same for you. I bet all the boys took very cold showers after dancing with you. I know I will be later."

Her lips part and she laughs, the sound like honey through my veins as we continue to move around the floor.

"I was a nerd in high school. Big glasses. Braces. Frizzy hair."

I stare at Harper as she draws in her lower lip, lost in thought. "I got the impression at lunch with you and Mia that there's something about high school you're not telling me."

Harper looks thoughtful for another moment before she shakes her head. "It doesn't matter now."

"You sure?"

"One hundred percent." She grins and her eyes light up. Those eyes I can't stop staring into.

The music slows, the singer crooning about lost love, and I pull Harper close. Across the room, I catch the glare from her preppy ex and resist the urge to flip him the finger.

Being with Harper is easy. We laugh and joke and dance and the night slips away. When the band stops, Harper leans her whole body against mine and whispers in my ear, "Take me home?"

"To Mia's?" I ask. And even though I've spent the evening telling myself all the reasons why I need to keep my distance, I hope it's not what she means.

She pauses, looking uncertain for a moment. Then she smiles. "Might as well head back to the ranch with you, since you're here."

Relief hits and I smile. "Yes, ma'am."

Out on the street the air is biting cold, our breath coming out in little white puffs. The streets are empty of people and vehicles. Christmas lights flash in office windows and shop fronts.

When Harper shivers, I lift my arm, beckoning her close. I think she'll give me that look that tells me she's remaining professional and doesn't need my help, but instead she steps into my body. The perfect fit.

"Thank you for making a difficult night fun," she says.

"Anytime," I reply, meaning it as we head toward my truck.

The radio plays old country as we make the drive home. Harper undoes the straps of her heels and sighs as she rubs the back of her feet. I'm acutely aware that we're heading back to an empty ranch. I wonder if Harper remembers. I wonder if that's why it feels like there's a loud, palpable tension crackling between us.

As we pull up to the ranch, there's a break in the clouds and the house is bathed in moonlight. Across the driveway, icicles hang from the eaves of the barn.

I climb from the truck and as I move around to open Harper's door, the first flakes of fat snow drift down from the sky. I open the door and Harper swings her legs out. The red silk of her dress rides up, exposing the smooth skin of her thighs. She dangles the straps of her red heels from her fingers and pulls a face as she glances at the ground and then the shoes in her hand, her expression so comically pained that I laugh.

"Would the gentlemanly thing to do be to offer you a lift?"

"Gentlemanly? You?"

"Hey, I've been your knight in shining armor tonight." I raise my chin, pulling my own face at her.

She grins. "True." She glances to the ground again then back to my face, her eyes dancing with mischief that shoots something electric through my body. "What kind of lift are we talking? Because if it's a fireman's carry—"

I roll my eyes. "Come here." And before she has the chance to talk herself out of it, I slide one hand around the bare skin of her back and one under her thighs, just below that fucking perfect ass of hers, and I lift her up and stride toward the house. All I can think about is the heat of her body in my arms. Then Harper sticks her tongue out and tilts her head to the sky and I can't help but laugh.

"What?" she asks with a grin. "Haven't you ever tried to catch snowflakes on your tongue before?"

I shake my head, watching the white fluffy snow float in the air. "Can't say I have."

"Come on, try it with me." She laughs.

I stop moving and we both let the snowflakes land on our tongues, so cold they feel like they burn for a second before melting into nothing. The way Harper's eyes shine with delight makes me think I've never seen anything so beautiful.

We're still laughing when we reach the porch and I place

her down on the cold planks of wood. The way she's biting her bottom lip is sexy as hell and feels dangerous.

"Don't look at me like that, Cassidy," I say as we step into the kitchen. Familiar aromas of fresh bread and coffee and home fill my senses. Buck's tail thumps from his bed in the corner of the kitchen, but he's half asleep and doesn't leap up to greet us. I go to him, scratching his ear briefly, and when I turn around, Harper is standing in the doorway between the kitchen and the hall, snowflakes still resting in her hair. Fuck, she takes my breath away.

"How am I looking at you?" she asks in a way that makes my dick stir.

I move toward her, resting an arm against the doorframe above her head, brushing a hand through her hair, moving it from where it's fallen over her face. Her lips pop open a fraction and I know by the way she's staring up at me, by the bob of her throat as she swallows, that she wants this as much as I do. I breathe her in. The wildflower perfume, the coconut scent of her shampoo, the feeling of being this close, of wanting her more than I've ever wanted anything in my life.

I'm rock-hard in seconds just thinking about what I want to do to her, but I swallow a groan. It takes every ounce of my self-control to keep my promise. I move closer, brushing my lips against her cheek. "Goodnight, Cassidy."

I push away from the door and step past her, into the hall. My willpower is hanging by a thread and if I see the desire in her eyes one more time, if she calls me back, says another word, I won't be able to keep my promise...

There are a million reasons why I should let Jake go to bed. Why I should step back into the kitchen, grab myself a glass of water, and do the same. But then I think how Jake showed up for me tonight. I think about our kiss in the hotel room and how much I want that feeling again. A small voice in my head whispers, "*Fuck it*," and it's so Jake-like that I smile. Instead of thinking about all the reasons why I shouldn't stop Jake from walking away, I think about the reason why I should. Because I want to. And right now, in this moment, that reason is enough.

"Hey," I say.

Jake turns back, hovering at the bottom of the stairs. He's undone his collar, the tie of his tux hanging loose. His dark hair has fallen over his face. It's his eyes I focus on and the hunger I see in them—the want that matches my own.

"You didn't answer my question. How am I looking at you?" I say, holding his gaze.

His lips part and he pulls in a breath. In the beat of silence while I wait for his reply, every nerve ending in my body feels charged, humming with electricity, waiting, hoping.

He moves slowly, crossing the hall—drawing near. He doesn't stop until he's so close my back is against the wall and I can feel the heat of his body on my skin.

"Cassidy, I promised I wouldn't kiss you again," he says, voice husky in a way that has me completely undone.

"Jake." His name is a whisper, full of need.

He tilts his head a fraction, his eyes never leaving mine. "Do you want me to break my promise?"

Longing is pounding through my veins. I lick my lips and nod.

"Say it," he growls, cupping my face in his hands.

My next words come with a confidence I didn't know I possessed. "I want you to kiss me."

His pupils darken, but still he holds back. Only when I don't think I can stand it for another second does he move. His lips brush lightly against mine. The kiss that follows is slow and so intense, I feel it between my thighs. I feel it in every part of my body. His tongue pushes lightly into my mouth and his hands move into my hair, tugging gently, then trail down my naked back to pull me against his hard body. I can feel every taut muscle through the fabric of his tux. One of his strong thighs nudges between my legs and I push against him, craving friction.

Jake's kiss grows more searching as a low groan rumbles in his throat. I feel his hardness press against me, solid and thick, straining against his pants. *God*, I want him. I want to feel all of him, skin on skin. I want him inside me, filling me.

I moan into his mouth as the kiss deepens, his tongue still stroking mine. My hands slide under his jacket, digging my fingertips in, pulling him even tighter against me as our kiss turns feverish.

And then suddenly Jake is pulling back, the pressure against my lips is gone, and I'm breathless, head spinning with desire, trying to work out why he's pulled away. He steps back, raking a hand through his hair.

"Harper…" Jake swallows. "Are you sure you want to do this?" he asks, tone low and serious despite the obvious bulge straining against his pants.

For a fleeting second all those reasons why this is a bad idea threaten to come crashing back into my thoughts. But the fact he's asking me, that he wants me to be certain, tells me everything I need to know. I don't speak as I push the straps of my dress from my shoulders, letting the red silk fall to the floor. I'm not wearing a bra and Jake sucks in a sharp breath, eyes filling with lust as he takes in the sight of my bare breasts. My nipples are hard from desire and the chill in the air. All I'm wearing now are my skimpy red lace panties.

"Fuck, Harper, you're so beautiful," Jake murmurs. His eyes rake over my body and I shiver under the intensity of his gaze, my skin tingling with anticipation and need. I've never wanted anyone as badly as I want Jake Sullivan right now. Still holding his gaze, I hook my thumbs in the sides of my panties and slowly slide them down my legs, kicking them aside.

"I want you," I say when I'm standing before him, naked and exposed.

My words light a fire in him. He moves toward me, sweeping me into his arms. His lips press hard to mine as he picks me up and I wrap my legs around his waist. In five strides, he's lowering me down on the living room couch. He follows me down, holding his weight on his elbows braced either side of my head.

"You have no idea what you do to me," he rasps, shrugging off his jacket and flinging it away before capturing my lips in a searing kiss that leaves me dizzy.

Lowering his head, he starts a trail of kisses along the column of my throat. Lips and tongue and the softest graze of teeth. I gasp and sink my fingers into his thick hair, arching into him. Every kiss sets a flaming torch burning down to my core as he moves his lips from my neck to my collarbone. He pauses, breath hot on my skin, making me shiver with anticipation. Then slowly, torturously, he dips his head and draws one hard nipple into his mouth. I draw in a sharp breath as his tongue swirls and flicks. Pleasure burns between my legs. He sucks harder and I cry out. I'm lost to the desire he's drawing out of me. Only one thought races through my mind: *I want him. I want him. I want him.*

"Jake, please," I beg, not even sure what I'm asking for, just knowing I need more. More of his hands and mouth on my body. More of this feeling winding me tighter.

He releases my nipple with a final flick of his tongue and lifts his head to look at me. His eyes are dark pools of desire that send another jolt of need pulsing between my legs.

"Tell me what you want, Harper," he commands, voice rough like gravel. "I want to hear you say it."

I'm so far gone, I don't even hesitate. "Touch me. I need your mouth on me. Lower."

A wicked grin spreads across his face. "With pleasure."

He starts kissing down my stomach, swirling his tongue around my navel. My abs quiver under his touch. Lower and lower he goes, until he's nudging my thighs apart and settling between them.

I tremble with want as he slowly runs his hands up my inner thighs, fingers softly pressing. Then his thumb brushes gently up and over my center, a barely there touch that makes me whimper.

"I'm going to take my time with you," he says, breath hot as he takes his thumb away and kisses my inner thighs, teasing, slowly moving with licks and nibbles until his mouth finds my opening and his tongue moves in one long sweep up my center to the bud of nerves I need him to be touching. His tongue is urgent and searching and I grip the couch cushions as my orgasm builds like a tight coil, ready to spring loose. Just when I don't think I can take any more, as my breathing turns ragged, Jake pulls back, tongue lazily stroking more gently, moving back to kiss my thighs, letting me catch my breath. My legs shake and I swear every part of me is throbbing for him.

"Jake," I cry. "Don't stop."

With a rumbling hum, he moves his mouth back to my center, one finger sliding into me as his tongue continues to drive me wild. I gasp at the feel of him inside me. The pressure builds and builds, my thighs trembling, toes curling as Jake's tongue works and he adds a second finger, stretching me and stroking inside me, sending sparks shooting through my body. I gasp, the pleasure coiling tighter and tighter in my core. Jake groans against me and the vibrations coupled with his relentless touch send me hurtling over the edge.

My orgasm crashes over me in a tidal wave, every nerve ending igniting. I arch off the couch, crying out Jake's name as it pulses through me. I feel myself clench around his fingers, my body no longer my own. I've never come so hard for anybody in my life. It seems to go on forever, aftershocks rolling through me until I collapse back against the cushions, boneless and spent.

With a satisfied smile, Jake presses a final soft kiss to my clit, making me shudder again, before lifting his head. I'm still quivering, mind blissfully blank, as he trails kisses up my body.

"That was... incredible," I rasp when he pulls back. My voice is hoarse from screaming his name.

Jake's eyes are heated as they roam over me, taking in my flushed cheeks, my heaving chest. "I could watch you fall apart like that all night."

A shiver runs through me at his words, at the promise in them.

"Take me to bed," I whisper, running my hands over his shoulders. "I want you inside me."

Desire flares in his eyes. In one smooth motion, he stands, scooping me into his arms. I loop my arms around his neck, pressing my face into his throat and breathing in that woodsy citrus scent that has become so familiar as he carries me effortlessly up the stairs. I'm so aware of the fact he's still fully clothed while I'm completely naked.

When he reaches the landing, he strides down the hall and shoulders open his bedroom door, kicking it shut behind us. The room is shadowy, illuminated only by the moonlight filtering in through the window. I catch a fleeting glimpse of a large bed before Jake is lowering me down onto cool sheets. He stands over me, eyes never leaving mine as he unbuttons his shirt in a slow, measured way, like there's no rush at all. Like he knows how desperate I am for this and wants to make me wait again. He drops his shirt to the floor, the planes of his muscular chest rippling in the moonlight. I've seen it before, but still my eyes snag on every sculpted groove and that trail of dark hair disappearing into his pants. Slowly, he undoes his belt, letting the rest of his clothes fall to the floor before kicking them aside. My mouth completely dries out. There is nothing that could compare to the sight of Jake naked, his dick rock-hard and huge in a way that makes my heart pound.

I reach forward and grab his hand, pulling him down toward me. Jake lowers himself onto the bed, skin pressing against mine. The weight of him is delicious, igniting my nerve endings all over again. He kisses me deeply, making my body forget it just had the best orgasm of my life and wanting more—*needing* more. The length of him nudges against my entrance, already slick for him, and I gasp. Jake reaches to his bedside table, fumbling in the drawer before pulling out a foil packet. He rips it open and sits back on his heels to roll the condom on. My eyes follow the movement of his hands over the impressive length of his dick. I can't stop the whimper from escaping my throat.

His eyes lock with mine as he moves over me, pushing my thighs apart with his knees. "How much do you want this?" he asks with a slow grin.

I bite my lip. "More than I've ever wanted anything in my life," I reply honestly. Then I sit up, pushing him sideways and back onto the bed, moving so that my legs are on either side of his, so I'm straddling him. His eyes flash in surprise as his head hits the pillow. Then slowly—so slowly, wanting to draw out this moment—I slide myself over him so just the tip of him is resting at my opening. I move another fraction and Jake closes his eyes and groans. I swallow down my desperation, my eyes tracking every bob of his throat, and move again. A sharp breath escapes my lips as he starts to stretch and fill me, inch by delicious inch. Then Jake's eyes snap open, his gaze fiery as his strong hands reach around my back, pulling me down the rest of the way. I cry out at the way he fills me.

"Fuck, Harper," he growls once he's buried to the hilt. "You feel so good."

I clench around him, reveling in the feel of him inside me. I move up slowly before pushing back down, starting a steady rhythm that has me seeing stars. Each drive hits a spot deep within me. I'm gasping as Jake's hands wrap around my ass, guiding me further each time. Every movement is exquisite and intense. I lose myself in the rhythm, throwing my head back, rocking over him, my aching clit rubbing against him with every stroke.

"Fuck," Jake bites out, sitting up and bringing me with him, kissing me fiercely as he drives relentlessly into me. He shifts the angle of his hips and pleasure explodes through me like fireworks.

"Don't stop!" I cry.

"Never," Jake grits out as we pick up pace. I move with him, meeting him thrust for thrust, climbing higher and higher. With one hand gripping my hair firmly, he moves the other in between us, his thumb rubbing tight circles on my center. His touch is my undoing. With a loud cry, I shatter, my inner muscles clamping down on him like a vise as ecstasy crashes over me.

TWENTY-THREE

JAKE

Harper's pussy clamps around the length of me, her body quivering against mine. Her breath comes fast and ragged as she rides her climax. The way her tight heat pulses around my cock has me teetering on the brink, pleasure coiling deep in my groin. But I'm not ready for this to end yet. I slow down and catch my breath as she finishes riding her wave. Then I move us around, laying Harper on the bed and positioning myself over her. I grip her hips and push myself all the way in at a new angle. She groans with pleasure and her legs wrap around me.

"Jake..." Harper's voice is a breathless whisper. Hearing her say my name feels so fucking good.

I capture her lips in a kiss, my tongue exploring her mouth as I start to move again, rocking into her with long, deep strokes. Fuck, she's so wet for me, arching up to meet every thrust. I tangle my fingers in her hair, tilting her head back to trail kisses down the column of her throat. Her nails rake down my back, shooting another pulse of pleasure through my body.

The sound of Harper's whimper is enough to send me hurtling over the edge, emptying myself in her as I welcome the heat flooding my body.

My head is still spinning as I catch my breath and twist us around so we're lying side by side, my dick still inside her, not wanting this moment to end. Her hand reaches up, pushing a strand of my hair away from my forehead as I press a tender kiss to her shoulder.

As we lie there, hearts pounding, I savor the feel of Harper in my arms. The scent of her hair, the softness of her skin. My thoughts are scattered, still buzzing from the release. I never thought this would happen with us, but now it has I swear in this moment, right now, I've never felt so close—so connected— to another person in my entire life.

Harper's fingers trace along my jaw, her touch feather-light but still sending shivers through me. I gaze down at her, studying the curve of her lips and the lines of her body. There's something about Harper that draws me in, makes me feel more awake—more alive—when I'm around her. The women I've dated or spent time with in the past have always stroked my ego and kissed my ass. But not Harper. If I'm being an idiot, she'll call me on it without hesitation.

And damn is she sexy as hell when she's arguing with me, cheeks flushed and eyes flashing with passion. I thought I wanted easy and fun and uncomplicated, but there's a reason none of my relationships have lasted longer than a few weeks or the occasional month. Harper challenges me in ways I never thought possible. More than that though, she has a way of stripping away all the hype that comes with being a pro athlete. The fame, the gossip stories, the fans—none of that matters to Harper. And the more time I spend with her, the more certain I am that none of that matters to me either.

She lifts her face to mine. Even with bed hair, skin glowing from what we've just done, she's radiant. A shy smile brushes her lips as she runs a hand across my chest. "That was... wow."

I grin back at her. "I'm slightly offended by the surprise in

your tone, Cassidy. You thought football was all I was good at?"
I quip.

She rolls her eyes. "You're ridiculous."

"That's not what you were saying a few minutes ago when
you were screaming my name."

"Shut up!" She huffs a laugh, burying her face against my
neck. I love being the one to make her laugh. Hell, I love being
the one making her scream my name now too.

I trail my fingers up and down the smooth expanse of her
back. "I agree, that was incredible," I say softly. "You're
incredible."

We stare at each other in the darkness of my room and I
want to whisper in Harper's ear that tonight—us, this—is just
the tip of the iceberg with how things will be between us. The
thought surprises me and scares me in the best possible way.

But even with only the dim light of the moon streaking
through the window, I see something change in Harper's eyes,
like her walls are going up. I take her hand, entwining her
fingers with mine, wanting to tell her she can be vulnerable with
me, wanting to reassure her, but Harper gets there first.

"I mean..." She smiles but there's a harder edge to it now as
she lifts one shoulder in a shrug. "Obviously this is just sex," she
says casually. "Really, really good sex. But you've got your
games and I've got my feature to write. And we've only got
twelve days left..." She trails off, searching my face as her words
land.

I feel like a bucket of ice water has been dumped on my
head. Realization washes through me. I've just blown any
chance of showing Harper I've changed, that I'm not the player
she thought I was. How could I have expected her to want
anything more from me than just sex, when she thinks it's all
I'm capable of?

I force a smile, ignoring the hurt and frustration radiating
from my chest. As always, I fall back on humor. "Sure. But just

remember, that was two orgasms you had. If you're adding it to the feature, I mean."

She barks a laugh and swats my chest with her hand before heading for the bathroom. She returns wearing one of my white tees, the material grazing the tops of her thighs and looking so goddamn sexy I want my mouth on her all over again.

We move around each other and it's awkward. We've crossed a line and now we have to find our way back. However much I want to stay this side of the line, Harper has made her feelings crystal clear. And maybe she's right. Maybe it is better this way. The hard lump of disappointment in my gut tells me otherwise.

For an awful moment, I think she's going to go back to her room to sleep. I can see her thinking about it. I drop back to the bed and pat the covers. "Come here," I say.

A soft smile touches her lips. "Just sleep now. You've worn me out, Sullivan," she says, slipping into the space beside me, her body warm and firm next to mine.

"Did I not mention I'm a stallion?" I quip with a wink, wishing away the disappointment.

She rolls her eyes and snuggles into the crook of my arm. "Goodnight, Jake."

"Night, Harper."

I lie awake for a long time, staring at Harper's face, wanting to pull her closer, never let go. But I don't. I have no claim on her. This didn't mean anything to her and I have to respect that.

When I wake the next morning to bright sunlight streaming through the window, my hand finds cold, empty space in the bed beside me. Harper's gone, leaving only the soft scent of her perfume on my covers and a night I won't forget in a hurry.

I flop onto my back with a heavy sigh, thrown by how much

it hurts that she left without a word. The truth hits me like a shoulder barge to the gut. Last night might've meant nothing to Harper, but it meant something to me. More than something. It meant everything.

TWENTY-FOUR
HARPER

MIA: *Should I take it as a good sign that you didn't come back to my place last night?*

HARPER: *Did you know Jake was going to be there?*

MIA: *I might have made sure his name was on the list.*

HARPER: *And you didn't tell me?*

MIA: *Where's the surprise in that? Are you walking like a fifty-year-old bull rider this morning?*

HARPER: *Pleading the fifth!*

MIA: *Fifth or filth? Tell me everything.*

HARPER: *I don't kiss and tell.*

MIA: *OMG! You gotta give me something. Was it good? It was, right!*

HARPER: *BDE.*

MIA: *I knew it!!*

~

DAD: *Something's come up and I'm leaving for New York this morning. Rain check on lunch?*

HARPER: *Sure.*

Notes for article: Jake Sullivan is the best wingman anyone could ask for.

When I woke up earlier, I found myself in Jake's bedroom. In Jake's bed. Wrapped in Jake's warm embrace. Bright morning daylight pushed in through the window. If I was expecting another bedroom like Chase's—football memorabilia and something teen-like—I was wrong. Jake's room, like him, is all man. The walls are a deep navy. The furniture dark wood, solid and sturdy. The hardwood floor is covered by a thick gray rug, and on the wall is a striking black-and-white photograph of the mountains. The room is dominated by a large bed with white sheets I was tangled in.

Memories from last night flooded my body. It was an effort to keep my breathing even. The last thing I wanted was to wake Jake. I needed a moment to collect my thoughts, and I couldn't do that while resting in the crook of Jake's arm, breathing in that woodsy masculine scent as my body tingled with desire. And so slowly, silently, I slipped out of Jake's embrace.

Now, in the familiar surrounds of Chase's bedroom, I breathe a little easier. It's still early. Jake isn't due at Stormhawks Park until this afternoon. There's time for me to escape. For a little while, anyway. I throw on my running clothes and pull my hair into a high ponytail before heading downstairs. In the hall, I see my dress—a puddle of red silk on the floor. I scoop it up along with my underwear and heels. My gaze strays to the living room as I pass the doorway, to the couch Jake laid me down on. The heat of the memories burns my skin and I hurry to the safety of the kitchen. It feels strange to find it empty. Last night I was grateful we had the ranch to ourselves, but this morning I miss Mama's calming presence. She always seems to know the right thing to say, the right time for the coffee to be ready and something tasty just out of the stove. I drop last night's clothes on the table and grab a glass of water.

From the corner of the room paws clatter on the floor and I turn to find Buck's floppy ears and wagging tail moving toward me. "Hey," I coo, running my hands over his soft fur. "You wanna come for a run with me?" I take a step and Buck dances around my legs, beating me to the back door.

Outside, the day is bright, the sky a pale blue. Last night's snow covers the ground like a dusting of powdered sugar. Buck bounds ahead, his paws leaving prints in the shallow snow. Cold bites my face and hands as I bounce on my toes, tighten my ponytail, and heave in a breath of fresh mountain air before following after Buck in the direction of the lake.

As blood pumps through my veins, the cold gradually loses its edge and my mind takes me straight back to last night. The sex was... I don't have the words. Heat pulses through me and it has nothing to do with how fast I'm running. It was the best sex of my life. Amazing, perfect, mind-blowing. The kind of sex I didn't think existed. Even thinking about it makes my body ache for Jake's touch.

Ahead of me, the spruce trees stretch toward the sky, casting long shadows over the untouched snow. Tiny mountains of white sit on the branches and I turn my gaze to the horizon and the real snowcapped peaks of the Rockies, painted shades of orange and pink by the rising sun. The view is breathtaking but it's not enough to stop the next rush of memories hitting me.

Obviously this is just sex.

My words from last night twist in my gut. I knew Jake would be thinking the same—letting me down gently by starting to tell me how incredible I was—and so I said it before he could. Self-preservation, maybe. He's Jake Sullivan—a star football player at the height of his career. He could have any woman he wanted and even if his reputation is no longer deserved, it doesn't mean he's suddenly the type to settle down. He has the world at his fingertips.

And then there's me. I'm a junior sports journalist, still trying to find my place in that same world. Following in my father's footsteps, but not really sure if journalism is truly my calling. I feel like I'm so far out of my depth, I'm drowning. I keep waiting for the feeling to pass, but so far it hasn't.

Then something else occurs to me and a fresh wave of horror floods my body. My heart pounds for an entirely different reason. I feel sick. Light-headed. I'm in so much trouble. I've done the one thing Tim told me not to do—I slept with the assignment. Oh, God. How could I have been so unprofessional? Top of the list for why we shouldn't cross that line, and last night I ignored it. If Tim finds out about this, I'm gone. Fired twice in six months for inappropriate behavior. Even if the first time was all a lie, no one will believe it because last night was definitely all me.

I can't lose another job!

The cold air burns in my lungs as Buck lopes easily beside me, his nose to the ground. As I run around the lake, the weak winter sun glints off the ice-crusted surface, fracturing into a million diamond pinpricks of light.

Jake and I come from completely different worlds. Last night was incredible, but it can't happen again. If there's any chance of me salvaging my career, I have to start acting like the professional I'm always trying to be. If only Jake hadn't come to the dinner last night, calling himself my wingman. It's easily the most thoughtful thing a man has ever done for me. He made the night not just bearable, but actually fun. Seeing the look of disbelief and annoyance on Scott's face when I was dancing in Jake's arms was pretty good, too.

Suddenly my mind is filled with thoughts of Scott and my dad. Last night, for the first time, I told my dad what I really thought of Scott. I wonder if Dad remembers, if he was even listening. For an award-winning journalist known for his investigative skills and attention to detail, he's turned a blind eye to his own daughter for most of her life. I wonder if he canceled our lunch in favor of spending time with Scott.

I shove the thought aside and push my legs faster, reminding myself of all I have. A best friend like Mia. And her mom, Gloria, who's always welcomed me like a second daughter. Even Dad is still my dad. I remember what Lori told me last night about how he took my stories with him on his trips away when I was a child. He might not show it, but a part of him must care.

I round the corner and the ranch comes back into view, bathed in the morning sunlight. The thought of spending five weeks here felt like a lifetime at the start, but with only eleven days left of the assignment, I know I'm going to miss staying here. Last night I asked Jake to take me home. It was only when he raised a quizzical eyebrow that I realized I meant here—this ranch, a place that in just a few short weeks feels more like home than anywhere I've ever lived. The thought of a time when this assignment is over fills me with an emptiness I can't wrap my head around.

Five weeks no longer feels enough. In eleven days the Stormhawks play their penultimate game of the season, marking the end of my time with Jake. The truth is, we've spent so much time together, talked endlessly about his childhood and his dreams, his life playing football, I have almost everything I need to write the profile on him, and I can tell already it's going to be good. It's going to be everything Mama wants it to be. Everything Jake needs it to be.

The only thing left for Jake to talk about is what happened with the cheerleaders in the parking lot last year. Whatever it was, it was bad enough to nearly destroy his career and completely change his lifestyle, and I want him to tell me about it in his own words. According to Jake, he moved home to the ranch after what happened and gave up the wild parties and the women. Until last night anyway. Until me.

At the start of all this, I thought getting to the truth about who Jake really is would be his downfall. Even two weeks ago, Jake sleeping with me would've been all the proof I needed that he's the womanizer his reputation says he is. But when I look back at last night, I think of Jake walking away. I think of me being the one to call him back. How he asked me if I was sure I wanted it. All last night proved is how fucking amazing Jake is in bed.

I force the thought away and think again of what's left for us to talk about. I'm not sure how much longer I can avoid asking him about what happened last year, but considering how awkward today is going to be for us, surely a few more days won't hurt.

Buck scampers up the porch, pushing through the back door, me at his heels. I need coffee and a shower and to write up my notes in a way that won't sound like they were written by the sixteen-year-old version of me with a huge crush on Jake Sullivan. The readers of *Sports Magazine* don't want to hear about Jake's dance moves or the mini fireworks display that goes on in my stomach every time he looks into my eyes.

The earthy smell of coffee hits me as I kick off my sneakers and pad into the kitchen. The first thing I see is Jake. He's by the coffee machine fussing over Buck. My heart skips a beat, and I wish I could blame it on my run and not on how gorgeous this man is. His dark hair is mussed from sleep and from my fingers raking through it last night. His stubble is thick and his gaze as he looks at me is intense and searching.

"Hey," I say, aiming for breezy but it comes out a breathy gasp.

"Morning, Cassidy," he says, sounding as cool and collected as I was aiming for.

He hands me a mug of coffee and I take it gratefully, ignoring the pang of want that hits my gut when our fingers touch.

His gaze rakes over my body, one eyebrow raised in question. "So, clearly I didn't wear you out enough last night?"

I huff a laugh of surprise at his remark, my face aflame. Of course he doesn't skirt around what happened. I search for a retort, but my mind is stuck on the images his comment unleashes.

"Something like that," I mumble, taking a grateful sip of hot bitter coffee. And even though I wish the floor would open up and swallow me whole, I grit my teeth and push on. "About last night..." I start, wanting to say again that it was just sex and reinforce that boundary I know we should have between us. But staring into the dark pools of Jake's eyes, the words ring hollow, even in my thoughts. Despite what I said last night, it didn't feel like just sex. It felt like... like more.

Jake gives a small shake of his head, his smile easy. "You want to keep things professional," he finishes, looking at me over the rim of his mug.

I nod, grateful for the rescue. The silence stretches between us, filled only by the soft sounds of Buck's tail thumping against the floor as Jake absently rubs his ears. I wish again that I could read Jake better. Beneath the easy smile and nonchalant words, I sense an undercurrent of something else.

Disappointment, maybe. Or regret? Does he wish last night hadn't happened?

I make for the door before I can ask the question. "I'd better grab a shower and work on my notes before we leave for practice."

"Harper," he says, voice low, making me think of last night and his hands on my body, his lips pressing against my skin.

I spin toward him, the air between us electric again.

He sighs, raking his hands through his hair. "I don't regret what happened last night."

"Me neither," I answer honestly. However awkward this is, whatever mess it's landed us in, I don't regret it.

His eyes bore into mine. "I don't want a one-night stand with you."

My heart lurches. The air leaves my lungs in a whoosh. The want in Jake's eyes makes my legs weak. For a split second, I think about inviting him to join me in the shower. But then what? We have eleven days together, and however fun last night was, it's already going to be hard enough to walk away from the ranch and from Jake.

I roll my eyes playfully, hoping Jake can't hear the pounding of my heart in my chest. "I think we've mixed business and plea-sure enough. My job is on the line too. If Tim finds out about this..." I make a face. So much for a playful comment. "But don't worry, I get how much your rep is just rumors and gossip. You didn't ruin that last night. So far, this feature is going to be everything you want it to be. Let's just forget last night ever happened." I back into the hall.

"Harper, that's—"

"It's fine," I call, taking the stairs two at a time, only drawing in breath when I'm in the bathroom with the door locked. I strip off my clothes and step under the hot spray of the shower, trying not to think about what Jake wanted to say when he called my name.

I don't know if there's a chance in hell I can claw my way back to any level of professionalism with Jake, but I'm going to try. What happened last night can't happen again. There's too much riding on this feature for both of us. And now it's not just my job I'm worried about. It's my heart, too. When this is over, we both have to go back to our normal lives, and I can't risk having my heart broken by the same man twice.

TWENTY-FIVE
JAKE

DYLAN: *Mama says good luck.*

CHASE: *She's not watching?*

DYLAN: *She's with me at the ACL clinic in LA. I told her I'm a 30yo man who didn't need his mama by his side but you know Mama.*

CHASE: *Like the time I got sick in college and she insisted on coming to stay in my dorm, bringing her famous soup with her.*

JAKE: *When do we tell her we hate that soup?*

DYLAN: *We take that shit to our graves!*

CHASE: *I'm sure you'll have a cute journalist to cheer you on tonight, Jakey.*

DYLAN: *And the ranch to yourself until we're home tomorrow.*

CHASE:

DYLAN: *Don't forget to feed Buck.*

JAKE: *He's my dog. I'm not going to forget to feed him.*

There's nothing like playing Sunday night football to the home crowd in my own stadium. The buzz of the roaring fans and their support. It's indescribable. Like magic flooding my body with every stamping foot and clapping hand. We charge onto the field, leaping and whooping, stirring the crowd into a frenzy as we stand beneath the floodlights, our helmets under our arms, ready for this game.

The Las Vegas Desertraptors follow us out of the tunnel. Their away supporters are strong and they keep their heads high as they take their positions in their green and white team colors, helmets already in place. No cheering. No waving. They're telling us they're not here for showboating. They're here to win, but so are we.

My gaze moves to the skybox and I can't stop the smile from touching my lips as I see Harper standing at the front of the glass in her white Stormhawks top, hair tousled, lips painted her favorite red. *My* favorite red. Our eyes meet and she waves, her grin widening.

My mind drifts to the past week. After our incredible night together, things were awkward for a while. Neither of us seemed to know what to say, how to act. I tried to tell her that morning in the kitchen that I wanted more, but it came out wrong. Like all I wanted from her was more sex. But that's only a fraction of the things I want from Harper. I've never felt this way before about anyone and it terrifies me. I choked. Since then, I've followed Harper's lead and kept things light, ignoring how much I've wanted to pull her into my arms, tell her how beautiful she is. Make her scream with pleasure all over again.

I know her assignment with me will be over next Sunday, and as much as I never wanted this profile in the first place, now I'm not sure I'm ready for this to end. Last night we stayed up late talking on the back porch, wrapped in blankets, Buck's head in Harper's lap. It was easy, like we've known each other for years. I caught myself wishing time would pause so we could stay like that forever. But football waits for no one. I push thoughts of Harper aside as I fasten my helmet and put my head firmly in the game.

The Desertraptors win the toss and choose to receive. JT moves into position for the kick. The crowd is roaring, the lights are blinding, but I tune it all out. The whistle blows, the ball is soaring toward the Desertraptors, and we're off in a clash of bodies and adrenaline.

Within minutes, the Stormhawks have possession. The ball is snapped, and I burst forward. Rob draws the safety deep, opening up space for me. I cut inside, slipping past the corner-back. Billy sees me break open and fires a perfect spiral. It slices through the air, and I extend my arms. The ball smacks into my hands, and I tuck it in, my legs pumping hard as I sprint toward the end zone.

The safety angles in for the tackle, but I lower my shoulder and drive right through him. Nothing but green grass lies ahead as I cross the goal line. I spike the ball, and the crowd erupts. It feels amazing, but I keep my focus—there's a whole game left to play. And this is where I belong.

The rest of the first quarter is a defensive slugfest, but by the third quarter, we're up 14-7. The Desertraptors offense finally responds, marching down the field with quick, precise passes. But our defense stiffens in the red zone. Gordon blows up a run, forcing them to settle for a field goal. 14-10. As we hit the final quarter, the score is 21-17 after Rob scores another touchdown and then their own wide receiver does the same. Both extra points are good.

The crowd is wild and restless. With minutes left, we have the ball again. Billy steps up behind center, eyes scanning the defense. He calls the cadence, and the ball snaps clean. I explode off the line, chip the edge rusher, and break into my route.

I know this is my moment. I cut across the field, and Billy sees me. A split second later, he fires. The ball spirals through the air, right to where I'm heading. I stretch, make the grab, and turn upfield. Adrenaline takes over as I dodge one Desertraptor and stiff-arm another. My legs burn, but I keep driving forward until I'm finally taken down. The clock hits zero, and the crowd erupts.

Final score: 21-17. We've won. With two games left of the season, the Stormhawks are leading the AFC West. If we can hold on to the lead, we'll have secured a playoff spot. The Super Bowl feels closer than ever.

As the stadium explodes, I throw off my helmet and look to the skybox for Harper. When our eyes meet again, a beam of energy shoots through me. In that moment, I can no longer deny the truth. It has me grinning like a fool. I'm falling for this woman. And I'm falling hard. Which only leaves one question —what the hell am I going to do about it?

TWENTY-SIX

HARPER

*Notes for feature: Jake Sullivan is a man who knows what he
wants and who he is off the field. But put a football in his hands
and he's a God among men. Intuitive and unrelenting, he's the
difference between winning and losing.*

My heart is still hammering with the win as I make my way out
of the skybox. The noise of the fans leaving the stadium is loud,
clattering, and joyous. The air is charged with victory. The
feeling buzzes through me as I'm waved through security and to
the back corridors of the stadium to wait for Jake. Outside the
locker room, there are people everywhere and I tuck myself
against the wall.

I can't get over how Jake played. Every step seemed like
magic. I shiver thinking of the way Jake's eyes landed on me
from the field. Even with the distance between us it felt intense.

To my surprise, the awkwardness after our night together
settled fast, but it hasn't stopped the heat that feels as though it's
shimmering in the air between us when we're alone. And it feels
like all the reasons why we shouldn't be together fade into the
background.

Coach Allen props open the door and begins his victory speech to the team in front of their loved ones and friends. "Men, that was one hell of a game! You went out there and left it all on the field. Every single one of you played your hearts out. Jake, the way you led the team tonight was truly inspirational. You're playing the best football of your career."

Jake beams with pride as his teammates thump his back. He looks up and catches my eye through the open door, flashing me that sexy, crooked smile that makes my knees weak. I smile back, my heart fluttering.

Coach Allen continues heaping praise on the other players, but all I see is Jake. Then a loud cheer erupts and Coach waves his hands to settle them. "You all deserve to celebrate tonight. I want every single one of you at The Hay Barn. Let off some steam. Tomorrow is a rest day. Come Tuesday we're back at practice for the final two games. We will get to those playoffs." He claps his hands and the boys leap up, slapping each other's shoulder pads and chanting, "Stormhawks!"

"Sullivan," Coach shouts above the noise. "That goes for you too, but stay out of trouble."

"Yes, Coach," Jake calls back before disappearing into the mob of his teammates and their celebrations.

The locker room door closes and I lean against the wall, my face aching from smiling. I swear I'm as happy as every die-hard Stormhawks fan tonight.

"You'll keep an eye on him?"

My head shoots up and I find Coach Allen standing before me. He's a bull of a man. An ex-player who still looks like he pumps some serious iron in the gym. His bushy gray mustache twitches as he speaks. "Trouble always finds that boy," he adds.

I nod, hoping Jake won't mind me tagging along as a babysitter, but any fears are swept away when the team bundles from the changing rooms fifteen minutes later and Jake makes a beeline for me, wearing his familiar Levi's and a black fitted sweater that clings to his biceps.

"Enjoy the game?" he asks, his voice a warm caress as he throws an arm around me and leads us through the throng to the parking lot.

"You were incredible," I reply as heat radiates from his touch. It feels so right to be tucked into his side, and yet I force some distance between us, aware of how many people are watching. I feel Jake tense and want to explain that no matter what is happening between us, we have to keep it quiet.

But then Jake relaxes, flashing me an easy grin. "I *was* incredible tonight, wasn't I? You really are my good luck charm, Cassidy."

"You don't need luck with those moves," I smile. "Look, Coach Allen asked me to tag along to keep an eye on you tonight, but I don't want to cramp your style. If you want me to go..."

The intensity returns to his gaze and suddenly my mind is pulling me back to the moment Jake laid me on the couch in the living room of the ranch and stared at me just like he is now. His eyes darken like he knows where my mind has gone.

"Come with us," he says, voice gravelly from the shouting on the field. "Not to babysit. Come because you want to celebrate with me."

I blink and nod. "OK."

The parking lot is flooded with fans in Stormhawks jerseys waiting to catch a glimpse of their heroes. They shout Jake's name and his face breaks into an easy smile as he signs autographs while the rest of the team hurries toward their vehicles, eager to start the celebrations. I tighten my jacket against the bitter chill of the night air. Overhead, the clouds look swollen and heavy, threatening more snow that doesn't look like it'll disappear this time.

Jake throws a glance over his shoulder, a crease forming at

the sight of me shivering and the line of his fans still waiting for their turn to greet him. When I chose the tight black jeans, white Stormhawks top, and Mia's leather jacket, it was with Jake's lingering gaze in mind. But my outfit is doing nothing to ward off the cold.

"I'm fine," I mouth, forcing myself not to shiver.

He's about to turn back when he catches the eye of two of his teammates. "JT, Billy, take Harper with you to the bar. I'll be five minutes behind you."

"Sure thing," one of them calls.

Jake gives me a nod, telling me to go. "They're good guys," he says. "They'll look after you."

"Well, I am. I'm Billy Vargas, the quarterback you saw throwing that awesome pass to Jake tonight," he says and I laugh at his confidence. He has a head of black curly hair, a cheeky smile, and a vibe that makes me instantly like him. "You're the journalist, right? How's the feature on our man Jake going?"

"It's going well." I smile. It's true. I think of the pages of notes filling my notebook. They've gone from bitter and scathing to something far richer. They paint a portrait of a complex man navigating a high-pressure world with all eyes on him, judging his every move. A man who, despite the headlines, has a good heart. A man who makes my pulse race with a single smoldering look.

"Well, if you need some juicy stories, we've got you covered," Billy shouts.

"Don't listen to them," Jake calls over his shoulder, but he's laughing. Relaxed. These are his friends. He trusts them.

"Yo, Vargas," JT says from the other side of me. "Hope there's room in the truck for your ego."

They tussle a little as we walk across the parking lot. JT is the Stormhawks kicker. He's tall and muscular like Jake, but not as broad. He has short brown hair, a mustache that looks right out of an eighties TV show, and twinkling eyes. The drive to the bar is short but filled with laughter. Billy regales me with story after outrageous story about Jake—how he once came to practice wearing nothing but a jockstrap and the time he got stuck in the laundry chute after a dare. I can't help giggling, though I wonder how much is true.

By the time we arrive, the lot is already full and JT finds a space a way down the road. A biting wind whips down the street as we hurry into the warmth of the bar, which is heaving with fans and players. The jukebox is loud, the laughter louder. I see Flic behind the bar with three other staff. She flashes me a smile and nods her appreciation for my white Stormhawks top.

We join the huddle of those waiting to be served and I try not to watch the door for Jake. I long for him to walk in and throw his arm around me again like I belong in that space beside him. Even if I know we can't be seen like that together.

Billy and JT push to the front, and a minute later an overflowing glass of white wine is being pushed into my hands and I find myself wedged in with nowhere to go. Before I know it, Gordon is beside me.

"Hey, Harper, how's it going?" he asks.

I take a sip of wine. It's cold with a sharp tang that leaves me wondering if I should've stuck with a light beer. "Good," I reply. "Congrats on the win."

"Thanks. It was a team effort. Couldn't have done it without Jake playing like that tonight."

I was expecting another testosterone-infused, egotistical reply but the humbleness to his answer takes me by surprise. Maybe Gordon isn't as bad as Jake thinks. There's obviously history with the two men but I pegged Jake so wrong when I first met him, I'm done basing my opinions of people on the past.

"So," Gordon asks as we shift away from the swell of fans and players lining up at the bar. "You and Jake, are you together? Because I'd like to get to know you better if..."

Heat rushes through my body. Images of the night in Jake's bed flood my mind again. Jake and I haven't crossed the line since that night, but I'd be lying if I said there was nothing between us. Especially after that look from Jake on the field.

I start to reply, to squash the interest in Gordon's eyes without admitting anything. Except my gaze is caught on the door as Jake steps through it and a loud cheer breaks out from the players and fans. He grins, setting a dozen fireworks off in the pit of my stomach. My body takes an involuntary step forward, but then I catch sight of the woman beside him. Jake isn't alone. Hanging off his arm like the cat who got the fucking cream is the redheaded woman who took the selfie with him in here a few weeks ago. I watch as he leans down to whisper in her ear. It's the same easy gesture he's done with me a hundred times in the last few weeks. Whatever he says, she giggles, face lighting up, and she swats his arm playfully.

A crushing sensation squeezes my chest. I grit my teeth until the hurt passes. I was a fool to even think Jake was into me. To start to believe for a single second that what we shared the other night was anything more than sex. He's treating me the way he does every woman. The flirting and closeness I've felt grow between us these last few weeks—it means nothing, I realize as a knot forms in my stomach.

I sip my wine, anger burning in my veins as I swallow down the hurt and devastation and turn back to Gordon with a reckless smile. "No," I reply. "There's nothing between me and Jake."

TWENTY-SEVEN

JAKE

FLIC: *Stop sulking in the corner and go get your girl.*

JAKE: *I'm not sulking. And she's clearly not mine.*

FLIC: *Bullshit!*

JAKE: *Haven't you got drinks to serve?*

FLIC: *Haven't you got a win to celebrate?*

I shove my phone in my pocket and ignore the pointed glare Flic shoots me from across the room. I'm not sulking. I'm confused and I'm pissed. Something happened in the space of time between stepping away from Harper in the parking lot after the game and arriving at the bar. And now she's letting a dick like Gordon drool all over her.

What the hell happened?

I take a swig of my beer and watch Harper goofing around with Gordon by the jukebox. She's wearing a red lace bra beneath the white Stormhawks top. The flash of red strap and the swell of her breasts straining against the white fabric is sexy as hell, and there isn't a man in this bar who hasn't noticed. Gordon says something as he leans over the jukebox, and the way she smiles at him has my vision blurring with anger. I'd planned to tell her tonight how I feel—how I want more. I want everything. And now it's all gone to shit.

My jaw muscles tighten and I drag my gaze away from her. If I thought for a single second Harper needed rescuing, I'd be over there, but even in my fury I can see she's having a good time.

The bar is filling up. Every seat taken. The music is loud and Billy is cajoling a group into line dancing with him. He's found a wide-brimmed cowboy hat from somewhere, clashing with the green tartan golf pants he swears are the height of fashion. Somehow, he still pulls it off. If I wasn't so pissed, I'd laugh. Hell, I'd probably join him on the dance floor.

Across the bar, Cherry is leaning against the wall, drinking a bottle of beer and watching me. She catches my eye, slowing down her movements as her lips slip over the end of the bottle. Her eyes are suggestive and I know when she flicks her gaze to the door, what she's suggesting. I shake my head and she rolls her eyes.

She looks at Harper and Gordon then back to me. "Her?" she mouths, but I look away. I don't answer to Cherry. I told her earlier when she'd caught up to me in the parking lot and slipped her arm in mine that I wasn't interested. I was gentle about it, leaning in to tell her I was seeing someone and thought it could be serious.

Her response was to laugh. *Come find me when it's over,* was all she said before moving away. Now it's like she's daring me to make Harper as jealous as I feel right now. But that's not my style. Any fun I once found in the back of my truck after a win disappeared the night on the benches when I watched Dylan bust his knee.

Before I met Harper, I thought I was done with women. Now I realize I was done with the wrong women. It's a kick in the gut to see the only woman I want flirting with another man. And not just any man, but the biggest sleaze in Colorado.

"Pussy," a voice whispers in my ear, followed by a hand on my shoulder. I don't need to turn around to know who that voice belongs to. Flic.

"No idea what you're talking about," I say, biting off the words.

Flic fixes me with her pale blue eyes. Like always, she's dressed in a black tank top and black jeans. Today her long, ice-blonde hair is hanging loose down her back. "Yeah, right," she scoffs. "Admit it, Jake, you're too scared to go after your girl because you're worried your tender little heart might finally get broken."

I huff, taking another sip of beer. "It's got nothing to do with me. I just don't want to see Harper get used by the likes of Gordon. She's too good for that piece of shit."

"Spoken like a man who isn't jealous at all," she replies, sarcasm dripping from her voice.

"You know if you were Chase or Dylan, I'd be telling you to fuck off right about now," I reply.

She laughs. "Go ahead, Sullivan. I've heard worse from you over the years. And since your brothers aren't here and I am, let me tell you exactly what they'd tell you. You're full of shit."

"How do you figure that?" I ask, wishing I hadn't when I turn to Flic and find she's looking at me like I'm the biggest dumbass in the place.

"You don't think everyone was looking when you walked in with Cherry hanging off your arm? You don't think Harper was? What do you think she saw?"

"What?" I pull back. "That's ridiculous. You know what Cherry's like. She leeched on to me before I could move away. She's been trying to get into the backseat of my truck since I signed with the Stormhawks."

"Yeah. I know what Cherry's like. But does Harper?" Flic asks. "You don't think the way she's acting with Gordon right now is anything more than proving something to herself and you?"

My gaze moves back to Harper and Gordon. I hate that fuckwit. Having to work with him, having to trust him on the field when I know the kind of man he is off it, leaves me feeling all kinds of wrong. I should've been honest with Harper from the start about just how bad Gordon is.

The beats of a new song start and he pulls her toward him. Harper is still smiling, but she's shifting out of his arms, heading for the bar.

"Fuck this," I mutter, slamming down the beer bottle I've barely touched and striding through the throng, cutting her off before she can order another drink. "We're leaving," I say.

Her eyes flash with defiance and fuck me if that anger doesn't make my dick thicken. All I want to do is push her up against the wall and take her right now, no matter how many pairs of eyes are watching.

"Go if you want to. I'm happy here," she replies.

I step closer. "No way I'm leaving you with the likes of Gordon."

"I can take care of myself," she says just as the dickhead in question appears at her side, snaking an arm around her waist.

"Fuck off, Gordon," I growl. "This doesn't concern you."

"Woah." He laughs. "Cool it, Sullivan. Harper and I are just having a good time, aren't we?" The lightness injected into his tone does nothing to the break the tension building between us.

Harper looks from me to Gordon and back again. "Jake," she

says, pressing a calming hand on my chest. Her touch is hot and electric, and when our eyes lock, longing shoots through my entire body.

"We're leaving," I say again, wishing I didn't sound so much like a caveman.

"She's fine with me," Gordon replies. The smile is gone and there's an edge to his voice. "I'll make sure she gets home safely."

"You and I both know that's bullshit, now fuck off, Gordon, before I tell the journalist from *Sports Magazine* what kind of man you really are. I've kept your secrets too long."

"Hey." He steps forward, no longer smiling. "There's a code, man."

"I couldn't give a fuck about your code."

Our conversation has caught the attention of the nearest group. Eyes are on us and I'm not the only one to notice. Three things happen at once. I step forward, daring Gordon to come at me. Then Flic appears with a bottle of liquor and a leather strap looped over her shoulder with spaces in the leather where shot glasses are tucked. She shouts, "Free shots for Stormhawks fans," pulling the attention of the bar away from us. And the third is Harper grabbing my arm and pulling me outside.

Fury radiates off her. "I'm only leaving with you because I told Coach Allen I'd keep you out of trouble," she hisses as we step into the ice-cold night. The first new snowflakes drift in the air, already covering the vehicles in a fine layer of white.

We drive back to the ranch in stony silence. The knotty tension that settled in my muscles when I first saw Harper with Gordon is still pulling tight.

The ranch is in darkness when I pull up. I'm glad we've got the place to ourselves for the fight I'm certain we're about to have. It wasn't how I saw tonight going. I jump out of the truck and storm into the house. Buck shoots straight past me and dances around Harper.

"What the hell was that, Jake?" Harper asks as she steps into the kitchen behind me.

"That was me saving you from a massive mistake. You're welcome."

Her eyes flash with anger. "You're not my boyfriend or my wingman, Jake. If I want to make a mistake, I will. It's my life. And that's not what I meant, and you know it. Why were you acting like that in the bar?"

I grit my teeth. "Why were you all over Gordon?"

"You've got no right to be jealous. You walked in with a woman draped all over you."

Damn Flic for being right. "Cherry is nothing to me. She wrapped herself around my arm as I walked into the bar. What was I supposed to do? Push her off? Cause a scene?"

"You didn't have to look like you were enjoying it so much," she fires back.

Despite the anger, I can't stop the smirk from hitting my face. "Now who's jealous?"

She huffs a reply then shakes her head, pushing past me and heading for the stairs.

My muscles tighten another notch. "You sleep with me, but you won't trust me."

She stops in the doorway and turns back without a word as though waiting for me to continue. So I do.

"You see a fan sidle up to me and instead of giving me the benefit of the doubt or asking me about it, you immediately assume the worst. I thought you knew me better than that. What the hell have we been doing these past four weeks?"

"You expect me to trust you and yet you refuse to tell me what happened last year with the cheerleaders? I've got one week left with you, Jake. One week. I could write the feature on you tomorrow. The only thing missing is your side of what happened last year."

Anger and hurt rise up from the deep well inside me. It's no longer for tonight, but for that one stupid moment and all that came next.

"You really wanna know?" I growl. "Fine I'll tell you."

She folds her arms and fixes me with a fierce look. "I'm listening."

TWENTY-EIGHT

HARPER

Jake pushes a hand through his hair and looks like this is the last thing he wants to do.

"I'm a nice guy, Harper," he says, dark eyes boring into mine. "A good one. Those closest to me know this. I think deep down, you know it, too."

I force myself to keep quiet. Inside a voice is screaming, *Yes! I do know that.* But if I speak now, if I give in to my need to step into Jake's arms, we'll lose this moment. And I have to know the truth. Not just for the feature, but for me. Because Jake is right. I saw the redhead on his arm earlier and thought the worst.

"A few years ago, Billy dated a woman called Kylie Hutton. They were together for six months, but it ended amicably when she joined the Stormhawks cheer team. They weren't serious and as soon as Kylie was on the squad they both knew it had to end. There aren't many rules for what football players can and can't do off the field, but dating cheerleaders is one of them. Management takes it seriously. If a player and a cheerleader are caught fraternizing, they'll both lose their spots on the teams. But during those six months Kylie was dating Billy, she and I became friends. So when she found herself in a tough position last year, she asked for my help and I gave it. Or tried."

"What kind of help?" I ask.

Jake sighs like the weight of the world is sitting on his shoulders. "Kylie found out two of her squad mates were breaking the rules and were secretly seeing someone on the team. Worse still, it was the same man. She wanted to tell them and she wanted it to stop before anyone lost their job, but because the guy was a teammate of mine, she wanted me there for moral support, I guess."

It hits me like that cold wind howling around the ranch outside. "Gordon," I say, realizing why Jake reacted like that in the bar and hating myself. I fight back a groan and the apology dancing on my lips as Jake continues.

"We were supposed to meet at The Hay Barn, but practice ran late and by the time I finished, Kylie and the other two cheerleaders were waiting by my truck. It was clear the second I arrived that they'd already been arguing. Cheer rules are a lot stricter. Being seen fighting would be an instant dismissal, too. So I told them all to get in my truck, planning to drive somewhere quiet, but then it all came out, right there in my truck in the parking lot of the stadium.

"Kylie tried to keep things calm but one of the girls went ballistic at the other. Accusing her of stealing Gordon from her. She tried to smack her and I moved between them. I should've just got out the truck, but it all happened so fast."

A haunted expression fills Jake's eyes like it's not the first time he's tormented himself with regret over the things he didn't do that night.

"I guess a fan was near enough to hear the shouting, because they snapped the photo that hit the tabloids. Three cheerleaders and me in a truck, one of them screaming about how the other was stealing her man. The story broke that I'd been sleeping with all three of them." He shrugs like that's the end of it. "I was trying to help and it blew up in my face."

There's more to this. I can tell by the rippling tension still in the air around Jake.

"Why didn't you speak out and explain what was really going on?" I ask.

He rubs a hand over the stubble of his jaw. "Behind the scenes, I did. I told Coach Allen and Mama. Kylie backed me up and at least management believed me so I could keep my spot on the team. But it was a huge mess. The publicity guy got involved and decided it was the kind of fire that would be better to let burn out than add fuel, so I was told to say nothing."

"Except it didn't die out."

"No." Jake shakes his head. "With my reputation the story exploded."

"But wouldn't the press have known that nothing could've happened or you would've been fired? Like you say, you were still on the team, so..."

"That's what they'd hoped, but it wasn't the gossip sites anymore, it was the fans taking to their socials. People were saying the Stormhawks let me break the rules with the cheerleaders and it wasn't fair. The story completely blew up. People were saying stuff that wasn't even remotely true and their followers were believing it. There was huge blowback on me and on the team. But by then it was too late to deny it without looking like I was lying or causing a ton of journalists to start digging around for the truth."

"And Gordon?"

Muscles tighten in Jake's jaw. "He acted like I was protecting him because of some bro code. It wasn't that at all, but like it or not, he was my teammate and I wasn't about to throw him in the shit."

I see it so clearly. Of course Jake was trying to help. Of course he didn't ruin the careers of four other people. This man standing before me is good. He thinks of others before himself. He puts them first. Everything he's done in the last month has shown me that.

"Not that it mattered," Jake continues. "The two cheerleaders still got fired. Cheerleaders have to sign NDAs so even after they were fired, they couldn't say publicly who the football player was they were sleeping with. Kylie barely held on to her job and quit two months later anyway.

"Coach Allen asked me if I was prepared to tell him who the player was, and stupidly I said no. Gordon had come to me the night before and begged me to stay quiet. He swore it was a mistake and he wouldn't do it again. He was a mess, crying, saying he'd be nothing if he got fired. I didn't like Gordon then any more than I like him now, but I couldn't see what good it would do to throw him under the bus. So I told Coach I wouldn't. He understood my loyalty but felt he had to bench me for a game."

"Even though you did nothing wrong?"

Jake shrugs. "I was pissed, but mostly with myself and how stupid the situation was. I thought it was only one game. What difference could it make?"

Another cold shot of realization pushes through me. "Dylan," I whisper.

It's not a question, but Jake gives a small nod.

"That was the game you weren't playing in," I say. "The one where he tore his ACL. But his injury wasn't your fault."

"Dylan doesn't see it that way. The way we read each other on the field was nothing short of magic. Dylan thinks if I'd played that game, I'd have protected him from the tackle that ruined his knee, and the worst thing is, he's probably right."

"Does he know what really happened with the cheerleaders? That it wasn't your fault?"

"I told Mama not to say anything. Dylan was in a bad way

after the injury. I thought at some point we'd talk and I'd explain, but we never have. He's still furious with me."

Jake steps toward me. I think he's going to reach for my hand, but instead he moves into the hall.

"I'm going to bed," he says when he reaches the stairs.

"Jake?" I say his name with no idea what will come next.

He pauses, turning to look at me.

"I'm sorry for flirting with Gordon," I blurt, unable to voice my feelings.

His eyes fill with regret. "Harper, since we met, have you seen any evidence that I think only with my dick?"

I shake my head.

"Because I don't." He pushes a hand through his hair. "There aren't many things I regret, but I regret that day in the parking lot last September and Dylan getting injured. I regret not standing up for myself and letting my reputation take the hit. And I regret letting you walk away the morning after the awards dinner without telling you how I was feeling."

My heart feels like it skips a beat. "How were you feeling?" I ask, the words barely a whisper.

"I didn't want what happened to be a one-night stand with you because..." He pauses and I watch the column of his throat move before he continues. "Because I'm falling for you. Your humor, your smart-ass mouth," he says with a small smirk. "You see through all the bullshit. You're smart and unbelievably sexy and I haven't been able to stop thinking about you since you walked into my life in those stupid sky-high stilettos."

My mouth drops open. His words hit me with a force that takes my breath away. I search for a reply, but Jake continues.

"But you don't trust me, and even though it kills me, there's nothing I can do about that."

He turns away and walks up the stairs. A moment later his bedroom door shuts and I'm alone. I stand in the hallway, my heart racing as Jake's words echo in my mind. I think of the times we've spent together. The teasing banter, the charged looks, and the way he searches for me on the field between plays. That smile on his lips when our eyes locked across the stadium earlier.

I sigh and lean back against the wall. Part of me aches to be back in Jake's arms. But another part of me is terrified to let him in. I've hardly had the best track record. Pining for Jake when I was sixteen. Then a handful of unsatisfactory boys who all treated me like I didn't matter. Then Scott and his cheating. I thought Jake was to blame for my low confidence after high school and the crappy love life that followed, but the truth is, I never allowed men in previous relationships to see the real me. Never let myself be vulnerable. To risk getting hurt.

I don't know how. Or if I'm even capable.

With a groan, I push away from the wall and head up to my room. I slip on my ivory camisole and shorts set and pad to the bathroom to brush my teeth. In the mirror I stare at my reflection and the truth staring back at me. My heart is on the line, but if I'm honest, I'm already in too deep. If I walk away from Jake now, I know it'll hurt.

An urgency starts to pound in my chest. Seven days. That's all the time we have left on the assignment. Suddenly, I have to tell him the words he needs to hear. I throw open the door and step into the hall, only to find Jake already in the doorway to his bedroom, looking as tormented as I feel.

"I trust you," I blurt.

"Really?" A frown is pinching his brow, but he's smiling too. "You're not just saying that to get me into bed again?"

I laugh and shake my head. "Really," I say, taking a step closer. "I don't see you as a player, Jake. I see the man who comes to a black-tie dinner because he knows I'm going to have a hard time. The man who puts others before himself, always." My words come in a breathy rush.

"Harper," he whispers.

I take a final step forward as Jake's eyes lock with mine. He looks utterly gorgeous. His dark hair is ruffled from where he's raked his hand through it. The stubble on his face just as dark. He's wearing a white tee that clings to every muscle and those low-slung basketball shorts I lusted over on our first weekend together.

Jake's eyes burn with desire as he draws me into him. He lifts his thumb to brush across my cheek, tracing a line down my face, my neck, and all the way to the edge of my camisole. My nipples are pushing against the silk and I know he sees by the hardness of his dick pressing against my stomach as I lean slowly into his body.

Giving him time to turn me down, I reach up to slip my arms around his neck, and just as I think he's going to push me away, he reaches down and grips the back of my thighs, picking me up like I weigh nothing. I press my lips to his and wrap my legs around his waist, and he turns, carrying me into his bedroom with determined strides, kicking the door shut with his foot without moving his lips from mine.

TWENTY-NINE

JAKE

The need to have Harper right here, right now consumes me. She slips her tongue into my mouth and our kiss intensifies with the longing I've felt since the night we shared the hotel room together. Before that, even. I can't remember a time when Harper wasn't in my head, taking over my every thought.

I'm torn, pulled apart by how much I want to rip her silk shorts from her body and slide the entire length of my dick straight into her hot pussy until she's screaming for more just like she did the other night. But there's another part of me that wants to take this slow again, to savor every touch and kiss and feeling.

Her hands slide under my tee and around the waistband of my shorts. My dick is straining to be unleashed but I pull my lips away from hers and stare at her, eyes tracking over her beautiful face. Her gaze is heavy-lidded, filled with desire as I carry her to the bed, laying her down on the covers and standing over her so she's looking up at me.

"I want you so bad it hurts." My voice is half growl, half whisper.

A slow smile spreads over her face. "Jake Sullivan, I've

fantasized about being in your bed ever since I left the other morning."

"Just since then?" I tease.

She huffs a laugh. "Fine. I've fantasized about being with you for ten years. So don't you dare cut this short."

"No intention of that, sweetheart." I move onto the bed and kneel over her, allowing a hand to trail over her toned stomach, loving the way she shivers at my touch. "You've fantasized about this moment? Tell me what you imagined me doing."

Her smile turns coy. "There was a lot of kissing."

I lean close, brushing my lips against the side of her neck. "Here?"

"Yes." She makes a noise in her throat as I trace my lips to her collarbone.

"Here?"

"Yes," she says and this time her voice is a breathy whisper.

I hook my finger under the strap of her camisole and slide it down over her shoulder. Desire burns in me at the sight of her exposed breast, nipple hard and wanting. "Do you know how fucking beautiful you are?"

Before she can answer, I pull the other strap from her shoulder so I have a full view of both of her perfect breasts and dip my head to run my tongue over one nipple. She groans in pleasure and the sound makes my dick twitch.

"Did you imagine me kissing you here?" I ask, my tongue circling the tight bud of nerves.

She gasps. "Yes."

I move to the other nipple, enjoying the tremble of her body beneath me.

She reaches up, pulling at my tee. "You're wearing too many clothes."

I grin. "So are you." With both hands, I slide the silk of her camisole down her body, taking the cute little shorts with them and throwing them to the floor. I stand back, admiring every curve of her naked body on my bed.

"Jake," she pleads and the sound of my name on her lips is all the encouragement I need. I pull off my tee and slide out of my shorts. My dick springs out, thick and hard and jerking at the sight of Harper's eyes on it. I position myself between her legs, nudging her knees apart as I kiss her breasts, my hands exploring her body. As my fingers trail over her clit, she arches into me, hungry for more, and I oblige, sliding a finger inside her.

I let my teeth graze her nipple before I say, "You're so fucking wet for me, aren't you?"

"Hell yes," she groans as my fingers return to circling her clit.

"Tell me what you want," I murmur, looking up to meet her heated gaze.

"I want you inside me," she pleads.

I grin, my dick aching for the same. I'm still on my knees as I grab a condom.

Then in one move, I slide my arm beneath her, flipping her over, pulling her toward me so her ass is pressed up against me.

She gasps as I slide into her from behind, feeling the exquisite heat of her all around me. My hand trails down her spine, tracing the curve of her body as I begin to move. Every thrust feels deeper than the last, causing a fire to build in my groin. Harper gasps my name and damn it sounds good. My hand glides over the curve of her ass, squeezing, loving the way her body responds to me. My other hand moves to her breast, teasing her nipple between my fingers, tugging just enough to draw another moan from her lips.

I lose myself to the feeling of each thrust until I feel the heat of her body closing around my length. She's panting, her body trembling. She's close. I slide my hand lower, my fingers finding her center. I circle my fingers slowly at first, building her up, before quickening my movements, matching the rhythm of my hips as I thrust deeper and harder.

"Jake," she cries, her voice breaking as her orgasm builds and her body shakes. She's so close now.

I keep my pace steady, the pressure in my body coiling tighter with every second. I'm on the edge, but I hold back, needing to feel her come apart. "That's it, sweetheart," I murmur. "Let me hear you."

Her cries grow louder, her body tensing as the orgasm takes hold of her. Her pussy clamps so hard around my dick, I'm forced to slow down, easing in and out as she rides her wave. The sound of her lost in pleasure because of what I'm doing to her sends a surge of primal satisfaction through me.

In that second, I'm certain of two things. The sound of Harper's cries is the best sound I've ever heard—and I want to spend the rest of my life making her scream like this.

THIRTY

HARPER

The world seems to shudder around me as Jake pulls out, turning me around so I'm on my back, panting, undone.

I gasp for breath and peel open my eyes to find Jake staring down at me like he's enjoying the view. If I wasn't completely ruined by what Jake just did to me, I'd probably feel shy right now, but we're way beyond that. Jake pushes his hair away from his face and smiles.

"You're so fucking hot for me, aren't you?" he says like he's reading my mind.

"Yes," I hiss, pulling him to me. He bends down, trailing kisses up my neck until his lips find mine and we kiss deeply.

My heart refuses to slow down as Jake positions himself between my thighs. The anticipation builds as I feel the tip of his dick press against my opening. The need has me trembling, desperate to feel him deep inside me once more.

Jake's eyes lock with mine as he slowly pushes his huge, rock-hard length into me.

"Oh God, Jake." The words leave my mouth in a gasp as he continues to push further and further, filling every part of me.

"I fucking love making you come, Cassidy." He draws back

just as slowly, the feeling indescribable. "This is just the start," he says as he pushes forward again, a little faster now, and I don't know if he means this moment or us, but either way I'm here for it all.

As he fills me again, we both groan.

"Fuck, Harper, you're so tight. You feel incredible," Jake says against my neck as he pushes deeper. I draw in a sharp breath. It's the most exquisite pleasure I've ever experienced.

"Don't stop," I whisper. "Don't ever stop."

He hooks one of my legs over his shoulder, moving deeper. I gasp, unleashing a cry as the first pulses of another orgasm start to build inside my core.

"That feels so fucking good," Jake moans, leaning down to kiss me tenderly before picking up speed once more. I tilt my hips and the new angle has his thick cock hitting a spot deep inside me that makes stars explode behind my eyelids. I dig my nails into his back, the heat inside me winding tighter until I don't think I can stand it for another second.

"Jake... I'm going to... I'm so close," I pant, lost to the sensations consuming me.

"Let go, Harper," Jake growls. "I want to feel you come over my dick again."

His words send me over the edge. My orgasm slams into me. Wave after wave of pleasure crashes over me as I come so hard I swear my heart stops beating for a moment. Jake's hands grip my hips, holding me steady as the aftershocks of my orgasm ripple through me.

Jake wraps his strong arms around me, holding me close as I catch my breath.

"That was... incredible," I murmur against his chest.

"You're incredible," Jake replies softly, trailing his fingertips up and down my spine in a soothing caress. "I could fuck you all night."

"Is that a promise?" I smile up at him.

A wide grin spreads across Jake's face. "I'm nowhere near done with you yet, Cassidy."

With that, Jake begins to move again, slowly withdrawing until just the tip remains before pressing back in with long, hard drives. Each thrust sends new ripples of pleasure through my body. I wrap my legs around his waist, urging him deeper as my hands roam the muscular expanse of his back. His skin is hot to the touch, the hard planes of muscle flexing beneath my fingertips with every powerful movement. The headboard slams against the wall with the force of his movements but I'm too far gone to care.

"Fuck, Harper." Jake grits out my name and with one more deep thrust he's groaning with pleasure, his dick pulsing inside me as he comes.

We collapse together, both gasping for air.

Jake turns away to remove the condom before he scoops me into his arms and I snuggle against his broad chest, completely content and satisfied in a way I've never known. His fingers trail lazily over my body as a pleasant ache settles between my thighs. I can't stop grinning as I snuggle deeper into his embrace, relishing the solid warmth of his muscular body pressed against mine.

"You know," I say. "If someone had told me a month ago that I'd be naked in bed with Jake Sullivan, I'd have laughed in their face and called them crazy."

Jake laughs, the sound a deep rumble in his chest. "Hey, considering the murderous look in your eyes that first night I walked into the kitchen—"

"An hour late," I remind him.

"True." He chuckles. "But I hardly thought we'd end up here, either. Then I saw you in the kitchen in the middle of the night, lost in your novel, wearing a tee and not much else, and even if I didn't think it would happen, I knew I wanted you."

"That was…" I think back. "That was only our second day together. You've wanted me all that time?"

"Says the woman who's fantasized about being in my bed since high school."

I swat Jake playfully on the arm and laugh. "Watch it, Sullivan. I've still got my feature to write about you." For a split second I think about what's happening between me and Jake, and the line we've crossed. What people will say. If Tim finds out… But I'm done trying to fight the pull toward Jake.

"Mmm, I'll take my chances," he murmurs, dipping his head to nuzzle my neck.

We stay like that for a long time. Entwined, talking in whispers and laughing. Then Jake's lips brush my neck and a new wave of desire starts to stir in my core. Jake hums in approval as my hands wander lower, ghosting along the trail of dark hair below his navel. I feel his dick stir and harden against my thigh and let my fingers drift further, lightly stroking the impressive length of him.

"Really?" I grin.

His large hand slides down to cup my ass, pulling me flush against him.

"I can't help that this is what you do to me. Like I said, I've thought about fucking you for the longest time."

I prop myself onto my elbow and run a hand over his broad chest. "And what did *you* think about doing to me? Your turn."

Heat burns in his gaze. He grabs another condom, and in one motion he scoops me from the bed and presses me against the wall as he holds me up, kissing me hard. I think of the way Jake towered over me on our first night in The Hay Barn, my back to the wall. The ache of anticipation throbs in my core, already ready for him all over again. I wrap my legs around his waist as he enters me in one deep thrust.

We spend the rest of the night worshipping each other's

bodies. When we're both aching and exhausted, Jake pulls me into his bed and I fall asleep in his arms, under his covers that smell of citrus musk and something masculine and Jake-like.

THIRTY-ONE
JAKE

My dick wakes me. A morning hard-on so thick it's almost painful. I shift back, trying not to jam the thing into Harper's ass like some horny eighteen-year-old.

"That's one hell of an alarm clock, Sullivan," Harper murmurs in a sleepy voice from beside me.

I chuckle. "Sorry. Mind of its own."

She shifts around so I'm on my back and she's nestling against my chest, one leg hooked over mine. Her chestnut hair has dried wavy from the shower we took together last night. "What's the time?" she asks, stretching her beautiful and very naked body in a way that makes my dick go from hard to rock-hard.

"Still early. Seven, I think." I glance to the window, where the first streaks of dawn are cutting across the sky. We've barely been asleep three hours. I'm bone-tired and buzzing and the two feel so good together.

Winning our game last night puts us in playoff position. Considering how we started the season, to be here now feels nothing short of a miracle, and I know I've played the best football of my life this month. Harper brings out the best in me. And now she's in my bed and we have nowhere we need to be today. No more misunderstandings or holding back. Just us. And I plan to make the most of it.

Harper pulls herself up and my eyes fall to her breasts. My mind blanks and all I can think about is kissing her.

"You're so beautiful," I say.

She grins like she can read my mind. "I'm going to freshen up."

"You're coming back though, right?" I smirk.

"I wouldn't leave you with a hard-on like that, Jake. You could hurt someone walking around with that between your legs."

I laugh and reach for my phone as she disappears from the room. I fire a reply to Flic's message, and when her next one arrives, tension snakes through me. I open up the Denver gossip site, remembering squaring off with Gordon in the bar. I'm expecting a photo of that moment or even one of Cherry on my arm, but it's neither.

What the fuck? I laugh at the photo of me on the website. *Seriously?*

"What is it?" Harper asks from the doorway.

I look up and she's wearing an old Stormhawks jersey of mine. A grin spreads over my face. "Don't ever wear anything else," I say.

"I'm naked under this shirt."

"Even better. Come here."

She moves toward me and I reach up, pulling her into me and sweeping her from her feet, making her giggle. She smells of toothpaste and soap. As she presses her body against me, I realize this photo doesn't just affect me. It affects her too, and she might not be as amused.

"There's been a story about me," I say.

She shoots me a questioning look. "And you're OK about it? I seem to remember you were pretty unhappy last time."

"This one is different. It's..." I swipe open my phone and show her the screen and the photo of me from last night's game. I'm on the field in my Stormhawks jersey and shoulder pads, helmet under my arm. It's during one of the breaks. The camera has caught me searching the crowd with an expression of a lovesick puppy on my face. Harper swipes down to read the headline.

IS STORMHAWKS STAR JAKE SULLIVAN IN LOVE?

I can't stop the smile from spreading across my face as I read the speculation about the mystery woman in the skybox I was caught looking at during last night's game. The article ends with another question: WHO IS JAKE'S GIRL?

"Oh," Harper says, her body tensing. Something drops in the pit of my stomach. Her editor warned her not to cross this line with me. I hate that this story could affect her. Affect us.

"I'm sorry," I say. "I know you'd rather not be dragged into this."

She makes a face. "It's not that. It's just... enough people on the team know I'm from *Sports Magazine*, writing a feature on you. It's only a matter of time before my name gets mentioned and my editor, Tim, finds out."

"There are no rules against it," I say gently.

"It's hardly appropriate though, is it? In the next few weeks, Tim is going to choose between me and another journalist. There's only one job and Tim warned me not to sleep with you..."

"But if you write an amazing piece on me, he's hardly going to fire you, is he?"

Harper frowns. "Amazing or not, it looks bad for the magazine that we've formed a relationship. I'm supposed to be impartial. People will assume anything positive I write is because we're sleeping together." She sighs before turning her gaze on me, searching my face. "What about you? I thought you hated this stuff?"

"Yeah, when it's not true. But I *was* looking for you in the skybox."

Harper's cheeks flush and she gives a shy smile. I lean close and kiss her gently.

"Are you OK?" I ask again.

"There's not much I can do about it now. I'd better email Tim today and hope he doesn't fire me."

"I'm sorry I've dragged you into the spotlight," I say.

She shakes her head and swings her leg around to straddle me. "I wish it wasn't all over the internet, but I'm not sorry and you haven't dragged me into this either."

She leans down, pressing her lips to mine and I'm lost in her kiss. My hands find the smooth skin of her thighs then up her body, pushing the jersey higher. I take my time worshipping every inch of her. When I finally slide inside her, it's pure bliss. Like coming home. The connection between us is fire and heat, but there's a depth that adds an intensity I've never felt before. Like she can see right into the heart of me, the real me.

∽

"Tell me why we're doing this again?" I ask, scrunching my eyes against the bright sunlight bouncing off the two feet of brilliant white snow that fell in the night. "We could be in bed right now." The air is cold and fresh and invigorating despite thinking of other things I'd like to be doing.

Harper laughs, thumping my arm as snow crunches under our boots. "We've been in bed all morning. We need air and Buck needs a walk. And just look at this place..." She waves a hand to the paddocks, glistening with a blanket of white. Beyond it, the normally brown foothills are covered in fresh white like the distant mountains.

I draw in a deep breath and cold air hits the bottom of my lungs. The ranch is a picture-perfect winter wonderland, which Buck is doing his best to charge and jump through, his yellow fur stark against the white, tail wagging furiously at the delight of the changed landscape.

As we make our way toward the lake, I slip my hand into Harper's. She seems surprised for a moment, but a second later she's entwining her fingers with mine. The lake is covered with a layer of frosty ice. The trees around it are heavy with snow, their branches drooping under the weight.

"Have you ever seen anything more beautiful?" Harper says as Buck shoves his face in a drift of snow, appearing a moment later with a white nose, making us both laugh. I look down at Harper. Her cheeks are flushed from the cold, her hair beneath the white bobble hat still tousled from being in my bed. Her eyes dance with delight.

"Yes, I have," I say, wrapping my arms around her.

She laughs, loud and free. "Smooth, Jake. Very smooth."

I know without a doubt that I'm crazy for this woman. I'm not just falling anymore. I've fallen. I'm all the way gone. I want to tell her, shout it into the icy air, but I hold back. This feeling thrumming through my body is still so new. So I pull her tighter against my chest and pour my feelings into our kiss.

THIRTY-TWO

HARPER

Notes for feature: I'M THE GIRL.

I'm the girl.

I'm the one Jake looks for in the crowd. The one who makes him smile like that.

Even though I'm freaking out about what this is going to do for my career and what Tim will say, I can't stop smiling. My cheeks hurt from it. My lips are sore from all the kissing. My whole body aches because of this man. For this man. I'm supposed to be finishing my latest notes and sending them to Tim. I'm almost done and I've opened the latest chapter of my book, pouring my emotions into my characters. Writing is usually the only thing that makes me happy, but now I'm happy and writing for the joy of it, not to escape. I save the latest version and open the email to Tim to tell him Jake and I are dating. To apologize for the unprofessionalism and grovel for my job. Even if there's a chance my name won't get connected to Jake on the gossip sites, I want to come clean to Tim. No more lies.

A few weeks ago this would've had me spinning out, but it's

as though one of my own walls has come down in the time I've been with Jake. I can see that while I enjoy my job, while it's important to me, it's not everything. It's not the center of the universe. I don't want to be fired, but if it happens, I know I'll be OK.

I read through my pleading apology for the tenth time then leave the email unsent, deciding to distract myself by calling Mia instead. She answers on the first ring.

"Please tell me you gave Jake the celebration he deserved after his epic win last night."

I laugh. "Hello to you, too."

"Harper."

"Mia," I reply.

She cackles. "You know what, don't tell me. It's fine. I can hear it in your voice."

"Hear what?" I grin.

"That husky 'I've had all the sex' voice."

I laugh. "I don't sound like that."

"Yeah, but you're not denying it either."

"Fine. We had sex again," I reply, my grin widening.

The scream in my ear is piercing and injected with the same excitement of the thirteen-year-old version of Mia when we got tickets to the rodeo finals in Las Vegas.

"So what does this mean?" she asks. "I'm guessing you saw that photo of Jake in the news? Are you *together* together? Is this just sex? Are you *riding* off into the sunset?" she asks, adding enough innuendo to the word riding so I know she doesn't mean on a horse.

"I have no idea," I reply, although I know it's more than just sex. The way Jake took my hand on the walk. The way he looks at me like I'm the only one in the world he can see. It's a lot more. Just as I know that if I spend any time thinking about this, I'm going to dive into all the questions Mia just asked me. These feelings could tip in a heartbeat from exciting to scary, and all I want is to exist in this moment and be happy. The future is coming for us one way or another. I could be one email away from being fired. The Stormhawks have two tough games ahead of them to determine if they make the playoffs. And I have six days left with Jake before the assignment is over. I don't know what's going to happen.

"Where is Jake now?" Mia asks.

"We're at the ranch. Mama and Dylan just got back from LA and Jake's filling her in on last night—"

"Wha—"

I huff a laugh. "The game, Mia. He's telling her about the game. And I'm hiding in Chase's room, drafting an email to Tim with my latest notes for the feature, and since that story about Jake hit this morning, I'm also telling him we're..." I sigh. "Whatever it is we are, begging for my job and hoping he's not going to fire me for sleeping with Jake." A small part of me is hiding from Mama, too. Thankfully Jake and I were fully clothed and in the kitchen when Mama and Dylan stepped through the door, but we might as well have been naked for the knowing smile she gave us.

"It'll be fine, Harper," Mia says. "I know you care about your reputation, and yeah, Tim might not be too happy, but honestly, this stuff happens all the time."

"I hope Tim agrees. I'm going to offer to forgo the byline so my name isn't attached to the feature."

"Are you sure? Your career—"

"My career wouldn't even exist if it wasn't for Tim giving me a chance. It feels like the right thing." I sigh before changing the subject, needing a distraction. "How are you, anyway?"

Mia launches into a description of dinner with Edward's family and the pressure they're under to announce an engagement. I can understand the questions. They've been dating for three years and they're good together. But neither seems to want to take the next step. I'm listening to Mia as I finish the email to

Tim, attach my latest notes, and press send before I can find another reason to delay.

A sharp unease hits my chest as I start to close down the lid of my laptop. I didn't just... I wouldn't have...

Fuck!!!

"Mia," I hiss. "I have to go."

"Lover boy calling you to his bed?" she asks.

"I think I just sent the wrong file to Tim."

"What did you send him?" Mia asks.

"I... Can I call you back?"

We say a hurried goodbye and I open the sent folder. I was on autopilot. It will be fine. Of course I sent him the latest notes on the feature and not...

A sick feeling twists in my gut as I stare at the file I attached. Not the notes, but my novel. My entire novel. I was just working on it and I'm so used to emailing the latest version to myself for safekeeping, and I was talking to Mia, my head filled with Jake and... *FUCK!*

My fingers fly across the keyboard as I furiously type a second email.

Hi Tim,

Please IGNORE and DELETE the file attached to my previous email. Here is the correct one!

Harper

~

JAKE: *I miss you in my bed.*

HARPER: *No way am I sneaking around when Mama is in the house. Remember how thin the walls are?*

JAKE: *I'm booking a hotel!*

HARPER: *It's late and you're due at practice first thing.*

JAKE: *We could go to the barn.*

HARPER: *Goodnight, Jake.*

It's the middle of the night and I can't sleep. I refuse to sneak around the ranch with Mama and Dylan home, but that doesn't mean I don't long for Jake's hands on me. The knowledge that he's lying in his bed in the room next to mine—the bed we slept in together last night—is thrumming through my body. I flop against my pillows, but it's no use. I'm too wound up, my mind racing with thoughts of Jake and everything that's happening between us. And the email I sent Tim with my novel attached. As if telling him Jake and I are now seeing each other wasn't bad enough, I've just sent him a very spicy novel about vampires having all the sex. *He won't read it,* I tell myself. And yet, I'm still dying inside.

With a sigh, I throw off the covers. Maybe a glass of water will help settle my nerves. There's been no more snow yet, but the cold has permeated the ranch and I throw on a pair of sweatpants and a sweatshirt. I pad softly down the stairs, the old wooden floorboards creaking under my feet as I make my way through the house. Buck is lying by the dying embers of the fire in the living room. His tail thumps gently on the floor as I pass by, but he doesn't get up and I don't blame him. As I reach the kitchen, I'm surprised to find the light is already on. I pause in the doorway, finding Dylan sitting at the table, a bowl of cereal in front of him. He looks up as I enter, his expression unreadable. He's seemed more sullen than usual since he returned from LA earlier.

I imagine Jake being injured. Having his career ripped away

from him by a split-second tackle. A pang of sympathy hits my chest.

"Just getting a glass of water," I say.

"Can't sleep, either?" he asks, shoveling a spoonful of cereal into his mouth.

I shake my head, glad for the extra clothes I've thrown on.

"How was the treatment center?" I ask, filling a glass and taking a sip.

He grimaces. "Painful."

"Will it help?"

A spark of hope flashes in his eyes. "They think I might have a shot at getting back to football for next season."

"That's amazing."

"Yeah. But it means another op and another month sitting on my ass."

"But if it works..."

"Yeah," he mumbles, turning his attention back to his cereal. "So, you and Jake, huh?" Dylan asks and I don't miss the not-so-subtle change of subject.

Heat creeps over my face. Is it that obvious? I think of the way Jake and I were over dinner tonight. Unable to stop staring at each other. His foot resting against mine beneath the table. I don't know what to say, so I shrug and sip my water.

"Just be careful, Harper. Jake has a way of hurting those he loves."

My head shoots up in surprise. Dylan's remark is sweeping, just like Coach Allen's after the game. *Trouble always finds that boy.* It feels like they've both got Jake wrong.

I lean against the counter. "You don't have to worry."

Dylan pushes his empty bowl away. "If you say so. As long as you're not making the mistake of thinking you're special, you'll be fine. Jake can turn on the charm when he wants to, but he's only out for himself."

A flash of hurt cuts across my chest, but I push it aside and set my glass on the counter with too much force. I trust the man I've got to know in the last four weeks. The one I'm falling for. And I'm sick of everyone else thinking shit about Jake without bothering to see the truth.

"Are we talking about me being hurt or you?" I ask, folding my arms across my chest.

He shakes his head. "This isn't about me."

"Isn't it? Because from where I'm standing, you're the one who's lashing out and hurting the people that love you."

"How do you figure that?" He sits back, giving me a look like I'm full of shit. It only makes me more determined to defend Jake.

"You're so busy being angry with Jake about your knee injury, you can't see how much you're pushing him and everyone else away. I think you need to ask yourself if it's really him you're mad at or the situation."

He huffs but it's not a laugh. "You a psychologist now? For your information, I have every right to be mad at Jake. If he'd been playing that game like he'd been supposed to instead of thinking with his dick, he'd have protected me from the tackle. I don't know how the hell he didn't get dropped, but my whole life is over because of him."

Anger flashes through me, making my fists curl, as much for Dylan and his misguided fury as it is for what happened last year to him and Jake. The unfairness of it all. "And you haven't stopped to ask yourself why Jake didn't get dropped, even though you're saying he should've been?"

"Jake's always been good at talking himself out of trouble. You might be blinded by his charm, but I'm not."

I grit my teeth, forcing my voice to stay low. "You haven't asked him about it though, have you?"

"No need. Saw it on the news."

"Yeah, and that's never wrong." Sarcasm drips from my voice as I stride across the kitchen. At the doorway I turn back to Dylan. "Maybe it isn't me who needs to think about how well I really know Jake."

Dylan opens his mouth like he's going to fire back another retort, but he doesn't and I head back to my room and open my laptop, needing the escape of my novel as my heart continues to race. But instead, all I do is stare at the blinking cursor, unable to concentrate. I think back to Dylan's resentment and misplaced blame. Anyone can see how much Jake is hurting over his brother's injury. He blames himself as much as Dylan does. But I overstepped just now.

I close my laptop and flop onto the bed. Maybe I'm losing myself in their problems because it's easier than thinking of my own. Like Tim's reply to my email this afternoon.

We'll talk about this the next time you're in the office.

It's obvious he's not happy, but at least I still have a job. For now. But it only makes me feel even guiltier for letting Tim think in the interview that my knowledge of sports included football. Not to mention the small fact I didn't disclose my previous connection to Jake when he gave me this assignment. Something that seems a lot worse considering we're now sleeping together.

Then there's Jake. We need to talk about what this is between us. All I know for sure is however complicated a future with Jake might be, I've never wanted anything more.

THIRTY-THREE

JAKE

The weights clang as I place them back on the rack, my muscles burning from the intensity of the workout. Despite the vast space of the gym at Stormhawks Park and the blast of AC, the air reeks of the sweat of my teammates as the coaches push us through a grueling gym routine.

It's Tuesday morning and even though spirits are high from Sunday's win, every one of us is focused—our thoughts on five days' time and the penultimate game of the season against Chase's Kansas City Trailblazers.

"Looking good, Jakey-boy," Billy calls from the bench press beside me. "Trying to impress a certain journalist, eh?" He waggles his eyebrows at me and laughs. If there was a bad bone in Billy's body, I might be tempted to tell him to eat shit, but Billy is all about the fun, so I just roll my eyes.

"Any truth to those luuuurv rumors?" he continues.

I chuckle. "They're called rumors for a reason, Vargas." I turn away before he can see the smile I'm fighting. I might love Billy, but he's as discreet as Mama when someone is stupid enough to be standing in the way of her getting what she wants.

The reality is, I can't stop thinking about Harper. The way her eyes sparkle when she laughs at one of my stupid jokes. How soft her skin feels under my fingertips. I'm counting down the minutes until I can be alone with her again. It's great to have Mama and Dylan home, but I wasn't joking about getting a hotel room. I already miss the feel of Harper naked in my arms. Especially knowing we'll be apart from tomorrow as Harper spends Christmas with Mia. Maybe it's time I get my own place in the city again.

I have tonight to make the most of Harper—to show her how special she is before we spend three days apart. It already feels too long. I can't even think about the assignment ending on Sunday and not seeing each other every day.

It was a struggle to drive straight this morning with how much I wanted to pull over and kiss her. The only thing that stopped me was the knowledge that Harper deserves better than a fumble in my truck. That and knowing she's packed that red two-piece to join me for a swim later.

Music thuds from the speakers, drowning out the grunts of the team and the light ribbings. I throw myself into the weights, forcing myself to think of nothing but the workout until my thighs and arms burn. Only when Coach Allen calls us for the tactics talk do I catch my breath and grab some water and a towel, wiping the sweat from my face. We might be leading the AFC West, but with two games left, nothing's locked in. Our playoff spot isn't guaranteed yet. Coach is straight to business, jabbing a finger at the whiteboard covered in arrows. The passion in his voice is contagious as he talks us through the plays we'll be running ahead of Sunday's game.

When Coach wraps up, I lag behind as the team hits the showers, pretending to study the whiteboard as the locker room empties. I spend longer than I need to in the shower, and when I shut off the water, the locker room is silent. This close to Christmas my teammates are all focused on last-minute shopping and spending time with their families. I throw on a tee and a pair of shorts and go in search of Harper.

I find her in the corner of the empty lounge, sitting cross-legged on the couch, her laptop balanced on her thighs. Her hair is swept up into a loose ponytail and she's lost in concentration, biting her lower lip, fingers flying over the keys. She looks up as I stride toward her and the smile on her face makes my heart judder.

"Hey," she says, and I catch a glimmer of uncertainty in her features, like she isn't sure how to greet me. Is it because we're in public or because we haven't defined what this is yet?

"Hey yourself," I say with a smile. "I really want to kiss you right now."

She closes the lid of her laptop, a cute little smile touching her lips. "What's stopping you?"

I arch an eyebrow. "You OK to make this public? Because for the record, I am!"

"It's already public." She swipes her phone and shows me another story on the gossip site. It's my soppy face from the game and beside it is one of Harper in the skybox looking back at me with the biggest grin on her face. "I'm named in it now, too. They know I'm from *Sports Magazine*."

"Shit. Are you OK?" I search her face as I drop onto the couch beside her.

Harper frowns. "I hate that people might think I'm sleeping my way to a big scoop." She looks down, avoiding my gaze.

I gently tilt her chin up so her eyes meet mine. "Harper, why do you care what anyone else thinks? I know the truth. You know the truth. Screw everyone else."

She sighs. "You're right, but I've spent my whole life wanting people to like me and pretty much failing at it."

"Hey, not everyone. Mia likes you," I tease.

Harper laughs. "Mia is... different," she finishes with a grin.

"I guess... I might like you a bit too," I say, flashing her my Jake Sullivan smile. "So it's not everyone."

"Most people then. Plus, it's in the public eye. I'm feeling pretty judged right now by people who don't even know me on top of those that do."

"Trust me, I get it." I think back on all the rumors and stories that have swirled around me over the years. "But at the end of the day, the only opinion that matters is yours. Everyone else? Background noise."

Harper nods reluctantly.

"And you've still got a job?"

She nods again. "So far, although I'm not looking forward to my meeting with Tim after Christmas."

All I want to do is take her in my arms and kiss her, but I can tell there's more. "But?" I push.

"Even if Tim doesn't directly fire me for this, I'm still in my probationary period. At the start of January, he's going to choose me or another journalist, Callie. The truth is, Callie deserves it more than I do. I shouldn't have lied in my interview. I feel like I've made a mess of my fresh start."

"So talk to Tim," I suggest, slipping my hand into hers and giving a reassuring squeeze. "He loves the notes you've been sending him and you're going to write an amazing feature about me—"

"You don't know that. And I'm not exactly Tim's favorite person right now."

"I do know that. Come clean to him at the right moment and he'll probably understand. You say he's a good guy."

"Yeah. One I've spent the last four months lying to."

I nod toward her laptop. "Are you writing about me or are you writing about sexy vampires right now?"

Harper's face lights up and the tension lifts. "Vampires."

"It really makes you happy."

"It does. But don't worry," she adds, tapping the purple

notebook she takes with her everywhere. "All my notes about you are here. I want to wait until the end of the week to start writing the feature. Just to make sure I've got all the details."

"Sounds like you still need to get to know me a bit better." I flash a grin and run my thumb down the side of her face. "I'm happy to accommodate any interview techniques you have in mind."

She tips her head back and laughs. "Says the man who spent our first week together scowling at me."

I groan. "Yeah, sorry about that. Is there anything I can do to make it up to you?"

"What do you have in mind?" she asks with enough suggestion in her voice to wake my dick.

"Come for a swim with me."

Harper pretends to think about it for a beat. "See you in the pool."

Ten minutes later, I've never been so relieved to see a pool empty as Harper appears in that sexy red two-piece.

I give a low whistle of appreciation. "Damn, Cassidy. You're trying to kill me, aren't you?"

"You've seen me wear this before."

"That was when I was trying to be a gentleman and keep our professional boundaries."

She gives me a teasing smile. "So you're not trying to be a gentleman anymore?" She trails her fingers over my chest where my muscles are still aching from the weights.

"With you wearing that—definitely not."

Unable to resist any longer, I capture her lips in a searing kiss. She responds by wrapping her arms around my neck and pressing her body to mine.

"Are you sure we're OK to be here?" she says when we pull apart.

I nod, and when I speak, my voice is husky. "But maybe you should get in the water before I fuck you against this wall."

She turns and dives gracefully into the water. Then she swims like the last time—strong, even strokes, giving herself to the workout. This time, I float around, allowing the water to ease my muscles.

When Harper is finished, she draws to the side of the pool and catches her breath.

"Sauna?" she asks and I nod.

The heat hits me like a wall as I open the door, the air thick with the smell of heated pinewood. Harper steps inside and I follow, shutting the door behind us with a soft click. She takes a seat on the wooden bench, leaning against the wall. Beads of water still cling to her skin, glistening in the dim light. I sit beside her, our thighs touching. Anticipation crackles between us as my eyes roam over her body. She opens her eyes and catches me staring.

A sly smile plays at her lips. "So about me getting to know you better..."

"You had something in mind?"

She glances down to where I'm straining against my swim trunks and trails a finger down my chest, following the line of my abs. Her hand dips lower, skimming over the waistband. I suck in a sharp breath as she palms my length through the fabric.

Slowly, teasingly, she tugs my trunks down in the front, freeing me. My dick juts out, hard and ready, and she wraps her hand around the base, stroking upward. I groan at the touch, my head falling back against the hot wood of the walls.

She shifts to kneel between my legs, and holding my gaze she parts her lips and takes me into her mouth. The feeling of her tongue swirling my tip has me rasping out a low "fuck" as jolts of electricity race down my spine. I've been dreaming of having her lips on me since the first time I saw them painted in her favorite red, but I could never have imagined quite how good it would feel.

She takes me deeper, my tip hitting the back of her throat. Harper's lips work me with slow, sensual strokes, her tongue swirling and teasing. The feeling of her mouth around my cock combined with the heat of the sauna makes me gasp. Each bob of her head takes me deeper into the wet heat of her mouth. I groan, my fingers threading through her damp hair, gently guiding her rhythm.

The sight of her lips stretched around me is the most erotic thing I've ever seen. "That feels so good," I groan.

Beads of sweat trickle down my chest from the heat, but it's nothing compared to the fire Harper is stoking inside me. She releases me from her mouth and I almost whimper at the loss of contact. But then her hand is there, stroking me base to tip as her tongue swirls around my sensitive head and over the bead of pre-cum building there. I let out a growl as she takes me deep again. I'm so damn close already, but I need to feel more of her. I pull on the string of her bikini top, the red triangles falling away to reveal her perfect breasts. I cup them in my palms, tweaking her nipples between my fingers and she moans around my shaft.

"I'm going to come," I rasp as the pressure builds.

She draws her mouth slowly up my length before she speaks. "Good. I want to taste you."

Harper doubles her efforts, sucking me faster, harder. My muscles tighten as I reach the edge. Harper looks up at me through her lashes. Our eyes lock and the raw desire in her gaze as she takes me deeper into her mouth sends me hurtling over.

"I'm coming," I growl in warning, but Harper doesn't release me as I explode, pulsing down her throat. Harper swallows every drop of me, sucking me through my orgasm, and then slowly pulls back. She gives me a coy smile and I lean my head back against the wood and close my eyes, my head spinning.

Fuck, I am so gone.

THIRTY-FOUR

HARPER

MIA: *You're still coming to Mom's for Christmas Eve and staying over, right?*

HARPER: *Wouldn't miss it!*

MIA: *Great!!! Just checking you haven't had a better offer from a sexy tight end!*

HARPER: *PJs and watching a cheesy Christmas movie? What could be better?*

Notes for feature: I think I'm falling in love with this man.

It's my final night at Oakwood Ranch and I'm surprised when we return from practice to find a lump of emotion building in my throat. Tomorrow, I'll stay at Gloria's with Mia and the rest of their family. With only a few days left of the assignment after the holiday, and Chase home for Christmas and Sunday's game, I'm not coming back to the ranch but returning to Mia's couch. The only thing making the time apart from Jake feel bearable is knowing that Mia and Edward are visiting his family on Saturday night, meaning Jake is going to join me at the apartment for a night in the city before Sunday's game.

Later, as I help Mama with dinner, my gaze wanders to the window, watching Jake outside playing fetch with Buck. Mama is humming by the stove, stirring a beef stew. The fragrant aromas filling the kitchen are making my mouth water. I scoop my hair behind one ear and almost laugh at the loose plaid shirt of Jake's I'm wearing over a tight white tank top and my jeans. I look like a different person to the journalist in the suit and stilettos that sat in this kitchen nearly five weeks ago. I feel like a different person too.

I'm not sure how much of my change is down to the beauty of the landscape and the time away from the mess of my life. Or if it's staying in a home with this family and the comfort, love, and fun I didn't experience firsthand growing up. Or how much of it is Jake and the spark of electricity I feel between us whenever he's near. All I know is that a part of me I didn't realize was broken has healed. Maybe I don't know what the future holds, but right now I'm happy.

When the table is ready, Mama hands me a glass of wine and clinks it to her own. "And you're sure you won't stay for Christmas? Dylan makes eggnog we all pretend to love and Chase forces us to sing carols by the fire, even though none of us remember the words or can carry a tune."

I laugh at the image. "Thank you, but I always spend it with my best friend, Mia, and her family. After missing Thanksgiving, I don't want to let her down. I'm sure Chase will appreciate having his room back, too."

It'll be the most time Jake and I have spent apart since I first arrived at the ranch and I know I'll miss him. But I'm excited to spend time with Mia. I'm also determined to find time for apartment hunting. The idea of having my own place is growing on me, and it has everything to do with the thought of Jake in my bed.

Mama puts her arm around me, squeezing me to her. "I understand. Well, thank you for staying with us. I'm really going to miss the female company."

A wobble of emotion catches in my throat again. "I'm going to miss it here, too." More than I can voice.

"I'm sure we'll be seeing much more of you anyway." She gives me a knowing yet reassuring smile.

My cheeks heat. "I'd like that," I say quietly as I take a sip of cold, crisp wine and watch Jake through the window. Buck is having more fun getting Jake to chase him than he is dropping the ball to be thrown again. Jake catches my eye and my breath hitches. He's wearing a light blue sweater that hugs his broad chest. Despite the cold chill of the evening, his sleeves are pushed up, revealing his strong forearms. Dark jeans mold to his muscular thighs and... other parts of him that make my mind wander to dangerous places.

A boyish smile lights up his face, and a moment later he bursts through the back door with Buck at his side.

"Perfect timing. I'm serving dinner," Mama says as Jake grabs my hand, pulling me close and kissing me lightly on the lips. A zing shoots through my body, but the moment is broken by Dylan clearing his throat. When I step out of Jake's arms, Dylan is standing in the doorway in sweats, his beard and hair unkempt as though he's only just woken.

We settle around the long table, Mama and Dylan on one side and me and Jake on the other. The pot of stew sits between us, surrounded by Mama's famous homemade bread, mashed potatoes, and bowls of steaming vegetables. We dive in and the food is as delicious as it smells. When we're finished, a tug of sadness pulls at my heart and I lift my glass.

"Thank you, Mama," I say, looking first to her and then

Dylan and Jake. "For this lovely meal and to all of you for allowing me into your home and making me feel so welcome."

Mama beams at me and takes a sip from her own wine glass. "Oh, honey. It's been an absolute joy. I'm just so glad we made the right decision in choosing you." She winks at Jake. "It's not often Jake and I disagree, but all's well that ends well."

I grin as Jake shifts uncomfortably beside me, remembering his comment on my first Friday at this table, when he mentioned expecting Kevin. He must be worried I'll be upset being reminded I wasn't the journalist he wanted, but I think it's funny. We've both let our walls down since I've been here.

I'm about to ask if it was the article on baseball I wrote at *Insight* that made Mama choose me, but then Jake takes my hand. "Thanks for sticking with me when I was a grumpy ass," he says, raising his glass. "And to the Stormhawks getting to the playoffs."

From the other side of the table, Dylan unleashes a loud sigh.

In an instant, the atmosphere shifts.

"What?" Jake demands, tension rippling between the brothers.

Dylan shrugs. "You haven't made the playoffs yet. If you lose against the Trailblazers on Sunday, you'll have to win the final game against the Steelguards to secure a playoff place. In case you haven't noticed, the Steelguards haven't lost a game this season. In fact, both teams are crushing it right now."

Jake sits back in his chair, jaw tightening. "And we're not, right? That's what you're saying."

"You've had a couple of easy wins, but your head's not in the game, Jake." Frustration edges Dylan's tone.

"That's total bull. I'm playing my best football."

"Doesn't mean your head's in the game. You're distracted." He throws me an apologetic look. "I'm sorry, Harper. For what it's worth, I think you're awesome and way too good for Jake."

I whisper a "thanks" even though it doesn't feel like a compliment so much as a dig at Jake.

"But this"—he waves a hand between us—"is distracting you. Whether you want to admit it or not. And distractions cause injuries and lose games."

Anger ripples through Jake's body, but he stays silent. Unease pushes through me. If Jake sees me as a distraction...

The thought is cut short by Dylan pulling himself to his feet, ending the conversation. "Thank you for dinner, Mama. I've got weights to do." I don't miss the limp as he moves stiffly out of the kitchen, closing the door behind him.

Jake blows out a loud exhale and rakes a hand through his hair. "I'm sorry you had to hear that," he says, shooting me a look filled with so much sorrow it melts my insides.

Mama sighs too and for the first time since I've known her, she looks deflated. "I wish you'd let me talk to him."

Jake shakes his head. "If he wants to talk to me about what really happened that night, he can. I don't want you to get involved, Mama. Dylan needs you. If he thinks you're taking my side, he'll feel even more alone than he does now."

I squeeze Jake's hand. "But it wasn't your fault."

"It doesn't change the fact that I didn't have his back the night he got injured." His shoulders drop and he swallows before turning to face me. "Hey, you OK on your own for a while? I've got something I need to do."

"Sure." I nod, hiding my disappointment. I hadn't expected to be spending my last night at the ranch alone.

I'm halfway through packing my clothes and wondering if I'll even miss Chase's Stormhawks bedspread when there's a soft knock at my door and a note slid beneath it. My name is scrawled across it in Jake's bold handwriting, followed by five words: *Meet me in the barn.*

A thrill zings through me. I grab my coat and slip silently into a cold, still night. My breath mists in the moonlight as I hurry toward the barn. Warm light spills from the open door, casting a glow across the frosted ground, and a gasp escapes my lips as I step inside. Strands of twinkling lights hang from the rafters, bathing the cavernous space in a romantic shimmer. A nest of thick blankets and cushions are spread over the ground beside a glass-cased lantern with the flame of a candle dancing inside. Two glasses and an open bottle of champagne sit in a bucket of ice nearby. And in the middle of it all stands Jake, looking utterly gorgeous. "Surprise," he says softly. "I wanted your last night to be special."

"It's magical," I whisper. I walk into his open arms and he pulls me in close, his body solid and warm. "Thank you."

Jake looks at me and his gaze is so deep, so intense, I feel like he's seeing right into my soul. He smiles, kissing me gently before reaching for the champagne. When the two glasses are full and we're sitting on the cushions he's laid out, he points to the roof.

"Look," he says and I follow his gaze to an open shutter high up in the barn. "It's the perfect view of the night sky."

I stare at the inky blackness, awash in a sprinkling of stars, bright against the dark canvas.

"Wow," I breathe. "It's stunning."

"I used to come here a lot when I wanted to think about my dad," Jake says quietly. "Being here, looking up at that big open sky—it made me feel closer to him somehow."

Emotion swells in my chest at the vulnerability in his voice, the poignant memory he's sharing with me.

Jake turns to me, eyes glinting in the light from the lantern.

I smile back at him. "And to think, I thought this was all about getting me into bed one last time before I leave," I tease.

Jake laughs, a deep rumble. "That too," he admits with a roguish grin. He sets down his glass and takes mine, placing it beside the ice bucket. Then he leans in, one hand coming up to cup my face, a thumb stroking my cheekbone. "But mostly, I just wanted to be alone with you on your last night here."

My breath catches at his words, at the undisguised longing in his gaze.

Jake's eyes drop to my parted lips. Slowly, deliberately, he lowers his head until his mouth hovers a mere whisper from mine. "Harper," he murmurs, my name a gravelly caress. "I'm going to miss you so damn much."

"I'll miss you, too."

"Does it have to be three nights?"

I laugh. "It's Christmas, remember? Chase is home. You'll forget about me. Besides, we're spending all day Saturday together and Saturday night at Mia's apartment." *Then it's the penultimate game and the end of the assignment,* I add to myself, feeling the disappointment knot in my chest.

I think Jake might kiss me, but instead he hands me my glass and taps his chest and I snuggle against him.

"When the assignment ends..." Jake says like he's reading my mind. He trails a hand down my back as I stop breathing, waiting to hear what he's going to say. "I wondered if I could take you out on a date."

A smile tugs at my lips. "That depends. What kind of date?" Like there's a chance in hell I'll be turning him down.

He makes a noise in the back of his throat. "I'm thinking... the kind of date that involves a bookstore and a really good burger and ends with a very big bath with candles and champagne."

"Hard to say no to that." I grin. And even though it isn't all the answers to what will happen next, it's something.

We sit in comfortable silence for a while. I enjoy the sharp fizz of champagne on my tongue as I lean against Jake's body and watch a plane tracking across the night sky.

"What are you thinking about?" Jake asks.

I smile. "I'm thinking about how I thought you didn't like me, and then you do something like this."

"When did you think that?" He huffs a laugh like it's the most ridiculous thing.

"After the kiss in the hotel room, you pulled away. You said we shouldn't."

He gives a half smile. "Because you wanted to keep things professional. I knew you'd put all your walls up and go into journalist mode. If promising not to kiss you was the only way to spend time with the amazing woman I was getting to know, then I was going to make it." He drops a kiss to the top of my head, his hand moving through my hair. "Why did you become a journalist?" Jake asks.

I take a sip of champagne before I reply. "Because it's what my dad did and I've always loved writing."

"But you prefer writing your novel?"

"Yes, but it's not that simple. Only the best can earn a living writing novels. I don't know if I'll even write another one."

"How do you become the best at writing novels?" he asks.

"By writing novels, I guess," I reply. "Except harder. It's like me throwing a ball around for a few weeks and then trying out to join the Stormhawks."

"True," he says. "But do you know something? I was terrible at football when I was younger."

I shove his arm. "You were not."

He makes a face.

"Really? I'm adding that to the feature."

He chuckles. "Go ahead. It's true. Every practice Mama took us to was the same. I could throw the ball, but I couldn't catch the damn thing. I kept trying to quit because I knew I was terrible, but Mama wouldn't let me. She said, 'You love football, right?' and I did. And so she said, 'We don't give up on what we love.'

"I kept going back to practice. Week after week. Month after month. Dylan would spend hours in the evening with me, just throwing the ball back and forth. Eventually, I got good at it. Then I kept practicing and practicing and then I got really good at it. What I'm saying is, I wasn't born a great football player. I wasn't destined to play in the NFL. I worked at it. I worked real hard and I still do, because it's what I love. So if writing novels is what you love, you need to keep working at it, right?"

I stare at the night sky and let Jake's words settle into me. Less than six months ago, I was packing my bags from a New York apartment I couldn't afford and coming back to Denver half destroyed. For a long time, the thought of doing anything more than sleeping on Mia's couch, hitting the gym, and then showing up at a job I didn't feel I deserved seemed impossible. I started my novel as a way to escape, knowing even as the pages filled that I was too scared of what people would think to ever try to publish it.

I know I'm stronger now. Part of that is Mia's unwavering support. She's the one person in my life who gets me, who has always had my back, no matter what. And now there's Jake too. He believes in me when I barely believe in myself. Am I prepared to put myself and my writing out into the world and see what happens? I draw in a long breath, uncertain but excited too, for a future doing what I love. A future with Jake in it.

THIRTY-FIVE

JAKE

The string lights twinkle above us as I draw Harper toward me and into a slow, tantalizing kiss. My dick starts to press against my jeans as heat builds between us. I'm always so damn ready for her...

I trail a line of kisses down her neck. "I know it's cold out here, but..."

"It is pretty cold," she replies as my hand moves over the curves of her body through her clothes. "But it's warm under these blankets."

"And we can make our own heat," I murmur.

She laughs softly, but it turns into a small gasp as my lips find the sensitive spot just below her ear. I pull her closer, our bodies pressed tight beneath the blankets. My hands slide under her sweater, meeting the smooth, warm skin of her back. I take my time exploring her body, feeling her shiver at my touch as our kiss deepens, the electricity between us sparking brighter with every passing second.

"Jake," she breathes, arching into me. The way she says my name—that need—makes my dick stir. I tug her sweater over her head and unhook her bra, freeing her perfect breasts. Her nipples are already taut in the cool air, and I lower my head, taking one in my mouth and swirling my tongue around the sensitive peak. Harper moans and tangles her fingers in my hair, tugging.

I lavish attention on her other breast before kissing a path down her body. Unbuttoning her jeans, I peel them down her legs, along with her panties. Harper shivers slightly and I grab another blanket, draping it over us, creating a private cocoon of warmth.

"You're so fucking gorgeous."

I settle between her thighs, kissing a slow path down her stomach. Her skin quivers beneath my lips, and when I reach her center, I take a moment to admire how ready she is for me too.

"Let me warm you up," I murmur against her skin before running my tongue along her slit in a long, deliberate stroke.

"Fuck," Harper whimpers, her hips lifting off the cushions.

I stroke her clit with the tip of my tongue. She's so wet, so responsive. Every sound she makes telling me she wants me to give her more. I slide a finger inside her tight heat, pumping in and out as I bring her closer to the edge with my tongue.

"Jake!" she moans as her thighs start to tremble. She writhes beneath me as I continue licking and sucking. I slide in another finger, curling them just right to hit that sensitive spot inside. Harper cries out, back arching off the ground.

"So fucking beautiful," I murmur again before sealing my lips around her clit. I pump my fingers faster, flicking my tongue rapidly. She's close, so deliciously close. Which is when I draw back, moving away and trailing my lips along the smooth skin of her inner thighs. I take my time, licking and nipping playfully, teasing her sensitive flesh before slowly returning to her center. Slowly at first, letting her pleasure build again until her thighs start to quake and tense around my head. Then I pick up speed, licking and sucking as my fingers slide into her tight, wet pussy once more.

"Jake," she cries out, but I don't stop. A few more firm strokes and she shatters with another cry, her walls clenching rhythmically around my fingers as I work her through the waves of her orgasm.

As she starts to come down, I place a final soft kiss on her center before I kiss my way back up her body until I reach her lips so she can taste herself on me.

"I need you," she whispers against my mouth. "Now."

I strip off my sweater and jeans, my cock straining as I cover her body with mine. Her warm hands roam over my chest, her nails scraping lightly against my skin as I reach for a condom from the pocket of my discarded jeans. Then her hand is on my arm, and I pause, my eyes meeting hers.

"I have an IUD," she says, her cheeks coloring a little even after everything we've just done. "If you didn't want to... I mean, we could..."

Her voice trails off, and I grin, brushing my lips against hers. "I'm good with that if you are?" I reply. "But I've never not used one before. Mama drilled consent and safety into us from the moment we hit puberty." I chuckle, shaking my head, remembering the long and awkward talks she gave me and my brothers. "Am I killing the mood?"

A playful smile touches Harper's face. "I think I can bring it back."

Before I can respond, she presses a hand to my chest, pushing me back as she straddles me. My breath catches as her soft skin brushes against me, her hand wrapping around my length.

"You're so hard," she whispers, guiding the tip of my cock to her entrance, her heat tantalizingly close. My hands move instinctively to grip her hips and bring her down over me, but she shakes her head, pushing them away. "My turn to play now."

I groan, my body aching with need.

She leans down, lips brushing my neck. "Tell me, how much do you want this?" she whispers as she pulls back, her hands running over her breasts, fingers tweaking her own nipples. One hand moves back to my dick, the tip resting just outside her pussy as she strokes a hand down the length. The feel of her touching me, of being this close to claiming her, is almost enough to make me lose my mind.

"So fucking much," I groan as she wiggles her hips, keeping me right at her hot entrance. "Harper." My jaw tightens as she moves just enough to drive me insane. "What do you want me to do?"

"I want you to tell me what you want," she replies, her voice like a challenge.

I lock eyes with her, raw hunger pulsing through me. "I want you to take my cock."

Her breath hitches, and with a sultry smile, she presses down slowly, taking my tip then stopping. "Like this?"

"Fuck. Yeah..."

Harper runs her hands over her body, wiggling a little, making sure to keep my dick just at the opening of her pussy. I grit my teeth, fighting against the burn in my groin. "What else do you want, Jake?"

"I want you to take *all* of my cock, Cassidy. Every fucking inch of it." I can't stand another second of not being inside her. I grab her thighs, pulling her down hard onto me. Heat pulses around my dick. She's so fucking wet for me and I feel it all over my length as I slide all the way to my hilt, Harper whimpering with pleasure. It's like nothing I could've imagined.

She moves then, riding me with slow, deliberate movements that make my vision blur. Each time she lifts herself, her slick heat tightens around me before sliding back down, sending shocks of need through my entire body.

"Do you like this?" she asks, her voice breathless and taunting.

"Yes," I growl, driving into her harder. "Fuck, Harper, yes."

Her cries grow louder as she moves faster, our bodies tangling together in a rhythm that pushes us both closer to the edge. When she slows, pulling herself up so just the tip of me is inside her, she leans down, her hair brushing against my face. Our lips meet in a deep, searing kiss.

"I'm done playing," I say as I nip her bottom lip with my teeth.

In one movement, I flip her over, hooking her legs over my shoulders, thrusting into her with a primal need, and now it's me in control and Harper crying out my name, begging for more.

"You want me to go harder?" I murmur, pushing deeper into her.

"Yes," she hisses as her body tightens around me. She's close to the edge. We both are.

"Come for me, Harper," I say, my voice rough and commanding as I reach a hand between us, circling her clit with my thumb. "I want to feel you come all over my cock."

Then there's nothing but the exquisite feel of Harper's pussy and the rhythm of my length pushing deeper inside her, over and over.

Harper shatters first, clenching tightly around me as she gasps my name into the night. I bury my face in the crook of her neck, muffling my groans against her skin, burying myself to the hilt and exploding into her with a guttural moan.

We cling to each other as the aftershocks slowly subside, our ragged breaths mingling in the chilly air.

I roll us to the side and Harper curls into me. In one movement, I pull the blankets around us, cocooning us in warmth once more. Harper tilts her head up and meets my gaze, her eyes luminous in the glow of the lights. I brush a strand of hair from her cheek and stroke the delicate line of her jaw.

We lie like that for a long while, exchanging gentle caresses and drinking champagne.

"This has been an amazing end to my stay," she whispers sleepily and it makes my heart swell inside my chest. I hold her close as she nuzzles into me.

"It's only the beginning for us," I say, meaning it with every part of me.

I look at Harper's face to see how she's taken my words, but her eyes are closed, her breathing even. I grin to myself. It's the most I've ever told any woman how much they mean to me, and of course Harper's asleep.

There will be other times. A lifetime. So I lie back against the cushions, this perfect woman sleeping in my arms. Thoughts of Sunday's game and my fight with Dylan are still spinning in my head, but in this moment all I can think is how much I'm going to miss Harper over the next few days and how I'm going to spend the rest of my life proving to her that she's my world.

THIRTY-SIX

HARPER

MIA: *Have fun with Jake today!!!*

HARPER: *Can't wait.*

MIA: *Glad the lovesick pining is over.*

HARPER: *I wasn't lovesick or pining.*

MIA: *Yeah right! You're annoyingly cute.*

HARPER: *You're sure you don't mind us staying in your apartment?*

MIA: *Of course not. It's only sitting empty.*

HARPER: *Have a good time! I'll miss you!*

MIA: *Ha! A good time? With Edward's stuffy family? No way! At least it's only one night. And you'll be far too busy having ALL the sex to miss me. See you tomorrow!*

A cold wind blows through my hair as I push through the doors of the Arquette Media building and onto the street. It's Saturday and the business district of Denver is quiet. Cherry Creek Mall and the shopping areas will be heaving with shoppers searching for bargains in the sales, but here it's almost deserted.

I could've waited until Monday, but with it being the weekend and Tim on vacation until after the New Year, the *Sports Magazine* floor was unsurprisingly empty, giving me time to tidy my desk and type up the rest of my notes, ready to start writing Jake's feature next week. The thought causes a ball of anxious energy to form in the pit of my stomach. There's so much riding on it for Jake. I want it to be perfect.

Ahead of me, a delivery truck trundles down the street. It snowed again on Christmas Eve and clumps of dirty snow are melting in the winter sun, leaving the sidewalk icy in places. I pull my bag over my shoulder and tuck my hands in the pockets of my thick black parka as I watch for Jake's truck.

We're meeting for coffee and a walk in the park. He's staying at Mia's with me tonight and heading straight from there to Sunday's game against the Trailblazers.

I can't wait to see him, to be in his arms. I can't wait to show him the studio apartment five blocks from Mia's I've found. Someone was supposed to move in last week but changed their mind, and now the landlord is eager for me to sign the lease. It's available straightaway if I want it.

I've thought about it all through Christmas. Even while throwing on the matching red tartan PJs Gloria made the entire family wear. Even while playing charades and eating too many chocolates. After missing Thanksgiving, it felt extra special to be with them, even if my mind was on Jake and my future the entire time. Our future. Gloria and Mia may not be my family by blood, but they're the closest I have, considering all Dad sent me was a Merry Christmas text with a cryptic message about a gift I'll know about soon. Another empty promise, I think.

"Harper?"

A shot of unease pushes through me. I know that voice and it isn't Jake's. I turn to find Scott stepping out of the doors of the Arquette Media building.

"Fancy bumping into you," he says with an unnerving smile. His brown hair is styled and he's wearing a suit, but the tie is askew and there's a shaving cut on his chin. He looks wired and unkempt.

"You look stunning as always," he says, eyes trailing over my body.

Prick.

I wrap my coat over the cute green sweater and jeans I'm wearing. "I'm waiting for someone." I glance again at the street, searching for Jake's truck.

"Ah yes, Jake Sullivan, right?" Scott says. "You enjoying slumming it with a brainless jock, Harper?"

A pulse of anger courses through me. "He's ten times the man you are, Scott. What are you doing in Denver, anyway?"

"Didn't you hear? I've got an interview for a job in sales at Arquette Media on Monday. A friend of mine works there and just showed me around. I thought I'd spend the weekend getting to know the city. I like what I see so far," he adds, smiling in a way that makes my skin crawl. "I think the corporate side of media will suit me better."

A sinking dread settles in my gut. Scott working at Arquette Media? In the same building as me? I can picture it now—seeing his smarmy, self-satisfied face smirking at me in the elevator every morning.

"Good luck with that," I say, not meaning a word as I turn away, wanting distance between us before Jake arrives. It's still in the back of my mind that I haven't been entirely honest with Jake about Scott. The thought squirms in my stomach. It's never felt like the right time to explain, but that's sounding more and more like a weak-ass excuse.

Before I can move, Scott's hand reaches for my arm. "You could put a good word in for me, couldn't you? With your friend, Mia, and her mom?"

I'm surprised by the faint note of desperation in his voice as I shrug his hand away. "Why would I do that?"

He purses his lips. "Because I could very easily tell your new editor—Tim, is it?—what it says on your HR record at *Insight.* Considering what's going on with you and Jake Sullivan now, he might be interested to know it's not your first dalliance with inappropriate behavior."

It's the exact thought I've had more than once over the last few weeks, worrying what people will think of my relationship with Jake—what Tim will do—but I'm not about to let this weasel blackmail me.

I grit my teeth and step back. "You're a piece of shit, Scott. There's no way I'm helping you." I also make a mental note to message Mia to make sure Scott doesn't get the job. "You and I both know that HR record is bullshit."

He continues like I've not spoken, tapping his chin as he speaks. "Funny how you're writing a feature on an NFL player, now I think about it. The last time I checked, you didn't know a thing about football. Didn't you always say you hated the game? You wouldn't have lied to get the job, would you, Harper?"

My cheeks flush pink and Scott's smile widens.

Fuck.

"Thought so." He steps close again. "How about we get a drink later and talk about how we can have each other's backs here."

Unease slides down my spine. I haven't been honest with Tim or Jake about my past and now it feels like it's all coming crashing down. I just never thought Scott would be the one to topple it. I've really messed up. The thought makes me want to bury my head in my hands and come clean to Jake and to Tim right here, right now. I see now I should've trusted both of them to see through the bullshit. I'll tell them everything, I promise myself. The next time I see them. And just hope they forgive me...

A car door slams from behind me, and when I turn, Jake is there. My heart leaps at the sight of him. He strides toward me, seeming somehow taller and more muscular in his fitted black wool coat. His dark hair is styled away from his face, and his stubble is trimmed, highlighting his strong jaw. But it's his eyes that take my breath away—those eyes that seem to see straight into my heart.

Jake shoots a quick, assessing glance at Scott, his eyes narrowing slightly, before he sweeps me into his strong arms. I melt against him, breathing in his woodsy citrus scent, until the rest of the world fades into nothing and there's only Jake.

He buries his face in my neck and whispers in my ear, "I've missed you so much."

"I missed you, too."

He pulls back. "Ready to go?" he asks, and I love how he's not asked why Scott is here or paid him any attention at all.

For a moment, I think we'll get away without a scene, but a second later Scott holds a hand out to Jake's and dread pools in my stomach.

"Hi, I'm a big fan. I'm Scott Harrington," Scott says followed by a pause, and then, "I was Harper's editor at *Insight*."

The world stops.

There it is. The thing I didn't tell Jake. The thing I've been trying to ignore since I returned to Denver. Scott isn't just my cheating, asshole college ex. The man my dad helped build a career for. He's also the editor I worked under during my internship at *Insight*. It was his slimy hand that reached for my thigh that night I was working late. He thought because we'd dated in college it gave him the right to proposition me.

I can't breathe. I swear the temperature drops another degree as the truth lands in the silence.

Jake ignores Scott's outstretched hand, shooting me a look. Confusion flashes in his eyes. I open my mouth to speak, to explain, but Jake gets there first.

"Harper's douchebag ex?" Jake looks back to Scott, his face a mask of calm.

Scott chuckles, not reading the tension rippling in the air. "That was a long time ago. We were all young and wanting to sow our wild oats once, weren't we? I know someone like you gets that."

A muscle ticks in Jake's jaw. "And her editor in New York?"

The first lines of worry form on Scott's brow. Like he's only just realized I might've told Jake the real reason I was fired from *Insight*. He must've thought that my humiliation in New York would stop me from telling people the truth.

Scott coughs. "Well, yes. We made a good team," he says, giving me a sharp look, reminding me of the veiled threat he just made to tell Tim his version of what happened. "In fact, knowing Harper is here is one of the reasons I thought Arquette Media would be a good fit for me. You don't mind putting a good word in for me, do you, Harper? I scratch your back and all that."

"Why do you even need my help getting a job?" I ask. "Don't you usually rely on my dad for that?"

Scott's face darkens. "Maybe you should ask him."

Realization hits. I remember the offhand comment I made about Scott at the awards dinner. I didn't think Dad was listening, but of course he was. He must've read between the lines, canceling our lunch and jumping on a plane the very next day to none other than New York. I can imagine him digging around and learning the truth...

And even though I'd prefer a dad who was in my life more—one capable of showing love like a normal father—I know he cares in his own way. It's in the stories I wrote as a child that he took with him on his trips. It's in getting Scott fired, too. Even without proof, I know he's had a hand in that from the fury in Scott's eyes. It's not conventional love from a parent. Not nearly enough. But it's something.

Suddenly Scott's desperation makes sense. It seems it was just as easy for Dad to destroy Scott's career as it was for him to build it in the first place. Now Scott wants to work at Arquette Media because it might be the only place he can get a job, if he can get a recommendation from me. The one person he thinks he can still bully...

I gather my strength, refusing to let Scott push me around. "I don't care what you say or who you say it to. I know what really happened in New York and that's all that matters. People can think what they like." My voice is as cold as the air stinging my face. I'm surprised by how true the words feel as they leave my mouth. How much I've changed in the time I've spent with Jake. I reach for Jake's arm. "Let's go," I say.

But as I'm stepping away, my foot slips on a patch of ice. The world tilts and for a split second I'm off balance, falling. Out of control. Then Jake's strong arm wraps around my waist, steadying me before I can hit the freezing sidewalk.

"I got you," he says. Of course he does.

I barely have time to flash a grateful smile before I register the clatter of noise and my bag slipping from my shoulder, the contents spilling into the slushy snow.

"Shit," I mutter, dropping to the ground and grabbing my purse. Jake kneels to help, his large hands making quick work of retrieving the pens and two lipsticks rolling toward the street. When Jake stands once more, he casts an assessing gaze first to me and then to Scott.

Whatever Scott reads in the look, he holds his hands in the

gesture of peace. "Hey," he says. "Whatever Harper has told you, there are two sides to every story. Surely you know that better than anyone?"

"Fuck off, Scott," I say before turning back to Jake. "Let's go."

Before we take a step away, a smirk twitches on Scott's face. "Bet you didn't realize your little girlfriend is quite the office slut."

Jake moves fast, taking a menacing step forward, forcing Scott to lurch back, slipping on the icy sidewalk just like I did and falling on his ass. His face is a mask of fury and hate.

Jake cocks an eyebrow. "I know a slimy fuckwit when I see one."

"I could have you charged with assault," Scott splutters.

"Look around you." Jake waves a hand to the Arquette Media building. "There are security cameras everywhere. You don't think one of them caught you falling on your ass of your own accord? And for the record, the only reason I haven't hit you right now is because you're a weedy little asshole and I'd probably kill you. But speak about Harper like that again and I won't hold back."

Jake takes my hand and moves us back.

"Your career is over, Harper," Scott hisses at me. "I thought we could help each other here, but I'm going to ruin you. You'll never work in journalism again."

From the scowl on Jake's face, he's about two seconds away from breaking Scott's nose, which would land him in a whole world of trouble because of me.

"Give me a second," I say quietly to Jake, adding strength to my voice.

Jake nods, stepping back just far enough to respect my wishes, but staying close enough should I need him. Always the perfect wingman.

When I turn to Scott, he's on his feet and brushing off the

wet snow from his coat. Even through the anger pulsing through me, I see his words for what they are—empty and desperate. I think of the love and support I have from Mia. I think of Jake's steadiness by my side. Whatever happens next, whatever Tim decides to do when we talk next week, I know I have the strength to face it.

"Actually," I say with a dark smile, "I think you'll find it's you whose career is over, Scott. You'll never get a job at Arquette Media or anywhere else I imagine, knowing how reputations have a way of spreading in this industry."

Scott's face darkens. "If I'm going down, I'm taking you with me." Then he turns away, disappearing down the street.

I move toward Jake, wanting his arms around me, wanting to say I'm sorry for not being honest about Scott. But when my gaze lands on him, his head is dipped and his focus is on a purple notebook open in his hands.

My purple notebook. With all my notes about him. All the anger and hate I wrote in those early weeks of the assignment.

Panic lances through me. It must've fallen from my bag and Jake has picked it up. He lifts his face, and when his eyes find mine, they're two dark pools of hurt. "Jake is a dick," he reads out before turning the page. "Jake hasn't changed at all. Jake deserves what's coming to him. What exactly is coming to me, Harper? What game have you been playing with me?"

THIRTY-SEVEN

JAKE

Pain carves through my chest as I scan the pages of Harper's notebook and see the words she's written about me. Her true feelings. What the hell is this?

"I can explain." Harper's voice rings out on the empty street.

I lift my gaze. Hurt and confusion battle for space in my head. Her face is pale, eyes wide with what looks like fear. Instinctively, I want to go to her, but I'm rooted to this one spot. I know we got off on the wrong foot. Hell, Harper wasn't exactly my favorite person to start with either, but the hate in these words takes my breath away. It's so much more than two people who didn't want to spend time together.

"Go on then," I say, my voice tight. "Because it's not just this I'm confused about. Why don't you start with why you lied to me about Scott? Why didn't you tell me he's both your college ex and the editor in New York who harassed you?"

Harper swallows, her hands trembling slightly at her sides. "It's not exactly something I like to talk about. Scott was my editor, but before that he was my boyfriend, and on top of that he's close with my dad. It made things complicated. When he told HR that I'd come on to him, he made this big point about how we'd dated in college, like it was evidence I would do something like that. I was humiliated and angry and hurt. I knew what people thought of me at *Insight*. They saw me as someone trying to sleep my way to a promotion. By the time I felt like I could trust you enough to open up about this stuff, we were already... growing close. I didn't want you to think I was sleeping with you to get the feature or a promotion..." She trails off, but I see where she's going and it cuts me to the bone.

I scrub a hand over my face. "You thought because Scott made up some bullshit about you, I wouldn't be able to see past that when it came to us?"

When my reputation blew up last year and I went from playboy to sleaze, it cost me. I've had to live with the knowledge that maybe I'm the reason Dylan got injured and might never play professional football again. I've had to live with people thinking and talking shit about me. The comments whispered behind my back. The disappointment in Mama's eyes when she sees a lurid bullshit headline about me. I've had to live with the grillings from Coach Allen and the Stormhawks management. The warnings to clean up my act or I'd be cut from the team. No one gave a damn the stories weren't true. But no matter how much I hate it all, it's nothing compared to how much it hurts Harper could think for one second that I'd side with a prick like Scott.

"I'm sorry," she whispers. "It was before I got to know you properly."

I shake my head, the muscles in my jaw tightening. "Maybe that's true, but you didn't tell me after you got to know me either, did you?" I tap the notebook. "You'll never trust me. You never have."

"That's not true. I—" She breaks off, shaking her head. "You weren't supposed to see that, Jake. Those were my private thoughts."

"Meaning your true feelings about me? What the hell is all this? There are *pages* of notes about how much you hate me. How writing this feature will be my downfall. 'A chance for the world to see the Jake I know him to be,'" he reads. "What did I ever do to you?"

"Look, it was a stupid thing and it doesn't even matter now." She draws in a long breath. "Back in high school... I wrote this article about you. I wasn't ever going to publish it in the school newspaper, but I poured my feelings for you into it, and I wanted you to read it before you left for college. So I slipped it into your locker." Her words come fast. "You were the only one I gave it to, so when copies of it were plastered all over school, I thought you'd done it as a joke to humiliate the person who wrote it."

"It was anonymous," I say quietly.

"Yeah, but seeing the whole school laughing at my feelings when I was already a lonely and shy kid still hurt. Then I over-heard you tell your friends—" She shakes her head. "It doesn't even matter now. Yes, at first I saw this feature as a chance to get even. But only because I thought you were a player. I thought reporting the truth would be reporting that. I was wrong. If you read—"

"For the record," I cut in, raking a hand through my hair in frustration, "I didn't make those copies. One of my idiot friends snatched your article out of my locker before I got a chance to see it, and as I've already told you, I know I was an idiot back in high school too. My friends were ripping into me about the arti-cle. What did you think I was going to tell them?"

"I know that now. It was easier to blame you for my insecu-rities and all the things that weren't going well in my life after high school than it was to admit I needed to change."

Tears pool in Harper's eyes and I find I have to clench my

hands by my side to stop myself reaching for her. Even now, when I'm hurting this bad, when I'm so fucking pissed, I still want to protect her.

She takes a shaky breath. "This isn't an excuse, but you have to admit, you weren't exactly welcoming at the start. You hated me from the moment I set foot on the ranch. Of course I thought you were still that same boy from high school. But then I got to know you and I saw you weren't like that. I realized I was the idiot for holding on to a high school grudge. I changed my mind, Jake. *You* changed my mind. Look at the rest of the notebook. Look at what else I've said about you."

"I think I've read enough." I take a step back, needing distance.

"Please, Jake," she cries. "Look at the rest of the notebook. The feature is going to be the truth. It's going to be about the man who I thought was nothing more than his reputation, but in getting to know him, I found not only was I wrong, but that you are someone who cares about others, who is kind and generous and everything this world needs in a human. You have to trust me."

We stand in silence. I want to believe Harper, but how can I trust what she's saying after she's lied to me? All I can hear is the betrayal roaring in my ears. Those words from her notebook spinning in my head.

Jake is a dick.

Jake hasn't changed at all.

Jake deserves what's coming to him.

I've never let anyone in. I've never wanted to. But for the first time in my life, I actually give a damn what someone thinks about me. And this is what I get. My heart feels like it's tearing down the middle. I swore I'd never let myself feel hurt like this again after my dad.

I take another step back. "You want me to trust you when

you've been lying to me this entire time? Trust you like you trust me, you mean?"

I drop the notebook back to the ground and stride to my truck. Harper calls out and I falter, because a part of me wants to go back and hear her out—believe what she's saying. But another, larger part of me wants to be as far away from this street, from Harper, and this hurt as I can get.

THIRTY-EIGHT

HARPER

"And you haven't spoken since?" Mia asks the next day as she drops onto the couch beside me after I finish telling her what happened with Jake. She only arrived home from her visit to Edward's family ten minutes ago and hasn't even taken her jacket off yet.

A look of horror crosses her face as I shake my head.

Before I can explain, Edward clears his throat from the doorway. "I'm going to leave you ladies to it and check my emails."

Mia gives him a grateful look.

"While you're both here, I want to say thanks again for letting me stay here for the last few months." I look between them. "I signed the lease on the studio apartment today, so I'll be out of your hair in a couple of days." I look around the living room and the place which has become my haven once again this week. Mia's penthouse apartment might only have one bedroom, but it's by no means small. The rooms are huge and decorated in Mia's eclectic taste of vintage and modern. There's an antique brass floor lamp in the corner and a sleek glass coffee table in front of the couch. Bright green wallpaper with pink flamingos on it covers one wall and there's a fluffy white rug on the floor. Somehow it works with the huge L-shaped couch I'm sitting on that takes up two walls. It's a gorgeous, dark green velvet, the color of the spruce trees bordering the lake at the ranch. Fuck, everything reminds me of the ranch now...

Edward smiles, pushing his glasses higher on his nose. "No thanks needed and no rush. We like having you here. Mia is much happier when you are." I wonder if I imagine the barbed edge to his comment, but he's gone and Mia is talking before I can question it.

"I love you, Harper, but you're an idiot. You need to talk to Jake and clear this up," she says with a shake of her black braids.

Disappointment lies heavy in my gut. I know I'm in the wrong. I should've told Jake the full truth about Scott and trusted him to take my side. And maybe I shouldn't have written all my negative thoughts about Jake in my notebook. But we both hated each other at the start. As soon as I saw who Jake really was, my thoughts and my notes changed, and with it any idea that the feature would act as payback disappeared. But that doesn't change the fact I hurt him, and I'm the first person he's ever let in like this... I can't imagine what he's thinking—or if he'll ever be able to let me back in.

I sigh. Frustration and hurt battle for space in my mind. I know it was hard for him to open up—it was hard for me too—but if what we had was the start of something special, how can he walk away from it so easily?

"Look," Mia says, giving my hand a gentle squeeze, "I get that you and Jake didn't exactly hit it off. And I can see why your notebook would say some pretty scathing things about him—"

"It says a lot of good things too if he'd bothered to look," I cut in.

"Yeah, except he'd just been blindsided with the whole Scott being your editor thing. And by the way, Scott is never working at Arquette Media. But you can't really blame Jake for not wanting to listen straightaway, can you?"

I groan, hollow sadness stretching inside me. I've spent the last twenty-four hours flipping from angry to sad. Fuming at Jake for not giving me more time to explain and show him the rest of my notebook. It's been easier than facing up to the fact that I've fucked everything up by not being open with him. In five minutes with my best friend, everything seems different. Clearer.

I really have been an idiot. I draw in a long breath and try to explain. "What happened with Scott was the most humiliating thing that's ever happened to me and I'm only just putting my life back together. Not telling Jake was more about me than him."

"But did you explain that to him?" Mia asks with a pointed look. The same look she gave me when I cried on her bed over Jake ten years ago. *How do you expect him to know who you are if you won't walk up to him and say hi?* She had a point then too.

I bury my head in my hands. "No. I didn't get the chance, and I tried to call but he didn't answer," I say in a muffled voice.

"Believe me, I'll be having a word with him about answering his phone when I see him later."

My head shoots up. A spark of something ignites in my chest. Excitement? Hope? "You're seeing Jake later?"

She looks at her watch and nods. "And so are you if you get in the shower and make yourself look less like you've spent all day wallowing on this couch with a family-sized bag of Cheetos."

"You know me so well." I smile. "But how are we—"

"We'll miss the start, but we can still get to the skybox to watch some of the game and you can see Jake afterward. And then the two of you can talk properly, even if I have to bang your heads together."

"Will you be allowed in?"

Her cackling laugh fills the living room. "I'm a VP at the biggest media firm in Colorado. You don't think I get a pass to every event in Denver? So what are you going to do?" she adds like there's only one answer.

I hesitate. I know I have to be the one to make the first move, but what if Jake rejects me? What if it really is over? What if he thinks I'm the worst human in the world? Except the Jake I know would never think that. He's wrong. I do trust him. I trust him to be the man I've come to know over the last five weeks.

I give a slow nod. "Everything else aside, today's my last day covering Jake for the feature, so I really should be at that game anyway."

"Right, then." She stands and pulls me from the couch. A Cheeto falls from my lap onto the floor and we both laugh before I hurry to the bathroom to shower and change.

As the warm water cascades over me, my head spins with thoughts of Jake. We barely saw each other yesterday. I've missed his teasing smile, the way his eyes light up when he looks at me. Most of all, I've missed the way he makes me feel—cherished, understood, alive in a way I never have before.

I turn off the water and wrap myself in one of Mia's fluffy towels. When I catch my reflection in the mirror, my eyes are troubled and unsure but there's still that spark of hope, that need to hurry. Maybe I've blown my chance with Jake, but I owe it to myself and him to find out.

I dress quickly in woolly tights, a cute denim skirt and my red Stormhawks tee beneath a black cardigan, teamed with a pair of heeled ankle boots. I swipe on some mascara and add concealer beneath my eyes. I don't have time for anything else except to add my favorite red lipstick, grab my notebook, and hurry out the door with Mia.

Mia's clarity has strengthened my resolve. I need to apologize to Jake for not being honest about who Scott was from the start. I'll do a better job of explaining my vulnerability, and I'll force Jake to read the rest of my notebook. My stomach knots remembering the hurt in his eyes. I need to make him see that I don't think that way about him anymore. Looking back, I'm not sure I ever truly did. It was easier to blame my failings and bad choices on one past event—on Jake—than it was to face them head on. I've been such a fool. And yet, the flickers of a smile touch my lips as we hit the parking garage and stride to Mia's Lexus. I'm already imagining Jake seeing me from the field, shooting me that smile. Then later, the way he'll pull me into his arms and we'll be alright again.

THIRTY-NINE

JAKE

Shouts and whistles pierce the air as I charge onto the field with the team, cleats crunching on the frozen turf, my breath fogging in the cold air. The stands are a sea of red and white, and even though I told myself I wouldn't, my gaze flicks to the skybox. Families and friends stand in front of the glass alongside a few celebrity fans. I spot a country singer and an actor from *Game of Thrones.*

I see Mama's gray-blonde head of hair and Dylan's hulking frame beside her. It's the first Stormhawks game he's come to since his injury. I know he's here for Chase and not me. It's a kick in the gut, but it's nothing compared to the knowledge that Harper isn't beside them. No beautiful smile. No Stormhawks tee clinging to her perfect curves. And even though I didn't think I wanted her here, didn't think she'd come, disappointment and regret snake through me.

Our fight races through my mind as I take my position. After all the time we spent together, getting closer than I've ever let anyone, I thought she saw the real me. But maybe it was all a ploy to get me to open up for the feature. Was her plan all along to write something bad about me because she's always hated my guts?

The questions are followed by a whispered voice, reminding me that I didn't exactly make it easy for her at the start. I was rude and arrogant and pissed at having a journalist up my ass for five weeks. Maybe some of her notes were justified, but not all of them. And maybe deep down I know there was nothing fake about the way Harper looked at me on our last night in the barn. Nothing fake about the electricity that shoots through me when we touch. But as I drag my eyes away from the skybox for a final time and slip on my helmet, I remind myself I have a right to be angry. The question is—can I get past it?

I sigh and force my thoughts to settle. All I've done today is think about our fight. I need to focus. Our chance of making the playoffs if we don't win today feels impossible. We need this win.

We take our positions opposite the bright white jerseys of the Trailblazers. Across the field, I see Chase in his crouch, ready. For the next sixty minutes, he isn't my brother, or me his. We're opponents both fighting for this win.

The whistle blows, and the game begins with the kickoff. The Trailblazers kicker sends the ball soaring high into the air. It arcs against the stadium lights before descending toward our end zone. The kick returner signals for the return, and catches, tucking it tight as he charges forward. The Trailblazers defense swarms, but he powers through to the twenty-five-yard line before they bring him down.

Adrenaline courses through me. It's time to make our first drive. My fingers flex inside my gloves, muscles coiled and ready. The ball is snapped, and we're in motion. Billy executes a perfect pass that spirals into Rob's hands. A split second later, he's speeding down the field. I charge forward, ready to block, taking out a linebacker coming from his right side. This is where I'm most alive—in the heat of the game with a stadium full of screaming fans. The Trailblazers defense comes at us with everything they've got. We're stopped short of the red zone, so JT comes in for the field goal. He kicks it and the ball arcs through the air, slicing through the uprights for three points. The crowd roars. The scoreboard lights up. The score is 3-0 to the Stormhawks.

We battle back and forth. A touchdown and extra point from the Trailblazers puts them in the lead. 3-7. Then a touchdown from Rob followed by the extra point to make it 10-7. We're winning, but it's tight and it's relentless. Sweat pours down my forehead despite the cold. As we take our positions for the third quarter, it's a tie at 17-17. Just before I pull my helmet on, I can't stop my gaze from dragging back to the skybox. Even from the field, I can see the tension radiating from Mama and Dylan. Then a swish of glossy brown hair catches my eye. Is that Harper? Before I can look again, the ref is calling for the quarter to start. I clip my helmet and try to focus.

Trailblazers have possession. The ball snaps and Chase drops back, eyes scanning the field. He launches a long pass, sailing high over our defenders. It's good. Their wide receiver leaps, snagging the ball out of the air. He hits the ground running, weaving through tackles. He makes the twenty-yard line, the ten, the five. Our safety dives, but it's too late. Touchdown.

They line up for the extra point, and it's good. 17-24. We're down by seven.

Fuck!

My heart pounds in my chest as we line up for the fourth quarter. We're so close to the playoffs. I can feel the pressure mounting as we huddle. My eyes flick to the skybox again. I swear I saw Harper. Those red lips. That Stormhawks tee Mama gave her.

I have to focus. The game. It's all that matters right now.

We drive the ball forward, closing the gap 20-24 with a field goal. We have possession with minutes on the clock. We need a touchdown. The huddle breaks, and Billy takes his place behind the center. He calls out the cadence, voice steady despite the pressure we're all feeling. I line up, heart hammering, eyes locked on the defense, looking for coverage shifts or signs they'll blitz and charge, trying to disrupt play. The ball snaps again and Billy drops back. The pocket holds. His arm cocks and the ball spirals through the air to a spot ahead of me. My legs pump as I charge downfield, hands reaching, catching the ball and tucking it tight as I pick up speed.

Thirty yards. The Trailblazers defense comes at me, but I see a gap. My cleats dig into the turf and I slip through, adrenaline surging. Twenty yards. I hear the roar of the crowd, the pounding of my heart. Two safeties close in. I search for one of my team, but I've raced ahead and I'm alone.

I fake left and cut right, but they're ready. One safety brushes my jersey—a near miss. I'm so close. Ten yards. Five. The end zone looms. One safety left, and he's in my path. I need this win. Not just for the Stormhawks and the playoffs. But for me. I need to prove to Dylan I'm not distracted.

I can make it.

I can—

The thought is knocked from my head as a savage weight slams into me. The breath whooshes out of my lungs as we crash to the ground. Pain erupts across my body. I stretch my arm out as far as it will go, desperate to cross the line, but the ref's whistle blows. I'm just inches short.

The clock hits zero.

We've lost the game.

The safety pulls himself up, his hand out for me to take. I try to reach for it, but white-hot pain explodes from my neck. Something is wrong. I can't move. Faces appear around me. Billy and then Chase, kneeling down, a hand gripping mine. As they stretcher me off the field, I catch a glimpse of the skybox again. It is Harper. I can see her face clearly now. Her hands covering her mouth. Our eyes meet for a split second before I'm carried into the tunnel and all I can think is that my head wasn't in the game. If I'd gone left instead of right, I could've made it. I can see my path to the end zone so clearly. I let Harper distract me. I made the wrong choice. I lost us the game.

The room is finally quiet. Mama has gone to find the doctor and the X-rays on my neck we're waiting for. I'm flat on my back, a fat white collar around my neck, and a warning not to move. I stare at the ceiling and try not to think about how bad it is, but my thoughts take me to dark places of never playing again. Never walking again. I close my eyes and grit my teeth to the anger and fear pounding through my body.

I don't hear the door open and close, but I catch the scent of Harper's wildflower perfume, and a second later, her soft fingers squeeze my hand. I don't squeeze back. Not because I can't, but because I won't. If she'd trusted me, if we hadn't fought, if my mind had been on the game instead of her, would we have won? If we'd never crossed the line from professional to something else, would I be lying on my back right now, my entire future uncertain?

"Jake?" she says, emotion quivering in her voice.

I open my eyes and look at her. Harper's hair falls around her face, her eyes bright with tears. Faint mascara lines streak down her face, and yet she's still beautiful. My chest aches, but only one thought fills my mind. I let myself get distracted. I lost us the game and maybe our place in the playoffs for the first time in four years. It might not be Harper's fault, but it doesn't make it easy to look at her right now. So I do the only thing I can do—I close my eyes.

"How are you feeling?" she asks.

"Like I've had two hundred and fifty pounds of muscle slam into my body."

"Is there anything I can do?"

Leave, I think, barely managing to keep the word in.

She squeezes my hand again. "Jake, talk to me."

"There's nothing to say." My voice is gravelly. My mouth is dry, but I'm not about to ask Harper to get me ice chips.

"I'm sorry for what happened yesterday," she blurts out. "I'm sorry I didn't tell you about Scott and I'm sorry for the notes I made before I got to know you. I'm sorry I ever thought this article would be payback for a stupid thing back in high school that wasn't even your fault. I brought my notebook. Let me—"

"Doesn't matter," I reply through gritted teeth.

"But if you'd listen—"

"I'm all good."

A tense silence fills the room. I hate the feeling of Harper's hand in mine. I don't want her apologies or her pity.

"You should go," I say.

"I want to stay."

"The assignment's finished. You've got what you need from me. There's nothing left for us to say so just go, Harper. Go back to your life and I'll go back to mine." My chest feels like it's cracking open, but I lean into it, relishing the hurt.

"Please don't push me away." Her voice is quiet, almost a whisper. I can hear her pain. It makes me want to reach for her, bury my face in her hair. But I can't move. Fear and frustration boil over into hot rage.

"You shouldn't have come," I push again. "You're a distraction, Harper. I never should have let things go this far between us." I force myself to look at her. I'm many things, but I'm no coward. If I'm going to inflict pain on someone, I'm going to face it head on.

Hurt flashes in her eyes but she doesn't let go of my hand.

"You don't mean that. I know you're scared right now, but pushing me away won't help."

"Won't it?" I growl. "Ever since you waltzed into my life, I haven't been able to think straight. I was off my game tonight because I couldn't stop thinking about our fight, and look what happened."

"That's not fair," she says quietly. "You can't put this on me."

"My head hasn't been right since the moment I met you. You've fucked everything up, Harper. My focus, my career. I might never play again because I let myself get distracted by you!" Then I drive the final nail into the coffin of our relationship. "We were nothing. Just some fun. This..." I grit out through the lump in my throat, "It was a challenge to see if I could get you into bed and I did, so you might as well go."

"You don't mean that," she says, finally dropping my hand, backing away.

"The hell I don't."

Tears streak down her face but she steps to the door without a word. A sudden panic seizes my chest. I want to beg her to stay, but my anger wins out. A red mist covering my thoughts. I lost the game. I was distracted. I don't know what's going to happen with my injury. These thoughts spin on an endless loop. There's no room for Harper's feelings, for her at all in my mind right now.

When she's gone, I lie in the silence for a long time, waiting for a relief that doesn't come. Mama returns with the doc and it's only when I catch the smiles on their faces that something eases in me, a knot loosening.

"Good news, Mr. Sullivan. The tackle caused a pinched nerve. It can be excruciatingly painful, but not serious. I'm going to send the team physical therapist in to manipulate your neck, and with some rest and some meds, you'll be fine."

"Can I play in next week's game?"

"There's no reason why you shouldn't be able to. If the nerve moves back into place and I expect it will, you should be back to normal in no time."

I close my eyes, relief sweeping through me, ice-cold wind to the red mist of anger.

"Let's get the neck brace off you now we know there's no spinal damage." The doc frees me from the brace and I reach a hand slowly to my neck. A sharp pain shoots down my left shoulder, bad enough to twist my gut, but at least I'm moving.

An hour later, the physical therapist has worked his magic and I'm sitting up in the bed, waiting for Mama to finish talking to the team docs and drive me home. When the door opens, my heart lurches with hope that takes my breath away. It crashes down at the sight of Dylan in the doorway. I sigh and close my eyes. A lecture from my big brother is the last thing I need.

"I come in peace," he says.

I tentatively open one eye and he huffs a laugh.

"I mean it," he says as he drops into the chair beside the bed. "How are you feeling?"

"Like a ton of bricks landed on my neck, but the doc says I'm good."

He nods. "You always were a lucky son of a bitch."

"Yeah." Something makes me think of Dad in that moment. How he saved my life the night of the storm but lost his in the process. The memory consumes me in a familiar grief. Like always it's tangled with a raw, unforgiving guilt. I'm the reason my father died. Harper's voice plays in my mind.

I bet anything, even if he knew the outcome, he'd still have done it a thousand times over.

Her words are a soothing ointment, despite everything going on between us. I take a shuddering breath and let the guilt go for now.

Beside me, Dylan shifts in the chair, his hulking frame looking out of place in the small room. He clears his throat, eyes darting around before finally settling on me. "Look, Jake, I owe you an apology."

I raise my brows. Dylan apologizing? That's a first.

He rubs a hand over his face, the scruff of his beard rasping against his palm. "I've been a real asshole to you. Ever since my injury, it's been easier to blame you than accept what happened. Seeing you out there tonight, watching you go down, I was terrified you were injured. It made me realize how awful I've been."

I swallow past the lump in my throat. I want to brush off his words, make a joke like I always do, but something in his eyes stops me.

"I finally talked to Coach while we were waiting for news on your neck," Dylan continues. "He told me what really happened with the cheerleaders. How you were trying to help them and it blew up in your face. I should've known better than to believe the stories in the press. I should've had your back."

"Yeah, you should've," I say, the words coming out harsher than I intend.

Dylan nods, accepting the jab. "You're right. I let my anger cloud my judgment. Then when Coach moved you to tight end, I felt like you'd stolen my dreams."

"It's not like I had a choice. I didn't ask to be tight end."

"I know. But all I kept thinking was, even if I make it back from this injury, I don't have a position to come back to."

"Coach had to fill it, Dylan."

"Yeah. I'm not saying my thoughts were logical, alright? I'm just trying to explain."

I ignore the shooting pain and clap a hand on his shoulder. "I'm sorry, too. I wanted to protect you in that game."

He shrugs. "Could've happened anyway and we both know it. I'm sorry, Jake. Truly. And hey, if things go to plan, we'll be playing together again next season."

I study my brother's face, the sincerity in his eyes. Then I smile. "If I'd realized all I needed to do was get my neck crushed for you to stop being the world's grumpiest ass, I'd have done it months ago."

He laughs. A deep, booming chuckle I've missed hearing. "Well, that and Harper giving me shit."

"Harper?" Even her name has my heart lurching.

A smile tugs at Dylan's mouth. "She didn't tell you? We bumped into each other in the kitchen the other night at the ranch and she gave me a talking to. God knows why, but she's crazy about you. Really has your back."

I think of the notes I read and our fight, and the thought of her having my back rails against me. But then I think of the hurt in her eyes as she walked out the door earlier. My heart sinks with shame as I realize I've done the same thing Dylan did to me—I pushed Harper away. Blaming her for my own failings, or for something nobody could have helped.

"Where is she?" Dylan asks, glancing around the room as if he expects her to materialize out of thin air.

I look down at my hands, regret burning through me. "I might've made it sound like I blamed her for me getting injured."

Dylan shakes his head. "You fucking idiot." He stands and makes his way to the door. "Well, are you coming? Or are you going to sit here and wallow all night?"

I ease myself from the bed, gritting my teeth to the throbbing ache in my neck. And that's when I see Harper's notebook sitting on the edge of the bed. Her words from earlier this week whisper in my ear.

Look at the rest of the notebook. Look at what else I've said about you.

Tentatively, I lift the cover, skipping past the first pages of her anger, and read on. The words swim in front of my eyes. Pages and pages of stories I told her and observations.

Jake doesn't even realize the kind things he does. Helping Mama with the shopping. Opening his truck door for me.

Jake Sullivan is the best wingman anyone could ask for.

Jake Sullivan has spent his life wanting the approval of one man—his father. With Harry Sullivan's tragic death when Jake was just ten years old, it seems as though Jake coped by deciding that without his father, he wouldn't be seeking approval from anyone else. Jake will say he doesn't care what anyone else thinks of him, and while a part of that is true, it's important to recognize that not caring what people think isn't the same as not caring, because Jake cares deeply about his family, football, and his friends.

And then my gaze lands on the last entry and it steals my breath.

I think I'm falling in love with this man!

I scrunch my eyes shut, a well of emotion gripping me by the throat. I see it so clearly. Harper is the best thing that's ever happened to me, despite how things might have started out between us. There's a reason she's the first person whose opinion I care about. The first woman I've let see beyond the bravado. She's funny and smart and cute as hell. And maybe she isn't perfect. Maybe she makes mistakes, but that makes two of us. Because I just told her she means nothing to me.

And when I think of the hurt flashing in her eyes, I realize I've just made the biggest mistake of my life.

FORTY

HARPER

JAKE: *I'm really sorry for what I said.*

JAKE: *Can we talk?*

JAKE: *Please meet me.*

JAKE: *The team is going to New York early for some press events ahead of Sunday's game. We're leaving today. Can we please talk when I'm back?*

It's the first day back in the office after New Year's and everyone is quiet. The atmosphere is sullen. People staring down the barrel of a long, cold January, wishing they'd booked the extra vacation and started the year next week. I'm the only one glad to be back. Routine and focus. That's what I need.

I've spent the last five days avoiding Jake's attempts to contact me. I stayed nearby even after he'd pushed me away, just until I'd spoken to Mama and knew he was OK. She gave me a tight hug and told me she'd see me soon, and I turned away before she could see my tears. I get that he was upset, but those words came from somewhere real.

We were nothing. Just some fun. It was a challenge to see if I could get you into bed and I did.

Maybe someone else in my position could forget it. Chalk it up to a moment of anger. But I can't. I don't have a big life, a big family, people I can depend on. But for a while, I thought I had Jake. For the first time in my life, Mia wasn't the only one I could turn to, and that meant something. And now he's gone. In his wake is a hollow emptiness. A reminder of how so very alone I am in this world.

I've buried myself in my novel this week, turning down Mia's invite to a New Year's Eve party and staying home alone, escaping into my characters. I wrote the final chapter this morning before work, the words pouring out in a rush of emotions as my characters found the happy ever after I couldn't. The novel is finished and the excitement I feel is almost enough for me to ignore the emptiness. When I first started writing this novel, it was in secret. I was embarrassed, telling myself it was just a distraction and I'd never do anything with it. But now... I don't know what the future holds for me and my writing career, but I know I'm going to carry on. Jake might not be in my life anymore, but I know his confidence has rubbed off on me. I no longer care if people think I'm a sellout. Writing sexy vampire stories makes me happy and that's all that matters.

I wish Jake's feature would write itself just as easily. I've spent the morning at my desk, staring at the blank screen of my computer. I have all the notes I typed up over the weekend. I have funny anecdotes, quotes, and memories from his child-hood. But I no longer have the direction. The feature Tim is expecting is one which starts with me believing Jake is his repu-tation, then me seeing the real Jake—the man behind the bravado—who is kind and sweet. Except after Jake told me I was just a challenge, I don't know how true that is or how to write this feature. I can't bring myself to write either version—the one where Jake is good, or the one where he isn't.

If I could find that perfect opening line, I think the rest will follow. I know a part of me is reluctant to start because starting will lead to finishing. The feature on Jake is the final thread that holds us together. Despite the hurt, I'm struggling to let it go. Let *us* go. Yet I couldn't answer the phone when he called. Another number has been calling too that I don't recognize and I haven't dared answer in case it's Jake.

Mia called last night to tell me Jake stopped by her apartment yesterday. With our fight and then Jake ending things between us for good, I didn't get the chance to tell him I'd found my own apartment. The studio is small but airy, overlooking a park. It's only a few blocks from the gym and Mia's place. When I first saw it, I thought of me and Jake dividing our time between the city and the ranch. I even wondered if Buck would like the park, but it's just me now. Mia has helped me shop for furnishings and already it's a mishmash of colors. If I block out the beauty of the ranch—those green paddocks, the lake, and the distant mountains—the apartment almost feels like home.

My eyes drag to my phone and the empty screen. Jake's message from this morning is still there. He's leaving for New York. This weekend is the final game of the season. It's against the undefeated Steelguards. The Stormhawks need this win to make the playoffs. Despite everything, I want it for them. For him.

I steel myself with a deep breath and focus on my computer and the blank document waiting to be filled. *Just start typing*, I tell myself. *Damn you, Jake Sullivan. Why did you have to make me fall for you?*

There's a shout of joy from the office kitchen and I look up, glad for the distraction. It's Callie. "Oh my God, there are donuts. Whoever brought these is my new best friend."

She pokes her head of red curls around the door as I hide my smile.

"Alison, was it you?"

The senior reporter shakes her head. "The only thing I leave in the kitchen in January is salad. But I'm starving, so I'll take a donut. Diet starts next week, I guess."

"Kevin?" Callie asks like she already doesn't believe it.

"Yeah, right," he scoffs. "But if you're offering one."

Eventually her eyes land on me and I give a wave. "Hey, bestie."

She looks taken aback. "You bought donuts for the office?" she asks with the same level of disbelief as if I'd announced Taylor Swift was my sister.

I shrug. "First day back after New Year's. I thought we could all do with the boost."

Alison gives a cheery thanks, her mouth already full of sugary dough, and Callie offers me a tentative smile. Not smug. Not mean. Just nice. I almost fall off my chair.

"Thanks, Harper."

For the first time, I wonder if the cold shoulder she's always given me is less to do with her and the fact we're competing for the same job, and more to do with how much I've been hell-bent on keeping my head down, acting professional, and making sure no one learns the truth about my football knowledge or that I was fired from *Insight*. It's quite possible my behavior has been misread as cold-hearted bitch.

I cringe inwardly as Callie takes her seat at the desk across from mine, placing a donut and a coffee on my desk.

"Thanks," I say.

"How's the feature going?" she asks.

"Good," I reply instinctively before slumping back in my chair and looking at Callie. "The truth?"

She gives a nod of encouragement.

"It's hard. I've got so much I want to say, but..." I trail off, unable to explain the mess of my thoughts.

"You'll get there," she says. It might be the nicest thing she's ever said to me.

"As long as you've got your red pen ready," I say, my tone light as I remember the marked-up notes left on my desk last month.

She snorts. "Just a little joke," she says with a smirk.

"It got me, too. But..." I narrow my eyes a little. "That hotel room you booked for me in Atlanta, did you cancel it the morning I was due to stay there?" The answer doesn't matter now, but I'd like to know.

"What?" She looks aghast. "No way! Seriously, Harper. I might not be your biggest fan, but canceling your hotel room would've been a step too far."

I laugh and remember the desk clerk mentioning a computer glitch. "Good to know."

"What did you do?" Callie asks. "Did you find another room? I had so much trouble getting you that one because there was—"

"An Irish dance competition," we say in unison.

My cheeks heat remembering that night with Jake and our first kiss. "Don't worry. I found something."

"Good." She smiles, turning back to her computer. "Hopefully that something involved a gorgeous football player."

My mouth drops open and she flashes me a wide grin. "Oh, come on. I saw the story about the two of you. I'd totally have done the same if I was given half a chance to fall in love with a hunky tight end."

Heat creeps over my cheeks, but I smile. I've been so worried about trying to prove I was a professional, maybe I should've spent more time being myself and trusting people to like me.

It occurs to me that whatever bridge is being built between

me and Callie is too little, too late. I glance toward Tim's office. He's gone to a meeting with management on the twenty-fourth floor, but when he's back, he wants to see me. No matter what Callie says, I crossed a line with Jake, and Tim has every right to be mad about that. It's not just my reputation, it's the reputation of the magazine too.

I sigh. Even if I come away from it with my job intact, I'm going to come clean about lying in my interview and allowing Tim to believe I knew as much about football as I do about other sports. I avoided anything to do with football after high school and my misguided hate toward Jake, but even with everything falling apart between us, I can't deny I love the game.

I'll offer to finish the feature on Jake, take my name off the byline, and clear out my desk. It's the right thing to do. There's only one position for a junior reporter on the magazine and it belongs to Callie.

I'm about to tell Callie that Jake and I are over, but then the elevator pings and Tim is striding across the floor, face like thunder. I freeze, pulse roaring in my ears. Walking beside him, a smug grin on his face, is Scott.

Mia shut down Scott's interview chances last week. There's no job for him at Arquette Media. So what the hell is he doing here? Scott glances my way, and in the knowing look he shoots me, I have my answer. Anger floods my body. He thinks he's here to take me down.

"Harper," Tim barks across the floor. "My office, please."

My legs are jelly, but I stand and keep my head high as I straighten my skirt and walk into Tim's office. No doubt Scott will have told Tim his version of New York. And he'll have told him I lied about my football knowledge. I hate that he's getting there before I've had the chance to do it myself.

"Take a seat, Harper." Tim waves to one of the chairs, his voice tight.

I perch on the edge of the chair, hoping I look more poised

than I feel. Scott throws himself into the other chair, slouching back like he owns the place. He examines his nails with a bored expression.

Tim pinches the bridge of his nose before fixing me with an intense stare. "Scott has told me something very disturbing, Harper."

My breath catches in my throat, but I force my voice to sound strong. "Tim, I can explain—"

He holds up a hand, cutting me off. "Let me finish." He turns his steely gaze on Scott. "This man has made some serious allegations against you. Suggesting you sexually harassed him in his workplace in New York."

Of course he did.

Scott sits forward. "You only have to look at how quickly she jumped into Jake Sullivan's bed to see she uses sex to get what she wants."

"Shut up, Scott," I hiss through gritted teeth, earning me another shit-eating grin from the man beside me.

Tim fixes Scott with a cold stare. "Let me finish. I happen to know that these allegations are bullshit for two reasons. First of all, I know Harper. I know the dedicated, hardworking journalist she is. I don't know you"—he points to Scott—"and I have no reason to believe you over one of my employees. And even if that wasn't the case, there's the second reason. I've also had a woman by the name of Genevieve Rose leave me several messages this week."

The name rings a bell, but I can't think why. Whoever she is, Scott's face pales.

"Genevieve is the head of HR for the media group that owns *Insight*. Apparently, she's been calling you, Harper, but you haven't picked up. She looked you up and found you were working here, which is why we spoke first thing this morning. It appears you were dismissed from your internship following allegations of sexual harassment from Mr. Harrington."

A smile twitches at the edges of Scott's face. I don't miss the look of relief either.

"However," Tim continues, "it has come to the attention of HR that these allegations are most likely entirely false. Following Mr. Harrington's dismissal a few weeks ago, several employees have now felt able to come forward with their own allegations against Mr. Harrington. Given the number of complaints, they're now looking back and considering that the one against you was also probably made up. Genevieve has asked you to call her to discuss reinstating your internship should you want it, although of course I'd rather you stayed here."

My mouth drops open. *Insight* wants me back. My dream life in New York is mine for the taking. I draw in a sharp breath, unable to fully process everything Tim has said.

Scott clears his throat. "The allegations against me will all prove false, I can assure you. What is undeniable, however, is that Harper has also lied to you to get this job. She might be a sports journalist but she knows nothing about football. Trust me. I'm afraid you've been manipulated, Tim." Scott smirks, despite the beads of sweat forming on his brow.

A dark rage bubbles inside me, but I force it down. He isn't worth a single drop of my energy.

"I'm well aware of Ms. Cassidy's experience, Mr. Harrington. So if there's nothing else, there's the door." He points across the room.

My head snaps up. *Tim knows? How?*

"Wh-what?" Scott splutters. "But she lied to you."

"I can call security to show you out if you can't find the way yourself," Tim says by way of reply as he flashes me a brief smile. There's a warmth there, a trust, that brings a lump of emotion to my throat.

Scott mutters something under his breath before striding to

the door and out of the office. I stay where I am as Tim stands
and closes the door before addressing me again.

"Harper—"

"I'm sorry," I blurt. "I was in a really bad place after being
fired in New York. I was desperate to prove myself. I'm sorry I
didn't tell you that I didn't know a thing about football."

Tim looks at me in the same way I imagine he does his children when they're in trouble. It's stern but not unkind. "Do you
think I didn't know you were full of shit, Harper? I've been
working in sports journalism for over twenty years. You evaded
every single question about football I asked, always bringing the
answer back to baseball and hockey."

I make a face before I ask the next question. "Why did you
hire me then?"

"Firstly, we all have different interests and experience. No
one is expected to be an expert on every sport. I hired you
because I read your work and I liked the depth you add to your
pieces. Sports journalism is a lot about reporting stats and
scores. Not everyone thinks to scratch the surface the way
you do."

"I knew Jake Sullivan in high school," I blurt out, cheeks
flaming from my confession or from Tim's compliment, I'm not
sure. "We weren't friends, but I was a couple of years below him
and I didn't tell you when you gave me the assignment."

Tim raises his brows.

"You knew that, too?" I say quietly.

"Mama Sullivan mentioned you'd gone to the same high
school when she asked for you. When you didn't bring it up in
the meeting, I didn't say anything either. I assumed you'd rather
the team didn't know. Most journalists with a connection to a
sports star can't wait to tell me. It gives us a great in. So if you
happen to have gone to college with Kelcie Grant or Joshua
Tiegan, now would be a great time to tell me that, too."

I manage a smile, shaking my head. Why the hell didn't I

trust Tim to accept the truth? It's the same with keeping the Scott thing from Jake, and even Callie and the team. I need to start letting people in. Trusting them to accept the real me.

"But Jake and I formed a relationship," I say, unsure why I'm trying to dig myself into a bigger hole, but unable to stop now the truth is coming out. "It was unprofessional."

"It was. And for the record, it's not behavior *Sports Magazine* condones. If it were to happen again, we'd probably be having a different conversation right now."

"You warned me about the lines getting blurred and I didn't listen. I'm sorry."

Tim sighs. "You think you're the first journalist who's fallen for the person they're interviewing? I've seen it before. As your boss, I wanted you to be aware and to act in a manner in keeping with *Sports Magazine*. And on a more personal level, I didn't want you to get hurt," Tim replies. I swallow down the emotion threatening to take over as Tim continues. "Look, Harper, I can't pretend what happened with you and Jake is ideal, but you were open with me about it, and you've continued to do your job. So I'm willing to overlook it this once."

"But—"

Tim sighs. "Harper, take the win. I'm not firing you. You're a fantastic journalist. Jake was right to ask for you to write his feature."

My gaze snaps to Tim. "It wasn't Jake who wanted me," I say. "It was Mama."

"I thought so at first, too," Tim says. "But Mama Sullivan called to sing your praises the other day and mentioned the request actually came from Jake. Apparently you wrote something about him once in high school?"

What?!

I feel like I have whiplash. Jake knew all along that it was me who wrote that article about him. I nod slowly. Suddenly, Jake's reaction over dinner on my last night at the ranch makes sense. He wasn't trying to change the subject because Mama wanted me to write the feature and he didn't. It was because *he'd* chosen me. He knew I wrote that story.

"According to Jake, you saw through the bullshit when you were sixteen and he felt certain you'd do the same now."

I briefly wonder how he found out I wrote that piece, but the question is swallowed up with the rising what-the-fuck anxiety threatening to take over. My head spins. I don't know what to make of everything Tim has said, but there's a new sense of urgency pounding in my chest, like I'm late for something. Like I have to go right now.

"I'll let you get back to work," Tim says. "But I hope you'll consider staying on now your probation has finished."

"You want to offer me the position?" My mouth drops open. "But I lied to you and I was unprofessional..."

He rolls his eyes again. "Are you trying to get me to change my mind?"

"No." I give a furious shake of my head. "But Callie..."

"Will be staying, too. Her ice hockey knowledge is better than mine. The plan is to have both of you, but you'll be focused on the longer features that go behind the scenes, if that's what you'd like to do? Take some time to think about it. I appreciate you've now got your old job offer on the table."

I nod, unsure what to say. I stumble out of Tim's office in a daze, my mind whirring with everything he's told me. Jake chose me to write the feature. He knew who I was all along and he wanted me to see the real him. And I have seen it, haven't I? The caring, generous, funny man who puts everyone else first. The man who looks at me like I'm his whole world.

And I've ignored all his attempts to contact me this week. I've focused on one moment of hurt, one outburst said in pain and fear, and I've let it cloud everything else. Every tender touch, every heated kiss, every joke and heartfelt moment between us. That's the real Jake. My Jake.

The realization crashes over me like a tidal wave. I love him. I am completely and utterly in love with Jake Sullivan. The second the thought lands, another is chasing at its heels. I have to tell him. I have to tell him now. Before it's too late and I lose him forever. I spin around and head straight back into Tim's office. He looks up in surprise.

"Um... I need to take the afternoon off," I blurt. "I have to go to New York. Not for the job... for Jake." My voice threatens to crack with emotion and urgency.

"You want half a day off after being back in the office for all of three hours?" he asks, pretending for a moment to be annoyed before the smile tugs at his lips. "Go. But you'll have to make it up to me."

I heave a sigh of relief. "Thank you. I'll work on the feature over the weekend. You'll have it first thing Monday."

Tim chuckles. "I know."

Relief and gratitude surge through me. "Thank you," I reply.

"Oh, and Harper? I almost forgot. That novel you sent me. I assume it's yours?"

I freeze, slowly turning back to face him. My face burns crimson at the thought of Tim reading about my sexy vampires, but I nod. "Sorry about that. You weren't supposed to read it."

"Well, I did. I can't say I know much about those er... fantasy novels, but my sister-in-law is a publishing director for one of the big publishing houses. She was visiting over Christmas and read some of it. She wants you to give her a call if you're interested in talking more. Maybe she can help. I'll send you her number."

For the second time this morning, I'm lost for words. A publishing director read my novel. They want to talk to me. "I... I don't know what to say."

He shrugs. "Say, 'See you Monday, Tim.'"

I laugh. "See you Monday, Tim."

As soon as I'm out of his office, I'm racing to my desk to grab my things. Callie gives me a curious look, but the usual venom is gone. There's no time to explain as I run to the elevator. I'm jamming my finger against the call button, urging it to hurry, when the opening lines of the feature land in my thoughts.

When I was sent to Jake Sullivan's family ranch to meet the man himself, I assumed I was meeting a privileged football star. A man with an ego. A man with a reputation he deserved. I thought I knew all there was to know about Jake before I set foot on Oakwood Ranch. But I was wrong. Jake Sullivan is nothing like I expected. He's so much more.

FORTY-ONE

HARPER

It's close to midnight in New York when the yellow cab hits Manhattan. As the taxi weaves through the busy streets, I stare out the window, feeling the same awe I felt arriving in New York this time nearly a year ago. Towering skyscrapers stretch like beacons into the pitch-black sky. The stars I marveled at from the skylight in the barn with Jake are lost to the bright billboards and flashing neon signs advertising everything from the latest Broadway shows to nightclubs and restaurants. The city pulses with an electric energy that seeps in through the cab windows and seems to charge the air. It stirs something within me. This is the city I spent so much of my life dreaming about. This is the city where I thought I could carve out a life that was truly my own.

"Where to?" the driver asks from the front of the cab.

"I..." A dawning horror hits me. I spent the three-hour flight furiously writing Jake's feature. With the first lines in place, the rest has slotted together exactly as I hoped and I emailed a draft to Tim as the plane taxied across the runway at LaGuardia. I already know it's my best work. But it meant I spent no time thinking about what I'd do when I actually reached New York. I have no idea where Jake is. And even though I could call him, something holds me back. I don't want to give him a heads-up. I need to see him. To see his reaction in real time. To stand before him and tell him I love him. If he decides to walk away, I know my heart will shatter into a million pieces and maybe I'll never recover, but at least I'll know I gave it my all.

I'm staring at my phone, wondering what to do, when a message arrives. It's from Callie.

When I was arranging your hotel, the Stormhawks travel coordinator sent me the travel itinerary for all of their games. Thought you might want to know the team is staying in The Manhattan. Jake is room 341. Good luck.

I grin—her timing couldn't have been better—and send back a hurried thank you as I tell the driver where he's going. Maybe Callie and I will become friends, if we give each other a chance.

My phone is still gripped in my hand when it rings.

"Jake?" I say by way of hello.

"No. I'm sorry. This is Genevieve Rose from the HR department connected to *Insight*. Is this Harper Cassidy?"

"Yes. Hi."

"I apologize for calling late, but I've been struggling to reach you for the last few days. I wonder if you have any time next week to come into the office and discuss your dismissal. We believe a grave error may have occurred and we hope you may consider restarting your internship with us, Ms. Cassidy."

It's not news. Tim told me as much in his office earlier today, though I still can't believe it. My gaze draws back to the window and the bright city lights cutting into the darkness. Even now, heart racing, urging the taxi on, desperate to reach Jake, I feel the pull of this city. And yet, it's not home. However much this city might hold a piece of my heart and my past, it's not my future.

"Thank you for the offer," I say at last. "I'm really grateful for the opportunity, but I have a new position I'm happy with."

Genevieve wishes me luck and we say goodbye as the taxi turns onto 7th Avenue. The truth hits me. I've spent so many months worrying about keeping my job that it's only recently I've realized how much I like working at *Sports Magazine*. And I like the idea of writing in-depth features. It's the kind of work I enjoy and it gives me time to continue writing novels if I want to. The thought sends a new buzz of energy humming through my veins. I think of the contact details Tim emailed me for his sister-in-law. A month ago, I'd have deleted the email, convincing myself I wasn't good enough to be a novelist.

As the taxi draws up to the imposing glass entrance of the hotel, I decide I'll call her next week. I've spent most of my life chasing a dream I thought was mine but was really my dad's. I've also spent far too long hiding myself away, blaming my past for my hang-ups, wanting people to like me without ever opening up to them. That ends now. It's time I started living my own life. Chasing my own dreams. *And not just in my career*, I think as Jake dominates my thoughts.

I take a deep breath and stride through the revolving doors into the huge lobby of The Manhattan hotel. I'm still wearing my office skirt and stilettos and my heels tap the floor as I rush to the elevators and jab the call button. My heart pounds against my ribcage as a sickening dread seizes me. What if I'm too late? What if, after everything, I'm the one who's pushed Jake away for good? I stab the elevator button again, willing the doors to open.

I find room 341 and raise my hand to knock. And then the doubt seizes me again. What if he tells me to go? What if he meant what he said and we were nothing?

I squash the fears down and tap lightly on the door before I can change my mind. A second later it opens and there is Jake. Bare-chested and wearing that pair of low-slung basketball shorts that always make my pulse skyrocket. He's so achingly familiar and gorgeous with his hair mussed from bed.

"Harper?" Jake's eyes widen with surprise. "What are you doing here?"

"I..." Now that I'm standing in front of him, the words clog in my throat. I feel the hot press of tears behind my eyes. I am utterly floored by this man. My throat aches as I remember his words the last time I saw him.

We were nothing.

"You chose me for the feature," I blurt. It feels like the least important thing I could say and yet they're the only words that come. "You knew all along it was me who wrote that article in high school."

He nods. "Even then, you saw through my bullshit. I only got to read that article after one of my idiot friends had made those copies. I couldn't believe someone I'd never spoken to had managed to see me for who I was. I went to the classroom you suggested we meet in, but you weren't there."

My heart pounds in my chest. He came. "I heard you tell your friends..."

"Harper, I've said it before and I'll say it again. I was an idiot in high school. My friends were ripping into me about the story you wrote because they could see it got to me. I said the first thing that came to mind to get them off my back. I never meant for you to hear it and I'm sorry you did."

"Why didn't you say anything?"

He shrugs. "Probably for the same reason you didn't either. We've both done a pretty good job of building our walls up since high school."

"But I never put my name on that article. How did you know I wrote it?"

"When you didn't show, I went to the newspaper office. I figured whoever wrote it probably wrote other stuff too. The teacher..."

"Mr. Lamerton," I say, remembering the stuffy English teacher who helped with the newspaper.

"I showed him the copy of the article and he told me the only person he knew who could write that well was a sophomore called Harper Cassidy." Jake's eyes shine as he smiles. "I wasn't going to forget the name in a hurry. When Mama showed me the list of journalists at *Sports Magazine* and I saw your name, I couldn't believe it." He chuckles. "Gotta say, I was pretty surprised when I walked into the kitchen at the ranch that day expecting to find a starry-eyed journalist ready to write about how amazing I was and found you shooting me death glares."

I laugh. "They weren't death glares."

Jake makes a face and I laugh again.

"OK," I admit. "Maybe they were death glares."

We fall silent. I'm not sure what to say or where we go from here. But then Jake is moving, pulling me into his arms, hands moving up to cup my face, those intense eyes burning into my soul.

"I love you." And just like that, he says the three words I flew halfway across the country to say, only to trip on at the last moment. Of course, Jake caught me.

"I love you, too," I breathe.

Jake pulls me into the room, kicking the door shut with his foot as his lips find mine for a kiss so tender and so deep, I absolutely *melt*. He pulls back after a moment and looks at me like he can't believe I'm really here.

"I'm so sorry," he says, his voice raw with emotion. "I'm sorry for pushing you away." He shakes his head, eyes filled with regret. "What I said keeps me up at night. I haven't been sleeping, I can't stop thinking about how much I hurt you."

I notice the dark circles under his eyes, the weariness in his posture. He really does look exhausted. My heart clenches. I did this to him.

"Jake..." I start but he continues on.

"I didn't mean what I said, Harper. You have to know that. You're not nothing to me. You're everything."

Tears well in my eyes and spill down my cheeks.

"Please tell me they're happy tears?" he says and I huff a laugh and nod as he brushes them away with his thumb.

"I'm sorry, too," I manage to choke out. "I'm sorry for not being honest with you from the beginning, for letting my fears and insecurities get in the way of us. I was so caught up trying to be the person I thought I had to be, I almost let the most important thing in my life slip away." I reach up to cup his face, his stubble tickling my palms. "I love you, Jake Sullivan. I love your big heart and the way you make me laugh. I love how you see me, the real me, even when I'm trying to hide. And I am so, so sorry for ever making you doubt that. For thinking for a single second that you were anything but a good man."

A slow smile spreads across Jake's face. "That's a relief then, because this is it for me, Harper. You make me want to be the best version of myself. I don't know what the future holds. I don't know if we'll win or lose against the Steelguards. If I'll get injured and never play again. Whatever happens, all I know is that my future is nothing without you in it."

I tremble with the rawness of the emotion throbbing through my body. Jake has laid himself bare for me and all I want to do is give the same back to him. I've finally learned to let somebody else in.

I stroke a thumb across his cheekbone. "Every game. Every scowl. Every injury and touchdown. Every walk around the lake and ball thrown for Buck, I want to be by your side. You are my future."

FORTY-TWO

JAKE

The stadium lights blaze down on me as I jog onto the field. This is what I was born to do. The roar of the crowd fills my ears —80,000 strong packed into the Steelguards stadium for the biggest game of the season. Of my career. The Steelguards have been undefeated all season, and while the Stormhawks have had some wins, we've had more than a few setbacks. This is it. We need this win to make the playoffs.

Despite grabbing only a few hours of sleep the last couple of nights for some seriously needed makeup time with Harper, I'm pumped. Focused. Ready.

Still, I can't help sneaking a glance at the skybox. Harper stands at the glass, her sexy white Stormhawks top hugging her perfectly. Her hair falls softly to her shoulders, and her red lipstick practically shouts, "Victory!" Wedged beside her are Dylan and Mama, all grinning at me in a way that makes me laugh, even now. I know they're going to rib me later about how whipped I am. I wish Chase was here too, but he's playing his own season finale tonight.

The ref's whistle pierces the air, and I'm locked in.

The game blurs into a war of tackles, charges, and relentless plays. Their defense comes at us hard and fast, but we give it right back. The Steelguards score the first touchdown, but we respond immediately. I burst off the line, giving the linebacker a solid chip block before breaking into my route. Billy launches a perfect spiral. I leap, snatch the ball from the air, and turn upfield. The defense closes in, but Rob finds a space. I pass the ball and he powers through for a touchdown. The crowd roars as he takes a punishing hit but clutches the ball tightly.

By the end of the third quarter, the Steelguards are up 22-18. As the whistle signals the break, I pull off my helmet and gulp down water. We huddle up, Coach Allen shouting plays we already know by heart. We don't need a speech. We need action.

As we take the field for the fourth quarter, I glance up one last time. Harper flashes a radiant smile, and the rest of the world disappears—the screaming fans, the pressure, the players around me. There's only her. I know the cameras are on me, my face plastered across the big screen. I couldn't care less. In that second, it's just me and Harper. A grin spreads across my face. My lips move without thought. "I love you," I mouth, tapping my chest and pointing at her. She smiles back, making a heart with her hands. The crowd erupts, igniting a fire inside me. I'm about to give the Stormhawks fans exactly what they came for.

The ball snaps back to Billy, and he scans for an open receiver. The defense collapses in, but Billy releases a quick pass. The ball wobbles in the air, a loose spiral. I see it before anyone else and charge forward, stepping in front of their running back. My hands reach out, and the ball slams into my grip. I turn and sprint, legs pumping. The Steelguards scramble to catch me, but I'm weaving between defenders. Thirty yards to go. Twenty. Ten. My lungs burn, my heart pounds. The final seconds tick down.

One defender dives. I leap, twisting midair to avoid his

grasp. I stretch out as the ball slams into the turf just inside the goal line.

Touchdown!

The ref's arms shoot into the air as the stadium explodes. 22-24. The clock hits zero. JT's kick is good. 22-25.

The team piles on top of me and JT in a wave of celebration. We did it! We won the AFC West. The Stormhawks are in the playoffs.

In minutes, the field is full of coaching staff and press and cameras. I spot Mama striding toward me. Her face shines with pride. Dylan reaches my side and thumps my arm hard. "I knew you'd do it," he says.

And when he steps to the side, there's Harper. Radiant. Beaming. I pull her into my arms.

Nothing else matters. Not the screaming fans, the flashing cameras, the reporters clamoring for a quote. Harper is in my arms and we've made the playoffs. I tilt her head up, pressing my lips to hers. Long and deep and intense. Like it's our first kiss. Like it's our last kiss. And I know, without a shadow of a doubt that this moment, this kiss, these feelings for Harper are better than the greatest touchdown of my life.

A LETTER FROM BELLA

Dear Reader,

Thank you for choosing *Score to Settle*. I hope it made you swoon, sigh, and possibly fan yourself a little (or a lot).

I had so much fun writing Jake and Harper's story. I loved the banter, teasing, and humor as they went from "out for my blood" to "I love you," with a lot of fun and some serious spice along the way.

If you want to stay up to date on future releases, you can sign up for my newsletter here:

www.bookouture.com/bella-north

I must confess, I spent a solid portion of my writing time hopelessly obsessed with Travis Kelce and Taylor Swift. I was watching every Chiefs game, replaying every cute reel, and goofy-smiling over their love story while writing about Jake and Harper. So if there's a little extra longing in these pages, you can thank the Kelce effect.

I love hearing from readers, so if you enjoyed this book, please consider leaving a review on Amazon, Goodreads, or just texting your bestie "OMG, YOU HAVE TO READ THIS." Every bit of book love helps!

You can also find me on Instagram and Facebook—come say hi and tell me which book boyfriend has ruined you the most.

With love, gratitude, and ALL the swoons,

Bella x

 facebook.com/BellaNorthAuthor
instagram.com/BellaNorthAuthor

ACKNOWLEDGMENTS

To every reader, blogger and bookish creator who devours romance like it's chocolate and shouts about book boyfriends from the rooftops—thank you. Your enthusiasm and support mean the world! I'm endlessly grateful for every post, message, and review.

Huge thanks to my editor, Lucy Frederick. Your insights make everything sharper, swoonier, and a hell of a lot hotter. And to the entire Bookouture team for sharing in my excitement for this series! I appreciate you all so much. Please take a moment to read the credits page and see the names of just how many people added the magic to this story along the way.

To my agent, Amanda Preston. Once again, your unfailing belief in me keeps me believing in myself. And to the whole LBA team behind the scenes, you are amazing!

To Lila Whatley for your NFL knowledge and support in the creation of this book—thank you! All mistakes are entirely my own, but hopefully you were all too busy swooning to notice.

To Sarah, Carol, Catherine, and Kathryn, who endure my constant book chatter, particularly when it involves the spicy kind—thank you for your enthusiasm. And to Pippa Nixon, my go-to spice pal. The support and humor we share is such a joy!

And, of course, my ride-or-dies: Zoe Lea, Nikki Smith, and Laura Pearson. You keep me sane, keep me writing, and keep me laughing. I love the voice notes and I love you all.

Finally, my family, who put up with my head being in fictional worlds most of the time. I love you!

PUBLISHING TEAM

Turning a manuscript into a book requires the efforts of many people. The publishing team at Bookouture would like to acknowledge everyone who contributed to this publication.

Audio
Alba Proko
Melissa Tran
Sinead O'Connor

Commercial
Lauren Morrissette
Hannah Richmond
Imogen Allport

Cover design
Ink & Laurel

Data and analysis
Mark Alder
Mohamed Bussuri

Editorial
Lucy Frederick
Melissa Tran

Copyeditor
DeAndra Lupu

Proofreader
Elaini Caruso

Marketing
Alex Crow
Melanie Price
Occy Carr
Cíara Rosney
Martyna Młynarska

Operations and distribution
Marina Valles
Stephanie Straub
Joe Morris

Production
Hannah Snetsinger
Mandy Kullar
Ria Clare
Nadia Michael

Publicity
Kim Nash
Noelle Holten
Jess Readett
Sarah Hardy

Rights and contracts
Peta Nightingale
Richard King
Saidah Graham

9 781805 500179